THE DANCER
AT THE END OF HIS BED

MILA DOUGLAS

BODONI
BOOKS

For Steve
He believed I could, so I did.

The world breaks everyone and afterwards many are stronger at the broken places.

Ernest Hemingway
(A Farewell to Arms, 1929)

Chapter One

CLAUDIA

Fremantle, Western Australia, 2018

Three fruitless tours of the hospital's multi-storey car park. Especially today, when finding a parking space is a matter of life and death.

My short fingernails pierce my palms as I tighten my sweaty grip on the steering wheel. Time to change tactics. Ambush rather than chase. I reverse into the no-standing zone to watch. I open the window for much needed fresh air; instead, a whoosh of stale exhaust fumes sends my already dizzy head into a spin.

A *beep, beep, beep* interrupts my stealth mission. Maybe it's a message about Dad? As I wrestle wallet, house keys, and glasses to retrieve the phone buried underneath, my hand shakes.

> Heya Claudia. Don't worry about dinner tonight, I'm going shopping. Hope everything goes okay.

Shopping? Oliver never goes shopping. But, aww. I welcome his act of kindness, especially in my current state. I tap the screen and begin typing a message to my husband, but I'm interrupted by the sight of a man clutching car keys emerging from the lift. I chuck the phone and track him to his vehicle.

"Be there soon, Dad," I whisper.

I idle a few spaces away from the reversing car. But while I'm preparing to pounce, a dust covered yellow car screeches past, cuts in front and steals my blinking spot.

My sister's all too bouncy curls taunt me from the driver's seat. I restrain the urge to hit the horn with a left, right, left jab. Today's not the day to start pointless battles. Anyway, why am I even surprised? Bonnie's personalised number plates say it all: **FUQɪT**.

Under my breath, I mutter **FUQɪT** over and over, my frown lines deepening as I return to the no-standing zone which has become a no-starting zone.

I finish the text to Oliver.

> Okay. I might end up coming home early. Bonnie's her usual selfish self.

Stress is turning me into a whinger. I stare at the message for a moment and delete the last sentence before I press send.

Bonnie saunters through the maze of vehicles. Despite only a two-year age gap between us *her* brow is smooth and youthful. She flashes an enormous smile before hopping into the car. Nothing has happened in Bonnie's world. It's all sunshine. How does she do it? Our father is terminally ill. Surely, she could stop smiling for a blinking minute and allow a few clouds of grief.

She kisses my cheek. "Sorry about nicking the space. Didn't see you."

I wipe away the inevitable make-up smear. Of course, she didn't see me. The closer I get to fifty, the more invisible I become.

She jabs the air with a painted fingernail. "Empty spot. Over there. Surprised you didn't nab it. Maybe you need glasses?"

She knows I already wear glasses.

Teeth clenched, I swallow back unspeakable words and move the car.

I'm about to open the car door when Bonnie drops a boxed lipstick in my lap. "For you. A freebie. Two for one." She indicates the orange-red blaze across her lips.

I read the label and shake my head. *Flat Out Fabulous*.

"Don't pull that face until you try it. It'll bring out the red in your hair. You'll have *less* bad days wearing brighter lippy."

'*Fewer*,' I mouth, shoving her gift in the ashtray. I'll eventually chuck it in the drawer with Bonnie's other attempts to transform me. I choose lipstick for the moisturising properties. Worn the same shade for years. I rack my brain for the name—*Fairly Bare?* or *Barely There?*

"Come on, Claudia darling. Hurry. Dad's waiting." Bonnie hooks her arm through mine and drags me towards the lift.

My internal voice yells, 'Screw you, I'd already be in his hospital room if you hadn't stolen my spot.' Out loud, I say, "Dad sounded... normal on the phone. You think he's done *a Wilf*?"

Bonnie screws up her face, yet still manages to look pretty. "Is W.I.L.F an acronym?"

"No. Wilf Poole—the guy Dad worked with. Remember? The doctors abandoned all hope, then he woke up feeling great. The cancer had gone. Vanished." I nod my head encouragingly, but she doesn't nod back.

"No, Claudia, I don't think Dad's done '*a Wilf*'. He's going to die, no matter how much you hold his hand. Time to let go."

She's starting to sound like Oliver. Mum, too. But it wasn't a mistake giving up my job. I can't buy back precious time with my father.

"Did Dad tell you he'd written letters?" I ask.

"Letters? When I saw him two days ago, he could barely lift his hand."

The lift doors open to let in more passengers, so I use my quietest voice. "He said he needs to talk to us. Urgently. He's gotten a second wind."

Bonnie megaphones her reply, "You sure you didn't mis-hear? Probably said he'd passed wind. For the second time."

When she laughs, her mirrored earrings reflect the overhead light, making me squint.   Half the elevator's occupants smile. The others frown. I fix my stare on the directory of hospital floors, trying to conjure a new listing. A button saying *Beam me outta here*.

We hurry down the corridor for Dad's ward. My soft shoes creep. Her heels clatter on the polished vinyl.

Dad's hospital room door is open a crack and I stop millimetres short of knocking. He's talking to someone. His voice low and intimate

"Listen," I whisper to Bonnie. "Dad's got a visitor."

My plan is to wait outside and give them some privacy, but Bonnie races in and pulls back the screen. Dad's still in bed. Still grey. Still sick. Alone.

His face lights up and he holds his arms towards me. A glimmer of hope warms my heart and I nudge Bonnie with my elbow in an *I-told-you-so*.

"You're a sight for sore eyes," he says. "I'm so glad you came."

"We're both here," I say. "Me and Bonnie."

For a long moment he closes his eyes and drifts off. Bonnie grabs a chair while I hover, wondering whether to wake him.

"Sit down, Claudia. He's not got a second wind."

Bonnie plays a game on her phone while I will Dad to wake up.

Suddenly, he pulls himself upright, stares beyond me and Bonnie, beyond the privacy screen, beyond the door.

I babble about my dizziness at driving round and round the carpark. I'm hoping Dad will make his usual joke: "Where did *Verti-go* and, has *Verti-gone* yet?" But he's staring at the wall.

Bonnie nudges me and points to Dad's face. He's smiling. His eyes full of life. They twinkle as if the young man hiding inside his old body is trying to break out.

He sniffs the air and chuckles. "There's mint growing around here. Remember how we crushed it under our feet when we were canoodling?"

Bonnie twirls her finger in front of her forehead, mouthing the words '*sensory hallucinations*'.

"I wrote a letter to you, my love," he whispers, tears

rolling lazily down his cheeks. "I'm so sorry for what happened. I've had a lifetime of regret."

He's silent for a moment, and I squeeze Bonnie's arm.

He blows a kiss into the air. "I didn't expect you to come. I kept our promise and never told a soul."

"Who's he talking to?" Bonnie hisses.

"Shhh."

When Dad reaches out his hand, it's like watching a scene from a movie where a character has been digitally removed.

I'm surprised to see Bonnie's lip trembling. I hold her hand and lead her until we're half hidden behind the screen. As we watch and listen to our dying father speak to a non-existent woman, we cover our mouths to stifle the sobs.

"You are so beautiful." The shimmer of tears sparkle his weary eyes. "Put the music on, let's dance again. Oh. How we danced." He hums an unrecognisable tune and tries to climb out of bed, stumbling and pulling at the needles in his arm. He extends his arms towards the woman in his dreams.

I can't just sit there. I race to him and wrap my arms around his shoulders. I press my tear-streaked face against his clammy cheek. "You can't get up, Dad."

He reaches beyond me, tries to push me away. As he fights, blood spurts from his arm, filling my nostrils with a sweet, metallic odour.

There are nothing but clouds across Bonnie's face when she pushes the emergency buzzer.

I exhale the last gasp of optimism.

Dad's not doing a Wilf.

A man in medical scrubs guides me and Bonnie towards the door. We hover outside, straining to hear what's going on, but the corridor is too full of hospital noises.

"He'll be okay," I say, willing Bonnie to smile. She doesn't.

The door eventually opens, and a female doctor gives us a practised look of reassurance. "Your father's back in bed. He's sedated."

In the second before the door closes, her professional mask drops, and she exchanges a micro-glance with a colleague. The look doesn't bode well.

Bonnie strides off, as if she's found purpose where there's none. "Let's head to the visitor's room."

I follow, not caring that she's leading us in the wrong direction. After a full circuit of the ward, we flop into plastic chairs only spitting distance from Dad's room.

"Was Dad dreaming?" I ask.

"It was real, I reckon. Reliving old memories."

"What about the letters? Should we ask a nurse?"

"You saw the state he's in. He imagined writing letters." Bonnie shrugs, searching through her giant handbag and producing a comb. Sensing today's makeover attempt number two, I lean my head against the wall. But she never takes a hint.

She folds my hair under—presumably testing a shorter style—before I bat her away.

"Our good ole Dad has a secret," she says.

"No way. Not Dad," I say. "But I admit, it was strange."

"Who was he talking to then? It couldn't be Mum," Bonnie says. "How many times have you heard her complain about him never dancing. Not even at their wedding. He stuffed his knee in the war."

"There was no woman," I say. "There was no one there. Like you said, sensory hallucinations from the cancer."

The medical staff warned us this could happen, but I wasn't prepared for it to feel so real. I could taste Dad's love and sadness and regret.

"You don't think Dad had an affair then?" Bonnie's stare is intense.

"No. Dad's not that kind of man."

She laughs unexpectedly. "I hope I don't reveal my secrets before I die. I'm glad my outrageous phase was before social media."

"Don't lie. You wear shenanigans like badges of honour."

She dissolves into laughter. "True."

We sit quietly for a minute, then she attacks my limp locks again, lifting them from my shoulder and twisting them in an up-do.

"Give up." I push her hand away. "I'm a lost cause."

"No. You're only a lost cause if you give up on yourself. Dad always said you looked like his Mama. It's the chestnut hair."

"My hair's not chestnut." I jerk away.

"Watered down genes. But that new lipstick would bring out the red."

"I'm too quiet for that."

She assesses me with a sideways stare. "It's the quiet ones you gotta watch. What secrets are you hiding, Claudia?"

I give what I hope is a *that's-for-me-to-know* shrug. Bonnie's eyes widen for a moment, then she says, "Nah.

You got nothing. Oliver was your first and only. You don't even swear."

"I do. I'm cursing at you right now. Inside my head."

She rolls her eyes. Bonnie is onto me. I'm forty-six years old and I've yet to do anything remotely scandalous.

"Back to those letters," I say. "If the mystery dancer was real, the letters might be, too. Maybe they were intended for her?"

"So... you're not discounting the idea of Dad having a floozy on the side?"

A nurse approaches and speaks gently, as if talking to small children, "We've called your mother. Your father can't have any other visitors. You might as well go home."

"Will he be okay tomorrow?" I swallow the lump in my throat.

"I'm not a doctor, so I don't know the full details." Her expression suggests she does know, but the news isn't good.

I try to stand but my legs are too shaky. My throat too tight to speak.

"You need some medicine." Bonnie offers me a box of chocolates, but I turn away. When I hear her rip the plastic film, my heart shreds, too.

"Here." She holds a chocolate to my mouth. "This will cheer you up. Hazelnut swirl. Isn't that your favourite?"

I'm surprised she knows. "You bought those for Dad."

"Dad won't be eating them, Claudia."

"Morning," Oliver mumbles.

Accepting the cup of tea, eyes half-closed, I slide the morning papers out of the way to plonk my elbow on the table, cradling my chin in one hand. An awful sleepless night, but at least there hasn't been a phone call.

Without looking up, I know Oliver's toast is cut into triangles and he's reading the daily headlines. Normal. A few sips of tea and everything will be okay.

I inhale the scent of freshly unrolled newspapers—the mixed aromas of hot-off-the-press news and Earl Grey are familiar, comforting smells.

We're probably the last people in Australia to have newspapers delivered, but it's a habit we don't want to break. My husband's made a sport of finding contradictions in news reports.

Last week *The West Australian* provided details of a major drug haul, sophisticated equipment, result of complex investigation. Yet, *The Daily Telegraph* reported the seizing of thirteen marijuana plants at the same address. Oliver finishes every comparison with the same statement: "Facts should be facts."

I sip my tea, waiting for today's example, but Oliver doesn't deliver his daily report.

"Can't you find anything?" I lift my head to look at him. What's he wearing? Before I check again, I rub the corner of my eyes. Purple. Definitely purple. After twenty-odd years of dark blue, light blue, and every shade of in-between-blue, my husband's wearing a purple shirt. I tilt my head, feeling slightly off balance. "New clothes?"

"Yes." He looks pleased with himself. "Late night shopping, on my own, while you were sitting with your dad at the hospital... again."

"It's different. The colour suits you."

He points forked fingers towards his face. "Thanks. Someone at work noticed my eyes." A smug smile. "You know only two percent of the population have green eyes? Apparently wearing purple makes them appear greener." He lifts the newspapers, revealing a stack of holiday brochures. "I stopped at a travel agent, too. The Greek Islands? A cruise?"

"We can't afford it."

His frown lines deepen. "You need to get another job so we can save money and go away."

"Not yet...I'm waiting until Dad gets better."

"But what if..." He clears his throat. "It will be a year from when you start a new job until you can take annual leave. We should..."

"Hang on," I say. "Phone."

I kiss Oliver's forehead and walk into the living room.

No caller I.D.

"Hello?"

"Our deepest sympathies. Your father passed away early this morning. He went peacefully."

Chapter Two

KATERINA

'The Figs' Residential Care Home, Sydney, New South Wales, 2018

When the wavy-haired nurse checks me for the umpteenth time, I throw my book on the bedside table. "Solitary confinement's one thing," I say, "but how can an old woman concentrate with all that racket outside?"

"It's an industrial cleaning team. Trying to stop the spread." She winks. "Deaths in old people's homes are bad for ratings."

Joking about death, under these circumstances, shows poor taste. My folded arms don't go unnoticed.

"Sorry for the wise crack. I'm new here, and sometimes when I'm nervous, I choose the wrong thing to say." She checks my pulse and her eyes crinkle in a smile. "You're fine, but we're stuck wearing these until the all clear." She pulls down her face mask, exposing smooth skinned cheeks.

I touch my own face, more bone than flesh; thin

papery skin. "I'd rather be in the fresh air," I moan, pointing to the manicured gardens. "If the plague doesn't kill me, the disinfectant fumes might."

"It's not the plague, it's the flu."

Young people think they know everything. "The Spanish flu was a plague of sorts."

I squint at the temporary name badge—printed with a label-making gadget—white raised letters on shiny green tape. It's good manners to use someone's title, but she has none. Just IzzyAugust, no gap between first name and last. I imagine they ran out of space.

After fussing with the bedcover, IzzyAugust inserts a thermometer device in my ear and checks her phone. At first, I think it's a new-fangled phone with an inbuilt computer to record my temperature, but she's typing a message. If the young viewed life through their eyes instead of their phones, they wouldn't miss those fleeting precious moments. And unless IzzyAugust concentrates on what she's paid to do, she'll never wear a permanent badge bearing The Figs insignia.

"Any 'empty beds', today?" I ask, arthritic fingers forming crooked quotation marks. I can't, I cannot, bring myself to call a spade a spade. We all know we're leaving this place in a box, but the word *dead* gives me the dithers.

Izzy nods seriously. "One. What's the saying about jumping into someone's grave? It's been filled by an Italian woman with dementia. The public hospital was desperate to move her out, but it's shocking timing. Being locked inside a strange room is the last thing a frightened woman needs. Can't understand a word she's yelling, but at a guess, there's a bucket load of swearing.

Hopefully, she'll settle, but at the moment she's kicking. Literally."

Maybe it's what the doctor ordered, someone to shake the place up after days of nothingness. I smile at the framed picture of my dearest friend, Anna. She was always good for a stir. "Which room is the new resident in?"

"Across this corridor, almost opposite. We've taped a poster of the *Leaning Tower of Pisa* on her door."

I do not point out the Catch-22. Pictures help residents remember their rooms, but only if they can remember which picture.

I tilt my head at the outburst of screaming and yelling outside. "Ooh, a kerfuffle," I say. "I bet that's her."

My door bursts open to two people; surgical masks hiding much of their faces, but their hair and eyes are so much alike. I'm sure they're related.

Izzy helps restrain the woman who looks too small to be the source of such big noise. The man holds the wild one at arm's length, pulling down his mask to apologise.

"Sorry, I'm Joe... my mum... Maria... I was... she escaped."

"What's your mother saying?" Izzy asks.

Joe shrugs and lowers his voice. "I only understand a handful of words. Mum spoke English... before she... anyway, she's reverted to Italian."

The wild woman with grey-streaked dark curls escapes her son's grasp and lunges towards me, stopping at the end of my bed. Her stare, especially with the muzzle-like surgical mask, reminds of a time at the zoo when keepers removed a baby gorilla from the enclosure and the mother gorilla pressed her face against the protective glass. The beautiful creature and I shared a moment, understanding each other's sadness. Now, Maria's intelligent dark-as-night eyes hold my gaze. *There's a lot going on in my head*, she seems to say, *but I'm trapped.*

I turn to the man. "I don't speak Italian, but I know your mother does not want to be locked up, because I feel the same." I offer my hand. "I'm Katerina."

Joe locks one arm tightly around his mother's waist and shakes with the other. "Pleased to meet you, Miss Katerina."

"Let her go," I whisper.

He looks at Nurse Izzy.

"Go on," she says. "I'm up for a chase."

When he releases Maria, she skips around like a young woman. Her eyes narrow at my wheelchair, and before Joe can stop her, she's trying to lift me out of bed.

After a clumsy wrestle, he grasps his mother's hand.

There's an uncomfortable imbalance. He's become the parent and she the unruly toddler.

"Sorry. Mum's changed. She's never been aggressive."

"No need to apologise. Her brain is playing cruel tricks, but the mother you love is still inside. I see mischief and kindness and fun."

"Thank you." Joe's voice warbles with sadness.

Izzy takes Maria's other hand. "Rules are rules. It's back to your room."

Maria wriggles out of their grip and hugs me.

"It will be okay," I say. "We can sit together once we're allowed out."

She nods and smiles.

Joe's eyes grow wide. "It looked as if Mum knew what you were saying."

"Only a fraction of communication is through words. The rest is tone of voice and body language."

He touches his throat and swallows. "I'm bringing Mum's favourite treats for afternoon tea on Wednesday. I think Mum would like you to join us. *I'd* like you to join us."

"That's if this darned quarantine is over, and as long as I'm still alive."

When Joe's shoulders slump, I add. "It's a joke, Joe. But I am in my nineties, and we've all got to go some time."

Is boredom fatal? Another day in here and I'll probably find out.

With the residents in lockdown, there's no need to conduct my daily audit where I make sure nothing's gone missing. But I check anyway, just for something to do.

The framed pictures are in their place at each end of the sideboard, and my pile of books sits intentionally off-centre. I chuckle every time the cleaners move them back to the middle, but I slide them as soon as they've left. Just enough off balance to be annoying. No-one mentions the nonsense. It's a harmless wheelchair accessible game. Too difficult these days to get out and throw rocks at lampposts.

Usually, when I scan the window wall, I blink to avoid the cylindrical brass calendar calling from the sill.

But monotony is a born troublemaker, and it bullies me into a momentary glance.

Father's paperweight.

I abhor the blasted thing, but today I not only look, but touch. Aligning the rings, I form a date. October 10th, 1945. A Wednesday. A day of dreadful woe.

Why didn't I cover my eyes as he committed the words to paper, or block my ears as the metal nib scratched and scrawled across the page?

"They won't believe it," I remember saying.

Shuddering, I put the perpetual calendar down, wishing I could leave my room. Residents gather to recite poetry on Mondays, but the administration staff at *The Figs* have followed protocol and cancelled communal sessions.

Many residents get lost on the way to the dining hall, but remember song lyrics from sixty years ago. Holding Father's blasted paperweight has recovered a different rhyme. I press play on an eight-decades' old recording and chant a verse my teacher made us memorise.

> Monday's child is fair of face, Tuesday's
> child is full of grace,
> Wednesday's child is full of woe, Thurs-
> day's child has far to go,
> Friday's child is loving and forgiving,
> Saturday's child works hard for a
> living,
> But the child which is born on the
> Sabbath Day,
> Is bonnie, blithe, good and gay.

Suddenly, I'm eight again, racing home to ask Mother which day belongs to me.

"Friday," she says.

For the next ten years, I embraced Friday like a special friend, and my life was full of *love and forgiveness*. Perhaps it was my mother's imperfect grasp of English, or perhaps my day of birth was insignificant. But she was wrong.

As a teenager, while helping my father relocate his office, I hefted the paperweight and spun the concentric rings. Father stopped packing to explain it was a perpetual calendar. After he showed me how to locate a chosen year, month, and day, I dialled my birthdate to discover with both certainty and disappointment that I came into this world on a Wednesday.

Wednesday's child is full of woe.

Not long after that, woe claimed me.

Chapter Three

CLAUDIA

Fremantle, 2018

It's barely a fortnight since Mum simultaneously dabbed at tears and complained to everyone about the roughness of the funeral director's complimentary tissues.

Although our solicitor's appointment isn't scheduled until eleven, Mum nods her head as if she's keeping time with the second hand on her watch. With Mum, if you're not ten minutes early, you're unfashionably late.

A conference room overlooking Dad's favourite park seems a fitting venue for the reading of his will. I turn from Mum and seek comfort in the view. Norfolk pines, the Indian Ocean and endless empty skies. The park holds memories of Dad and my sons playing cricket with pinecones. The scenery is picture-perfect, but today it's like a postcard without a personal message. A reminder of who's missing.

I examine the miserable office décor. A better match for my mood.

You never realise how much space people take up until they're gone. Now, my life is woefully underpopulated. Anger seems inappropriate, but I'm mad Dad didn't do a Wilf. Then Oliver's attitude this morning? If he hadn't waited until the last second to say he couldn't stomach another family gathering, I would have demanded a proper explanation or insisted he come along. For better or worse, in sickness and in health?

Bonnie squeezes into a non-existent gap between her husband, Matt, and Mum when there's room at the table for twenty.

"Where's Oliver?"

"Not feeling well," I whisper, not wanting to involve Mum in this conversation.

I'm staring at the vacant chair next to me, when Mum slaps the table. I jump.

"The lawyer mentioned your father writing letters. What letters? Did he say anything on that last day?"

That last day? Mum says it without so much as a shudder. We were warned Dad might seem better just before death, but the heads-up didn't help. I wasn't ready.

I take too long to respond and Bonnie replies for me, "Dad was too far gone to say anything. We'll find out from the solicitor."

I owe Bonnie for that. For not talking about Dad. For cutting Mum off.

"We will find out if the solicitor ever gets here." As my mother speaks, I stare at the brittle line of her mouth. "Lawyers are good at taking money, but too cheap to spend any. It wouldn't hurt to air-condition this place."

I'm not sure where Mum finds the strength to

complain, but she's right. It's summer for God's sake and although the overhead fan clatters a dismal beat, it doesn't move a wisp of air.

"Are we waiting for Oliver?" Mum snaps.

"No. Something important came up."

Bonnie looks up from scratching Matt's shoulder, and gives me a glance-and-a-half.

I should have used the same excuse both times. I'm not exactly lying; I have no idea why Oliver didn't come.

Bonnie opens her mouth to question me, but Matt groans and she goes back to dancing her fingers over his back.

"Higher," Matt says. "Left. No, higher..."

I try to not to think about Dad being dead or about my grown sons, Josh and Aaron living in other states, and especially not about Oliver deciding now's a good time to be an arsehole.

Matt snuffles and snorts and I check what Bonnie's up to. "What's that smell?" he asks, sniffing for the source. "Naphthalene?"

"What?!" Bonnie's screech causes my temple to throb. "I hope you can't smell burning feathers?"

It's a joke from some old movie we watched together when we were young. She's suggesting Matt has a brain tumour like Dad, and it's not funny. Fortunately, her remark goes over everyone else's head.

"No. Naphthalene," Matt repeats. "Mothballs. Can you smell mothballs?"

"I don't know." Bonnie giggles. "I've never been that close to a moth."

I sigh, Matt sniggers, and Mum hisses, "Stop. The lawyer's arrived."

"Ahem." A man in an ill-fitting suit clears his throat.

It's not cheap, just too big. I wonder if he has cancer, too; I look for the signs in everyone, now. Not that I know what I'm looking for. Dad looked healthy on the outside almost until the end. He joked about being like a supermarket apple; cold storage unblemished skin while he rotted on the inside.

The lawyer introduces himself as Gary Kovacevic, and Mum *oomphs*, no doubt dissatisfied he doesn't have a 'good Australian' name.

"Are all beneficiaries present?" The manner in which Gary scans the room suggests he'd rather be somewhere else.

We have something in common.

In her usual grating manner, Mum takes over, "Claudia and Bonnie." She waves emphatically towards us. "These are Philip's daughters."

I'm surprised she doesn't make us put our hands up.

"Bonnie's husband, Matthew." She points at him, even though he's the only man there. "Claudia's husband hasn't bothered," she continues, "not that he'll get a mention in the will. And I'm Hillary, wife of the deceased."

Mum could be auditioning for a role in a legal show, and I cringe at her use of *deceased* instead of my father's name.

Mr Kovacevic explains the contents of the will and, as expected, most of Dad's possessions go to Mum, but a previously unknown deposit is to be divided between me and Bonnie.

"What money is this?" Mum asks, far too sharply for the occasion. It's a pity she never tells her facial expressions to use their inside voice.

The lawyer looks uncomfortable. "There's a personal letter attached to the legal papers. Philip asked for everyone to think about what's important." He reads it aloud, and although he sounds nothing like Dad, I hear Dad's voice:

> *My dearest Claudia and Bonnie,*
> *Money does not buy happiness, but I'm leaving an inheritance I couldn't bring myself to spend. It's money from a life I was forced to forget, from people I had to leave behind.*

Dad's words echo... Forced? Not chose? He left a life behind? Is Bonnie right about Dad having a secret past? Does this have something to do with the hallucinations? I try to catch Bonnie's eye, but she's busy filing her fingernail. Probably snagged it on Matt's blinking back.

"What life left behind?" Mum interrupts. "What does he mean?" She tries to snatch the letter, but Kovacevic pulls it away. "How much money was my husband holding on to? Do either of you know anything about this?"

The lawyer faces his palm towards her and continues:

> *We have only one life to live, and my dying wish is for everyone to take stock of theirs. I'd like you all to think about what matters most. Remember, while a ship is safest in the harbour, it was built to sail the ocean.*

Mum's expression is similar to the time Dad brought home a pig claiming it would make a great house pet. She told him he'd lost his marbles and made him take it back.

She's still muttering 'ship?' and 'harbour?' when the lawyer interrupts.

"I've set a three-minute timer as per Philip's request to provide a period of reflection." He holds a finger to his lips showing us the time has begun.

Sweat beads on my top lip and I fan my face before resting my elbows on the table to contemplate the money. It would be useful if there's enough to tide us over until I get a new job. But I don't think Dad would want me thinking about that. Forget the bills. I'd like to see more of Josh and Aaron. And not just at funerals. We need to take the family holiday Oliver's been dreaming of. I know Dad's leaving the harbour advice was a metaphor, but we could take a cruise. We could go to the Greek Islands like Oliver's travel brochure. We need some joy. I'll convince Josh and Aaron to come.

The timer buzzes and the lawyer indicates it's the end of the reading by holding out copies of our paperwork. "Your father's deposit is unusual in that it's held overseas. I've enclosed an informational leaflet. You'll need to contact their office and provide notarised copies of your birth and marriage certificates, along with your father's birth and death certificates. It should be straightforward."

I'm the first to sign the receipt. I need to get home to empty-nester, television-filled normal.

Mum blocks the doorway, her voice sharp. "Do you know anything about this past life rubbish? If your father was going to tell anyone, it'd be you."

I exhale to the count of five. "No, Mum. I'll call you tomorrow."

I hurry down the stairwell, expecting relief at my narrow escape, instead there's a niggling feeling of heading towards something worse.

At home, Oliver's planted in his usual armchair and he doesn't look up when I toss the legal paperwork on the coffee table. Checking his phone again.

I fling myself onto the couch. "Dad left a confusing message."

He doesn't take his eyes off the screen.

"And we had to think for three minutes."

He nods without looking and I chuck a cushion, narrowly missing his head. "Oliver? Are you listening?"

My playfulness didn't have the desired effect.

He bites off his words "What was the message?"

"Well...he asked us to take stock of our lives. He's left some kind of deposit. We don't know how much until it's processed. But I thought about a family holiday. All of us. You, me, and the boys." My words spill out in a nervous cascade.

Oliver's continued lack of eye contact makes my stomach writhe.

"Is everything okay?" I ask.

"I need water."

As he rattles around in the kitchen, there's an oppressive emptiness. I talk loudly to fill the space. "Dad said the money was from a life he left behind. Mum knew nothing about it. A secret stash? Why would Dad leave a life behind?"

Oliver nurses his glass of water but doesn't sit down. "Maybe your father was unhappy and wanted to start again."

I laugh a panicky laugh. "Life's not a dress rehearsal."

"No, it's not," he says without a smile. "Look... Claudia..." He bites his lip.

"Has something happened to one of the boys?" I brace myself for bad news.

"They're fine. Forget it." He shrugs dismissively.

This would be a good time to ask what's going on but I'm scared.

He shifts his weight from foot to foot and takes a deep breath. "I feel as if I've been standing on the edge of a cliff waiting to jump."

His words echo, but I push them away. "I'm sorry for being so occupied with Dad. I'll make more effort."

"Caring shouldn't need an effort."

"No," I say, covering my ears. "Not now. I'm going to rest."

On the floor of the bedroom, at the foot of the bed, a suitcase mocks me. It wasn't there this morning. I remind myself to breathe then pick it up hoping it's empty. My arms shake as I carry the heavy case out. "Are you going somewhere?"

"I'm leaving you." His voice is almost drowned out by the ticking clock, and I fight an urge to rip it off the wall and chuck it at him.

When Oliver picks up the bag and opens the front door, time slows.

I could yell, or wrestle him, or throw the fucking clock. But I'm trapped inside my head with his parting words.

The catch clicks softly as he abandons me.

The Earth's tilting the wrong way, and I'm the only one who didn't know it was about to tip. My will-reading outfit is two-day-creased and stained with tea and tears. A teetering pile of dirty cups on the coffee table reminds me of how much I've drunk. I've used all the everyday cups, I'm beyond the good set reserved for visitors, and onto the fine bone china I inherited from Grandma Rose.

I stared at the door for hours expecting Oliver to come back, fooling myself into believing he'd calm down once he'd driven around the block. Surely, it was a mix-up. All those high emotions after Dad's death.

But he didn't come back.

There was a pinprick of hope when I remembered switching my phone to silent in the lawyer's office. I desperately rummaged in the depths of my bag anticipating a screen full of missed calls. Oliver, professing his terrible mistake. But *Nada*.

My calls went unanswered, so I sent a carefully worded text to his sister Wendy, to find out what she knew. Wendy is also—inconveniently it seems—my best friend, and while I can see how this puts her in a difficult position, years of friendship should count for something.

No response.

The unopened legal envelope is wedged between unwashed cups. Some, dangerously close to the edge. They remind me of Oliver standing at the edge of his fucking cliff.

A swift kick at the coffee table and they tumble, shattering a precious cup from Grandma Rose. Now, at least, I'm not the only broken thing in the room.

Chapter Four

KATERINA

'The Figs' Sydney, 2018

Nurse Izzy pokes her head around the door.

"Seems the crisis is almost over. If there aren't any cases tomorrow, the Health Department will clear us for business as usual." She makes a celebratory hand flourish. "You'll be able to breathe fresh air again instead of staring outside like a dog begging for a walk."

I find her straightforwardness strangely refreshing. The usual practice of *wrapping the oldies in cottonwool* can be smothering.

She turns to leave, then reaches into her pocket. "I almost forgot. Someone sent you a personal letter."

"I doubt it? Personal letters are scarcer than hen's teeth."

"It's definitely yours," Izzy says, in the self-assured manner of the young.

I tap my finger on the envelope, ready to point out

her mistake, but when I turn it over, sure enough, the post office redirection sticker details are mine.

Ms Katerina Tremaine
The Figs Garden Village Residential Care Home
Abernathy Road Sydney
NSW Australia

I crease my brow, muttering half to myself, "How would anyone find my current address?"

Izzy shrugs. "In this electronic age, people can find anything and anyone."

After she closes the door, I tilt the envelope under my bedside lamp. Originally addressed to a house I left decades ago, the handwriting is almost obscured by crossing-outs and redirections, but my heart races at his unmistakable script. Each word meticulously penned with tall, thin letters like an avenue of pencil pines, a blustery breeze slanting them ever so slightly backwards. His writing is shakier than it used to be—but it's definitely him.

Philip.

I fumble with the sticky tape for an age, then wait to catch my breath. After so many years, a few extra minutes won't hurt.

My hands tremble unfolding the paper, just as they did with his war-time correspondence. I didn't know then what his letters would bring, and I cannot imagine what he has to say now.

It's been so long.

My Dearest Katerina,

Please allow me to call you dearest one last time.

I'm sorry we won't meet again, but you have my reassurance I've kept our secret. I'm concerned my daughters will follow the unavoidable document trail that comes with death, but you do not have to reveal the truth.

My life has been good, yet despite our promise to forget, I never did.

Farewell and love,

Philip McLeod

He's changed his last name, but it's unmistakably the Philip I've fought to block out. Once I made the decision, I resigned myself to a lifetime of burying every damn memory. Until now, I've done an admirable job.

Before returning it to the envelope, I smooth the paper and press my lips against his words to kiss the memory of the man.

I drop it immediately.

It's only a feeling, but feelings should never be ignored.

Philip is dead.

To stop the memories rushing back, I crumple the letter into a ball. I want to let go, but my fingers obey my heart rather than my brain and bring it to my chest. My heart tingles with a mixture of fear, sorrow and love. All at once beautiful and cruel.

I flop back onto my pillow, fists pressing my breast. "No. Not you."

I open my eyes to Izzy fumbling with her mask, no

silly comments made before she disappears down the corridor.

"I'm not ill," I call, but my voice is drowned out by the emergency buzzer. I give up and wait for the doctor.

As the doctor checks my pulse, Izzy explains, "She was clutching her heart. Her colour was poor."

He barely examines me before calling an ambulance. As far as doctors are concerned, a patient of my age is one stretcher trip away from the morgue.

I muster as much vigour as I can. "I'm not going."

"But Ms Tremaine," he begins.

"I'll sign a waiver." I hold up my index finger, hoping to make my point clear. "I'm not dying, and even if I was, I'd rather die here at The Figs."

I've been on this Earth long enough to know that, like the rest of us, doctors aren't infallible.

I'm not having a coronary. This is the untangling of my heart.

Philip's letter has released the knot of lies, anguish, and terrible deeds I've bound tightly for seventy-two years.

Izzy checks my vital signs. "You seem fine, but I reckon you should be careful what you wish for in the future. When you complained about boredom a week ago, you were rewarded with a crazy lot of excitement. People dying, then Italian Maria bursting into your room, and the mysterious letter I reckon tipped you over the edge, bringing on your—"

"Funny turn?" My laugh is forced.

"Nothing funny about it and it's not quite over.

Since the letter, night staff have recorded horrific night-mares. For those episodes, you've won another prize—extra bed rest."

"No. Please, no. I'm okay, it's the new cook, there's been too much cheese in the evening. It disagrees with me."

"I'll give you the benefit of the doubt," she says and checks a message on her phone. She smiles and shoves it under my face but whisks it away before I have a chance to focus.

"Yippee," she says. "Management have sent through a provisional contract. Once they get a reference, I can stay on permanently."

"You got all that from the phone? I'm old enough to remember when phones were attached to a wall and could only be used for talking. And we thought that was a miracle."

She pokes out her tongue, but the silly effect is spoiled by the loveliness of youth.

As Izzy studies the new employment details, I get an idea. "Excuse me. You said people can find anything if they know where to look. Can you search for death notices on that fancy phone?"

"Give me a name and a place."

The results are a bitter-sweet success. Although for the past seven days I've been emotionally sure of Philip's passing, I'm shocked to see the proof in black and white.

MCLEOD PHILIP

Philip passed away peacefully surrounded by family. Treasured husband of Hillary, beloved father of Claudia and Bonnie. Philip, my vase shall remain empty. Thank you for fifty-three years and countless bouquets of Geraldton Wax.

If I had a mirror to check, my face would be green with envy. Philip led a normal life. He gave his wife flowers.

Claudia and Bonnie. My mouth goes dry. His daughters. Philip's letter warned they might come looking.

Izzy touches my arm gently. "Are you okay, Katerina? I planned on bending the rules and allowing you out for afternoon tea with Maria and her son, but looks as if you're overdoing it again.".

"Keeping busy is better for my health," I say. "I'm happy to give you a reference. I worked in the medical field myself, many years ago."

"That would be lovely, but there's no need."

"Help me into the wheelchair." I plead. "I'll be sensible. I'll wait quietly in the 'Sunny Corner' for afternoon tea."

I park myself in front of the open window and drink in the birdsong, get lost in the wispy ribbon clouds, then watch fallen leaves somersaulting across the brick path. I force myself to focus on anything but the prickling and prodding memories.

I must stop my fear echoing in nightmares. Who knows what I'll scream from the shadows?

Chapter Five

CLAUDIA

Fremantle, 2018

Nothing looks, or tastes the same anymore, and I can hardly keep anything down. I return my triangle of vegemite toast to the plate, and imagine the rolls of newspapers piling up outside my front door.

I glance at the fractured pieces of Grandma Rose's cup I'd set in front of a family photograph. Aaron was fifteen when he captured a burst of candid shots. This picture has always been my favourite.

Oliver's happily building a limestone retaining wall, while Josh, my oldest son, pushes a wheelbarrow of potted ferns. I'm smiling a dirty-faced, messy-haired smile, carrying buckets of mortar to lay the capping tiles. After setting a timer, Aaron's peeps a tongue-poking-face into the frame. Dad in the background, has beer in hand and sits low in a picnic chair like a film set director.

He's not overseeing us now, at least not from Earth.

I close my eyes to escape into the photo, back to a time when all of us were happy.

"You're telling the boys," I say, tapping the glass over Oliver's face. "I can't do it. I don't even know what happened."

Tilting my head upwards, I talk to Dad, in case his spirit's hovering. "Do you know what's going on? Why did Oliver leave?"

Bile-infused tea hits my throat and spews over the floor. I curl up next to the mess and cry.

The phone rings constantly, but I can't move. I know it isn't my husband.

Hours pass before I find the strength to force one foot in front of the other and clean up the mess. I'm putting the mop and the bucket away when it rings again. The damned thing stops before I pick up.

Missed calls: Oliver zero, Mum four, and Bonnie ten. I listen half-heartedly to the voice messages. Mum's tone is increasingly irritated. "Too busy out spending your father's money to call your mother back?" Bonnie's latest message makes me want to bash my head. "Claudia, if you don't phone back within the hour, I'm ringing the police. I'm worried."

She doesn't make idle threats and the thought of police at my door is unbearable. I don't want to talk, but I have no choice. After splashing my face with water, I return her call.

"What do you mean, Oliver's left?" Bonnie sounds agitated. "Is there another woman? Don't even answer. There's always another fucking woman."

I lack the energy to both breathe and talk.

Met with my silence she yells, "Claudia?"

"He...didn't say. I... didn't ask."

Her voice softens. "Claudia? Are you okay?"

I try to smother my ragged breath, but animalistic sobs escape.

"That's it. I'm coming over."

The phone goes dead. No point ringing back—she'll be halfway to **FUQiT** and here in twenty minutes if she takes the backroads past the beaches and old factories. I walk outside and lean against the tree stump where Aaron had balanced the camera for the photo.

Staring at the place where we sat as a family pours salt on my wounds. But I need the pain. That's when I notice the weeds. Oliver has always been obsessive about keeping the garden manicured, but the place is neglected. Was he even home while I sat at Dad's bedside? If not, where was he?

I collapse on the un-mowed grass and don't move until Bonnie announces her entrance with a ten-kilometre whistle. "Claudia! Your door's unlocked. Someone could have broken in and bashed you senseless."

Good.

She drops her bags on the limestone wall and stares down at me. "Jesus, you look like you've already been assaulted."

I wipe snot and tears across my jacket sleeve. I'm beyond caring.

"Do you need a doctor?"

I shake my head.

"Come inside, then."

While I lie on the couch, she cleans frantically, as if putting my house in order will fix my life. She stops mid-whirl holding a mess of teacups and points to the solicitor's envelope with her nose. "You haven't read it?"

I shake my head.

"You're wearing the same clothes?"

I nod.

"Get in the shower." She sounds like Mum. "You have fifteen minutes to rinse and dry while I make us something to eat. If you're not back in sixteen, I'm coming in to carry you out."

The ridiculous idea of twig-like Bonnie carrying tree trunk-like me, makes me laugh. It's a feeble laugh, but it pokes a tiny bit of air through the smothering despair.

Following orders is easier than thinking, so I trudge to the bathroom.

When I emerge from the shower, the living room is full of Bonnie's energy. She jitters around, hitting high notes that, under better circumstances, would be almost bearable.

Grandma Rose said Bonnie had way too much electricity. Grandma Rose was right. A few minutes ago, my house was dead—flatlining, but I need calm. Not this madness.

"Don't you want to know what's in my carry bag?" she asks, her lightning-bolt earrings jiggling as she empties the contents onto the newly cleared table. Her bag is hand painted with Munch's Scream. It may as well be a mirror.

She produces a bottle of port and two small crystal glasses. I watch as she pours, adding drop after drop until the burgundy liquid surface domes above the rim.

"Remember this?" she asks. "We're going to suck the meniscus off the port. It's a sisterly tradition."

Anything we've done once is a tradition to her. Arguing is pointless, her comebacks are like lightning-fast zaps from a cattle prod.

I empty the glass in a single gulp.

"Have another," Bonnie says. "Port's a great replacement for tears—similar chemical composition."

I know these are 'Bonnie-facts' but I drink another. "Maybe I should stop replenishing my supply," I say. "Let the tears dry up."

"No. Your heart might dry out, too. You'll end up like Mum."

It never occurred to me Mum might once have been softer. My God. I've become my mother. Is that why Oliver left?

We suck the meniscus until Bonnie gets wobbly, and puddles of port pool on the pale timber of the coffee table. She spreads the spills with a silver-painted fingernail. "What do you see?"

"I'm not in the mood for a Rorschach test."

"Come on, squint and tell me."

"Will it give me answers about Oliver walking out, or Dad leaving stupid advice to assess our lives?"

She takes the last swig, turning the bottle upside down to dribble a red cross over the splotches. "No fucking idea. But things always get easier."

Bonnie doesn't sound convinced.

"Not without money or a job." I pick up the unopened envelope. "How much money did Dad leave?"

"You needn't bother checking; I imagine we have the same letter—it's addressed to both." She tears it out of my hand and rips it open. "Yep. Same. A Premium Bond. I tried to phone the office in London but forgot about the time difference."

Along with the letter there are certificates for two-thousand pounds of English premium bonds, bought in 1962. Three years before he met Mum.

"What do you reckon they're worth, now?" Bonnie asks.

"I don't know, but that would have been a lot of money back then."

We make telepathic eye-contact.

"Mum's going to crack it," she says.

I sit in the added-on conservatory, with its French doors and wall of books, it was once my favourite room. It's lost its charm. Bonnie must have left early this morning. Not that it was difficult to leave before I forced myself out of bed at three this afternoon.

Everything gives me a headache. Even the once cheery sun heckles me. I move into the darker living room to text Oliver.

Again.

> Are you ready to tell me what happened?

> Have you told Josh and Aaron yet?

Last time I phoned the boys, I delivered the news about Dad's death. I refuse to be the bearer of more unhappiness.

I send a third message to Oliver.

> What's up with Wendy? You leave and she stops talking to me?

Dad used to say you only need one good friend. He was wrong. A few days ago, my life was sparsely populated. Now it's a fucking ghost town.

As if on cue, keys jangle at the front door—first one, then another, and another.

It's not my husband. Not unless during the past week he's inexplicably forgotten the front door key is the one with the square end.

Leaning numbly against the arm of the couch, I ignore the rattle. A violent intruder would be a quick solution.

Bonnie bursts through juggling an overnight bag and several packages.

"You moving in?"

She grins. "Just visiting. I collected your spare keys from Mum."

"You can't spend every day babysitting me," I say.

Bonnie ignores me, emptying the contents of the Scream bag onto the coffee table. I brace myself for another mess of shot glasses and alcohol, but today's survival kit is a waterfall of buttons, wool, and multi-coloured-bobble-headed pins.

What is she thinking?

"Craft? I'm not in the mood."

"You've been stewing in your own juices for long enough."

"That's okay coming from you. Matt hasn't walked out and you still have Will to keep you company. This house is emptier than empty. Couldn't my sons have happily grown up and lived around the corner instead of moving to different states?"

"I'll happily hand over my kid—" She stops mid joke and pats my arm. "I can't fix any of that, and I can't hold Mum back forever. But we can and will fix fuckhead Oliver. Where are your scissors?"

"What do you mean fix? We can't sew a marriage

back together." I'm talking to myself. She's left the room to rummage in the kitchen. "Scissors are in the third drawer. Lefthand side."

Bonnie returns, making stabbing motions with the scissors as she spreads the bits and pieces table. "We're making voodoo dolls out of socks; you'll get that bastard out of your head and very soon he'll be in a world of hurt!"

"Nope. This is silly and I don't want to play."

"No choice. We're doing it."

She shows me her Pinterest collection of homemade dolls. Button eyes, ragged stitching and embroidered hearts pierced by pins. "The curse won't work unless we include something personal."

She says this as if it's perfectly normal and rather than think of an appropriate response, I wander around the house wondering if my world has totally flipped. Now I'm looking for sorcery stuff.

Bonnie claps her hands with delight when I return holding socks, a pair of underpants from the dirty wash, and Oliver's nose hair trimmer.

"You've outdone yourself. The only thing more personal would be a stool sample."

I almost laugh, but it's too dangerous—laughter is an entrée for tears.

Bonnie screws up her face as she taps out strands of nasal hair, and makes a disgusted yelp as she touches his underwear "I should have brung gloves."

"Brought," I say, realising immediately that I'm the loser in our ongoing contest. On purpose, she'll say something like 'could of' instead of 'could have', and every time I correct her, I lose the game.

I try for a smile, but although I'm only days out of

practise it's an effort forcing my mouth into the correct shape.

We concentrate while we're sewing, and I'm transported back to when Bonnie and I were kids, making clothes for our dolls. Given the ridiculous things we're creating now, there's an unexpected but welcome period of calm. For a heartbeat or two I forget. *Thanks Bonnie.* Sometimes she does know what I need.

After attaching strands of woollen hair, I get the urge to stab pins through the doll's head. Voodoo-Oliver stares coldly with soulless blue button eyes. "A perfect likeness." I poke pins in each of the holes, but instead of satisfaction there's a wave of remorse. "I hope this doesn't blind him."

Bonnie gasps disapprovingly. "You're supposed to be enjoying this, not worrying about Oliver."

I shrug off the guilt and stab in a cathartic frenzy. "I fucking hope his eyes explode."

"Swearing out loud? Good girl. But eyes? There are better places to stab."

Raising my eyebrows is all the encouragement Bonnie needs. Her furious voodoo-puppet attack is concentrated between its tiny sock legs.

I prick my finger, checking for sharpness, then position my pins where it should hurt the most.

Bonnie puts her hand out to stop me. "OMG, what if Oliver's dick falls off? You wouldn't take him back then."

"I'd feel sorry for him."

"But SEX, Claudia. SEX!"

"It's been months, maybe a year."

Bonnie tilts her head, staring like a dog who can't understand human language.

"What's wrong?"

There's a long pause. "Nothing. Go ahead."

Repeating one of Dad's favourite sayings, "Cruel but fair," I puncture the spot where a heart would be, if Oliver had one. Then I stab the doll's groin. "Another to the to the private parts."

Bonnie laughs hysterically, slapping her thigh.

"What?" I ask.

"The private parts? Surely that's not what you call it?"

I glare at her and she glares back double-strength. What is she waiting for?

"Penis? Is that better?"

"No way, woman. Too anatomical. From now on it's either cock or dick."

"So now you're an expert of acceptable and unacceptable terms for genitalia?"

"Never say genitalia. And, unless you're at the doctors, you never, ever say penis. How did you get into your forties without knowing this? You need an education." Chuckling, she puts up her fingers, one by one. "Schlong...knob...plonker—"

"Stop."

I'm not sure whether I'm laughing or crying, but Bonnie joins in and the giggling turns to tears. I'm glad she's here crying with me.

I panic at my phone suddenly ringing—what if Oliver's in the hospital emergency department with sharp stabbing pains in his...knob?

Bonnie answers, "Hello ...Mum ... No... No, it's not Claudia, it's Bonnie ... Yes, I am crying... No, nothing's wrong with me ... It's Claudia ... Oliver's left."

Bonnie listens to Mum and I study her face for clues.

"No ... no ..." Bonnie is annoyed at whatever Mum is saying. "He followed Dad's lead. You know, assess your current life, build yourself a new one."

I'm glad I can't hear the whole conversation. I can't deal with Mum blaming me. I think back thirty years to Bonnie being chosen as a princess in our school play. Mum couldn't wait to sew her a fancy costume, but she was horrified at me being given a masculine role. Dad jumped to my defence. *"Be proud of playing a woodcutter. You'll grow into a strong woman like my mother."*

Dad would be disappointed if he could see how weak I am now.

"No...," Bonnie continues grunting in response to Mum's questions. "Claudia's not okay, but I'm looking after her...no, now's not a good time."

My hands tremble as I pack up the Voodoo stuff.

"Time for bed." Bonnie herds me into the bedroom and is walking out when she changes her mind, resting on the bed beside me.

Holding my Voodoo-Oliver, pins and all, I close my eyes.

I hate Oliver... I want him back. I'd cry myself to sleep, but she'd hear me. Maybe Dad would hear me too, and I don't want him to be sad.

I talk to Bonnie in the dark like we did when we were children. "Don't wish away your time with Will. I did that and look at me now."

"Claudia, stop blaming yourself for everything. You were so proud when Josh got the job with the Federal Police. He had to move to Sydney."

"I could be just as proud with him living next door...

Aaron moved too. I looked after my family, but they've all left me."

"Sleep," Bonnie whispers.

After placing the voodoo doll in the nightstand drawer, I put a pillow over my head, thinking about Bonnie's reaction to our sexless marriage. Surely, it's normal for couples to stop. It's not like Oliver begged and I knocked him back. It wasn't the other way, either. When the boys were here, we were busy, they left home and we were both lost, then Dad got sick...there was no abrupt ending...our desire simply faded and neither of us tried to bring it back.

"Bonnie? Is there something wrong with me?"

Her answer is a gentle snore.

Chapter Six

CLAUDIA

Fremantle, Western Australia

I wake up to mid-morning glare, a clattering from the kitchen, and the memory of Bonnie. For a few indulgent minutes, I bury my face in the mattress, but denial's pointless. She isn't the type to leave me be.

Before she marches in and drags me out of bed, I untangle myself from the mess of sheets and head to the bathroom. The fluoro-lit mirror highlights my puffy under-eyes, but there are positives. Compared to yesterday, my eyes are pink-rimmed instead of fire engine red. An improvement.

I'm not ready for a full-on smile as I wander out to find Bonnie, but hey—baby steps.

She holds a cup of coffee towards me. "Ta Da. Here. I heard you getting out of bed."

"I drink tea."

"I know, but you're getting coffee." She points out

the post-it-note stuck on my cup: *A NEW START. A NEW CLAUDIA.*

It's too early to complain, so I take a cautious sip, but the smell reminds me of Oliver.

"Thank you," I mumble, forcing another mouthful.

"You slept forever. . . which is good . . . you look . . . better." Her unusual hesitancy suggests she'd rather say, 'you look like shit.' I'm surprised. My tactless sister has never considered anyone's feelings before.

"While you slept, I did more digging about Dad's money."

"It's too early to think."

"What you mean to say, is thanks for chasing up the Premium Bond deposit."

"What did you find?"

Bonnie drops two slices into the toaster, smiling smugly. "I'm glad you asked. I phoned the office in London. The woman was helpful-ish. She couldn't be specific about amounts, but did say there's been no communication with Dad for years. She explained how all profits are regularly moved into a building society holding account."

"Did she give you details?'

"Confidentiality rules apply. So . . . no."

"Where the money originally came from?"

"No idea. She was professionally cautious. Took my email address to send more information and sent something immediately."

My scatterbrain-princess sister is taking control. I rub my eyes to check who's talking.

"You want me to tell you the key bits?"

"Please do."

"Premium bonds are like a lottery," she explains.

"The shared interest earned by investors is lumped together and winners are drawn at random, like lotto. Chances are you'll get a few small wins, maybe even a big one, but a win isn't guaranteed. The winnings are paid as dividends, and the initial deposit is never touched."

So, not a normal interest earning account. I roll my confused head. "So, we could be rich?" I ask. "Or it's worth only what Dad deposited."

"Until we provide proof of identity, the account is worth nothing to us. And that's not the only bad news.

"What?"

"Mum's coming over this afternoon." Bonnie pokes out her tongue. " Don't look at me like that. I'm the one who called her then had to hold the phone at arm's length. She wasn't impressed when I told her the money was deposited in 1962. Mum refused to start a family without a proper roof over their heads, so Dad and her saved for years to buy a house. Mum's going to be seriously pissed off if it turns out all that time he was hiding money they could have used as a deposit."

I shudder. "That bad?"

"Worse, she talked about bringing Dad back from the fucking dead just to kill him."

"I'm not often on Mum's side," I say. "But I'm with her on this one. Why would Dad hide money when they were broke?"

"Maybe he was a secret hit man? Or a bank robber worried about leaving a money trail?" Bonnie takes a mouthful of toast and chews while she talks. "Dirty cash. He couldn't spend it."

"No way. Dad would never steal. There's a simpler explanation."

"Then why the intrigue?" She waves her toast, showering a drift of crumbs.

I wish I could float like a crumb, not worrying about loss, deceit or money. "Dad knew he was dying, so why didn't he sort out this mess?" I ask. "He could have deposited it in a normal bank account instead of leaving it for us to resolve."

"Drink your coffee then log on to the Centrelink site. Now's as good a time as any to register for an allowance. We're not getting our mitts on any money today."

"I'd rather wait."

"Do it. You need the money."

I don't argue because Bonnie's like a pit bull; she never lets go. She might have written Oliver off, but part of me hopes he'll come to his senses.

"Sign yourself up," she says, looking at me as if she can read minds. "That's one problem out of the way. As for the *being forced* to leave an old life behind shit, and the woman Dad wanted to dance with on his death bed, that mystery's not easily fixed." Bonnie grabs her car keys and kisses my cheek. "I've got to go. I'm ducking in to work for a couple of hours. I'll be back before Mum gets here."

"I'm fine," I say, mostly to myself, as I tip out the coffee and make myself a cup of tea.

After logging into the computer, I look around at the only remaining constant. This house. I can't keep it without money, and I won't grovel at Oliver's feet.

My throat tightens as I record my online status as newly single and unemployed. Centrelink will start paying an allowance in four weeks. There's a waiting period because I resigned from my last job, and the payments are conditional on me searching for a new one. I've seen myself in the mirror—the current Claudia is far from appealing to prospective employers.

I finish submitting the request as Bonnie returns.

"I've done it," I say, smiling weakly. My smile falters. Mum's standing behind her.

In through the nose, I say to myself, breathing in additional oxygen to deal with what's next. "Hello Mum."

I cross my fingers under the table. Please don't start about Oliver or tell me you suspected something was going on.

"I thought you'd make more of an effort with your appearance, now you're single," Mum says.

"Thanks." I position my feet towards the door.

"Ask Bonnie for help," Mum continues. "She always does her face nicely. She'll advise you how to do the best with what you've got."

Always the same: beautiful Bonnie, plain old Claudia.

"What did Josh and Aaron say about Oliver leaving?" Mum asks.

"I haven't spoken to them. It's Oliver's job."

While Mum tuts, I clench and unclench my jaw, trying to release the tension.

"Don't look at me like that," Mum says. "You've always been too sensitive."

She sets a sturdy cardboard box on the table. The one she and Dad used to store important documents.

"Good. You've got the birth and death certificates" I say.

Mum shakes her head as she produces a handful of papers. "I've found inconsistencies I can't believe I missed. You know I pride myself on noticing details."

Bonnie leans in to look and Mum flashes a look of self-importance.

"Here's our marriage certificate. Your dad gave his mother's maiden name as Bridgett O'Patrick, but twenty years ago, when we applied to get the pension—lo-and-behold her name was Healy."

Mum makes a hand gesture suggesting, '*What the fuck?*' But she'd never use those words, they're too straightforward and honest. Mum's body language carries a harshness beyond swearing.

I check the names myself. "This is unbelievable. Dad could remember every horse that ever won the Melbourne Cup, yet he forgot his mother's name?"

Bonnie repeats one of Dad's countless sayings, "If my memory serves me correctly and it usually does... my mother's name was—"

"Exactly. No one would forget their parent's name." I glance warily at Mum.

She growls from the back of her throat. "Better not be any more contradictions. No wife likes to be deceived."

I look away. I'm not going there; it would open a whole new conversation. Me and Oliver.

"What's on Dad's birth certificate?" I ask. "Surely that has his parents' correct names?"

"He never had one," Mum says. "We applied to the register of births, deaths and marriages in Melbourne, but they couldn't find any record."

Mum doesn't miss the exchange looks between me and Bonnie. "They explained it wasn't unusual in those days for births to be unregistered."

"It doesn't make sense," I say. "There's something fishy."

"Really fucking fishy," Bonnie says. "Where are his army records Mum?"

"Don't swear." Mum slaps Bonnie's leg. "He lost his records. Your father moved a lot in his younger years."

Bonnie sends me a message using eyebrow code.

"He worked his way around Australia." Mum's grasping to find a valid explanation. I understand what she's doing—defending the man she trusted for years. I know the feeling. I'm fighting the temptation to make excuses for Oliver.

"Dad, the sneaky bugger," Bonnie says. "There's no evidence of him existing before he married you. I bet he was using an alias, Mum."

"There could be lots of reasons for the different names." My words don't block the sound of Mum grinding her teeth. "Maybe his mother remarried?"

"Thank you." Mum nods in my direction. "Your Dad made careless errors with names; that isn't illegal. He wasn't using an alias."

Bonnie stands. "I'll ring Kovacevic. See what's next."

While Bonnie talks to the lawyer, I whisper to Mum, "What exactly do we know about Dad? We grew up knowing Grandma Rose and Pop, but never met Dad's family. None of them. He talked about his Mama but said she died years ago."

Mum twists a fabric belt tightly around her fingers. I'm torn between stopping her from cutting off her circulation and wrapping it around her neck.

We're silent as we wait for Bonnie to reappear.

"Ladies, we can't bury our heads up our arses. Philip McLeod was covering his tracks. He said as much in his letter."

"Is that what the lawyer said?" Mum asks.

"Course not. The highlights of the call are actually lowlights. Without proof of identity the money isn't claimable... unless we have a birth certificate or something to connect Dad to the person who deposited the money." Bonnie's more serious than I've ever seen.

I shake my head "So, we can't claim it? I can't deal with this."

"You'll have to. We'll have to."

Bonnie stares to the left. She always does this when she's concentrating. "Mum? Is there anyone who knew Dad as a young man?"

"The only friends your dad had were from the bowls club. He was over ninety. What chance is there of his childhood friends being around?"

"Buckley's," Bonnie says. "And fucking Buckley's chance of ever finding them."

Chapter Seven

KATERINA

'The Figs' Sydney, 2018

It's a month since Philip's letter and although I expected to push away my worries and get back to the normal-run-of-the-mill, the nightmares are worsening. Nurse Izzy makes my bed so taut you could bounce a sixpence on it, and while I like to see a job well done, this is a waste of time considering my plan to get back in and stay all day.

"Do you mind helping me fold the spare blanket?" she asks. "It's easier with two."

I regard her with suspicion. Izzy can fold blankets perfectly well on her own, but I hold the corners and wait. She's going to ask me about last night. The terror was real. I woke every resident within cooee of my room and the night staff were run off their feet. I clench my hands around the blanket as if tightening my grip around the memories. They sneak out whenever I let down my guard.

"Mrs Carmichael was telling me about your keen mind," Izzy says.

I wait for her to add the usual qualifier—for your age—but she doesn't. Izzy may be too curious for her own good, but she isn't patronising.

"I call Mrs Carmichael... Matron," I say. "It's a proper title for the woman in charge."

"Well, whatever you call her, she's worried. About you. We're both worried about you. Mrs Carm...Matron is properly concerned."

"Give me a sleeping tablet then. Knock me out."

"It's not just about what's happening at night, Katerina. It's your whole demeanour. It's been ages since you washed your hair, and you're spending too much time alone. Neglecting selfcare. Avoiding other patients. Together, these are bad signs."

"My hair is fine. There are parts of the world where people never wash their hair." I've no idea if this is true, but it gives Izzy something to consider.

Nurse Izzy tilts her head, lost in thought.

"Maybe I could sit with you in my break, and you could tell me what's on your mind."

"No."

I pick my novel off the night stand and pretend to read, hoping she takes the hint.

"Are the nightmares about the accident?" She points to my wheelchair, but I ignore her. I've reread the same page of this book several times since Philip's letter, but the words won't sink in.

"I'd love to hear what you got up to when you were young."

She must think I'm either stupid or senile. I'm not falling for that and I have no intention of sharing stories of my youth with anyone. Anyway, people Izzy's age are more interested in the style of shoes and clothes than actual events. What could an old lady have to say? The young think they invented love and sex and heightened feelings. Old women are the wrinkled keepers of knitting, mashed potatoes, and lavender soap.

"I could write your memoir. It might help," she says. Her voice carries a familiar softness. She reminds me of Mama Bridgett—Philip's beautiful mother—my nanny as a child, then my confidante when I could trust nobody else. But this is not Mama Bridgett, it is Izzy and she's prying.

I strengthen my resolve and shake my head. "No."

"Well, if you change your mind, let me know. I've been doing a creative writing course and it would give me practise."

I smile. She'll be wanting to write light and airy tales, but I cannot help her there. "If I ever need someone, I'll ask."

"Almost forgot, Maria's been looking for you. She's knocked on your door several times."

I'm tempted to snap, 'I'm old, not deaf', but kind Izzy doesn't deserve my moods.

"She's waiting for Gentlecise class to begin. Are you sure you won't go?"

It's the third time someone's asked this morning.

"Not today."

"You don't like the sessions anymore?"

"At the moment, I'm irritated by you trying to get me out of my room. And for the record, Gentlecise isn't a word. Would it be too much effort to say gentle exercise?"

Days like these I'm tired of change. I only have a

short time left on Earth, so surely, it's not too much to ask the world to stop turning. I was slipping out peacefully until Philip's letter arrived.

"I love a good portmanteau," Izzy says.

"I'm confused. Why have you changed the subject to luggage?"

Occasionally, Izzy sounds as incoherent as some of the residents. No doubt a side effects of spending too much time on the phone.

"Portmanteau has another meaning. Two words blended together to make a new one." She eyeballs me and smiles. "My favourites are *bromance* and *mansplaining*. Bromance is a combination of —"

"I know what it means. I just do not see the point in making up new words."

"Okay. I get the hint."

But she obviously doesn't. She calls back on her way out, "Aldesco, a blend of alfresco and a desk. Eating at work."

I hear her chuckle as she walks down the corridor.

A month ago, before the letter, I might have chuckled too, but I'm consumed by visions of a seventy-year-old event. There's no room for joy.

Once Izzy's gone, I take out my notebook. Writing in my journal, pretending to talk to Philip is my only hope of easing the pain.

Dear Philip,

I need to talk to you. Feel free to send me a sign to let me know you're listening. I'll take anything.

I'd buried the memories deep, but the seeds

were only dormant. Now, they're sprouting in the night like a godawful jungle of terror and guilt.

I expected to pine for you, maybe even fade away and die for you, but surprisingly I kept living and you did too... a wife, two daughters... a new name. This pleases me but frightens me, too. I've an awful feeling someone will discover what we hid.

"Katerina." Izzy puts her head around the door and I hide my notebook under the blanket.

"Yes."

"Can you please help with Maria?"

"Is this another ploy to get me to leave my room?" I eye her suspiciously, but she looks genuine.

"She's having a meltdown because Gentlecise ... sorry...exercise class was cancelled."

Maria is one of the few residents of The Figs who loves to prance about. I suppose it's understandable in someone whose muscles are still cooperative. For me, stuck in the wheelchair—waving my arms around and lolling my head in time to the same bunch of unmelodic tunes is a waste of time.

"I'll see what I can do." I pull myself out of bed and follow Izzy.

Many years ago, I worked for a research doctor, taking notes on treatment and results. The old habit's still with me, though these days the notes are stored in my mind. I've noticed a pattern: the more active Maria is the more stable her mood. I wonder what else might trigger her tantrums?

"I'll take her outside," I say, wagging my finger. "Make sure you let Matron know where I am. That way, she can draw a smiley face on my behaviour chart with a note saying: Katerina left her room."

Izzy grins and gives me the thumbs up.

Once outside, Maria races ahead of me, almost running along the garden path as I roll. She gets twice the exercise and I get to admire the gardens at a leisurely pace. It suits us both.

It's cruel how the only part of Maria's body to age is her brain. When I get back to my room, I'm going to start a proper set of notes, recording everything that improves her mood. Helping Maria will help me forget.

Maria grabs my wheelchair like a demon and zooms along the rough pathway against the boundary wall, gloriously lined with yellow-dressed wattle trees. From the corner of my eye, I notice Izzy, watching like a mother hen. I wave to let her know I'm safe.

"Wait a minute," I say to Maria, holding my hand in the universal stop signal. "The wattles are magnificent."

I cross my hands over my chest, letting Maria know how much I love the yellow blooms. They remind me of when I was young, before the time of woe.

She makes a heart symbol with her fingers and I smile proudly. She understands. Shaking the branches, she coats the pathway with petals then scoops up the strands of gold, as I pick a perfect flower.

Mama Bridgett described them as floral bursts of sunshine. I loved stories of her life before Philip was born. She'd seen illustrations of Golden Wattle in a book from the library of a grand English house where she'd worked with her fiancé. He'd asked her to marry him and move to Australia, where he promised she'd see them for real.

"Katerina," Matron calls and beckons us to come inside.

What now? Is she planning to issue Maria with a speeding ticket for pushing a wheelchair too fast?

Matron has a different agenda. "I've made you a doctor's appointment."

"No need. I'm fine. I can see the regular doctor next week."

"You can't wait," Matron says. "I've found someone with experience treating night terrors." When she wears this look, Matron won't take no for an answer.

I argue, "I've had a sudden upset, but I'm sure it will get better if we give it time."

"You're going today. There are departmental procedures to follow."

"But it's Wednesday," I say. Although I do not feel like chatting over afternoon tea with Joe and Maria, I'm looking for a decent excuse.

"You might be back before Maria's son leaves, but I can't guarantee it. This is more important."

Izzy, standing next to matron, looks away as if she's let me down. She takes out her phone. "Wait here while I take Maria to her room. I'll call the taxi."

———

Izzy holds my hand in the doctor's waiting room. Her youthful skin is smooth and perfect against my age spots and bruises. Where did the years go? I am the oldest patient here by a long way. The magazines show pictures of movie stars I do not know, and Izzy is looking up something on her phone. Probably pictures of breakfasts. I hear that's what the young people do.

"Katerina Tremaine," a man wearing a casual blue polo shirt calls my name. Doctors once instilled confidence by wearing white coats with stethoscopes hanging from their necks; not only does this doctor dress down, he looks young enough to be refused service of alcohol. But then again everyone looks young these days.

While Izzy hands over the charts she's brought from 'The Figs', I look around his consulting room. His framed diploma looks genuine. He isn't too young, I'm just so old that everyone's beginning to look like a child. I was surprised to find Izzy's in her thirties.

"Any loss of appetite?" he asks.

"Only when they serve food I do not like," I say.

He ignores my sarcasm and continues reading Matron's letter.

"Muscle weakness?"

"I'm having trouble with my legs," I say.

He looks up with interest. "Since when?"

"How long is it Izzy?" I ask.

Izzy suppresses a smile. "About seventy years."

The doctor intentionally drops his pen, then leans forward in his chair. He addresses his question to Izzy. "Mental confusion?"

She snaps back, "There's nothing wrong with Katerina's mind."

"I can see she's razor sharp at the moment, but minds aren't always stable." I expect him to give me a haughty look, but his face is concerned and sincere. "I'm trying to help you, Mrs Tremaine."

Feeling tremendously guilty, I swallow my flippancy and sit up straight.

"When did the sleep issues begin?"

"After I was reminded of something that happened years ago, but I'd rather not say."

"Well, I'm telling you to talk to someone. If your sleep's been affected for any length of time, you'll develop multiple serious problems."

"I started to write it down," I say.

He studies the chart again. "Whatever you're planning to do, do it quickly. The Figs home is a medium-care facility. You're able to look after yourself... despite the trouble with your legs..." He half winks. "But the nightmares must be under control."

Izzy squeezes my hand. "We'll work something out, Doctor," she says convincingly.

On the trip back to The Figs, Izzy is quiet. When she eventually speaks, she touches my cheek. "Why don't you tell Maria what's troubling you?"

"Maria can't understand. She cannot."

"Exactly. You're '*The Odd Couple*', Maria's desperate to remember and you're determined to forget."

I promise her I'll consider the idea.

But I won't. A promise is a promise.

———

Joe has finished packing away the afternoon tea, but he opens the white cardboard cakebox again when I arrive. I'd rather go straight to my room, but I'm obliged to socialise. I cannot afford another strike against my name.

While we eat the sweet Italian Cannoli, he tells me about the day dementia suddenly stole his mother's second language and most clear thoughts of her first.

While that may be true, every time Joe speaks, Maria's eyes shine. She especially lights up at a sprinkling of words in Italian. It would be splendid if she could hear phrases in her native tongue. Unfortunately, no one at The Figs speaks the language.

He is pouring the sparkling apple juice when Maria complains. Loudly. She does such a perfect charade of drinking wine I can almost see the grapevines.

"Pity real wine is against the rules," I say. "Before we were twenty-one, we were considered too young for alcohol. Apparently, now we're too old."

I mean it as a joke, but Joe looks sad. "Getting old is cruel," he says. "Can I talk to you, Miss Katerina?"

"Of course."

"Thank you for looking after Mum," he says, "but what about you? Are you okay?"

"Has Matron been talking out of school? What happens at The Figs stays at The Figs." I laugh without conviction.

"Only about Mum. She told me how good you are with her. But I already knew that from the first day." Joe stares like a headmaster extracting the truth from a pupil.

"I'm fine." I say, trying for a tone that's both chirpy and mentally sound. "But the Doctor could not or would not guarantee I'll live more than twenty years."

Joe doesn't laugh, so I rest my hand on his. "Maria's good for me, too."

"You are a dear, sweet woman. I'm glad there's someone here who remembers my Mum is human."

He looks at me as if I'm a saint.

If only he knew.

It's not exactly what the doctor ordered, but in the spare hour before dinner, I continue my journal entry. Writing is as much of a reveal as I'll allow.

I've barely picked up my pen when Izzy appears—a bouquet of Golden Wattle twigs in hand.

"I saw you admiring these, and I can see why. They're like tiny yellow fireworks."

I smile. Her description is both fanciful and charming.

"Your room needed brightening."

I'm not senile. The darkness she hints at is inside my head. "Are you suggesting my mood could improve?"

She opens her mouth and pauses for a moment. "I want to help with your nightmares."

"They're not magic. They're flowers." I immediately regret my snappy tone. "They are beautiful, though. Thank you."

Once Izzy leaves, I remove a twig of blossoms, inhaling the scent. It awakens such strong memories that I pick up my notebook.

Philip, I'm back.

Your mother always said to find joy where you can, and to look for the silver lining. I've tried. Part of me is thankful you found love, but another part wonders how our lives would have been if we hadn't gone to the house that day.

I read in the paper how you gave flowers to your wife and remembered the bouquet of wattle you left outside my door when we were ten. I didn't like you back then. I loved Mama Bridgett, but you were just the annoying son.

My silver lining for today was that memory. Had things been different, those bouquets could have been mine.

Philip, I need your advice. My nightmares are out of control and telling someone what happened might be the only way to stop them. If I told the secret to someone who could not repeat it, would you consider our promise kept?

An iridescent blue-black bird hovers outside my window. A superb fairywren. The first one I've seen in the grounds. I very much want it to fly towards me. If it does, I'll know Philip is giving me permission to tell.

The bird flies away.

Chapter Eight

CLAUDIA

Hearing from my sons is one of my few pleasures, but when Josh calls with a tremulous greeting, my throat tightens in response.

Oliver has broken the news.

"So, is it true? You and Dad have broken up? When were you planning to tell your kids?"

"I'm sorry. I left it to him. He wanted to explain." Technically this is a lie, but I don't want to say Oliver let me down. Or talk about the end of our marriage. Not to our children.

"It wasn't Dad who told us, it was Grandma."

Covering the phone, I whisper under my breath. "Don't bad mouth your mother to your son."

Blinking Oliver—he up and leaves, then shirks his responsibility to tell the boys. And Mum? Why can't she mind her own business?

"I am sorry, Josh. There must have been a misunderstanding."

"So, what happened?" he asks. "At Pop's funeral, you and Dad seemed normal. A month later, it's over."

"I'm not sure." I shrug. "Relationships end. It's something I'll have to get used to."

"What a thing to say, Mum. You can't give up a marriage without a fight."

He's not a boy anymore. I wish he was, because then I'd distract him with a new toy or a visit to the park. I rest the phone between my head and shoulder. "My words aren't coming out the way I mean."

"Grandma said Dad decided it was over and you just let him go. Aren't you planning to get him back?"

This is the same pleading tone he used when he saw injustice as a child. He wanted us to fix the world. Unfortunately, the maternal urge to make things better kicks in.

"I'll call your dad to see if we can work things out."

I stare at the phone after he hangs up. I've made a promise and now I have to carry it out, but first of all, I'm ringing my blinking mother.

"Mum. I need to talk to you."

"You've found something terrible. I can tell by your voice. Is it about the money?"

"No. It's about my sons. You told them about me and Oliver." I squeeze the tip of my nose to stop myself snorting like an angry bull. No. Not a bull. A cow. An angry mother cow.

"Oliver was too spineless to tell *you* why he left, so he wasn't going to tell my grandsons, was he? And you weren't up to it. I was doing you a favour."

"Don't do me any more favours." My hand shakes.

"Well, you could have told me that before I spent half the morning looking through the filing cabinet.

Your father hoarded everything. He wouldn't listen when I told him there's no need to save financial information beyond seven years. There's a folder here with old tax returns, dated back to before Noah built the ark."

"You've found something?"

"No. You know your dad," Mum says. "He still longed for the days when we paid in cash and spent in cash. It was none of the government's business knowing how much money he had or what he was doing with it. So, he got rid of it all."

"Thanks for looking." I close my eyes, hoping she has somewhere better to be. Regrettably, she doesn't.

"What other documents did the Bond's office people say were acceptable. Did they explain it to you, or just Bonnie?"

"Hang on, I'll look." I sit at the computer with Mum on speaker phone while I scroll through the Australian government website the lawyer suggested. "There's a list. Acceptable proof of identity Are you ready?"

"Yes. Read it."

"Do we have commencement documents?"

"What are they?" Mum sounds annoyed, even though she's the one who asked me to read it.

"Documents like a birth certificate, or evidence of passenger arrival in Australia?"

"Oh dear. That would be a no." Mum clicks her tongue.

"Old driver's licence? Any with photo ID?" I ask.

"No, your father stopped driving before photo IDs were introduced. Once he let the car wander over the wrong side of the road. I thought he was trying to get rid of me—"

I interrupt before she describes each of Dad's driving incidents in dodgy detail. "Passport?"

"No. He never wanted to travel."

I scan through the long list, shaking my head as I read, "A continuing bank account with Dad's signature?"

She says no so loudly, I flinch.

The lawyer promised this would be straightforward, but it isn't. I consider the possibility Dad deliberately covered his tracks.

"Thanks for helping," I say to Mum.

"I'm not helping you; I'm helping me. If Bonnie's right—and your dad had secrets, I want to know what they were and why he kept them."

An incoming call stutters in the background.

"What's that beeping?" Mum asks.

"Another caller. I've got to go. I'll talk to you tomorrow."

I'm not telling her it's Oliver.

"How've you been Claudia?" he asks.

"Fine."

"I wanted to apologise for hurting you."

He sprinkles a handful of *sorrys* into meaningless-talk about 'making arrangements' and I analyse his tone of voice. Oliver sounds normal. How can he sound normal? Why isn't he begging to come home?

"How are you feeling?" I ask.

"All good," he says.

I was hoping he'd complain of needle-like pain in his nether region. Bonnie and I did a lot of stabbing down there, but obviously not enough. I want to swear or hang up, but I remember my promise to Josh to give my marriage a second chance.

"Do you think we could talk?" I ask.

"I'll come and see you after work, I need to collect some things."

If I had an old-fashioned phone, I'd slam it down. "It's best if I go now," I say.

"I'll be over this afternoon."

Until Oliver mentioned his belongings, I'd never noticed the pieces of him dotted around this house; his antique globe and his favourite artwork—a world map covering most of the exposed-stone wall. The signs have been here all along; he's been looking outward wanting to explore new places, while I've been looking for satisfaction inside the house. No doubt, he'll mark his new territory with stickers and brag about locations visited without me.

Bonnie's probably right. There'll be another woman.

I'm so angry that I pull the world map off the wall, deciding it looks better on the floor. As I'm dragging it to a corner, I accidentally step on it seven times.

I'm not shutting the door completely to Oliver, but I won't beg. I'd like to keep some pride.

The now empty wall strikes me as the perfect place to set up a research board. Bonnie and I will piece this jigsaw together in no time and collect Dad's inheritance.

After unhooking pinboards from above the desks in the boys' old rooms, I hammer nails into the stonework, glancing at the clock as I finish. "Shit. I've been at this for ages. Oliver will be here in less than an hour."

Despite hating Oliver earlier, I find myself hoping he'll realise he's missed me. Maybe Mum's right, I need to make more of myself.

I stare into the dreaded drawer of Bonnie's unwanted make-up gifts, without any idea of what half of it does. What's contouring powder?

I do the best I can with my face, then open the still-sealed packaging of a hair-curling-device Bonnie bought three years ago. She and Mum buy me beauty stuff every birthday. I grit my teeth imagining their secret plot to end my plainness as I twirl the heated brush through my faded red hair, muttering to myself about the blinking effort. The gadget doesn't transform my hair into the bouncy curls worn by the woman on the box. Nor does it give me her radiant smile. I bet she's not the kind of woman a man walks out on.

Although I mostly wear trousers, I do own dresses. Some time ago, I was persuaded by bossy, blinking Bonnie to buy a body-hugging green dress. I changed my mind once I got home, but never returned it. *Body-con* the tag says—code for a dress size too small. I pull it off the hanger and throw it over my head. It fits perfectly. *Appetite-annihilating-grief has benefits.*

As Dad always said, "*Find joy where you can and look for the silver lining.*"

After a second check in the mirror, I replace my usual nude lipstick with '*Flat Out Fabulous*', then kick off my flats and squeeze into heels.

I spent less time getting ready for our wedding.

With the extra height, I'm taller than Oliver's five-foot-eleven and I strut into the living room ready for battle.

He's already here, making himself comfortable on the sofa.

Oliver stares like he's never seen me dressed before. "You look ... different, Claudia. But you know I'm only here to collect some things."

"Yes. You told me on the phone."

"You've gone to a lot of trouble. I wasn't planning a date."

His comment cuts deep into my hurt. If I could have a do-over, I'd wipe off the make-up to show I don't care. "Thank you for your kind invitation," I say, "but Bonnie and I are going out on the town."

This will be the first of many lies.

I turn my back to pin index cards and a picture of Dad on the boards. "I can't stop, I've got work to do."

Oliver stands too close as he runs his finger underneath my scribbled heading: *Philip McLeod*. He taps the board. "It looks like a scene from a detective show."

I've never been abandoned before, so I don't know the etiquette, but Oliver is too familiar for my liking. Especially since he doesn't want to be here.

He writes Dad's full name on a blank index card. *Philip Sean Victor Patrick Alexander McLeod*. "I always thought the six-name thing was dodgy. I told him, too. I asked for proof, but your dad laughed, saying there wasn't enough room on official forms to write the whole kit and caboodle."

"What are you doing?" I yank Oliver's new card from the board. I've lived with this man for twenty-five years, without realising he was a jerk. There's no way I'm talking to him about Dad. I will not speak to Oliver as if nothing's changed.

I point to his prized map on the floor.

"Yours."

"Footprints?" He lifts a disdainful eyebrow.

"An accident." My second lie comes easier than the first.

Oliver rolls the map carefully, scanning the room for other personal effects. "You said you wanted to talk?"

I look up after what I hope passes as a couldn't-give-a-fuck pause. "Will it change anything?"

"Probably not...I don't think I have... but we can't ignore... we have to discuss ..." He ends his jumbled nothingness with an awkward laugh.

I bite my bottom lip. "Don't bother. I'm not convinced you'd tell the truth."

"Try me."

"Is there someone else?" I force my voice to remain steady.

"I've always loved you, but ... maybe love's not enough... I guess I got sick of living side by side. I've longed for someone who wanted the same things."

"Yes, or no?" I ask.

"It's not a yes or no answer, Claudia," he says.

I feel sick when Oliver says my name. It sounds indecent coming from his mouth. He's not allowed to say it anymore. Not when he's found someone else.

Oliver drops his face into his hands, but I'm not buying it.

"Something's missing and has been for a long time."

"So, after all these years, you're after bright and shiny without ever telling me how you felt or asking me what I wanted."

My shoulders drop of their own accord and I find myself staring at the ridiculously high shoes. "Text me before you come over for the last of your stuff and I'll be sure to leave before you arrive. I've left cardboard packing boxes in the bedroom."

As I say this, I wonder why I'm organising a man who's organised himself out of my life. I draw myself to my full height. "One more thing," I call as I march out.

"Ring our sons and explain why you left. Maybe one day you can explain it to me."

I might not be strong or brave, but I faced Oliver without crying.

I drive aimlessly around the streets, then after circling for ten minutes I pull into the beach carpark. Stunning sunsets a short trip from home—why haven't I made the effort to watch them?

In my right mind, I would have removed my shoes before hitting the sand, but I wobble towards the shore, my heels sinking in. I stumble; no doubt looking drunk.

A few metres from the water's edge I sit, watching a lone surfer silhouetted against the fiery sky. He misses a wave, and I hold my breath as he disappears under the foam before being dumped onto the shore. Poor bloke. But he lifts himself out of the water, shaking his hair like a wet dog. His teeth gleam white against his tanned skin and, even in the failing light, I recognise his joy at being alive. It's a timely reminder that we can be swamped and come up smiling.

I smile a thank you, then flatten my gadget-curled hair and make a feeble swipe at my make-up. It'll have to stay on until I get home. And I can't go home until Oliver's gone.

Deciding enough time's passed, I brush the sand off my clothes and cross the carpark, passing the surfer changing into dry clothes. Despite his wetsuit dangling around his waist, he's not at all self-conscious. Close-up, with the street light shining on him, he looks older than I thought; late thirties to early forties at a guess. It's hard to pinpoint the age of a man. They seem to flatline at *boy-man* stage for years. Then around fifty, they step off the edge of youth.

They say women over forty fade until they're invisible. But that can't be totally true—the surfer is smiling. At me. Maybe Bonnie's right about the lipstick. I'm tempted to explain why I'm overdressed for the beach, instead I say, "This visit was unplanned."

"Finding your way to the beach was a good move. I'm teaching myself how to surf. It might even be therapeutic if I ever get the hang of it." He grins.

Despite gravelly stones sticking into my bare feet like pieces of dropped Lego, I smile as I walk to my car. Nothing miraculous happened. It hasn't been a *barely there* to *flat out fabulous* day. But it hasn't ended badly.

Oliver's car's still in the driveway, so I park down the street and watch through the rear-view mirror. Spying on my own husband doesn't sit well, but after my '*going out with Bonnie*' lie, I can't go in until he leaves.

It's not long before he appears; carrying boxes with a spring to his step. Is this the walk of freedom?

I duck down as he drives past, then I shuffle my sore feet inside and pour myself a glass of wine.

Oliver's pinned a message on the noticeboard:
Claudia, I am sorry. Oliver.

You didn't look sorry as you skipped your way to the blinking *car.* I tear up his pathetic apology, and I'm violently shredding the pieces when my phone rings.

"Hey," Bonnie says. "I've had another thought. Dad liked us discovering stuff for ourselves. He probably left us this mystery on purpose. A project for his girls to work on together. We should create a command centre and call it *Finding the Old Man*."

"I'm a step ahead. I've already set one up."

"This could be more exciting than getting the money," she says. "I bet Dad's left hidden clues like he did with our Christmas scavenger hunts. We'll be a famous duo."

"Like Bonnie and Clyde?" I ask.

"No shit! Bonnie and Claudia—Bonnie and Clyde. I love it. I'm going to call you Clyde from now on. Did Dad give us these names on purpose? We could rob banks together. You know? Followed in Dad's footsteps."

I'm still shuddering when she adds, "It's a joke."

After hanging up, I search for a target. Do I aim the screwed-up paper at Oliver's face in the family photo? Or do I chuck it at Dad?

There better be a blinking good reason for this lack of identity caper.

Chapter Nine

CLAUDIA

Fremantle, 2018

Today's a scorcher. Not a whisper of airflow to make it bearable. If the local sea-breeze—*The Fremantle Doctor*—doesn't make a house call soon, I'll report him for malpractice.

The back lawn desperately needs a drink and I need to cool down, so I strip to my underwear and turn on the sprinkler. At first, it comes out of the hose hot enough to make a cup of tea, but once cold water clears the pipes it's refreshing enough to lose myself for an hour, ignoring the phone ringing in the kitchen.

Bonnie, Mum and I have examined so much in the last three weeks our command station is dotted with index cards. All rubbishy dead ends. The lawyer suggested we put together a collection of documents such as house title, marriage certificate, death certificate, Dad's pension card, Bonnie and my birth certificates, and a copy of the English Premium Bond deposit.

We handed over what we had, but haven't heard anything back.

Within minutes of being back inside, the water-cooling effect disappears and I flop like a liquefied candle onto a dining chair to listen to voicemail messages. As I lean forward to open another packet of index cards, to write down Mum and Bonnie's new leads, there's a slurp at the break in suction between sweaty skin and leather.

I replay Mum's voicemail, and smile as she recalls some of Dad's stories. They aren't much use, but I scribble much-shortened versions of the anecdotes.

Dad got in trouble for riding a horse into a classroom.

He was ordered to say a hundred Hail Marys when caught drinking sacramental wine.

The police asked for proof of his ethnicity in the early-fifties., so he flashed his bare lily-white arse in a Darwin pub.

Another lot of thinner than flimsy clues. I groan. None of this leads to anything. If I believed cardboard-cuts were more lethal than papercuts, I'd stab the index cards into my forehead.

After chucking them on the table, I return Bonnie's calls.

"I've remembered half the name of Dad's favourite football team—the Sydney *somethings*—rabbits or roosters." She says this with the keen smugness of someone who's deciphered ancient hieroglyphs.

"I need something concrete." I shake my head. "It's

nice to reminisce, but it won't help us prove Dad's the man who deposited the money."

"You're missing the point, Claudia...I mean Clyde. Dad insisted real football was rugby league not that frickin AFL aerial ping-pong. This surely means he grew up in New South Wales?"

"I'm not following."

"Mum and Dad checked for a birth registration in Victoria. What if they looked in the wrong state?" "I'll get on it, now."

A good old Google search connects me to the NSW Births Deaths and Marriages site. But birth records aren't released for a hundred years. Dad would have chuckled at being considered too young. I get lost down an endless rabbit-hole of search threads, only giving up when my eyes turn to grit.

It's after midnight when my mobile rings. I cover my ears with my pillow, but it doesn't let up. The caller ID flashes Bonnie's name.

"Please tell me this is important, it's too late for a social call."

"An email from the bonds office just arrived."

"Details. Quick." I dash to the command centre for pen and paper,

"Okay. They've evaluated our proof of identity and based on British rulings it's enough to release the two-thousand pounds initial deposit into an Australian building society account in Dad's name. The same place they've sent any dividends."

"That is good news."

"Except Australian financial institutions require a birth certificate, or a passport, or Dad going in with minor identity documents and signing in front of them."

"None of those are much help. What now?"

"At first, I considered giving up, thinking two thousand pounds isn't worth us chasing our tails, but the Bond mob sent us a method of estimating typical profits over time. Want me to read it?"

"Yes. Of course, I do."

"Assuming average winnings; premium bonds double approximately every seven years."

"Sounds like a sales pitch. Averages are useless in a lottery. Some will win lots and some none."

"Humour me," Bonnie says. "You're the finance officer. Let's make an estimate before we give up."

"So, Dad deposited it... fifty-five years ago?" I scratch my head. "Eight lots of doubling?"

"Don't ask me, I don't do numbers," she says.

"That's right, you don't." I start counting on my fingers. "Two, four, eight ..."

"Shouldn't that be two, four, six?" Bonnie interrupts.

"I'm doubling, not counting in twos. Shush."

I write it down, not trusting the calculation in my head, and check it twice. "That's around five hundred and twenty-eight thousand. Two hundred and sixty-four thousand dollars each."

"They're *British* bonds, Claudia. Not Aussie dollars. Pounds."

"What's the exchange rate?" I ask.

"I wouldn't know. You just pointed out I don't do numbers." Her voice carries an edge.

"Hang on. I'll put you on hold."

After checking the exchange rate then inputting the figures into my calculator, I try not to get too excited, but my heart races.

"Bonnie?"

"Well?"

"If Dad's deposit is 'average', there's more than $900,000 sitting in the building society."

"Wow. Fucking *wow*. Enough for Matt and me to pay out our mortgage and take a holiday."

"Don't count your chickens. There's a good chance it will be less. Or worse. There's a chance there's more money, and we're never able to claim it."

Chapter Ten

CLAUDIA

Fremantle, 2018

After unsuccessfully phoning government organisations for advice about our next steps in collecting Dad's inheritance, I visit a local branch of the building society he apparently used.

The waiting line in front of the enquiry desk is empty, but a young male employee, gestures for me to take a number.

When he eventually listens to my story, he scribbles notes in his pad, then taps the keypad several times before speaking, "About all I can do, is confirm the existence of an account in the name Philip McLeod. But because all financial statements were returned unopened, we put a hold on withdrawal from this account, pending identity checks." He raises his eyebrows at the screen. "Years ago."

"Can you tell me the original address?"

"I'm afraid not. I can tell you the account was

opened in a different state. For further information you will need to put your request in writing."

My face drops and I fight back tears, "Can I speak to the manager?"

The employee shows the first sign of being human. "He'll say the same as me: For further information put your request in writing." He's leans across the desk. "I can tell you this much. Due to regular deposits from an overseas company, the account is still active."

I lean in closer, trying the mum look I used to give to the boys when I wanted the truth. "Do you know the balance?"

He smacks his lips as if he's just sucked a lemon and shakes his head.

"It's okay," I say. "I'll put my request in writing."

My temple's throbbing by the time I head out into the street.

To unwind and clear my head I walk the city block. My phone beeps and I lean against a shopfront window to read it.

A text from Wendy.

> Claudia, I'm sorry. I hope you're okay, but we can't be friends. My family would think I'm siding with you over my brother. You understand, don't you? Blood is thicker than water.

I catch my hopeless expression in the hair salon window. My hair couldn't look worse if I'd washed it with floor cleaner and forgotten to rinse. Their brightly painted slogan speaks to me: *Life Isn't Perfect but Your Hair Can Be.*

Within minutes, I'm perched on a black leather and

chrome chair grimacing at my reflection, regretting the decision to walk in. Sitting less than an arm's length from a mirror is a cruel example of *in-your-face*.

"You're going to look fabulous," Kiki, the hairdresser, gushes.

Although I usually dislike hairdresser chitchat, my friend-pile's so thin I don't mind listening to meaningless conversation.

But when she asks if I'm getting my hair done to meet someone special, my eyes well up.

"You all right?" Kiki asks.

"It's the hair colour. Chemicals make my eyes sting." I thought I'd settled on the crying front, but Wendy's message has reopened wounds.

She narrows her eyes. "It might help to talk."

Words spill from my mouth. I tell her about Dad, about Oliver leaving, about losing my best friend.

"So, hubby's gone, eh? How long you known him?"

"We met through his sister Wendy; she's been my best friend since we were nine."

Kiki continues applying the colour that promises to brighten my life.

"Nine?" She studies my face. "That must have been...err... a long time ago."

"It was." I'm not telling her my age, because no matter what she actually thinks she'll tell me I don't look as old as that. They probably run faux-compliment classes for hair stylists.

"Remember the good. Tell me all about meeting him. I love a good hook up tale," Kiki says.

So, I tell it. "My family moved south from Port Hedland, and I was put in Wendy's class. She offered to look after the new girl, then shared her collection of

'Babysitter's' books with me. We've... we'd... been friends ever since."

My throat hurts, so I pick up a gossip magazine and pretend to read. Kiki doesn't take the hint.

"Was it love at first sight with your husband, then?" she asks.

It seems a slightly cruel question, but what the hell. "No. Oliver was in the background as Wendy's older brother. I was just another annoying girl. It was like that for years. Things changed when Wendy and I planned our year twelve formal. We'd agreed to do our hair the same and buy the same dresses. But days before she told me a boy had asked her to the dance, and our matchy-matchy thing wouldn't work unless I could find someone to go with me."

"Let me guess, *you* asked her brother?"

"No. I've never been that brave. I'd never let someone know I liked them. Wendy announced I'd be going with Oliver; apparently, he owed her a favour." I shrug my shoulders under the protective cape. "It's an unromantic getting-together story."

She stops applying the hair colour, "But... you realised, he was actually gorgeous and had been under your nose all along?" She looks at my face in the mirror, her eyes wide with interest.

"Not exactly. When Mum drove us to the dance, she whispered, '*Here's your chance. He's taller than you. With your height, you narrow the field of men by at least three quarters.*' In my mind, I was doomed to be alone. That was it, really."

Kiki grimaces as if I've ruined the ending of a movie. "Let's get you under the warmer to speed up processing."

I'm relieved this prevents further conversation about my love life, or lack thereof. Kiki leaves me alone, but I see her whispering to another stylist. Her voice, no doubt, dripping with pity.

I fan myself with the magazine to stop feeling sick. Until I saw Kiki shudder, I hadn't realised our relationship was doomed from the start. The fireworks didn't fizzle, they were never there.

Wendy gave Oliver a push. He told me how nice I looked, and I said the same to him.

That was our lukewarm Cupid's kiss.

Chapter Eleven

KATERINA

'The Figs' Sydney, 2018

Maria's not doing well and neither am I.

We've taken walks, attended exercise class, and I've reminisced about the days you could buy a serving of fish and chips wrapped in real newspaper, for less than a shilling. But I haven't opened up about Philip, and the nightmares have worsened. I fear they're eating moth-ball holes into my sanity.

For the past month, I've recorded everything that has a positive effect on Maria's mood. But today, something's distressing her beyond anything we've seen before. She won't listen to me at all. Izzy tried her best to calm Maria, and although Matron's reluctant to call on family for help, she phoned Joe.

He looks uneasy when he sees her. "What is it, Mum?"

She pushes him away, continuing to wail. Whatever's wrong, she's pointing in my direction.

"Maria's never been like this with me," I say, taking out my notepad.

I'm set on finding the magic cure. Something guaranteed to soothe her. Matron's given me more leeway than I deserve, but I'm preparing this in case I'm moved out. I want to leave a record so the nursing staff can help Maria.

"What's wrong?" I ask again.

Her entire body shakes as she cries. She won't look at me.

"I think she's worried about you, Miss Katerina."

My throat tightens. For the past few nights, my nightmares have worsened, and I worry that she's listening from across the hall. If things don't improve, Maria will be moved into a secure wing, and I'll be moved into a different aged care home. I can't, I cannot let that happen to either of us. Maria and I need each other.

She holds her index finger under one eye. "*Occhio*," she says.

"I don't know that word," Joe says. "And I can't look it up on my phone because I don't have a clue how to spell it."

She changes the position of her fingers, making a signal like a science fictional greeting.

Fortunately, Joe recognises this sign. "*Malocchio*. The evil eye. A curse."

Maria stares with wide, frightened eyes.

"What is it, Mum?"

She rocks against the wardrobe, crying into her hands.

Joe reaches for the notepad in my hand. "Do you

mind? Mum used to design wedding gowns. She was always drawing."

He passes it to her. "Draw. Draw what's worrying you."

Maria sits straight, repeats the sign of the curse, then sketches a bed with a woman screaming. I'm astonished at her talent. A few lines and the picture is clear. She stabs her drawing with the pen... then points it at me.

"Mum believes you're cursed." Joe suggests.

"What sort of curse?" I ask.

Joe shrugs. "Mum's had these ideas before. When she began losing her mind, she was convinced she'd been given the evil eye. An incident back in her youth when she lived in Italy. She told me a man had shown her too much interest, causing a woman to put a curse on Mum. She became certain the curse was strangling her brain." Joe lowers his voice to make a sad joke, "Fifty years later? It must have been a slow acting spell."

"Is she worried my mind's going too?" I ask. Maria *has* been listening to my nightmares.

"Ignore Mum, she's talking rubbish. It's the dementia." Joe laughs nervously but stops when he sees my tears. He gulps as if swallowing his words.

"I'm sorry, Joe. I'm the problem. I'll try to sort it out."

I wheel myself back to my room, needing a moment alone. The last few days have been nightmarish in every sense. There's no sugar-coating the truth. My fears are punishing Maria, and I must do something about it.

The little bird from yesterday hovers near my window, and I whisper, "Give me a sign, Philip. Please."

I focus. Willing the bird to land on my windowsill.

It does.

"Thank you."

I have permission to end the seventy-year silence and tell Maria. But where will I start?

I remember everything about a certain date: Tenth of October, Nineteen-forty-five. A Wednesday. I smell Father's tobacco, feel the coolness of the marble floor against my feet, and hear the screams.

This was the Wednesday my real woe began, but it would be way too painful to start my story there.

Moving along the corridor towards Maria's room, I decide to nibble around the edges of what happened, hoping to push back the fear.

"Come, Maria," I call. "I need to tell you a story."

Chapter Twelve

KATERINA

Sydney, 1940

Although a year had passed since my family huddled around the wireless listening to the special address by the Prime Minister, the memory of Father nervously tuning out the static and Menzies saying the words, *Australia is at war*, still wrenched my stomach.

Father shuddered, then raised his voice. "It no is good for Australia to become involved." In times of stress, Father's Russian accent was more pronounced.

For months, my parents never smiled, and I hoped the war would end soon. The arguments between them seemed never-ending. Their raised voices often carried down the grand staircase, through the ballroom, to the stand of eucalyptus and beyond. While the high walls and large gates insulated us from talk of the war, a personal battle raged within. My parents had fought for as long as I could remember, but since the war, everything annoyed Father, and Mother's migraines grew worse.

Often my older brother, Nick, and I were sent outside to give them peace and quiet. My parents didn't hold with the saying 'children should be seen and not heard', preferring 'children should neither be seen, nor heard'.

At fourteen, any joy at exploring the grounds had disappeared. I wanted to spend time reading in my bedroom instead of being banished from the house along with Nick.

On one of those evenings, I took my book to the converted stables where Father parked his Bentley, climbing the ladder to the platform above. The garage for the car gleamed with new siding, but the loft remained unchanged—filled with bales of straw, once used for the horses, but now to mulch the vegetable patches.

"What are you doing up here?" I asked when I saw Nick. This was my place; he usually took his football to practise his passes and kicks.

Nick ignored me but picked up a seed pod from a pile at his side, throwing it through the opening once used for loading the straw. I'd barely settled into my book when he aimed for the roof, watching and listening as the pods rattled against the wooden cladding.

"Do you mind?" I covered my ears. "Are you trying to annoy me, or does it come naturally?"

Nick usually talked incessantly about rugby and his favourite players, but the sullen mood of the household affected him too.

"Only a year until I leave this place for university."

He continued to hurl the pods. "The time can't come soon enough."

Angered by the constant racket, and the thought of being left alone with my parents, I grabbed the warning bell hanging in the loading space. "I'll ring this if you don't stop."

Nick grabbed the bell to mute the sound. "Father's already on edge. Don't trigger his temper."

"Surely, we've been outside long enough?" I said. "I'm going back."

I half-climbed, half-jumped from the loft with Nick following. We ran to the house, but I stopped outside when I heard Father shouting and Mother crying. Nick tugged at my ponytail, and as I spun around, he grabbed my sleeve to drag me away.

We returned to the loft without a word about the argument. I went back to my book and Nick to throwing the seeds. As annoying as this was, hiding was a better alternative than going home.

Our parents didn't call us inside until long after dark.

———

A telegram arrived from my Uncle Viktor and the atmosphere in our house improved immediately. Because of the war, he was taking an extended break from captaining a passenger ship that sailed regularly around Europe, and occasionally made a voyage from England to Australia. He was planning to spend time with us.

Viktor was Father's first cousin, so technically not

my uncle, but as he and father had grown up together in the same house, Father thought of him as a brother.

His imminent visit gave everyone something to look forward to. Mother was set on throwing an extravagant welcome party, but my parents disagreed as usual. I could not speak fluent Russian, but their shouts wove a path from their bedroom into mine, and I understood enough to get the gist.

Father did not want a party. He considered it an overindulgence, especially during wartime. Instead, he wanted to host a dinner at home for a small group of family and friends. After cross words, they reached a compromise and I was surprised that Father smiled as he left the house. Viktor's upcoming trip put Father in a much better mood. I watched through the window as he paced the boundary walls, eventually resting against the tall, silvery trunk of a eucalyptus tree. As he stuffed his pipe with tobacco, his stance was surprisingly relaxed. I took the opportunity to join him outside. I wanted to talk to him alone.

As much as I loved my uncle, I knew there would be long stretches when Nick and I would be sent away leaving the adults to talk without children. I wanted my new friend, Anna, to keep me company, and knew Father was more likely to agree than Mother.

"I love the smell of tobacco," I said hoping to get on Father's good side.

He shook his head disapprovingly, crushing a handful of eucalyptus leaves between his fingers. "The smell of these are better suited to a young woman. Ladies do not smoke."

"Father?" My voice trembled. I was no longer sure of my timing.

"Yes, Katerina? You want something?"

He appeared calm, so I forged ahead. "You've heard me talk about Anna, my best friend from school."

"And...?" Father asked.

"May I please invite her over when Uncle Viktor arrives?"

Father enjoyed every opportunity to introduce Viktor to others. He smiled. "Of course you can. Viktor and I will enjoy meeting your friend and it will be good for you to have the company of someone your own age."

On the morning of Viktor's arrival, Mother was the happiest I'd seen since the war began. She said spring had saved the perfect day for this special occasion.

I was sent to the corner shop, armed with a list and a book of ration stamps. The usually gruff shop assistant giggled and blushed as she asked if it was true my handsome uncle was arriving soon.

Our house buzzed with preparation. There were to be drinks and canapes in the garden, and an extra table set up in the almost disused, formal dining room. The guest list had grown larger than originally planned.

"Walk with Katerina to collect her friend," Mother said to Nick. "But come straight back, there are jobs to be done."

Nick was annoyed, but not stupid. He didn't disobey her, instead, he knocked on the old cottage door.

"Want to come for a walk?" he asked Philip, pulling an indignant face in my direction. "I have to escort Katerina to her friend's place."

Philip mirrored Nick's expression. "Sure. I'll leave Mama a note."

"I hope I'm not expected to sit with her and her friend all day," Nick said when Philip came out. There were sniggers and whispers as we walked, but the boys walked several paces behind as if I was contagious.

Anna had written down her address but told me it was easy to find. "Just look for the enormous tree and rope swing."

She was outside when we arrived, swinging like a female Tarzan, her long black plait tucked into the belt at her waist. She shouted my name, adding jungle sounds for effect.

Adults were laughing and chasing each other in the front garden where all the neighbours could see. I rubbed my eyes to make sure they weren't just over-sized children.

A woman wearing men's trousers sauntered towards the fence and called, "Hello, Katerina. I'm Vivian, Anna's mum. Come and join us." She took a long slow puff on a cigarette. "Who are these handsome young men?"

I shrugged, wondering who she talking about. "Oh. My brother, Nick, and Philip."

"We're having a bash here too," she said, blowing smoke rings in the air

"We have to get back to help Mother get ready for the dinner party," I said nervously, but I was in awe of this woman who let children call her by her first name. She wasn't acting at all ladylike. Definitely not smelling eucalyptus leaves instead of tobacco.

Fascinating. Maybe not all women followed men's rules?

Holding her cigarette like a stylish accessory, she looked upwards at Anna, dangling from the rope. "You'd better get down, my love."

Anna let go and leapt the low fence to stand at my side.

Nick and Philip stared—mouths agape. They didn't distance themselves from us on the trip home. In comparison to the uncomfortable silence on the way to Anna's, the walk home was lively. She never stopped talking, and the boys barely stopped grinning.

"My mother's wearing father's clothes to make a point," she said. "A protest against all the jobs women aren't allowed to do."

There were times when she said the strangest things, but I loved how Anna bounced along, finding joy at everything she saw.

When we got home, I was surprised that neither Nick nor Philip raced off to practise their football skills as they usually did. Instead, the boys sat within earshot of Anna. They watched her, then whispered, but whenever I caught them staring, they looked away. It seemed they didn't want their interest in Anna to appear obvious.

"Do you usually sit outside with your brothers?" she whispered.

"Only one brother. Nick. Philip's mother works for us," I pointed to Mama Bridgett's cottage at the front corner of our property. "They live over there."

"Don't mention this to my parents," Anna said. "They'd accuse your family of keeping a slave."

"Mama Bridgett isn't a slave. She works for us. She's also the nicest, kindest adult I know."

"I'll bring you a book about slavery. You can read it at school."

I creased my brow. Mama Bridgett was a paid worker and free to come and go as she pleased.

Mother called out to Nick, explaining how she wanted candles set along the pathway. She waved to Anna but didn't acknowledge Philip at all.

We watched the boys set candles into sand filled brown-paper bags. They made frequent glances in our direction.

"Who do you think will finish the job faster? Nick asked. "Me or this runt?"

I compared Philip to Nick. At sixteen, Nick was two years older than Philip, but Philip was catching up in height.

Anna stood with her arms akimbo. "Why do boys make everything a competition? I'm not picking a winner in advance, but I'll judge. Finish one side of the walkway each."

"I've got it in the bag." Nick snorted, pushing Philip over.

Philip punched Nick's arm. "You're on."

They worked up a sweat—carrying armfuls of candles and positioning them a pace apart on the long walkway from the gate to the house. I was mesmerised by the way Philip dropped the bags in an easy rhythmic motion. I could not pick a winner either. Despite Nick's confidence of a win, Philip looked a strong contender.

Although Nick finished first, Anna declared Philip the champ. I could tell she was teasing my brother. "The criteria I used wasn't just speed. Philip's candles are evenly spaced and align perfectly with the edge of the path."

"Not fair," Nick argued, but Anna shoed him away.

The boys didn't go far. They climbed a ladder to the top of the old stable and took turns jumping from the upper platform onto a pile of hay bales they'd thrown to the ground.

"And that is why you're both losers," Anna called. "It's a wonder the males of our species actually survive."

Nick and Philip touched fists in solidarity, jumped together, then disappeared.

Once they'd gone, Anna asked, "How long have Philip and his mother lived on your land?"

"I'm not sure. I remember them being here forever, but they can't have been. Mama Bridgett cooks and cleans now, but she looked after Nick and me when we were little. The cottage they live in was the original house, before Father had the big one built."

"Let me guess. Philip's father is your butler?"

"You're mocking me. We do not have a butler, and I think Philip's father is dead, but I've never asked."

Anna pushed her nose upwards using her index finger. "I am teasing you. But I've decided that we should have a kissing game, I'll take your brother and you get to kiss Philip."

"No. You have the silliest ideas. I don't want to. Besides my parents would never allow it."

"Don't tell anyone else that you listen to your parents. It will ruin your reputation."

I was about to ask what she meant, when I heard a familiar voice calling from the house.

"Nick. Katerina." It was Uncle Viktor carrying a canvas satchel and smiling the broadest of smiles. Nick and Philip reappeared from behind the stables.

"Look how much you've grown." He pretended to

pick me up, grunting and acting as if I was too heavy. He twirled me around instead.

He stopped to give firm handshakes to Nick and Philip, before bowing to Anna. She giggled, curtsied, and fell to the ground.

"I hadn't realised how old you were now, so I hope your presents aren't too babyish. A toy truck and a doll." He winked and laughed.

I watched as Nick opened the gift Viktor had produced from his satchel.

"Cor," Nick said as he held up a pocketknife.

"A Russian folding knife." Viktor ran his hand over the handle, pointing out the carving. "A Siberian wolf."

He handled my parcel very carefully. "This was my mother's, your great aunt."

I peeled back many layers of paper and unfolded the inner protective wrapping. One of Uncle Viktor's cravats. Inside was a porcelain egg, painted with snow covered houses.

"It is beautiful," I said.

Uncle Viktor smiled. "St Petersburg, Leningrad now. The city I live when I'm not at sea. The place where your parents were born."

"I will treasure it forever, Uncle." I handed back his cravat.

"Keep that too," he said.

"Pity you don't have two." Anna held her arms imploringly.

I put my hand over my mouth at Anna's forwardness, and hoped Uncle Viktor wouldn't tell my parents. But he slapped his thighs in laughter instead. "I'm so pleased you've found yourself a courageous role model,

Katerina. And she is right. How rude of me not to give presents to all of you."

He sat on the ground to search through the side pockets of his satchel. After a few minutes, he handed Anna a handful of overseas coins and Philip some foreign stamped envelopes.

"You could both start collections. Coins and stamps from around the world." Uncle Viktor patted Philip's back.

Viktor seemed in no hurry to get back to the house and he answered many questions from Anna about coins and the countries he'd been to.

Philip was more interested in the goings-on of the boat, and my uncle happily provided details of rough seas and even rougher men. I was reminded why everyone enjoyed his company. Uncle Viktor was not only interesting, he took a genuine interest in others.

"There's something I must discuss with your father before the guests arrive," he said. "And Katerina, your mother wants you to help Bridgett."

After putting my gift away, Anna and I raced to the dining room.

Mama Bridgett showed us how each place setting should be arranged. She explained about the final polish to the silverware and the need to take care not to leave fingerprints on the glassware.

"You look like the mermaid in one of my fairy tales," Anna said as we worked.

Mama laughed and lifted her long skirt. "But I have legs."

"It's your rust-coloured hair, pale skin and heart shaped face. You are beautiful."

Mama Bridgett's face turned pink. "Thank you."

"When did your husband die?" Anna asked.

I stepped on her toe and glared.

"It's okay," Mama Bridgett said. "It was a long time ago. Months before Philip was born."

Anna seemed intent on asking more questions when we heard raised voices. Father and Uncle Viktor were speaking in Russian and I was the only one who understood.

I eavesdropped as they argued. Father had hoped Viktor would stay for a while, travelling back to Russia, only when it became safe to do so, but he'd made other arrangements.

"There's been a change of plans," I heard him say. "I received a telegram this morning. The *Armenia* is undergoing conversion from passenger liner to military hospital. I've been offered a position as Captain."

Father tried to convince him that it was foolish to even consider such a posting.

"The conversion hasn't yet begun, and it will take many months before it is suitable for transporting wounded soldiers, but I'm returning to Leningrad. I can oversee the project and spend time with my family before I take charge of the ship."

I knew immediately our high spirits would end. Viktor's news was not the celebration our household desperately needed.

After reluctantly translating the gist of the conversation to Mama Bridgett and Anna, both of their smiles disappeared.

Anna said, "Brave, selfless and handsome, but what a

pity—I was hoping the lovely Bridgett and dashing Viktor could marry."

"Anna," I said. I was mortified. "I'm sorry, Mama Bridgett."

"You've been reading too many fairy tales, Anna," Mama said. "In real life, rich people never marry poor."

Chapter Thirteen

CLAUDIA

Fremantle, 2018

Yesterday, Bonnie gave me a stern talking to. Told me it's time to move on. And just in case I lapse without in-person nagging, she's dotted 'Bonnie-notes' all around the house. Reminders for me to lift my game. I guess she's sick of my misery-guts, and to be honest, I'm sick of it too.

I find my first inspirational reminder half shoved under the canister of tea bags on the kitchen bench: *Give coffee another go.*

All right, Bonnie. I'll make myself a coffee even though it isn't to my taste. Maybe there's a bitter blend that suits rejected tea drinkers?

The coffee gnaws at my already raw gut. Oliver's new floozy probably grinds her own beans between youthfully smooth thighs and serves him all sorts of exotic flavours.

I wonder what she looks like—the new woman he's not yet admitting to. Imagining her as young and delicate makes the old 'woodcutter' incident sting once more.

'You're so tall and sturdy.' Mrs Lillywhite said this to twelve-year-old me like it was a compliment.

If Bonnie could read my mind she'd say: *Let that crap go.*

She's right.

I plonk my cup too hard on the table and splash the coffee, burning my hand. Swapping tea for coffee feels too much like Oliver trading me in.

I tip the dregs down the sink.

While sipping good old friendly tea, I check the random clues Mum, Bonnie and I pinned on the 'Dad's Life' command station. So many unanswered questions about Dad, about life. I show the board my displeased back, and look at the house instead, this time with fresh eyes.

When the boys lived here, I loved this place. Not liked it—loved it. Now, the residue of Oliver taints it like undetected termites, working away to undermine my foundations. A breath stalls in my throat, and I begin a text: *Oliver, do you think we should put the house on the market?* I'm about to press send when I spy a Bonnie-note stuck to the window. *Be assertive!* A waft of air shakes the note and it may as well be Bonnie's bossy, waggling finger.

It works. I delete then reword my message: *We're selling the house. It has bad vibes and I can't afford it. I'm phoning a real-estate agent.*

Send.

I'm not sure if whether it's the newfound assertiveness or the cooling breeze, but I get a burst of energy and decide now's as good a time as any to start the declutter and clean.

The living room and conservatory shape up nicely, but Oliver's negativity lingers.

As tired as I am, I need to eradicate every trace before I rest.

I dump his stuff from the bedroom in a messy pile outside the door: the painting Oliver liked; the elephant statue he bought in Thailand even when I turned up my nose more than the elephant's trunk; his every-shades-of-blue shirts, his favourite pillow—the complete kit and caboodle. Begone.

Then I scrub the walls like I'm preparing the room for surgery.

It *is* surgery. I'm amputating a husband from my life.

Although the sting of cleaning fluid brings tears to my eyes, they're good tears, they're the tears of a woman clawing back control.

The ugly clock-radio Wendy bought me will have to go, too, but I allow it a last gasp and crank a song up to high volume, dance-cleaning like no one's watching. Which, of course, they're not, because I'm entirely alone.

When I'm done, I strip off my clothes and switch the ceiling fan to helicopter speed, then lie on the bed to stare into space. 'Bite my naked body!' I yell to the bedbugs, even though I'm not sure what they are or where they'd be hiding. Either I'm going a bit crazy, or this is the new Claudia.

I notice a wallpaper covered box on top of the wardrobe. So far back I couldn't see it from the ground. I glued that paper on when I was about fourteen, matching the box to my bedroom. What's inside? Definitely Furry Monkey—the toy that co-starred in every picture of me as a baby, and probably my old stone-washed jeans. I bet it's where the stamp collection got to, but what I really hope is it's the hiding place of my magic medal.

Dad hung the medal around my neck because he found me crying about moving towns and losing friends. 'This is a magic medal,' he said. 'It will make everything alright.'

First thing tomorrow I'll find that magic medal. It's exactly what I need.

When I wake up the air seems cleaner; and I spring out of bed, scaling the wardrobe shelves to retrieve the box.

With my monkey pal under one arm, I unpack the rest. Dad's old stamp album—bulging and bowed, tied up with string. It strikes me as odd that Dad held on to an inconsequential hobby-book but lost his army records and other identifying documents.

The contents at the bottom of the box are jammed, so I tip them out on the floor. My high school magazines, a concert ticket stub, a plastic bag full of coloured gel pens, and a Star Wars figurine of Princess Leia, still in its packet. But no magic medal.

Leaning my elbows on the upturned box, I drop my head in my hands and sob. It's not the medal, it's the loss of everything. This is much worse than changing schools: my sons are gone, Dad is dead, Wendy has cut me off.

'It's normal to feel sad,' I imagine Bonnie's voice.

Yesterday, she described the journey to wellness as unpredictable. I'm sure she'd just read it somewhere. She vowed to motivate me on what she referred to as 'your forward fucking journey'.

Blinking Bonnie should get a job writing adult only inspirational quotes: *The forward fucking journey begins with a single step, so fucking move it.*

There's a fine line between tears and laughter, and I chuckle as I head to the bathroom.

A note on the mirror tells me to: *Make yourself the shit-I need to-do list.*

When did Bonnie find the time? Assertive me shows the note my middle finger. No list-making happening. If I feel like indulging myself; eating chocolate fudge, or going back to bed, or walking along the beach, or reading a book; that's what I'll do.

List or not, I need to call Oliver. I don't want to contact a real estate agent without an idea of a listing price. But I shudder at the thought of Oliver's whiny voice. Funny how I once considered it radio-announcer, well-modulated, but now it has the tones of a lying bastard.

I call our local real estate agent, Mark Katter, and 'assertive me' tells him the deal includes him negotiating the selling price between me and Oliver. I brush my hands with satisfaction.

That vulgar word *money* crops up a lot when you don't have any. I'd rather abandon Dad's research, but I could use some of the inheritance to tide me over until I get another job. Since Bonnie's rugby team clue, we've decided Dad came from Sydney and narrowed the search criteria to New South Wales. Hints on the website link me to multiple sources:

census forms, other user's family trees, war records and a screed of other stuff that makes my head spin. Ignoring the twenty-four dollar download fee, I purchase multiple certificates with names matching either Dad's or his parents'. But after two hours of following a twisty rabbit-hole of clues, I'm empty-handed. Although the names in the document previews matched, the actual certificates were irrelevant.

There's more to this genealogy business than I imagined.

The useless certificates add more litter to my research than the cigarette butts on the pavement outside my last workplace. The expensive downloads have probably catapulted my credit card debt. Just looking makes my eyes sting and my brain hurt. I must find a job.

Reluctantly, I open the job search website. There are a few interesting positions advertised, but my old resume is years out of date.

If I don't clear my head, it will explode. Taking in the salty air worked before, so I change into shorts, singlet and thongs, and grab a hat. I consider driving north to Cottesloe, but settle for walking to the beach down the road.

This time, there's no sign of the smiling surfer. Obviously, I wouldn't expect him to hang around in case I drop by, but I feel a twinge of disappointment. A man smiling at me when I felt too unattractive to keep a husband was significant.

The temperature's perfect. The sun warms my skin while the gentle sea breeze cools it. Along the shoreline, water foams around my ankles and tickles the soles of my feet. With my big toe, I draw patterns in the sand for waves to wash away.

"Better off sending your thoughts in a bottle."

Without looking, I know it's the surfer.

"Hope I don't sound creepy, but I recognised you from over there." He points to an area near the limestone boulder break. "Salt air and seawater give me an appetite. I'm about to grab some lunch. Want to join me?"

Is this invitation in code? *Appetite?* I search his face, but his eyes don't glint like a predator. At least, not like those in television close ups.

"I'd like that," I say bravely.

"Troy." He extends his hand.

"Claudia." I grip firmer than comes naturally because Bonnie once told me a floppy-fish handshake is a sign of deviancy. I'm reassured by Troy's powerful grasp.

"You know the café on the road near Fremantle hospital? Brightly painted chairs?" he asks.

His teeth are so white and even. Could he be a dentist?

"Miss-Matched," I say.

"Yep. Exactly. Looks like someone's done a tip run and repainted other people's rubbishy furniture." When he laughs and shakes his head, his beach-salty-strands of scruffy blond hair remind me of an old doll I had as a kid.

"Miss-Matched is the name of the café." I laugh. "I know it well."

Oliver and I visited when it first opened. He complained the coffee wasn't very good.

A place Oliver hates is the perfect choice.

As Troy straps his surfboard to the roof of his ute, I wonder if we should meet in half an hour so I can get my car and put on some lipstick. I was wearing *Flat Out Fabulous* when he smiled at me. "I can meet you there if it's easier?"

"Nah. Hop in," he says, opening the car door. "With these quirky cafés breeding like rabbits, we could end up in identical coffee shops on different streets."

I bite my fingernail, wondering about going somewhere with a stranger.

"Look. If you'd rather, I'll meet you there."

If I stop trusting people, I'm left with nothing. I switch on a Bonnie-bright smile. "I'm fine."

I'm thankful for the short drive because I'm not good at initiating conversation. But when we arrive there are no mis-matched tables out on the pavement, and the café doors are shut.

Troy reads a sign on the window. "Closed. Family problems."

"Don't we all," I say. "Keep driving, I live around the corner and I'll make you a coffee for free."

His smile is so cheeky, I hope 'making coffee' isn't an invitation for sex. Until my youngest son, Aaron, asked me to stop saying it, I thought 'Netflix and chill' meant watching movies and relaxing.

To be safe, when I'm in my kitchen, I'll text Bonnie with his name and car registration.

We pull up outside my house and the safety message isn't necessary. Bonnie's waiting on the wall outside, and has been here long enough to create a flower crown using my Michaelmas daisies. She looks Woodstock ready.

"Here." I say. "The strange hippy woman is my sister."

As I step out, I twist my handbag's shoulder strap, avoiding eye contact with Bonnie. She might read it as an invitation to embarrass me.

"Saw your car in the driveway. Knew you'd be back soon."

Troy displays his splendid teeth and extends his hand. "Hi, I'm Troy."

"Bonnie," she says, tilting her head to me with a 'knowing' twitch. "I'm here cos I've thought of something for our forensic interrogation board."

"Uh-oh." Troy makes a face of mock horror, arms positioned like a runner on the start line.

"Sounds more interesting than it is," I say. "Bonnie and I are researching our dad's identity."

"It sounds intriguing."

I make two coffees, and a tea. Bonnie takes the mug with one hand, continuing to rearrange index cards and sticky notes with the other. She's made new headings: FACTS, POSSIBILITIES, and RUBBISH.

The RUBBISH section is heavily populated. The FACTS—barren.

I groan loudly.

"Mind If I take a look?" Troy asks.

"Go ahead. We can use all the help we can get."

"Anything to drink?" Bonnie asks. "If we're grappling with this mess, we need something stronger than coffee."

"Another night?" I suggest. "The real estate agent is appraising the house tomorrow."

"You're selling?" Bonnie asks.

"Yes."

Troy scans the board. "I hope you don't mind me adding my bit? Doing this sort of research needs a system."

"Oooh, a man with skills. I'll get you a beer to keep you here," Bonnie says.

"You've done this before?" I ask.

"Not really. My best mate's mum tried to find her birth mother, and she jumped all over the place following random paths that led nowhere." He leans back as he re-inspects our muddle of clues. "Her research was worse than this. You've kinda got a system."

"Thanks." I say.

Bonnie hands him a beer. "So, you're the knight in shining armour who figured it out for your friend's mum?"

"Nah." His face turns pink. "We taught her some basic computer skills, but it wasn't much use. Wasn't any use, actually."

"So, you put your ten cents in to tell us we're doomed?" Bonnie flaps her hand in a mock slap, and he plays along, protecting his face with an arm.

"It was all good in the end, a retired professor bloke, who does this sort of research part-time, sorted it all out."

Bonnie throws me a questioning look. "How much would a professional cost?"

I shrug. "We don't have any money, yet."

"Maybe you could hire a researcher who'd work on commission," Troy suggests. "Like lawyers who only get paid if they win the case?"

"You know someone who works for commission?" Bonnie clanks her beer to Troy's.

"Sorry. No." He takes a sip. "But I don't mind helping. Three sets of eyes are better than two."

"I'll have one drink then," I say.

Troy rests his elbow on my shoulder. "This is gonna be fun. First, we'll sort out a system for organising the research. It'll be easier if everyone follows the same method."

"You're coming back again?" Bonnie says, way louder than necessary, then gives me a wicked smile.

"I'm back to work next week, but we can make a start now."

After half an hour of reviewing our findings, Troy confirms what we suspected. We don't have the expertise to go further.

The realisation hits like a bucket of iced water.

Troy checks his phone. "Look, guys. I've got to go." He hands me an index card scrawled with his phone number. "If either of you lovely women would like a coffee, or a drink, give me a ring."

He's barely backed his ute out of the driveway when Bonnie corners me in the kitchen. To sidestep the questions I can tell are coming, I pretend I'm searching through the pantry.

"Where'd you pick up Troy the surfer?" Bonnie copies Mum's lie-detector glare.

"We met at the beach." I read the label on a bottle of port from behind a stack of out-of-date cans. "Twenty-five years in oak barrels. Another fifteen hiding in my cupboard." I uncork it.

"Backtrack a minute. You were at the beach?" Bonnie waves her arms dramatically. "You've always hated the beach. Nonstop complaining about sand between your toes... and that one time the sand got inside your bikini bottom and I yelled out, Sandy Vagina. Remember?"

She laughs and gets out the glasses as I open the port

"You weren't smiling when Mum spooned Hot English Mustard on your tongue."

Bonnie chuckles. "I got even. Bought the mustard-coloured car and bought the sweariest personalised plate allowed. Mum should be pleased she got off lightly. These days, she'd get a visit from child protection. Such cruelty."

"Nah. you deserved it."

"On a cheerful note," Bonnie says. "Oliver won't be happy when he finds out."

"About what?"

"I picture him coming home to throw himself at your feet and finding you've hooked up with a hunka hunka surfing love." Bonnie adds throaty emphasis, accompanied by an Elvis hip gyration.

"I haven't hooked up with anyone," I say. "And if I took Oliver back, I'd be waiting for the other shoe to drop. He might get over it, but I won't."

"Fair enough," Bonnie says. "So, what do you know about Troy?"

"Almost nothing. He has a surfboard and drives a ute with Western Australian number-plates."

"You got into a car with a stranger?" Bonnie shakes my shoulders and wrestles me off the chair. "Who are you? What have you done with my sister?"

"Stop it." I laugh as I push her away. "Don't worry, I've seen my movies. People are only abducted in black vans, and I would have run if his car had tinted windows."

Bonnie tickles me. "Claudia's three mystery men, eh?"

"Three?"

"Dad with his hidden identity, Oliver and his sudden pissing off, and a beachy toy-boy."

I smile. "For future reference, I prefer the term Troy-boy."

"Claudia—you made a joke. You *are* back."

I brush it aside, "Let's concentrate on Dad's past."

"You're not changing the subject that easily." Bonnie touches the seat next to her. "Sit here. Let's talk about the sexy dude."

"This isn't about sex." I slap her arm.

"But if I hadn't been waiting outside, you might have—"

"It was a cup of coffee." I drop my handbag over the card with his phone number.

"But he's cute. And you're single. And the best way to get over one man is to get under another." Bonnie makes ridiculous hip thrusts, her tongue hanging out one side of her mouth.

I grab the bottle and glasses. "No more drinks. No more personal questions. Research time."

"But we have nothing..." Bonnie whines.

She draws a sad emoticon on a sticky-note and writes a piece of Bonnie-advice: *There's nothing wrong about enjoying sex.* I watch her stick the message on a bookshelf.

No more wrestling. I'll remove it when she's gone.

I try sorting our clues. But I don't know what I'm doing. "This is a complete mess. I could contact a historical society to see if they can recommend a genealogist?"

"Please do," Bonnie says. "I'll pay the first payment."

My throat tightens at her generosity. "Thanks."

One thing's for sure, I won't be asking Oliver for money.

"We're out of choices," she says. "There's no inheritance without proving Dad's the same Philip McLeod who made the deposit."

"I'll pay you back when we get it."

Bonnie sweeps her hand across the board. "I'm starting to think there's something really dodgy about all these dead ends."

"Me too," I say. "You know what? It's not just about the money. I want to find the truth about Dad."

"We've found nothing to prove Dad even existed before he met Mum," Bonnie says. "I reckon that's really fucking dodgy."

I remember my box of keepsakes. "Hang on! I forgot. I might have something."

I race off to fetch the stamp album.

"Maybe there's something in here. Dad started this collection when he was a teenager." I produce yellowed envelopes with Australian stamps. "These were shoved in the back since Dad gave it to me."

Bonnie peers at an envelope. "Were they sent to Dad or did he buy them from a stamp collecting shop?"

"I don't know, but he said he kept the stamps on the envelopes to preserve the postmarks."

"Why are the sender and receiver's names blacked out?" she asks.

"Maybe he did buy them? The recipients' details could have been crossed out."

Grabbing another envelope and holding it up to the

window, I try reading the writing beneath. "They're too well scribbled over. But the stamps are intact."

"Claudia!" Bonnie's voice is a squeal as she points to a postmark. "Imagine if Dad's name is on this one. This stamp is dated before he deposited the money."

I bulldog clip the envelopes to our research board. "God. I hope these help."

Chapter Fourteen

CLAUDIA

Fremantle, 2018

I open the front door to an obscenely bright sun and the silhouette of a man. His mirrored sunglasses reflect my scrunched-up eyes, and it takes a few awkward seconds for me to realise he's extending his hand.

"Claudia?" he asks.

I nod and shake his hand, still squinting.

He removes his glasses, flashing a winning smile. "Mark Katter."

Ah ha! The real estate agent. His gleaming salesman charm should have been a clue. Perhaps they give *charisma lessons* at real estate school. The class next door to *Conversational Tips for Hairdressers*.

"My... Oliver's not here yet," I say, showing him inside. "Do you want a coffee while you wait?"

"I'll get a feel for the place if you don't mind?"

He turns in a slow circle, keeping up a running patter and adding notes to his clipboard. "So much potential. Lovingly maintained." The easy smile again—maybe it is genuine.

"It's refreshing to find a house where most personal items and clutter have been cleared. Most vendors don't understand how important it is for a potential buyer to picture it as their own home."

'There's nothing personal left here,' the voice inside my head screams. "Feel free to look around," I say out loud.

While Mark checks out the house, I wipe down the kitchen island for the fifth time. It looked spotless before he came, but from this angle there's another smear. I sterilise the dishcloth in the microwave, then give the bench a hot wipe, but stop myself from checking again. He's not a buyer. He's here to make an appraisal and a profit from the sale.

Without so much as a knock or a '*Yoo-hoo*' Oliver lets himself in. I wonder if he'll notice my new hairdo, but he doesn't even smile. Until recently, Oliver not saying anything was routine, but now his silence feels unnatural. I make a mental note to ask for his keys.

Mark returns, breaking the uncomfortable atmosphere. "Quiet tree-lined street. Beach-side living at its finest."

Quotes from the realtor handbook?

On his second circuit of the 'desirable-dwelling', Oliver and I accompany him.

"Did you add this yourselves?" Mark asks, indicating the glassed-ceiling mini-conservatory extension off the dining room.

"Yes. Fifteen years ago," Oliver says.

This area, just big enough for the old wooden table

and bookshelves, was my favourite place. I sigh. It won't be mine much longer.

"Character and charm, flooded with natural light" He adds to his notes.

"We call this the grand conservatory," Oliver says with a laugh.

I want to stab him for making our pet names sound pretentious.

"This place will sell. Some lush house plants and tidy up the backyard," Mark says with a broad smile. "If you don't mind, I have artwork in the boot of my car to brighten up houses needing help. Your house looks wonderful, but I've got a wall hanging perfect for covering whatever that workstation is."

Oliver clears his throat loudly as he looks at the mess.

I rearrange my face to present an air of confidence. I'm not giving Oliver the satisfaction of knowing I'm on a trail to nowhere. "Thanks, that will be helpful. It's research on my dad's family tree and I'd prefer not to take it down."

Mark nods seriously. "I'll duck out to the car and fetch the wall hanging and my list of recent sales in the area. No doubt you need time alone to discuss your plans for selling."

Oliver leans against the bookshelf with a familiarity he no longer deserves. "Do you remember when we built this conservatory?"

His shared memory smile makes me gag. I step back, increasing the distance between us. That's when I see Bonnie's note, stuck on the bookshelf, just above Oliver's shoulder.

My throat tightens when I realise he's seen what I'm reaching for.

He grabs it before I can. "What's this? *There's nothing wrong about enjoying sex.* Are you having counselling?"

"No."

"Then what?"

"None of your business." I snatch the note and tear it up.

When Mark returns, he's either unaware of the uncomfortable atmosphere, or he's practised at ignoring domestic tension. He places a rolled-up macramé hanging on the table. "Here. I'll get some paperwork started, then your house is good to go. I'll have it sold before you can blink."

Oliver blinks—and the two men laugh. I would have found this funny once upon a time.

He shakes mine and Oliver's hands to seal the deal. "I'll send you a market proposal, and a contract."

After we've walked Mark to the car, Oliver asks, "Do you have a few minutes to talk?"

"About?"

He kicks a weed in the garden that was once his pride and joy. "I don't want to sell."

I'm unreasonably angry. "Are you going to re-mortgage and keep it? Pay me out?"

"No, not a re-mortgage. I wondered if maybe *we* should wait, to be sure the marriage is actually over."

'*We?*' Bile rises in my throat. "There is no *we*, there is no *us*."

"That's what I want to talk to you about."

Who is this man? Is Oliver suggesting we get back together? I thought I knew him. But obviously not. I didn't know he was ready to leave, either.

"Fuck off, Oliver."

He grabs my arm. "Claudia. Your life's always revolved around the kids, or work, and then you spent so much time with your dad at the hospital. You've never had time for me."

"So, you're blaming me?" I gnaw at my knuckle to stop myself from screaming. It's too late to push back tears, but I channel my anger. "Stop fucking messing with me. You never spent enough time with the kids. It's always been about you and now your see-sawing is giving me the shits."

I'm surprised by my outburst, but it's worth it to see Oliver's shocked expression.

"You agreed to sell," I say, "and I want out."

"Thought you loved the house," he says, turning away like a petulant child. "If you want it sold, you organise everything."

I place my hands firmly on my hips and stare as Oliver gets into the car. I've never seen Oliver move so fast.

Chapter Fifteen

KATERINA

'The Figs' Sydney, 2018

Over the past week, my nightmares have eased, Maria's mood has improved, and I'm relieved beyond measure. Each time I relate my story we're both enveloped in relative calm.

Not that the calm has stopped Maria's antics entirely.

This morning, she was sent outside for ruining today's Gentle-cise session. She brought a brooch into class, which I believe shows logic and forethought. When we had to *tap-tap-tap* the balloons, Maria took the brooch from her pocket, bursting every single one. I found it hilarious; if I were more mobile, I'd be tempted to do the same.

As we sat together afterwards Maria said, "Screw them."

A definite mental improvement. 'Screw them' indeed. What sort of exercise are we getting? Perhaps they don't know the meaning of the word exercise. I need to improve my upper body strength, not play *tap-bloody-tap*.

Telling Maria about Philip is helping both of us, so I grab storytelling moments whenever I can. While Maria pushes me around the gardens, I anticipate telling her the next instalment.

I check the clock. "Maria, nearly time for your son's visit."

Today, I feel like a child at Christmas. I'm eager to share the good news with Joe. His mother has stretches of clarity and no major meltdowns.

Maria shuffles along the hallway ahead of me. Although she loves Joe's visits there's an element of sadness when he arrives. I imagine it's the anticipation of him leaving again. Dementia is barrier enough, but the Italian makes it almost impossible. I'll take the 'Screw you' anytime.

"*Vieni qui*," Joe calls, leading Maria to the table. He translates for me, "That means come here."

"It's a pity your mother didn't teach you to speak Italian when you were a child," I say.

His dark eyes look incredibly sad. "Unfortunately, she couldn't. My father was proudly 'Australian-Australian'—whatever that means." Joe shrugs. "Dad made Mum speak English, and only English to us kids, believing complete assimilation was for the best. According to him, moving to a new country meant leaving the old behind."

He surprises me by laughing out loud.

"I have learned a few Italian phrases. But I warn you, Miss Katerina, they're not exactly polite."

Although I've seen too much to be shocked by such

frippery as swear words, I ready my face with a taken-aback expression.

"When Mum was outside, I'd hear her speaking Italian to the dog, so my bit of Italian is limited to commands: *Eat. Stop. Come here. Sit.*"

"I imagine they've been surprisingly useful," I say.

"Yes." He smiles affectionately at Maria, then whispers to me from the side of his mouth. "But there hasn't been much call for *heel* or *fetch*."

Joe's and his mother's eyes are identical. Almost black. Not a depressing black, but a sparkly darkness, like the clearest of nights.

When he kisses Maria on the cheek, her eyes twinkle with intelligence, and I wouldn't be surprised if she understood the conversation about the dog.

If only Maria could remember how to speak English.

Joe opens his briefcase. "I've brought you a present, Miss Katerina. That song from the radio. I found a copy."

Such unexpected thoughtfulness makes me tear up. "Thank you," I say, covering my face with a hanky and pretending to sneeze.

"How are the nightmares?"

"Decreasing. Your mother's been helping," I say. "Talking to her about what's on my mind has relieved the worry, if only I could repay the favour. It's a pity no-one at 'The Figs' speaks Italian."

"There's Izzy," he says. "She's been great. She downloaded a translating app on her phone. She's used it to sort out minor things for Mum."

So, Izzy and her phone aren't all about posting pictures of food or taking selfies. My chin quivers and my shoulders slump as guilt drops by. I recognise guilt; an unwelcome but frequent visitor.

Once Joe leaves, I return to my room.

My new CD plays over and over, the music carrying vivid memories.

Izzy stands at my door doing an arm action I assume to be some sort of hammer dance. "You've been hammering that song for the past hour."

"Until last week, I hadn't heard it in years. Joe brought me the actual music. It's better than having it play over and over in my head."

"You caught yourself an earworm, eh?" she says.

"Caught what?"

"Not an actual worm. That's what it's called when a song gets stuck in your head."

"Did you find that out on your phone?"

Izzy tuts.

"Not a criticism this time," I say. "I've become aware that phones are magical tools of the future. Next, we'll all be teleporting." I laugh but feel guilty underneath for misjudging her.

She winks as she sits on the edge of my bed.

She's so generous, even to an old woman who sometimes thought of her as frivolous. "Could you please show me the Italian speaking thing on your phone? Joe told me about it."

"Of course." She types the phrase '*Katerina is one of my favourites*' and a robotic voice translates it into Italian.

I burst into tears. Not since Philip's mother has a woman treated me so kindly.

"Come on." Izzy passes me a tissue.

"Can it teach me how to say, '*Time for another story*'?"

"*Tempo per un'altra storia.*"

I practise all the way to Maria's room.

Maria's eyes gleam upon hearing her native tongue, and she rapid-fires words in Italian. When it's obvious I do not understand, she kicks the end of the bed and throws a pillow.

Izzy sticks her head in. "Did it work?"

"Not really. I think I've stirred her up. I'll take her back to my room."

I play the song twice through, and Maria relaxes on my bed, tapping her feet in time with the music.

Of course. Music soothes the savage beast. I take out the log I've created to record activities that have a calming effect on Maria and add music.

She's relaxed enough to give it another try. "Maria?" I repeat the Italian phrase, "*Tempo per un'altra storia.*"

This time she tilts her head as if she's considering my offer.

"Yes, or no?" I ask.

"*Sì.*"

"Good." I slide onto the bed next to her, taking her hand.

"There was a time before the wheelchair when I danced to this song. I can picture Philip, whistling, dancing and smiling to the very same tune. It's been years since I've felt the lightness music brings."

Maria's bounces my hand along with the beat.

I wait for the song to end, then close my eyes. "They say only the exterior changes and the young person hides within, but that's not true for me. The sweetness of youth carried hormones that lifted both the spirits and the skirt, without a thought for consequences. When it came to love, my feelings for Philip were spectacular. It was a time of great urgency and little caution, but it cost us so much."

Fancifully, I imagine Maria closing her eyes too, as she thinks back to her own youth in Italy.

"Forgive me if my mind embellishes the memories, but this is what I remember about those days..."

Chapter Sixteen

KATERINA

Sydney, 1943

Anna and I could speak freely under the tree at the far corner of the school grounds, because no one else dared sit at the old wooden bench where falling berries stained the seat. But Anna came prepared. Every day she brought an old towel, covered the mess, and created a private conversation space perfect for two.

"Where's the romance in our lives?" She held the back of her hand to her brow and heaved a sigh. "The situation is inexcusable."

"It's an all-girl school," I reminded her.

"But we're seventeen and neither of us has been kissed," Anna said.

"We never talk to any boys. Let alone kiss them."

She waved her hand dismissively. "We'll have to learn about kissing vicariously. I've nicked a book by Norman Lindsay. It's banned. Want to scan it for spicy bits?"

"You told me Norman Lindsay was an artist. A friend of your father's."

"Writing is an art form. He's an author, too." She pulled out the black-market copy of *Age of Consent* and looked around before she opened it.

No sooner had we begun reading, than a patrolling teacher headed our way. "Later," she whispered, hiding it in her bag.

I was secretly disappointed. Unlike Anna, my parents never spoke about such things. How would I ever find the truth about sex? Anna had offered dubious 'facts', but if what she said were to be believed, no one would ever do it.

"Come to the movie theatre with me," Anna said. "There's a wild dance film that's been playing for yonks at the *Century*."

"I'll ask, but I doubt I can go without an adult," I said.

"Come on, Katerina. Practise your persuasive patter. If we can't have romance of our own, we can at least watch it on screen."

I sorely wanted to see the movie 'Hellzapoppin', and mentally prepared for the enormous amount of cajoling it would take. I was surprised when Father agreed. But he made me promise to wait for Anna in the foyer of the Century Theatre, and not move until he returned to collect me.

If the movie had been about anything other than dancing, Father would have accompanied me. Luckily, he didn't.

I'd bought two tickets to save Anna waiting in the queue, but Anna didn't show. There was nothing I could do but wait. At least a dozen times I disobeyed Father by walking outside. Then, as the film was about to begin, I saw Philip walking along the opposite side of the road.

It had been months since I'd seen more than distant glimpses, and more than a year since we'd spoken. We attended different schools, had different routines, and I no longer visited Mama Bridgett.

To be honest, until I saw Philip across the street and felt a jolt of optimism, I hadn't realised I'd missed him being around. He looked the same, but different. He looked like a man. A handsome one, at that.

"Philip," I yelled.

He turned his head, then raced towards me, dodging traffic, looking like an athlete navigating a movable obstacle course. I held my breath, hoping he made it safely, but at the same time I was suitably impressed.

"Are you okay?" His forehead creased in concern.

"I'm fine." I waved the tickets in his face but didn't stop to explain. "Come with me." I linked my arm through his and hurried him into the theatre. He didn't ask what the movie was, but he smiled at me as I skipped the grand carpeted staircase two steps at a time. There was no way I was missing the opening scene.

It struck me as peculiar that I'd been worried about sitting and watching a movie alone but was brazen enough to hijack a young man. Anna would be deliriously proud.

As we followed the usher to our seats, I became acutely aware of Philip's arm. It was warmer than mine.

Firmer and stronger. He almost lifted me off my feet as he helped me sidle to our allocated spaces. I could have released him once we sat, but I held on.

I considered gazing into his eyes. Not that I wanted to, but I was thinking of the story I'd share with Anna. A gaze would make it sound like a scene from the romance novels she'd stolen, but that would have been a step too far. She'd have to settle for a description of the sensation of Philip's skin brushing against mine.

During the interval, Philip dashed to the snack bar and returned with candy hearts in a white paper bag. The blood rushed to his cheeks as I took out the pastel sweets one by one, taking delight in reading each message stamped upon the heart-shaped faces.

Cutie Pie. Cheeky Boy. Be Mine.

I laughed and popped one into my pocket for Anna —she would shriek.

During the second half of the movie, I brazenly tapped the beat of the songs on his knee and danced the steps with my feet touching his. I squealed with delight when he joined in.

Before intermission, the characters up on the silver screen had been Jeff and Kitty, but in the second half of the film, Philip and I were up there too; doing the Lindy Hop.

I imagined him lifting me, holding my hands and pulling me close. Philip was no longer Mama Bridgett's annoying son.

When the movie ended, the cogs in my mind turned at full speed, devising ways to run into him again. I felt heartless about asking him to wait upstairs out of Father's sight, but he knew my family well and didn't argue.

I lied when Father asked if I'd enjoyed myself. I made a fuss about how disappointing it was that Anna hadn't shown, then I had to backtrack in case Father stopped me seeing her altogether.

But there was nothing disappointing. The night was a magical adventure from beginning to end.

Philip and I watched the same movie three times. With each viewing, our dance moves progressed.

On our last visit we found an empty row at the back, so as not to annoy the rest of the audience. We danced and wriggled as much as sitting allowed, but shushing patrons across the aisle forced us to stop.

The usher asked us to leave and told us not to come back.

There were still forty minutes until Father was due to arrive, so Philip waited with me in the foyer. He propped himself against the lobby wall, and I pretended to browse the notice board behind him. I leaned in so close I could see the movement of his heartbeat, throbbing in his neck. I was fighting an urge to press my finger to his pulse, when I noticed a flyer advertising a Lindy Hop dance competition at the Trocadero on George Street—my mind was made up immediately. We would enter. I just needed to convince Philip.

"But your father?" he argued.

"I won't tell him if you don't."

"We've never actually danced." His eyes widened with dread.

I shrugged my shoulders, not considering this an obstacle. "We'll learn. We'll practise."

I answered every objection, then grabbed his hand, covering his knuckles with innocent kisses. When he smiled back, his eyes shone golden, like water under sunlight, and suddenly the kissing wasn't a silly game. Perhaps I could tell Anna about this, but my parents could never know. Mother would find it terribly unacceptable, and Father would be furious.

Philip's eyes traced a line around my neckline, down past my waist, to my toes and slowly up again. I felt heat at every point, and my heart beat so fast I was worried he'd hear it.

"I guess we could give it a go," he said.

***

The weeks leading up to the competition were better than warm sun on a bitter-cold winter's day. I felt alive in a world full of promise.

On one of those weekends, my family planned an overnight beach trip. I mimicked what I hoped were the symptoms of an illness serious enough to prevent me joining them, yet not so worrying my mother sought medical attention.

My brother Nick gave me a suspicious look, but Mother and Father agreed I could stay home alone on the proviso I wouldn't leave the house. Father made firm eye-contact as he said this, but I returned his gaze without flinching. I was after all telling the truth. I planned to stay at home.

I was far from unwell; I had so much energy I was ready to burst. Even before Father's black car disappeared down the driveway, I imagined Philip spinning me across the floor as we followed the dance steps in the movie.

Within minutes of my family driving away, Philip crept to the back door.

How bossy I was. I made him sit with me on the staircase and together we studied my notes. Every step copied directly from those we'd watched in 'Hellzapoppin'.

When Philip creased his temple, I thought he was disagreeing with my routine. "What's wrong?" I asked.

"Something Mama said."

It seemed a cryptic answer.

I waited as he tugged his hair, messing up the usual sleek style, but he didn't explain.

"What did Mama Bridgett say? Is she sick?" I thought the worst.

"She's fine, but she spoke sternly as I was leaving, 'Know your place,' she said. 'It makes life easier in the long run.'"

I grabbed Philip's hands, pulling him to his feet. "You are in the right place. You're with me, learning to dance."

When we began practising, his feet moved slowly, as if his mother's words weighed him down. But youth is youth, and love is love. His warm hands firmed against my back, and he shed a layer of heaviness with every twirl.

As it got dark, the large window in the ballroom became a mirror. We watched the lines of our bodies, ensuring we echoed each other's moves.

"Are you alright," he asked suddenly, pulling back to look at me.

I blushed. I'd been staring at the reflection of our bodies snaking across the black and white tiles, and I'd moaned.

Would I dare to share this exciting, yet frightening sensation with Anna?

Chapter Seventeen

CLAUDIA

Fremantle, 2018

There's been nothing from Oliver since the house went on the market two weeks ago. Now, he's whining down the phone.

"Claudia, I can't find my favourite coffee mug. *World's Best Dad.*"

"I haven't seen it, but I'll look."

I feel a prick of sympathy about him wanting to hold onto memories of our beautiful sons. Despite my cleaning and culling frenzy, I haven't had the heart to part with a single thing either Josh or Aaron made me. I spent a whole hour reading, smiling, and crying over a pile of Mother's Day cards.

"Thanks," he says. "I remember when Josh gave it to me."

Josh? It was Aaron. I remember when he rode his bike to the shops to buy it. He used all his money, filling the mug with his dad's favourite lollies.

There's no prick of sympathy now, just an egotistical prick named Oliver.

There's a long pause, then he clears his throat. "I know you're angry. I made a mistake leaving you, but now I'm thinking of all the good times." Another pause. "I read an article recently about forgiveness being the highest form of love."

"Fuck off."

I hang up and walk outside to martial-arts-kick one of Oliver's favourite plants. Then, risking danger to my bare legs, I put the boot into a rose bush—a birthday present from Wendy.

Oliver and his sister are off my Christmas list.

It takes ten soapy minutes to remove my wedding and engagement rings. My finger has grown around them like tree-bark around a nail. I would have chewed them off if I'd had to. They're an unnecessary reminder of our marriage.

Instead of my usual hours and hours of stewing over arguments, I settle quickly. Maybe a touch of violence and some colourful language, à la Bonnie, is what I've always needed?

I call my new role model to tell her how I swore at Oliver, and describe my crimes against innocent plants.

Bonnie laughs through the entire phone call. "You're going through the six stages of divorce. Shock, denial, swearing, kicking, selling your rings. Next it will be finding a new man."

"I never know when you're making things up. You remind me of Dad."

"To be honest, I'm proud of you. I didn't think you had the guts."

"Neither did I." I manage a weak laugh. "So, stage

six is a new man, eh? I don't want a man, but I wouldn't mind friends. At forty-six it isn't going to be easy."

"I'm sorry Wendy turned out to be such a bi-atch," Bonnie says. "But you've got me. That's worth something. And I'm going to push you until you meet people."

I think about this long after she hangs up. Bonnie's right, but where do I start?

I phone the boys to tell them their father and I have agreed it's all over, but my calls go to voicemail. At the end of my message I add that we also agreed how much we love and miss our sons.

I'm reflected in the black screen of the television. There's a space surrounding me, like an expanding black hole, and people I care about are disappearing into it.

If only they had Platonic Tinder. If only making friends was as easy as swiping right.

I search through my handbag for the scrap of paper with Troy's phone number. New friends aren't going to appear from nowhere; it's up to me. Besides, it will give me a chance to ask the name of the genealogy man.

I inhale what I hope is bravery-infused air, then practise what to say.

'How about a drink?' *Corny and uninventive. I need to come up with something better.*

I run through several 'witty' opening lines, but they're more Bonnie than me. I finally decide on, 'How've you been?' with a follow up question of, "Do you want to try the coffee shop again?'

I input the first digits of his phone number, letting my finger hesitate over the last. *Come on Claudia, dial.*

I'm relieved when the call rings out and I can leave a message. This leaves Troy two options: either not ring back or be ready with a plausible excuse. I wish I hadn't called. He'll feel uncomfortable but won't want to hurt my feelings because he's nice.

Take a breath, Claudia. Stop overthinking.

I'm confused when the tune '*I'm winning the game of survival*' plays from nowhere. But then remember Bonnie fiddling with my phone settings—she's made it sing clichés from the bottom of my bag.

It's Troy.

"Hi." I try channelling something like estate-agent charm. Hard to pull off with a single word.

"Sorry, I missed the call. The breeze at the beach is crazy cyclonic. I was fastening the surfboard back onto the roof rack, and I thought I'd lose the board if I let it go."

"How are you?" I ask.

"Psyching myself up to go back to work on Monday. I'm flying out tomorrow afternoon. How about a drink?" he asks.

I smile at the uncomplicated request. Troy used the opening line I'd rejected as corny, but sometimes simple is best. "That would be nice." *That would be nice?* I sound like Grandma Rose accepting an invitation to bingo.

"There's a bar in town advertising live music and gin tasting."

"Great," I say.

I've got to work on my social skills. Too many single word answers.

"Happy hour is five until six. I'll pick you up at 4:45."

"Thank you." Two words. I'm improving.

One hour to get ready. Not enough time to over-think. I choose old but flattering jeans and a striped wrap top. Last time I wore this outfit, Bonnie, the self-proclaimed style expert, said I looked really good. I even add some make-up.

The survival song plays again. My shoulders drop as I get the phone. I bet he's changed his mind and I'm all dressed up and no place to go.

"Hello," I say, trying to hide my disappointment.

"Matt's been held up at work," Bonnie says. "Do you want me to come over and cheer you up?"

I press my lips together. I don't want to tell her about Troy.

"You there?" she asks.

"I phoned Troy," I blurt out. "We're having a drink."

"Good girl."

"You're welcome to come." I'm not sure I want her to.

"Noooo, but I have some advice. Try to enjoy yourself. He doesn't have to replace Oliver."

"I'm not looking for a replacement," I say.

"Forget your inhibitions and get yourself some sex."

"Bonnie. Stop."

"Well, you never know. Have you got condoms?"

"*No!* Stop! I'm planning to ask the name of the genealogist. Nothing else. He'll be here soon."

"I'll ring for a full report," Bonnie says.

That conversation was ridiculous. Sex is not on my list, and it's not a date, but it is an opportunity for me to practise my dating skills should I ever need them. *God, am I considering a stage six—finding a man?*

I've barely taken a breath when Troy knocks.

Calm down. Smile. I open the door and Troy leans in to kiss my cheek, then steps back to give me an appraising look. I put my hands over my thighs where they feel too snug.

"You look lovely."

"You too," I say. His hair's been cut, and he's lost the beachy windswept look. The plain cotton shirt and jeans make him look older. It makes me feel better. He's definitely over forty. I'd fall apart if someone mistook me for his mother.

We find a parking spot close to the bar, and Troy leans against his car. "Do you mind if we stand here for a minute so I can have a cigarette?"

"Not at all," I say.

He asks how I've been and I surprise myself by telling him how I miss my sons since they moved away.

"Distance can be difficult," he says. "I'm a fly-in, fly-out worker. Chef for a mine up north. Four weeks on, four off."

He's not a dentist, but he still has perfect teeth.

"Is it a good job?"

"Good for money, but not relationships. My wife thought she'd get into shape while I was away, but she found more than she was looking for in her personal trainer." He says this with a half laugh, but I sense the sad undertone. I like him better for not saying something dismissive, like, you'll never believe what my whore of an ex did." He lights another cigarette and I wonder how I'd feel about kissing a smoker.

"She found living apart difficult. I get that, but I wish she'd told me instead of leaving. She left him when she found out she wasn't the only woman he was 'training', but I'm not man enough to forgive and forget."

I could tell Troy about Oliver, but I'm not yet far

enough down Bonnie's stages of divorce, to do it without swearing or bad-mouthing.

The tables outside the tavern are full, so we head to the bar. A man carrying a tray of labelled shot glasses offers samples. "SIN GINS," he says, "The seven deadly gins—name your vice."

I check out the glasses of Wrath, Envy, Gluttony, Pride, Lust, Sloth and Avarice, reading the handwritten cards describing the not-so-secret ingredients.

"Envy," Troy says attempting to clink his plastic cup against mine. It's more a dull clunk.

"Before I forget." He produces a business card. "I chased down the details of the genealogy guy. I phoned him and he said he'll accept delayed payment."

"That's really thoughtful." I drink up.

There's a lull in the conversation and I spin the shot glass in my hands. My face turns red as I look at label. The pomegranate-elderberry-flower flavoured gin I selected has a LUST sticker on it. I try to hide it.

"Too late," Troy says with a grin.

"I chose it for the flavour," I explain.

He has a wicked laugh. "What does *lust* taste like?"

He knows I'm uncomfortable but seems to enjoy watching me squirm. Bonnie would have made a quick comeback, but I have none.

I sample another drink instead; this time *avarice*.

"Don't ask," I say flashing the label. "I honestly have no idea what avarice means. If it's something fun, then it's another thing I've missed out on."

"Aren't the deadly sins supposed to be avoided?" he asks.

"I don't know enough to comment."

"Another?" The waiter pushes the tray within reach.

"I'll take *pride*." I'm not used to drinking gin and my mouth drags out the words. "I've never understood what's so bad about pride."

Troy studies my face. "What about I buy us a non-alcoholic drink? We can pace ourselves."

I nod, but as soon as he walks to the bar, I chug a shot of *wrath*.

Troy takes ages and I tear a beer coaster into tiny squares while I wait. When I eventually look for him, he's leaning against the wall, in a quiet corner, talking on the phone.

He comes back with two tall glasses. "Soda water." He reaches into his pocket for a packet of cigarettes. "I'll be near the tree having a smoke."

After two sips of plain soda, I add the shot of gin Troy left untouched. I wonder if I'm allergic to the ingredients, because I'm slightly dizzy.

The tree branches look fuzzy, but he's on the phone again.

I jabber non-stop when he gets back, and even when I realise everything is sliding downhill, I don't shut up. I tell Troy about Oliver, how we met, how sad I was when he left. By the time I'm telling him about Dad and the cancer, tears are streaming down my cheeks.

A three-piece Irish band starts playing old ballads and my mood flips. I wipe my tears and grab Troy's hand. "Dance?"

He mouths something, but the music's too loud.

"I can't hear what you're saying."

He yells into my ear, "No. Time to take you home."

"Yes." I smile to myself.

Troy said I looked lovely. He smiled at me at the beach. He enjoys my company—now he wants to take me home. I've spent my whole life being careful—not a hint of scandal in my history—until tonight.

When we pull up in my driveway, he races to open my car door, but I step out too quickly and misjudge the distance to the ground. I slip on the gravel and my ankle crumples underneath me. My head spins as Troy half carries me to the front door.

"Put your foot up," he says once we're inside. "I'll get ice."

While Troy is in the kitchen, I decide on mood music, but my ankle won't make the trip across the room. I press random buttons on the TV remote, managing to find a channel playing 90's hits. I struggle to stand on one foot. My shoulders and hips roll as the room rotates.

"Come on, Claudia, put your feet up," Troy says.

"No dance?" I ask, my tongue feeling too thick.

"No." He helps me back to my seat.

"That's okay," I slur. "Lots of men hate dancing."

He presses ice against my ankle.

"My Dad used to say I was a great dancer. I got it from him. He said he won a big competition for some fancy swing dancing, but he hurt his knee in the war."

When Troy lifts my leg to put a cushion underneath it, I wriggle my bottom over until we're close, then turn to face him.

It's now or never.

"Thanks for a lovely time." I thread my fingers through his hair and close my eyes. I'm wondering whether he'll kiss me gently or firmly, and whether the smell of cigarettes will be a turn on or turn off. But he pulls away.

"You need rest. I need to go." He kisses the top of my head.

I try to think of something funny or sexy, but he's gone before I say anything at all.

No matter how many times I replay last night's events, I don't find a version where I come out looking good. Thankfully, Troy left before I indecently assaulted him, and he was gone half an hour before I threw up. I owe him an apology, but there's no way I can face him in person.

Sorry. My favourite word. *Really sorry*.

Dad's voice throbs inside my head, "*Look for the silver lining*."

What Dad? There's no silver lining in this.

It takes all morning, but I do find one. If Dad won a dance competition, maybe we can track that down. Well, maybe not me. I have no skills.

When I remember the business card from Troy, I email the Professor, Dermot Gallagher, to explain our two-part search. First, we need to prove Dad's identity and then we want to find out why he was hiding his past.

The genealogist replies almost straight away. He's available.

I'm putting more ice on my foot when I receive a message from Troy.

I'm reluctant to open the text. Oh God. I'm so undesirable. At least Oliver walked slowly, my last recollection of Troy was him sprinting to the door.

What can he possibly say about my behaviour?

As my stomach churns and my self-talk develops nasty edges. I decide what Troy's actually written can't be worse. I'll die if it includes a #metoo hashtag.

> Claudia, Thanks for last night. Sorry about running off. The phone calls were from my wife. She asked me about getting back together. I didn't want to complicate things when I'm not sure. I absolutely wanted to kiss you last night, but it's clear you have things to work through, too. Besides I'd never take advantage of a drunken woman. LOL. I smiled all the way home. An attractive woman showing me attention has been great for my ego. –Troy.

I read his text three times. I won't see him again, but I'm okay with it. A man found me attractive. It feels as if he was an angel, appearing just in time to give me a boost. A reminder that all men aren't bastards.

Even though I'm sure Bonnie will tease me, I need to tell someone.

"So, you offered sex, but he refused?" Bonnie asks after I explain.

"Not quite. But kind of." My voice is quiet. Now Bonnie's put it that way, I no longer feel desirable.

"Did you take your clothes off?"

"NO!"

Bonnie giggles and her voice echoes as she says, "Then you don't have to worry. He didn't hate your naked body or get a shock at your vagina. But even if it's unattractive—surgery can fix it. They have vagina designers these days. I looked at before and after photos once—it was enlightening."

"Stop. I can't tell whether you're joking."

Bonnie laughs so loudly I hold the phone away from my ear. "I almost got you. Of course, I'm joking. You are an attractive woman, Claudia. When you're ready to meet someone, you will."

I change the subject. "Do you have time on Tuesday to meet the genealogist?"

"Don't you mean gynaecologist?" This time Bonnie's laugh's a guffaw.

"Enough jokes. I need you here in case he has questions only you can answer."

"Another man in your house, eh?"

"He's a retired professor, a friend of Troy's friend. He's probably eighty," I say.

"You've missed an opportunity to hook up. There must be some way we can get you laid." She stops talking to shush someone in the background.

That's when I realise there's been an echo. Bonnie's on speaker phone.

"You're not having this conversation in public, are you?"

"Not really." Her voice is unconvincing.

"Bonnie! I have to go."

So, this is the ditch my life has dropped into?

I've always kept personal things to myself. Now, Bonnie's let other people know about my drunken behaviour.

My humiliation isn't even a secret.

Chapter Eighteen

CLAUDIA

Fremantle, 2018

I feel awful holding a grudge against Bonnie. After ignoring two text messages, I cave and send her a reminder about the meeting with our genealogist. What happened wasn't entirely Bonnie's fault. I unloaded my embarrassment without asking where she was.

Besides, Bonnie gave me the consideration and level of privacy she'd have given herself. In my shoes, she would have laughed it off. Bonnie never changes, and I don't want her to. Grandma Rose was wrong, Bonnie doesn't have too much electricity, but she has enough to share when I'm in need of a jolt.

Dermot Gallagher arrives ten minutes early, briefly introduces himself, then immerses himself in the plantation of dodgy notes with barely a word. I hope Bonnie arrives soon; I've no idea what small talk I should make under the circumstances.

The moment Bonnie sets eyes on him, she grabs the

back of my shirt and pulls me into the kitchen. "Where d'you dig up that fella?"

"Troy. Remember? His friend's mother hired him."

I glance at Dermot. He's certainly not one of the suit-wearing professors in the movies. Bonnie purses her lips. I know the look. She thinks we should have found someone else.

"I think we're lucky to have him," I say. "He's a retired professor, he's giving us mate's rates, and he's willing to wait to for payment."

"Professor of what? Homelessness?" Bonnie stares at him, then back at me as if I've gone mad.

Perhaps I have; it never occurred to me to check his qualifications. Another personality flaw right there. I hear professor or doctor, and assume people are legitimate.

Bonnie and I edge around the corner of the kitchen for a better view.

"What the fuck is he wearing?" Bonnie looks like she's sniffing a cat litter tray.

I scan his clothes from the collar of his purple-swirl shirt, past his striped trousers and down to his odd socks. Not just navy and black odd, but one sock's argyle-patterned grey and one is plain red.

"Okay, I admit he's not well put together, but we're not hiring him for his fashion flair."

We watch as he removes our evidence cards and anecdotes from the pinboard and sorts them into piles on the small table in the conservatory. I imagine each clue organised according to: A) unrelated documents B) kernel of truth; or C) actual facts.

There's one large pile—my money's on category A.

"He hasn't said much, just looked at our evidence

and written in his notepad," I whisper to Bonnie. "I hope he has mad skills and can crack Dad's case. The quicker the better."

"What's his name?" Bonnie asks.

"Dermot."

"Oh no. I can't bear the name Dermot. Remember when Pyro-Dermot burnt half our school down. He gave me the creeps. God, I hope it's not him."

"It isn't," I say. "He hasn't got Pyro-Dermot's hooked nose, and he has an accent." I study the side of the professor's face to be sure.

"Do you remember that Dermot incident?" she asks. "Someone said he was fiddling as the school burned. That's disgusting." The volume of Bonnie's voice turns up a notch.

"Shhh, Bonnie." I touch my lips. "It was a reference to Nero fiddling as Rome burned."

"I know. How sick is that?"

"You do know the saying means Nero was playing a violin, don't you?"

"OMG, I thought he was mas—"

"Bonnie!" I put my hand over her mouth. "This man is ten years older than Pyro-Dermot. This Professor Dermot's in his fifties."

"Heat is aging. It's the fires. Bad for the skin." Bonnie laughs.

"Don't try to distract me from the Nero comment, it won't work." I touch my forehead. "It's locked in here forever."

I'm surprisingly pleased to have something over Bonnie; it almost counteracts the teasing potential she has about my embarrassing encounter with Troy.

Bonnie presses her finger in a silent *Shhh*, then slides

closer to where Dermot is working. After rummaging through the dining room sideboard, she produces three of the rose-bud teacups. Clearly a ploy for a closer look.

Back in the kitchen, Bonnie nudges her shoulder against mine to whisper, "He's not wearing glasses. No one over forty-five has eyesight that good."

"Contacts?" I shrug.

"What about wrinkles?"

I take a better look. "He has some, but overall, he has lovely olive skin."

She drags me into the laundry so forcefully I almost fall onto the washing machine.

"Oh my god, Claudia. You've let down your ponytail, taken off your glasses and lowered your neckline."

"What are you talking about?"

"You know. In the movies. Sensible woman suddenly single. No one notices how pretty she is underneath her clever disguise." Bonnie scratches her fingernails in the air and purrs. "The practical woman goes man-crrrrazy."

Terrified he'll hear, I shut the laundry door. "I commented on his skin because you mentioned wrinkles."

"You said lovely skin. Lovely, lovely, lovely."

"Stop. I'm opening the laundry door and I want you to behave."

I push her back into the kitchen, and she puts the kettle on.

"Tea?" Bonnie asks Dermot, carrying a tray into the conservatory.

He shakes his head and continues working.

"Excuse me," she says. "I'm Bonnie, Claudia's sister. Do you mind if I ask questions while you work?"

"It would be better if you wrote them down. That way I can concentrate."

Dermot's voice is definitely Irish, maybe watered-down, but I should have picked it straight away. He goes back to his notes. He's in the zone. His clothes might be a mess, but he has a laser focussed work ethic.

"Just one question," Bonnie says. "Any leads yet?"

"Nothing at this point." He taps his pen for effect. "Unfortunately, birth records aren't made public for a hundred years. I don't imagine you want to wait nine more for your Dad's to be released. I'm researching his parents."

Bonnie tilts her ear towards him. My money is on her listening to his accent rather than to what he is saying.

"If we find evidence of the parents, we might get the birth certificate you need. I'll check church records too." He holds up an index card. "Catholic, you think?"

"Yes," I say. "I thought about looking up church records, but didn't know how."

Bonnie laughs. "You wouldn't have known it if you'd seen Dad with a beer, but he was an altar boy. He hated Catholic boarding school. Here..." Bonnie grabs for his pen. "I'll write that down."

He holds onto it. "I'm grand. I'll put it in my notes."

"Can we help you? To cut down costs?" I ask.

"Not at the minute. I usually work on my own. I quoted for an identity search and I'll stick to that estimate until I'm either successful or decide to give up."

"You're already thinking of abandoning it?"

I must look horrified because he jumps in quickly.

"Not yet. But if your father was hiding something and didn't want to be found, we might not succeed."

Dermot reaches for a lunchbox. "Right-e-o. I'm going to take a break. I'll be out back."

The door is barely closed when Bonnie says, "He doesn't look like a pensioner."

"Retired isn't the same as being pension age."

"It's amazing how an accent can make a man fifty-percent more attractive. I would have rated him a five, but he's gone to a seven and a half. Could even be an eight with the right clothes."

"You can't do numbers with money, but you're an expert with attractiveness ratings?" I laugh, but when I glance through the window, I realise Bonnie's right. Dermot's not 'in-your-face' good-looking, but he is appealing.

Bonnie sidles over to the research table and flicks through Dermot's notebook.

"Bonnie! Don't." I take it off her. "You can't look through people's personal things."

"We're paying him. That's not the same as prying." She points at the label. Dad's name. "See?"

I look through the French doors to make sure the professor isn't looking. He's got his back to us.

"BDM." She points melodramatically to the first page heading. "Bondage discipline masochism? What on earth has he uncovered about Dad?"

"Births, deaths and marriages." I close the book.

"That was a joke," Bonnie says. "Let's not add that to my genuine mistakes."

"Put his stuff away before he comes back."

Food and fresh air obviously agree with Dermot, because he returns smiling.

"I've made a checklist and I'll come back tomorrow,

if that's okay?" As he packs up his belongings, he looks amused. "I initially leaned towards turning down this project. For some reason, your father changed key personal details, making it difficult to prove his identity. People usually leave a trail, but I think in Philip McLeod's case, I'll need assistance for the more time-consuming tasks. Fortunately, it seems I have two willing assistants. I'll take the job, but I can't promise results."

"I volunteer for homework." I put my hand up. "As long as you explain what you want done."

"The pile of old envelopes with the redacted names —can you see if there's technology capable of deciphering the blacked-out details? I haven't dealt with this before."

"We'll try," Bonnie says.

With that, Dermot is gone, leaving us staring at the door.

"Strange man," Bonnie says.

I pick up the stamp collectors' envelopes. "Where will I start? I don't want to fail my first assignment."

"Pity neither of us know anyone who works for the Police," Bonnie says with a cheeky wink.

"If only one of us had a kid in that field. You're a genius." I laugh. "I'll call Josh tonight."

I want to prove I'm capable of helping—now we have guidance, it feels doable. "It feels like a game," I say.

"A game?" she says. "Like Cluedo?"

A shiver runs up my spine. "We have our own Professor Plum in the conservatory. I hope we don't uncover a murder."

Chapter Nineteen

KATERINA

'The Figs' Sydney, 2018

My nightmares have almost gone. Although I still lie awake thinking about Philip and what happened, insomnia is a better option than sedation or being moved from The Figs. Sleep is less important to me than my need to stay and help Maria—the guilt of abandoning someone else would be too much to bear.

I've stopped rehearsing what I would say to Philip's daughters: Claudia and Bonnie, if they ever found me. I've read his death notice so many times I've not only memorised their names, I've imagined what they look like and how they'd speak. But they won't come. They're young and have their own lives. By the time they're old enough to become contemplative and interested in their father's early life, I'll be long dead—the secret buried with me.

I'd rather not be quizzed in person. Keeping something hidden is a different beast than lying to someone's face. Still, a part of me is curious about Philip's daughters. I wonder if they're anything like him, or more like their mother.

"Wakie-wakie." Izzy nudges me, bringing me back from my thoughts.

"I'm not asleep. I never snooze in the afternoon," I say. "It should be obvious I'm listening to music."

"In bed. Eyes closed," Izzy says. "If it looks like a duck..."

She picks up the paperweight calendar from the windowsill. I shudder, waiting for waves of negative energy to travel through time. Nothing happens. I've been afraid of the damned thing for so long, I've imagined it as more than just pieces of metal.

"I just asked you something," Izzy says. "But you were off with the fairies."

"Watch out, you're picking up old people sayings."

"I know. The other day I said I was *pleased as punch*." Izzy laughs, happy to poke fun at herself.

"What exactly does this thing do?" She turns the brass circles, then hands it to me.

I'm ready to recoil, but it doesn't leave a brand of shame. I exhale decades of fear in one long breath.

"It's a perpetual calendar. When you align the rings to any date, it gives you the day of the week," I explain.

"Why would anyone need that?" Izzy wrinkles her nose.

"Well, *back when Adam was a boy*." I waggle my finger putting emphasis on the old person saying, ensuring Izzy knows I'm throwing it in for effect. At my age, it would be easy for that kind of joke to slip through the keeper. "Before people had fancy phone computers, if you wanted to set an event more than a year in advance, it was difficult to find out what day a particular date fell on. Like planning a wedding. You might want to know which days are Saturdays."

I demonstrate, then pass it back to Izzy who imitates my finger waggle to perfection.

"Ooh, my birthday is on a Sunday next year. I'm a Sagittarian. What star sign are you?" she asks.

"A nonagenarian." I chuckle. Sometimes, you have to laugh so people know you've said something funny.

Izzy's laugh is warm and encompassing. She doesn't laugh at people; she laughs with them.

I hoist myself into the wheelchair. "Anyway, it's Wednesday. Joe and Maria day, and I need to put on my best clothes."

"Take the *thing-a-ma-jig* to afternoon tea with Joe."

"No. I'll leave it here." I reset the date before replacing it on the windowsill.

"Pity. You could have made the nonagenarian joke again. Joe needs a good laugh; he's worried about Maria. The duty nurse put in a complaint."

"About the fight when we watched the football?" I ask.

"Possibly."

"I'll explain it to Joe. It wasn't Maria's fault."

As I approach the table, I can see Joe is genuinely concerned, and Maria's nowhere to be seen. "Everything alright?" I ask.

"Fine."

He's lying. He's anything but fine.

"If it makes you feel any better, it's a full moon, and most of the residents are out of sorts," I say.

"She wasn't friendly with me just now either," he says. "I brought in her old iPad. She loved using it until the dementia. I thought it might keep her brain active. It could have been something good for you to record on that improvement chart you're keeping. I was feeling hopeful, but after hearing about the incident with the nurse, I don't think Mum's improving at all."

"Your mother's blow-up wasn't anything out of the ordinary."

"According to the complaint, she went completely crazy."

"No. You've only heard one side. Neither me nor your mother wanted to leave our rooms, but we were herded into the Welcome Room by the new carer. The expression on that nurse's face should have been a warning sign. *Beady scavenger eyes, like a bird of prey*," I say this part dramatically, pausing for a moment in the hope of seeing Joe's usual smile. It doesn't appear.

"The TV was tuned to a football grand-final, and the bird-like woman had pre-picked the teams we were to cheer for. She didn't ask our preference, just *squawked* a shrill command. When I flatly refused to wear the jersey, the carer pulled one over my head." I add, "Using her *talons*." I know I'm overplaying the bird analogy, but I'm hoping to relieve the worry by distracting Joe.

I've never seen him irritated before. Now the poor man is angry. "You can't be forced to join in. Surely, you have the right to refuse?"

"You might be able to with another carer, but you cannot argue with a *buzzard*." I flap my arms hoping he'll laugh. But he doesn't.

"Your mother tried to stop the woman dressing me up in team colours, and she started yelling and swearing in Italian. When the nurse insisted on English, Maria grabbed my wheelchair and began wheeling me away."

"I would have done worse, I would have pushed your chair into the nurse," Joe says.

"When the carer screeched, and commandeered my wheelchair, your mother saw red. She pulled the jumper off me, stole another resident's cane, and poked it into the ceiling fan. Everyone in the TV room screamed with delight. Except bird-lady."

Joe puts his hand over his mouth to stop laughing.

"Maria might not be the hero of all staff, but she's gained a few resident followers. George, the man who owns the cane, has been smiling at your mother ever since."

"Sometimes, I think Mum hates me for putting her in here." Although Joe's mouth is smiling, his eyes are slick with tears. "After hearing that story, I can see why."

I push the packet of biscuits towards him and take one myself. "I'll eat, while you show me the iPad gadget," I say. "What games does your mother like to play?"

"Solitaire?" he shrugs. "I'm not sure. I never took that much interest in what Mum liked. I tried showing her Izzy's translating app, but when Mum heard the robotic voice, she threw the iPad across the table. Then she started with her 'Ndrangheta rubbish. I reckon she was trying to put a curse on me. Her own son."

"As I said before, it's probably the full moon."

"I just wanted to communicate with her."

"She knows what's important. She knows how much you love her," I say.

"There's so much I don't know about my own mother, now it's too late to ask questions," Joe says.

"Is it worrying you that much?"

"There's guilt too. When I was young, I didn't realise how cruel it was that our father didn't let Mum speak Italian or talk about the old days. Now, I regret not challenging him. If she'd had a daughter instead of a son, she would have asked questions, and encouraged Mum to tell stories of her life."

I think back to my relationship with my own mother. "Not necessarily. Mothers and daughters do not always get on. You and Maria are very close. She's lucky."

"But I waited until Mum's mind was almost gone to take an interest."

"There are many things I wish I'd done or hadn't done, Joe. I'm twice as old as you. They say wisdom comes with age, but I've just used the time to make double the mistakes."

"But I don't know anything about Mum's life back in Italy, or why she came to Australia." Joe shakes his head.

"Lives aren't always tales of sunshine. Sometimes mothers are reluctant to tell their children about their youth. Or what they've done."

"Nothing Mum could ever do would shock me," he says.

I think of my years of shame, guilt and lies, and I'm tempted to tell him that in my experience people are capable of worse than expected.

Chapter Twenty

CLAUDIA

Fremantle, 2018

Dermot's worked from the same spot at the conservatory table for the past two weeks; methodically checking his research schedule and taking lunch breaks in the courtyard outside.

There's been buyer interest in the house, and Mark Katter thinks it will be sold before the week's out, so I've kept out of Dermot's way, packing belongings ready for the big move.

From the moment he arrived this morning, Dermot switched into a zone of concentration, and he's said very little since.

The only signs of progress on the research board are notations showing which leads are dead ends, and a couple of question marks denoting further investigation needed. Proving Dad's identity seems a distant hope.

Standing at the kitchen bench, wrapping breakables with newspaper, I absentmindedly watch him work.

He's dressed differently today. Dermot has exchanged the homeless look for neat and tidy. I wonder what prompted the change. He's never mentioned a wife, so, perhaps he's met a woman. I know nothing about him except he takes one sugar in black tea, and I assume he likes gardening because he often waters mine while he's eating his sandwich. The plants have all sprouted new leaves.

When Dermot suddenly spins his chair towards me, I pretend I'm inspecting one of the cups for a crack. My cheeks warm with the tingle of embarrassment. I hope I was quick enough, and he didn't see me staring.

"Claudia." Dermot gestures to the list of possible names we've come up with for Dad.

We've used many combinations of the lengthy name he used: *Philip Sean Francis Patrick Alexander McLeod,* along with *Healy* and *O'Patrick* from his mother.

"There's an overload of search options," he says. "The chance of hitting on the right one without facts is like the big win in lotto."

"Is there anything I can do to help?"

"Thank you, but at the moment it's better for me to keep track on my own. Anyway, it looks as if you've quite the job of your own." He takes an exaggerated breath.

"You're trying to let me down nicely, aren't you? There's more chance of being struck by lightning than winning Lotto, and even less chance of finding Dad's real name?"

"Ah, no. I'm not saying that." Dermot stares in my general direction but over my shoulder. I turn quickly in case another of those embarrassing inspirational quotes from Bonnie needs immediate destruction. Nothing there.

"I've crossmatched most of these names against available records," he says, his voice more upbeat. "But it's got me thinking. Last time, I asked about your dad's Ma. It wasn't just chitchat. From what you've told me, he adored his mother. I should have concentrated my efforts on finding her."

"But what if he changed her name too?" I ask.

"People who take on an alias, usually preserve the names of people they loved. To do otherwise would be like erasing their existence."

I nod, thinking about my sons. I'd never erase them.

"I'm fairly certain Bridgett was his mother's name. I have a feeling she could be an O'Patrick too, like your father claimed. It's not as if I've discovered anything, but sometimes this genealogy gig is more than leg work, it's sensing an inkling of the truth. Hunches often pan out."

"You're good at this work," I say.

His eyes twinkle and smile, and I try to work out the colour. They're unusual. Flecks of grey, green and blue, like Irish tweed.

He puts his head down and gets back to work.

After emptying two more kitchen cupboards, I consider interrupting him for a lunch break, but he's on a mission.

I wonder why he retired? Bonnie's interest in other people's lives is rubbing off, but unlike Bonnie, I'd never outright ask.

"Look at these," he says, drawing my attention to a list of codes.

It takes me an awkward moment to register he's

talking to me and even longer to look where he's pointing. Serves me right for being so inquisitive.

"These documents are worthy of further investigation," he says. "I'm optimistic a woman hiding amongst these names will be our Bridgett."

Although he's already refused my help, I decide to give it another go. "I could continue searching Dad's records. I might not have your skills, but I can follow instructions, and I'm careful."

"That would be grand," he says unexpectedly. "I'm warning you—it's repetitive. I started searching through old school and church records, but if you're fine with looking up every Philip, Sean and Harry, I'll do the Bridgetts."

He smiles another crinkly-eyed generous smile at his own joke. Greeny-blue, I decide.

I almost drop my laptop in my hurry to set up and start helping. I'm useful at last. Dermot's right about the monotony, but I find the repetition soothing.

Less than an hour later, he slides his chair over, looking over my shoulder at my two pages of notes. "Your investigative skills are excellent. Systematic and meticulous."

Instead of giving my usual 'No. Not really' response to a compliment, I manage a quiet thank you.

After a stretch of silent research, Dermot taps his hands on the table in an introductory drum roll. "I've found something."

"Hang on." I mark my place, then give him my full attention.

"This Bridgett O'Patrick, on shipping passenger records from 1926, is in the right age bracket." He points to a name. "And born in Ireland. Which matches your father's claim." He makes a note in his log. "It's the closest we've come to a lead, but I'll need a death certificate to see if she had any children. If there's a son around your father's age, it's worth pursuing further."

"If she had one called Philip, even better," I say.

There's a lot of ifs, but I'm not worried. I'm not sure if it's because I'm busy, or because we have a possible match to Dad's mother—but I feel positively buoyant.

"Yay," I say, and in an un-Claudia-like move I throw my pen in the air, but it slips through my fingers when I try to catch it, rolling under the table. I reach to pick it up and notice Dermot's wearing new shoes and matching socks.

"You look especially nice today, are you going somewhere?" I ask.

He eyes me questioningly. "No. Just here."

"But you're dressed up..." I stop mid-sentence to bite my knuckle. If a man said that to a woman, it would be considered out of line. I hope he's not offended.

He stands and turns, showing his entire outfit. "I'm glad you approve. A while back, I was given an unintentional shove about my unkempt appearance."

"Unintentional?"

He rolls his eyes and smiles a cheeky smile. "I wasn't supposed to hear."

I shrug. I have no idea what he's talking about.

"The first day here," he says with a laugh. "Your sister's voice is hardly a whisper."

I cover my face to hide my cheeks. They turn so red when I'm embarrassed, and I'm beyond embarrassed. Bonnie and her comments.

"For informational purposes, I was experimenting

with artistic clothing. An obvious fail." He throws his palms in the air. "I haven't worn glasses since the laser eye surgery, and I am much older than that other Dermot. Fifty-three and seven months to be exact."

He laughs, but I'm horrified.

"Oh my God. I'm so sorry."

"Don't be. When I told you I'd continue the project because I loved a challenge, it was a half-truth. That was the most interesting morning I'd had in years. I laughed all the way home. Especially at Bonnie's misunderstanding of Nero fiddling as he watched Rome burn. A man '*my age*' would be mad to walk away from such entertainment. Even if I was the butt of her jokes."

I'm mortified, but at least he wasn't insulted. "Bonnie is funny. You must be disappointed she's not often here," I say. Gawd. First, I apologise for Bonnie's nonsense, then because she's not here to amuse him.

"Oh, she's grand in small doses, but at my *advanced age*, I appreciate peace and quiet."

Before my nervous laughter makes me seem completely foolish, I make an excuse to go outside. I sit on the front fence to sort out my head. *Oh My God*. What just happened?

The mailman waves from his motorbike, stopping at my letter box. I hesitate before checking. No more bills please. Not until I get a job.

There's an official looking package from Josh. The stamp collection envelopes.

"What about we open this express post-pack together?" I suggest after hurrying inside. "My son used police connections. Although he phoned to say there was nothing obviously helpful, his colleagues have written a forensic report and my fingers are crossed we'll find something useful."

"I'd better open it then." Dermot smiles. "Too difficult for you—with your fingers crossed and all."

I watch Dermot read the report and write new entries into his notebook. He checks back through his records so many times I'm optimistic.

This time I cross my fingers for real.

"These ..." He holds up two envelopes marked A and B. "...are both addressed to Philip McLeod, one sender, a Miss M. or N. Alexander, the other a Bridgett O'— the rest of her name unreadable."

He hands exhibits A and B to me. "Hold these, we'll come back to them later."

Dermot flicks his thumb through a pack of other envelopes. "This group are addressed to a P. O'Sean— which could be P for Philip and a possible alias. They're dated before the money was deposited. The rest have Russian writing and are dated during the war."

"Is this good, bad or indifferent?"

"In my opinion, all the envelopes were of significance to your father and not just random stamps for the collection."

"And the A and B envelopes?" I ask, turning them over in my hands.

"The dates and addresses on these might prove his identity. They were posted to your father around the time he started the premium bonds. To an address in Darwin."

"You're worth every penny we haven't paid you," I say, bravely adding a wink. "I'll highlight this section of the police report. If this address is the same as the one

Dad used to open his account, maybe the bank will accept it as proof."

Dermot has barely left the house when I phone Bonnie to squeal about the moment where I wanted the floor to open up and swallow me.

"He heard everything?" she asks. "Even about the clothes?"

"Yes."

"Please don't tell me he heard about Pyro-Dermot and the fiddling."

"Okay, I won't tell you," I say.

"Aargh. That's fucking awkward. Lucky you're the one facing him on a regular basis." Bonnie laughs.

"I'll take this one for the team." I choose not to tell her how much nicer Dermot looked, and how interesting he is, because Bonnie would make smart comments. And Bonnie's teasing would ruin the easiness I feel about making a friend.

"So, no news on the search front?" Bonnie asks, moving on. She's already shaken off the highly embarrassing moment. She's a duck. Everything is water to her.

"A couple of leads on Dad's mother—nothing confirmed, but there was a breakthrough—"

"Spit it."

"Two of the envelopes from the stamp album were dated around the time of the mystery deposit. They have Dad's full name and an address in Darwin. Lucky, I didn't tear off the stamps as a kid."

"Woo, fuckity, foo, they could be the concrete proof we need," Bonnie says. "My left palm is itching, and Grandma Rose said that means you're coming into money."

"I hope Grandma Rose is right. They're only old envelopes, but I'll take copies into the branch of the building society with the official report. Hopefully, they'll accept it."

Do I really hope Grandma Rose is right? I want the money. I need the money, but I wouldn't mind a small delay. Getting my teeth into research is satisfying, and I'm enjoying helping Dermot. At least until I get a job.

My search for Dad isn't only about cash. I can't imagine leaving someone I loved. If Dad left people behind, I want to know who, and why.

Chapter Twenty-One

CLAUDIA

Fremantle, 2018

The building society rejected our application this morning, stating that further evidence must be provided, including Dad's signature on a document from the specified time period.

I phone Dermot to complain. "Where will we get that? Maybe we should just admit defeat?"

"I won't have a bar of it." He chuckles. "You're not getting rid of me that easily."

"But where do we go from here?"

"I know you're busy sorting your house, but you could check your mother's place. There could be something of importance."

"Like what?"

"I can't tell you without looking, but I have every confidence you'll recognise it when you see it."

I straighten my shoulders, strengthened by Dermot's belief.

The moment I hang up, I phone Mum.

Some of my newfound self-assurance dwindles while I wait for her to answer. I'm psyching myself for an interrogation, when she says, "Hello."

Without waiting for me to respond, she asks, "Have you heard anything about the money?"

Her bluntness isn't unexpected. "The building society turned us down. Do you mind if I look through Dad's old stuff?" I brace myself for a '*Yes, I do mind*,' followed by, '*What's going on with Oliver?*' But instead of criticisms disguised as questions, she says, "Of course, you can. Why don't you come for dinner? I'll cook your favourite."

I'm still gob smacked, three hours later, on the drive over.

Bonnie, gifted with rose-coloured glasses, always finds the positive in Mum. Perhaps if I hadn't spent so long looking through green-tinted lenses, I might have appreciated Mum's better qualities. I guess the truth is somewhere in the middle.

As I pull into the driveway, my mouth waters and my heart softens. Mum promised to cook my comfort food. Home-made buttered-potato-pie with mushroom gravy.

Her hug is the usual dutiful, but her expression is astonishingly tender. "We've both lost someone."

She hooks her arm through mine. "While dinner finishes cooking, I'll spend an hour clearing out your dad's clothes, and I'll empty his pockets for clues. You can pick over the junk out there."

I take a steadying breath when I open the door to the bedroom-sized metal lean-to Dad called The Shed. The sheer number of odds and ends he's crammed into such a small space overwhelms me and I lean on a shelf while I regain composure of my knees.

There might be hidden treasure, but it will take more than an hour to sift through a tenth of this stuff. I exhale. Tackle it one piece at a time, Claudia.

I open his collection of cupboards, then I clear two patches of floor. A small 'keep' space and a larger space for 'chuck'. Making piles feels like moving deckchairs on the Titanic.

Dad's saved every can of paint he's ever bought, and there's useless paraphernalia. I hear him correct me, 'Never know, luv, it might come in handy.'

I recognise the vintage leather suitcase under the back of his workbench, and prise open the rusty clasps with a screwdriver, revealing bowling trophies and a pile of old newspapers. The well-creased editions on top, protected between layers of brown paper, are from mine and Bonnie's births.

Slumping on an old milk crate, I fight back tears imagining Dad reading our birth notices in this very spot.

When I check underneath the pile, there are old photographs of me and Bonnie.

Dad was more sentimental than I realised.

A moth-eaten velvet-covered box contains my magic bronze medal. Dad told me it was magic; I believed him then and here in this shed, I believe him now. I loop the faded ribbon over my neck.

A large wooden box holds a plastic container full of old VHS tapes, Dad's slide projector, and cassettes of photographic slides. Tucked down the side is an oil painting; a scene at a lake signed, Philip.

Mum appears as I'm closing the lid. "Anything interesting?"

I hold up the canvas. "I didn't know Dad painted?"

"He messed around with it before you were born. Not a skerrick of talent, so if you're planning to auction his work at Sotheby's, you'll be disappointed."

She throws her hands in the air. "I nagged him for years to sort this jumble, now he's left it for me."

"This box and suitcase seem personal." I open them to show her, but Mum turns her back.

"I'll keep the old movies, but I'll order a rubbish skip for everything else. That's unless one of my grandsons wants his tools."

I open Dad's tool cupboard.

"Not now," Mum says. "Wash your hands to get rid of the germs and greasy cobwebs, then come inside. Dinner's almost ready."

As if she needs to remind me. I've been a germophobe ever since Dad got sick.

After storing the VHS tapes in the laundry cupboard, I heave the box and suitcase to my car.

I'm setting the dining table when Mum stops me. "Not tonight; we're going to eat on our laps in the best room."

"What if I spill it? You know I'm clumsy—I got it from Dad."

"I should have sat on the sofas while I still liked them. They might be in showroom condition, but they're totally out of date." Mum laughs a humourless laugh. "I'm going to buy what I want now. Your Dad's not here to tell me to save for a rainy day. Pity he's not here to enjoy it."

The aroma of Mum's pastry reminds me of her homemade bread. Buns straight from the oven, and Dad savouring every bite, throwing out compliments between mouthfuls. "You could make a fortune selling these, Hillary."

If he asked for seconds, Mum would remind him he needed to watch his weight. Dad would pat his generous belly and laugh. "I don't need to watch it, love, you're watching it for me."

One day, he asked for another one and she smiled. "Go on. Course, you can."

Bonnie, Dad and I formed a triangle of shocked stares. Dad wasn't smiling when he whispered, "Your mum scares me most when she's nice."

Right now, I know exactly what he meant.

"Would you like to watch a movie?" Mum asks, shaking her head in a no.

She's so sure I'll refuse; she's answering for me. She's right. I'd usually slip away as quickly as possible. The guilt makes my heart ache. "Go on, then. What's on TV?"

"Not the telly, a tape from the box you brought in. Your dad kept our collection of old black and white movies. We've still got the player set up and there's one I'm sure you'll love. To Have and Have Not. Bogey and Bacall."

Mum wears a peculiar smile. I wonder if she's thinking about the futility of waiting for special occasions. My stomach lurches. It's odd sitting here with Mum. Not just in the same room; we've done that many times. Now, we're somehow connected, and we're watching a movie together. Just the two of us.

I need a drink to cope with the guilt.

For as long as I can remember, the glass-fronted, mirror-backed cabinet has been for display only. Gleaming crystal, ornate decanters and unopened bottles of alcohol. I summon Assertive-Claudia and say, "Let's attack the drink cabinet."

"Good idea, we'll have a proper splurge."

Breaking the seal of a decades' old bottle of Cointreau liqueur gives me a strange sense of satisfaction.

Mum laughs heartily at the movie's witty one-liners and we both *ooh* and *aah* as the on-screen romance unfolds.

When it ends, I say, "Good pick, Mum, and talented actors too."

She smiles with self-satisfaction.

"He's obviously much older than her," I add. "But they played their parts so well, the chemistry was believable."

"Humphrey Bogart was forty-four and Lauren Bacall only nineteen." Mum wears her know-it-all grin. "And they weren't acting. They fell in love and got married in real life."

"Why cast stars with such an age difference? That's a bit iffy."

Mum laughs as if I'm a child saying something cute.

I consider the age difference between Mum and Dad, and wonder whether to risk ruining an enjoyable conversation by bringing it back to him. I decide to go with the 'You only live once' approach.

"Is that why you married an older man—because you grew up with these movies?"

"No. But your father did have movie star charisma." Mum blushes. "And compared to the Bogey-Bacall age difference—twelve years was loose change."

When I head to the cocktail cabinet for a top up, there's a spring in my step. Slightly wonky, but a spring just the same. Maybe Mum's wonky too, because she's talking in a woman-to-woman chatty way, as if it's something we've always done.

"Your father and I met at a dance. He didn't dance, not with his knee from the war, but he was standing at the bar, and he winked at me. I was sure he said he was thirty-five, but later when I found out he was thirty-nine, he told me I'd misheard because of the music. I accepted that then—but now with so many lies, I'm not sure I misheard at all."

"I was twenty-seven. Nowadays that's young, but my parents were already planning how convenient it was having one daughter, a spinster, to look after them in their old age." She puts down her drink; her voice harsh. "Of course, the age difference is where the fairy-tale similarities end. Your father had years to establish himself, but in those days young women didn't ask men about their finances. I wasn't exactly disappointed when I discovered he was broke. I'd half-expected it. I'd rather help a man save than be 'left on the shelf'. 'Squandered it all' he said, when I asked where his years of earning had gone. If I'd damn well known he had the bank deposit and wasn't sharing, there wouldn't have been any children. I wouldn't have let the man touch me with a ten-foot pole, let alone the pole he had."

I choke on my drink at her too much information. But I see the silver lining. Mum, the old bitch, has returned. Part of my life is back to normal.

Without asking, I pour her another. Instead of taking the glass, she stares at her empty hands. "I'll never see your dad again."

"Aww, Mum." I pat her arm.

"When we got married, I wanted a church, but your dad insisted a registry office was more practical." She wipes a tear with the back of her hand. "He never went to church as an adult, but he still believed. In the back of my mind, I think he chose the civil ceremony because he didn't want to marry me before God. Otherwise, he'd have to commit to me in the afterlife and I think he had another woman in mind for that."

"No, Mum." I hug her. "Dad loved you. He was canny with his money—it was the Scottish genes."

She rests her head back against the sofa, looking dejected.

I'm not prepared for Mum being emotional, so I pour myself another drink. I hope I'm not sick during the night, she'll never let me forget it.

"I knew your father was hiding something, but I never asked him outright. Maybe, I didn't want an answer."

"Mum." I wrap my arms around her awkwardly, giving the biggest bear hug I can. She needs my support. My gut says there's a chance Mum's right. Dad was keeping a secret.

After I call Bonnie about the interesting stuff in Dad's shed, she makes the trip to my place in record time.

She spreads Dad's things across the dining table. "Where d' you find all this?"

"Under Dad's work bench. Not exactly hidden."

Bonnie shakes her head when she picks up the painting. "Who knew Dad painted?"

"Mum did. She was relieved he never asked to hang it on 'her' wall because he was no Monet." I rearrange my lips to capture Mum's signature sucked-a-lemon pucker.

Bonnie laughs and does the same. "Let's take a picture of us looking like twins."

When we've finished with the double selfies, I go back to studying the crude picture of a man, woman, and child rowing on a lake.

Bonnie snatches it and turns it face down. "Any date?"

"No. but there's a title." I point out faded, pencilled words. "*An Almost Perfect Day.*"

"It's not going to help us, is it?"

I kiss the painting. "No. But it meant something to Dad and I'm keeping it."

"You were always closer to Dad than me." Bonnie flicks through the newspapers. "Here, look at our birth notices. Your page is more crinkled. He looked at yours more often."

"Don't be silly, Bonnie. Mine's older."

"Give me the packet of photos." Tears slide down her cheeks. "There'll be way more pictures of you."

My throat aches watching Bonnie sort them, moving a photo of a baby with a mop of blonde curls to her side of the table. "Definitely me." She flips the others like she's dealing my cards. "You, you, and again you."

"Irrelevant. Every first child has more photos because the parents have more time. You were the favourite Bonnie, always the prettiest, always making everyone laugh." I'm shocked she thinks otherwise.

"No, Claudia. Mum made a fuss of me because I never got Dad's attention."

"That's not true. Dad loved you." I reach out, but she pushes me away.

"It's not just Dad. You never really liked me either. It took Dad dying and Oliver pissing off for you to become desperate enough to spend time with me."

Tears stream as I pick out more photos off Bonnie. "Here you are, a whole pile." My voice breaks. "He loved us both exactly the same. I love you, too."

Her voice is accusatory. "I saw you put some aside."

"These? That's cos I have no idea which of us this is."

She inspects the photographs as if she's a face recognition expert. "Bingo," she says.

"I can't see what you're Bingo-ing. Old photos of Dad with a baby we don't recognise."

"You're not looking at the right face."

I frown. "What face?"

"Look at Dad instead of the baby, Claudia."

She's right. Dad is oh-so-young. These photographs were taken many years before Bonnie and I were born. "Perhaps a niece or nephew?'

Bonnie doesn't look convinced.

I'm leaning over to look again, when she grabs the medal hidden under my shirt "Is this the magic medal?" She pulls it over my head to take a closer look "*Trocadero.1944*." She turns it to read the words encircling its edge. "*First prize, Lindy Hop.* Is Lindy Hop a woman's name?"

"Maybe. Somewhere in my brain I've heard it before."

"Claudia!" She shrieks so loudly I jump back. "I think Dad told the truth about being a dance champion. And maybe Lindy Hop is the name of the dancer he hallucinated about before he died?"

Chapter Twenty-Two

KATERINA

'The Figs' Sydney, 2018

When I was a child, a day seemed an eternity, but the closer I get to my expiry date—time flashes by.

I blink, and it's Wednesday. Again. Maria will be waiting in the Welcome Room for Joe. Despite her faulty memory, she never forgets his visits.

I give them a few minutes alone, then pack away my cards. *Solitaire*—the perfect game for lonely old souls.

When Joe sees me, he smiles with relief. Maria is slumped against the table hugging herself.

"Mum's unhappy." His face is doleful.

"Her mood swings are out of your control, Joe," I say gently.

I wave my notebook towards Maria and hand her my pen. "I've put drawing on my list of things to calm her down," I say.

"Her wedding dress designs were beautiful." He lifts his chin, wearing a wide, proud smile.

Maria wilts further, pushing the notebook away.

I lean close to her, and use the soft, kind voice which calmed soldiers after the war. I point out a kookaburra and tell her I'm glad it's stopped raining.

When Maria sits up and smiles, I offer her the notebook again and this time she takes it.

Joe looks on curiously.

"What I say seems less important than the manner in which I speak," I say to Joe.

Maria sketches the kookaburra and begins speaking in Italian. Not a complaint; there's no yelling or pointing. She's telling us a story as she draws a picture of a man who looks a lot like Joe.

I look between Maria and her son. He smiles as she talks in her native language, with its rounded vowels and honest emphasis.

"I see what you mean." Joe smiles. "The tone of your voice settles her. She sounds so much happier."

He opens his mouth to add something else but changes his mind.

If there's one thing age has taught me—people will only talk when they're ready.

"Miss Katerina?" he asks eventually.

"Yes, Joe?"

He brings out the iPad he showed me last week. "What if Mum is actually making sense? I thought I'd lost the opportunity to learn about Mum's past, but maybe not."

I look at the gadget suspiciously. "It's too complicated for your mother. We've seen how much she despises the robotic voice. If you're not careful, you'll set her off again."

Joe nods, then gazes outside for a long minute. "I

have another idea." He hands me the iPad. "Not for Mum to play with, but for you. I should have thought of it last visit."

I watch as Joe demonstrates how to use it for games. He even shows me a game of Solitaire where I don't have to shuffle cards. When I was young, shuffling cards was easy. Now my fingers make hard work of the smallest tasks.

"These are the main icons," he says, pointing to small square pictures under the glass.

I laugh. "Oh my. The meaning of the word 'icons' has changed over the years."

He laughs too, but I sense he's holding something back.

"Come on Joe, spill the beans. What's your plan?"

"You've found a few things that help Mum. You're incredible, but maybe we can try another."

"I don't know," I say. "I'm too old to learn Italian if that's your idea. I could manage a few phrases, but then I'd never understand what Maria's saying back to me. She speaks so rapidly and I would never be able to write it down."

"Just a one-way conversation. Your voice soothes her. Please, Miss Katerina. If you familiarised yourself with the iPad and the translation app, we could record your voice in Italian. Mum responds beautifully when you speak English, imagine how powerful it would be if she understood the words too?"

Joe pleads with puppy dog eyes. "I'm desperate."

"Okay, I'll get to know how the gadget works, but there are no guarantees. Until I know what I'm doing I'll work with the tested and proven methods of improving her mood."

"Thank you." Joe kisses my hand.

"I think going for a walk beyond The Fig's walls will help," I say. "We've been stuck inside with bad weather."

"She'll try to escape, and I'll have to drag her back." Joe sags with worry.

"No, not you. There's an outing tomorrow."

I hold Maria's hand and look into her eyes. "Do you want to come on the bus. Ducks? A lake? Fresh air?"

"Yes," Maria says very clearly.

By the time I arrive at the bus, Maria is waiting in the queue, wearing striped yellow slippers and pink pyjamas. No one but me seems to notice these aren't regular 'going out' clothes, that is until *Bird-Woman* arrives. "We don't want to wear this do we, sweetie?"

I prefer this nurse when she's cranky. Talking in third person and saying '*Sweetie*' is condescending. I think *bird-woman's* been spoken to about her abrupt manner. Her eyes are still mean, but now she's a vulture disguised as a chicken.

George, one of The Fig's long-term residents, holds up the queue by blocking the steps to the bus. He's been following Maria since she stole his cane, and even though he is antagonising her now, it seems an attention-getting ploy rather than an act of spite.

I try to distract Maria, but Patience is not her middle name. She loses control and shoves George away. Unless I come up with a way to stop them fighting, Maria won't be allowed on the bus.

"Run," I say to Maria, but she stares blankly. I move

my middle and index finger like tiny legs and run them up my arm. Then I wave my hand in a circle towards the lawn, to indicate a slow jog of the grounds. If Maria burns off energy, she'll relax enough to sit quietly for the trip.

Maria's shoulders might stoop, but her legs are a marvel. She runs rings around the expansive lawn. Instead of getting on the bus, George stands on the grass and roars, "Go! Go! Go!" He could be cheering an Olympic athlete.

Maria returns with snippets of freshly mown grass stuck to her striped slippers. *Bird-Woman* makes a *clucking* sound, but Maria's glowing face is all smiles.

I touch her hand, as if to absorb her excitement.

"Come," she says in English.

"Maria. You spoke English again." I encourage her to say something else, "More. More"

"Yes, more," Maria says, but misunderstands what I want more of, and hijacks my wheelchair, pushing me off the path and over the damp grass. *Bird-Woman* wrestles me from Maria's grip, ending up on the ground. She brushes off herself off, and flies inside for back-up.

I'm stunned by Maria's energy, as she makes patterns in the lawn with my wheels. She continues the *figure eights* and *do-si-dos* until Matron storms outside.

Matron orders the nurse to shepherd the other cheering residents onto the bus, then calls out for Maria to stop. But my abduction isn't over, Maria speeds past the rose garden, around the fishpond and parks me at the edge of the raised herb bed.

By the time Matron catches us, Maria is dancing on the plants. There are delicious traces of basil and rose-mary, but mostly there's the overwhelming aroma of mint.

"No outing for you today," Matron says firmly.

"I'll stay with her," I say.

"Very kind," Matron says. "It's a pity she's spoiled your fun."

But the day wasn't ruined for me. The smell of trampled mint has awakened a vivid memory, and I plan to share it with Maria.

Chapter Twenty-Three

KATERINA

Sydney – The Trocadero, 1944

After the weekend of dance practice, it rained for days, which meant Anna and I had to sit inside during lunch break. I was bursting to tell her about dancing with Philip; his firm hand cradling my back, the way he lifted me in the air and spun me around until I was giddy. But I didn't dare pass a note in case it was discovered and handed to my parents.

When the rain finally stopped, we braved the muddy grass to meet at our whispering tree. Anna's first question was, "Well? Did you kiss?"

"No, but we danced like we were in a film. Only better."

She cursed under her breath. "If I'm living through you, my friend, you'll have to lift your game."

"Well, I have lifted my game," I whispered. "We're entering the Trocadero competition on Saturday."

Anna's eyes widened. "I expect a full report."

"I have one problem; I need an excuse to get out at night."

"What about telling your parents I've invited you over for dinner. Would that work?"

I hugged Anna on the spot. "Thank you. But you can't tell anyone the truth."

"I'm happy to lie for you, as long as you promise to kiss and tell me the steamy details."

During the hours before the dance competition, my stomach twisted in knots. This wasn't just bending the truth. I'd outright lied to my parents.

My concern was so strong that Philip and I turned back twice, but I considered carefully. Anna wouldn't tell. I knew she wouldn't. We'd rehearsed what would happen if Mother and Father came to collect me instead of waiting for me to be brought home. Anna reassured me she'd feign a sudden illness and tell them I'd gone to the movies with another friend. A last-minute change of plan we didn't think they'd mind. Why would my parents bother?

The fear of missing out held a stronger pull than the fear of being caught, and by the time we reached the Trocadero, I thought only of Philip and the dance.

The audience tapped their feet as we circled: hands almost touching; eyes locked. Despite looking for my instruction during practice, I knew Philip was the better dancer and there under the lights he improvised and lost all traces of self-consciousness. The crowd was dazzled as his limbs moved with liquid fluidity, mesmerising onlookers as he tap danced and jived and threw me around like a happy rag doll.

When the spectators whistled, I raised my skirt to show my knees and Philip played along, feigning shock. I lifted it a smidgeon higher in response to calls for 'more'. Energised by the audience, Philip leapt higher and faster.

In practice, we'd crashed with the more ambitious moves but on the night, we were a well-oiled machine. He took charge. Changing the dance. Leading me, inviting me to follow. I made small mistakes and he instantly accommodated, making me look more accomplished than I deserved.

We were in sync like the planets and the stars, heat crossing the infinitesimal space between us. Philip spun on one leg; twirling in a delicious blur as I bobbed and bounced underneath the other. The music slowed, and he pulled me close enough to breathe him in but stopped me when our lips were a hair's breadth from touching.

The pull was irresistible, and I no longer cared about the competition. I wanted that kiss more than the win.

For the finale, we hopped from one side of the dancefloor to the other, mirroring each other in a double arabesque. I trusted him entirely as he lifted me into the air and flipped me upside down. I savoured every moment of his strong arms pivoting me this way and that. As the last beats of our song played, he tossed me through his legs, and I slid across the ballroom. As I finished in the splits, I looked up at him, and for a beautiful second, we were the only ones in the universe.

Our laughter rang nervously over ragged breaths, as we bowed towards the gallery.

On the walk home, Philip and I held hands, dancing along the street. The moon was absent and there were more stars than ever before in living history.

"We won," Philip yelled, as he lifted his medal to the night sky. He pressed it to his lips with an exaggerated kiss.

I twirled the skirts of my cornflower-blue swing dress, closing my eyes to enjoy the swish-swish of the fabric against my legs. We'd won.

We skipped along the laneway that wove behind the houses near home, but instead of rounding the last corner, Philip pulled me through a broken picket fence and onto a leafy patch of mint growing behind an old shed. A dog barked nearby, but as I opened my mouth to silence it, Philip touched his finger to my lips.

"Shhh."

The dog calmed as Philip spoke softly. He traced the ribbon suspending the medal against my chest, running his finger lightly around the sweetheart neckline. His touch was whispery light, sending quivers through my body as it skimmed the curve of my breast.

"You are divine," he whispered.

When he wrapped his arms around my waist, I felt I could float into the night.

"My favourite part of dancing is holding you." His voice hummed against my ear. "Let's dance a few minutes more." He hummed the tune of our favourite song and pressed his thighs against mine.

We swayed in a new delicious rhythm. Under the starlight we brushed our lips against each other's cheeks. Our breathing became faster and my heart drummed in my ears as we re-lived the finale of our winning dance in slow-slow-motion.

His hand floated down my back and crept over the curve of my bottom as we kissed. My knees weakened and I leant backwards against the fence for support. When he pulled me closer, my legs turned to jelly, but we continued dancing.

"Do you want to go back now?" His fingers danced lightly against the back of my neck.

"No."

Our lips were soft and open when he touched his mouth to mine, and he wrapped his arms around my waist until I was on tiptoes.

"We should go," he said.

"No." I pulled him closer and pressed my lips hard against his. My feet left the ground as he lifted me to meet him and twirled me in the air. I grabbed his hair and he kissed me full on the mouth. It was an intoxicating mix of lips and tongue where the twinkling of the stars migrated from the night and sparked inside my body.

As Philip trampled the plants underfoot, the smell of bruised mint filled the air, and I could taste it in his kiss.

I didn't want the night to end.

When the dog barked again, it was in warning.

I heard my brother's voice, and we jumped apart as if we'd been scalded.

Nick was yelling, "Kat... Kat... Kat..."

Each time he called my name, it sounded clearer and closer.

"Something's wrong." I quickly smoothed down my

dress and fanned my face with my hands to cool it down. "I'm in trouble. I can hear it in Nick's voice."

Philip touched my lips then whispered, "It will be okay, we will tell Nick we met up as we were walking home." He yanked me back into the laneway, but it was too late; a few feet away, three familiar faces stared from underneath a streetlamp.

Mama Bridgett's cheeks were wet with tears, Father's expression was thunderous, and Nick silently mouthed, 'Holy Shit'.

As Father strode heavily towards us, a sick, frightened feeling made me dry reach. He studied me from head to toe with a look of disdain.

"Philip walked me home from Anna's," I lied.

My Father stopped for a second then snatched my medal with so much force the ribbon grazed my skin as it tore.

"Your Uncle Viktor is dead. Now, I do not know which is worse. His physical death or the death of my daughter's innocence and trust."

"But Father..."

"I went to collect you from Anna's and her mother told me where you were and who you were with. I should take a strap to the pair of you."

Tears streamed from my eyes, as Father grabbed both my arm and Philip's, dragging us towards home. Once through the gates he pushed Philip into Mama and hissed, "Bridgett, keep your bastard away from my daughter."

I looked back as Father hauled me away. I was surprised to see Philip holding up Mama Bridgett. Her face was pressed against his chest and she sobbed as if broken-hearted.

"Get inside, you liar," Father said to me. "And I do not want your friend, Anna, to step foot inside this house again. Do you understand?"

The night should have been remembered with incredible joy. Winning the dance competition, and my first, yet perfect, kiss. But all delight had been stolen, along with my favourite uncle who would never light our lives again.

Father screamed almost unintelligibly about the ship, *Armenia*, being torpedoed. He yelled about the loss of his cousin and spat on the ground as he spoke of his untruthful, disobedient daughter. When he threw me inside my bedroom and locked the door, the yelling didn't end. The arguing went on well into the night. Part of me didn't want to hear what my parents said, but I leaned my ear against the window listening to words stream from their room.

"What sort of devious daughter have you raised that she could lie and run around with that boy?" Father said.

"She is your daughter, too."

"When I'm not at the consulate, I am working from my study. It's the mother's job to watch her children. Especially daughters."

"Whose job is it to keep an eye on Bridgett's son?" Mother asked.

"If Katerina was here where she should have been. It wouldn't matter where that bastard was!" Father screamed.

There was a pause... one thump, then another. I imagined either a book thrown to the floor or a fist against a table. I'd heard these sounds before.

My throat tightened, and I curled under my blanket,

wrapping a pillow around my ears to block out the voices. After an hour, I become overheated and opened the window wider to let in breeze, but there were still murmurs.

This time it was Father crying and apologising.

"Stop," Mother said. "We can't go through this again. It was only a dance, and Katerina is safe. But the boy and his mother need to leave this property, and soon."

"I can't. I gave Viktor my word."

"We've looked after Bridgett for years. You've met the promise."

"But Viktor is dead, and I won't dishonour him."

"I will ensure Katerina does not leave her room unaccompanied, but you must come up with a plan to remove that boy."

During the first three days of confinement, I forced myself to replay the heavenly part of the night over and over, ignoring its disastrous ending. But then, I thought about Uncle Viktor. He would never bring me gifts or smiles again. I cried for him and I cried about Anna. I had to accept she'd told her mother where I'd gone, and that meant I could no longer share my secrets. I felt utterly, completely alone.

Until Father decided I could leave my room, my communication was restricted to notes. Fortunately, Nick was assigned the job of errand boy. He collected textbooks from school so I could study for the mid-year examinations. He also brought me news.

"Philip's gone," he said, plonking study notes and books on the table beside my bed.

"Gone where?" I gasped.

"He is finishing his final year at St Joseph's boarding school."

This was a calculated move by my parents, to keep Philip and me apart.

I threw myself onto the bed. "But that's miles and miles away."

I pulled my knees towards my chest, circling them with my arms, and buried my face to hide my tears. I considered Nick's news. How would I get to see Philip again? Did he even try to say goodbye?

Nick spoke kindly, "There's a note in your textbook from Anna. That should cheer you."

Kat, what have you done? Nick won't spill the beans so it must be racy. As your best friend, I order you to write back and tell all. I'm dying of curiosity. Please eat this message so we won't be caught.

This was typical Anna. Once I would have smiled, but not today. She, of all people, wanted to communicate in secret. But she hadn't kept her promise. To my mind at least, not telling a soul, included not telling one's mother.

"Write back if you like," Nick urged. "I'll deliver it."

"No." I ripped Anna's note and Nick backed up towards the door.

Then I had an idea. "Are you and Philip still on the same rugby team?"

"Of course," he said. "The team can't play without Philip; we'd miss our chance at the grand finale. Coach has organised for him to catch a bus down and play the last three games."

"Could you take a letter to Philip—at the next match?"

I saw fear in Nick's hesitation, but my outpouring of tears changed his mind. "Just once. If Father found out, he'd be beyond furious."

Chapter Twenty-Four

CLAUDIA

Fremantle, 2018

Dermot suggested moving our workstation to his house because each time a potential buyer is shown through my place, we waste time packing and unpacking our research. But now, standing at his front door, I feel I'm intruding.

In all honesty, I didn't mind the house viewing interruptions. I enjoyed walking with Dermot along the beach road, filling in time. On one of our walks, he told me he'd been a language professor and worked all around the world before settling in Australia. I wanted to ask if he was married, but by the time I'd worked out a way to say it that didn't seem too intrusive, he'd changed the subject.

Maybe his wife will be here, today. Since it's a late start, I've brought lunch for us to share. Enough for three.

I comb my fingers through my hair then drum my

fingernails against my thigh as I summon the nerve to knock. I pause to look at the garden beds in Dermot's front yard. They strike me as unusual. One side of the path is filled with a messy blend of wild looking plants, and the other has shrubs pruned into perfect domes.

I'm considering whether the imbalance of his garden indicates a personality disorder, when Dermot startles me by opening the door. "I saw your car pull up."

He leads me down a narrow hallway with black-painted walls, but the dungeon atmosphere ends abruptly as we enter a sun-filled room spanning the width of the house. One white wall is covered by sketches, hung gallery style, while opposite, large windows frame the terraced back garden. There are multiple levels, uneven retaining walls and varying shaped patches of lawn and flowers. I can't resist asking, "Your garden beds are so different. Did you design them?"

"No." He laughs. "My wife was an art teacher. Her mind free-form and uninhibited. Mine is boringly regular, and so are my designs. Leonie allowed me one orderly garden bed near the front door."

Was an art teacher? Retired? There's plenty of art on the walls, so she hasn't moved out.

"I haven't got an arty-farty bone in my body, as you might have guessed. Leonie encouraged me to experiment, and I was trying for unconventional hippy styling until you and your sister pointed out I looked homeless. I'm never going there again."

My face burns with embarrassment, but Dermot chuckles. I decide it's an Irish chuckle— full of mischief.

He points out the bathroom and kitchen. "In case

you need them."

My stomach announces lunch. Loudly.

Dermot looks towards my belly and laughs. "Hungry, are we?"

"Excuse me." My cheeks burn red and I pick up my cooler. "Do you mind if we eat first? I've brought food. Instead of making the sandwiches at home, I've brought the makings with me."

He cocks his head and grins. "Very fancy. Deconstructed sandwiches."

I laugh and begin clearing a space on his desk.

"Not in here. It's the perfect weather for sitting outside." Dermot disappears and reappears with a blanket.

I help spread the picnic rug on a triangular patch of lawn, arranging a selection of cured meats, cheeses, tomatoes and bread.

I use the hand sanitiser clipped to my bag, then hand it to Dermot.

"No thanks." He looks at me seriously. "Your dad died of cancer, didn't he?"

"Yes?"

"Before Leonie died, the chemo weakened her immune system to a dangerous level, and I was obsessed with cleanliness, too. Terrified of passing on germs. But she's gone now." He grabs himself some bread and cheese. "A bit of bacteria's not a bad thing."

As I take some food, Dermot shields his eyes from the sun. "She'd be pleased I'm sitting here with a friend."

Before Dad's death, I found it uncomfortable to say a dead person's name, but now it seems disrespectful not to. "How long has Leonie been gone?"

"Five years, but she was sick a long time. Too long. She was ready to leave before I was ready to say goodbye." His lip trembles.

"You have children?"

He looks at the ground. "Three. Two now. Our oldest son died in a car accident."

Clouds cover the sun in respect, and Dermot ducks inside.

He returns bearing two glasses of iced water.

"Leonie had this idea of designing our unique versions of heaven. I told her mine was having her healthy, and all three children living at home. Each patch of the garden represents a member of the family. In her last days, she finished this garden, leaving a special place behind."

My throat is so tight it hurts to swallow; I push my finger against the tip of my nose as if I'm pressing an on-off button for tears. It doesn't work.

Dermot rips paper towel from the roll. A piece for me, and one for himself. I don't look up because I can't bear to see him cry.

We eat without speaking and he packs away the picnic. "Come on, Claudia. Back to work. Your father's mystery won't solve itself."

I follow him inside. He closes the office blinds and shows me the seat facing a blank wall. He's set up Dad's old slide projector.

"A viewing?" I ask.

"Not today." He shakes his head and grins. "I offered to go through the slides because I thought I'd be quicker than you. I didn't realise how interested I'd be in someone else's family photos."

We exchange smiles before I look away.

"Did you find anything useful?"

"Well, after watching you and Bonnie grow up before my eyes, I found a slide cassette with much older photographs. So, the short answer is yes. I found answers but also more questions."

He turns on the projector and flashes through several slides.

"These three," he says, flicking backwards and forwards through photos of a young Dad, "are at the inauguration of the new airlines, Ansett ANA. On the slide frame someone has written Philip McLeod December 1957. Before he deposited your money."

"Will the building society care or believe we have pictures of Dad? He could have written the name himself, at a later date."

"Well, a quick Google search confirmed that Ansett and Australian National Airlines combined in 1957. There's a good chance they'd have drawn up new employment contracts."

"But Ansett closed down more than ten years ago." I slump in my seat. Another dead end.

"It's okay. I contacted *Trove*, to see if they had copies of the records." Dermot leans towards me, raising his eyebrows.

"And? They said?"

"Philip McLeod is on file and the original documents are in storage waiting to be digitised. They are going to dig them out and send us a copy of his signed employment form. When we get that, Claudia, my job is done. This is as much proof of identity as anyone has."

I should be jumping for joy, but I'm not.

Both the base of my skull and my stomach tense up.

I try to massage them at the same time and Dermot looks at me as if I'm doing the pat your head while circling your tummy trick. One thing's for sure. I am confused. Bonnie and I hired Dermot to claim the money and now, it seems likely we can. But what will I do if we stop?

This search has given me purpose.

Dermot pivots the monitor, displaying his spreadsheet. "I'll show you where I'm up to. I've copied it onto a memory stick in case you or Bonnie decide you want to look further into your father's history later down the track."

As he talks, I stare at the beautiful garden. Dermot's wife worked on this until her last day.

"There are possibilities here, but no definites," Dermot continues. "The medal wasn't traceable, but I did find names of dance competition winners for the Lindy Hop."

"Lindy Hop is the name of the dance. I knew I'd heard it before."

Dermot laughs. "I've downloaded Catholic boarding school records for Sydney and surrounds, but without your dad's birth name, they're not much help. Unfortunately, I haven't finalised my research on the passenger ship list for the woman I thought could be his mother."

He points out spreadsheet entries. Colour coded cells: factual green, hopeful yellow, improbable orange, and dead-end red. The highlighted pattern reminds me of flowers.

I look at the garden again. What a mammoth task for a dying woman? How much love did it take? My eyes fill with tears as I consider my life.

Oliver wouldn't have done this for me, and even

sadder is the realisation I wouldn't have done it for him.

Dermot misinterprets my sadness. "It must be difficult thinking about your father."

"Yes." I sniff, wiping a tear drop before it falls from my nose. "Dad's parting gift was a letter telling me and Bonnie to assess our lives and live the remainder to the full. My husband, Oliver left the same day, without warning."

Dermot lifts a stunned eyebrow. "What a gobshite."

He's a good judge of character.

"I wonder why Philip left such a letter?" he asks.

I shake my head. "No idea."

"If I wrote a message like that to my children, it would be because I believed they needed a change. He must have thought either or both of you weren't making the most of your lives."

"My life was good before Oliver left." As I say the words, I realise I no longer believe them.

"Back to your next steps in tracing our slippery customer." Dermot reaches into the desk drawer and produces two toothpaste sized boxes. "The big guns. DNA kits," he says. "We've already paid for them, it's up to you to decide whether to follow through."

I heft the boxes in my hand. "Not very heavy for guns."

Dermot's Irish chuckle warms my heart.

"Will we find a match?" I ask.

"It's hit and miss, but home DNA tests are becoming increasingly popular. They're easily available, and affordable, so there's a growing database. Unless you and Bonnie take one, you have little chance of finding someone related to your father. That's if you're planning to continue the search without me."

My hands shake. If we stop our research now, there'll be no more picnics like today.

I knock on the solicitor's open door and Gary Kovacevic looks up.

"Thank you for squeezing me in."

"No problem. I've wondered how your search has been going."

I lay out all the evidence, and Gary moves from envelope to envelope, checking and notarising. After a few minutes, he touches each pile. "Photo slides showing Philip McLeod during the correct time period. An employment declaration with a formally witnessed signature. The same address on the form as he used when he opened the account."

Kovacevic looks impressed.

"So, it's sufficient to prove Dad's identity?"

"You ladies have outdone yourselves," he said. "I can see no reason for the building society to delay payment. Take it all in as soon as you can."

"We didn't do it alone. We hired someone with skills. There's no way we could have done this without Dermot Gallagher, our genealogist and researcher."

"Leave me his business card. I might have some work for him. The thoroughness of this research would stand up in any court."

I phone Bonnie on the drive home and she almost wets herself with excitement. "We're going to get Dad's money, but how much? I hope it's enough to at least pay off Dermot."

My laughter rings hollow.

Chapter Twenty-Five

CLAUDIA

Fremantle, 2018

Bonnie shouts into the phone, her voice ecstatic, "Have you checked your email? We've done it, Claudia. The Building Society is ready to deposit our half-shares and need our personal bank details."

"I'll send my account number," I say, returning the milk to the fridge. This calls for something stronger than tea.

"Don't you want to know how much?" Bonnie yells.

"Just tell me."

Bonnie raises her voice to a high-pitched squeal. "$879,000. $440,000 each. Your estimate was pretty close."

I bite my lip. "And there are two offers to buy the house. It's all happening."

"You don't sound as if it's all happening. Get excited, Claudia. This is frickin' humungous news."

She's right, but the void is pulling me back. The search was about more than cash.

"What about the DNA tests? Do you really want to stop looking for Dad?" My heart misses a beat as I wait for her answer.

"There's no point continuing. It's not going anywhere," she says. "Dad clearly wanted to hide and there's nothing we can do about it."

I try to spark her interest. "Didn't you enjoy following the trail of clues."

"What clues, Claudia? We have next to nothing. It's time to move on."

I steady myself against the kitchen bench.

"Okay, then." Bonnie says, after a few seconds' silence. "Bring the DNA tests over. We've already paid for them; we may as well do them."

Three weeks later, I get a phone call from Dermot, sounding ready to jump out of his skin.

"Claudia! Your DNA results are in."

"Really? Did we find a match?"

"Something really interesting came back, but I'd rather tell you in person," he says. "Can I come over?"

I hang up and call Bonnie. "Get over here, quick. Our DNA results have been posted online and from Dermot's reaction, I think we've found a match."

Bonnie sounds unusually solemn. "Who with?"

"Dermot didn't say, but he's on his way to my place."

. . .

Dermot opens the results on his laptop with Bonnie and me peering over his shoulder. There are pie graphs, lists, family trees, and world maps with shaded blobs showing our heritage.

"Not surprisingly," he says, pointing to the DNA match list. "The pair of you share the most DNA. You're rated as siblings."

He scrolls down then up again "Hundreds of distant relatives. But look here." He taps on an entry near the top. "Viktoria Alexander."

"Last name Alexander?" Bonnie says, "Could be Scottish. Dad did say he was Scottish."

"Alexander was a name on the stamp collection envelopes," I say. "But it can't be Dad's mother. Surely she's long dead."

Dermot pats the two chairs on either side of him. "Sit down, while I explain. The DNA match-relationships are rated in levels. Viktoria Alexander is marked as 'close family'. By the number of points in common, it's likely she's your half-sister."

"Gosh," I say, holding my forehead, suddenly dizzy.

"This isn't a '*gosh*' moment, Claudia," Bonnie squeals. "It's a fuckity-fuck moment."

Dermot places his hand on my elbow. "It's okay to be shocked. I've looked up her profile and she lives in Melbourne. We could message her. She might have useful information."

There's a thud in my chest when I think about Mum. "Our Dad had another daughter?"

"The baby photos!" Bonnie yells. "They were pictures of our sister."

"Why would Dad leave a child and not tell anyone? I can't imagine Dad doing that."

Bonnie groans, then clenches her teeth. "A half-sister? Mum's going to lose her shit."

We stare at each other, then she starts humming a funeral march. I half cry, half laugh.

"Viktoria Alexander has created a public family tree on the Ancestry site," Dermot says, handing us a copy. "I've printed it out."

The first thing that strikes me as I scan the names, is despite Viktoria's Scottish surname, most of the entries are of Russian lineage. She's written her mother's name: Mary Alexander, but left her father's name blank.

"No father's name?" I moan. "I know you don't want to keep going, Bonnie, but can we contact her?"

Bonnie shakes me. "Of course, we will. It was boring when we had nothing to go on, but this is fucking amazing. This woman is a link to Dad's past life. We better hire Dermot again."

She turns to me, raising her eyebrows. When I nod, she slaps his back hard enough to make him cough. "Are your mad skills still for hire?"

I look at Dermot hopefully. "We can pay you now. That's if you're interested?"

"I've already drafted a message in case you wanted to contact her." He sounds intoxicated.

The happy, silly party-feeling envelops all of us and Bonnie pulls us in for a group hug.

When my hand touches Dermot's, my fingers become entangled in his.

He blushes and blinks, then focusses on the computer screen. "Before we send this request you need to think about the implications. Number one: Will you share these findings with your mother? Number two:

You've worked hard to claim your father's inheritance and another sister could want her share. Number three: The truth behind Philip McLeod's story could be painful."

"Do you want to meet Viktoria?" I ask Bonnie. "We'd have to tell Mum."

Bonnie shrugs. "Mum will be upset. And if we contact our half-sister, the three-way split's around three hundred thousand, rather than four-hundred-and-forty."

"So, you don't want to go ahead?" I ask.

"This is a lot to take in," Bonnie says. "I was prepared for discovering ancestors but not another sister."

Dermot asks, "Do you want more time? Sleep on it?"

The look between me and Bonnie is clear. A rock's been dropped into our once peaceful pond and the ripples can't be ignored.

"I've enjoyed getting to know my full sister better, but...we can't turn back now."

"And there's definitely room for more excitement in my life." I hug Bonnie so tightly she gasps for breath. "Righto, Dermot. Read us your draft."

Dear Viktoria,

DNA evidence suggests we're related.

We recently lost our father but he left a letter hinting at a hidden life. The resulting search led to you. DNA test results indicate a close match; so close in fact, we believe our father might also be your father.

Please contact us. We'd like to meet and share information.

Claudia and Bonnie

Chapter Twenty-Six

KATERINA

'The Figs' Sydney, 2018

Although it's only a month until summer, winter's fingers haven't yet loosened their frosty grip. It's cold everywhere except the sunny corner where the sun peeks through the glass, encouraging Maria and I to soak up the warmth.

Although, I still believe relying on a computer to remember facts sounds like a sure way of killing an active brain, I'm coming around to the new technology. It does offer advantages.

In the last week, Izzy has taught me to how to download audio books for free, and I've searched up a storm. I've checked the time in Paris, Moscow and Milan. Useless information. I've never been to these places and I won't visit now, but I'm happy losing myself in this virtual world.

I searched for Philip, but despite finding hundreds of people with that name, none looked like the Philip I remember. I did find photographs of Geraldton Wax—the flowers he gave his wife.

Solitaire in electronic form is convenient. No risk of falling from my wheelchair as I search for fallen cards, but there's one thing computer devices just cannot replace—interaction with friends. Maria and I still play her favourite game of poker, using real cards. She always wins.

As I mark down the score of our latest game, Matron hands me a package. "Your order has arrived, Katerina."

"Thank you."

Matron watches as I remove the outer plastic wrapping and she passes a message from Joe to Maria. "Your son will be too late for the family luncheon. Apparently too many of his co-workers have taken the day off for Melbourne Cup. He'll be here after work."

Maria grunts. Even if she understood English, it's difficult to tell whether she'd remember Joe promised to visit on Tuesday instead of Wednesday this week. Her mind is like a lamp, randomly switching on and off.

"No Joe for lunch," I say. Her face is blank; the lamp is off.

"I'll try the translator app again," I say to Matron. "I've been practising. I had a thought about me saying the Italian instead of using the robotic voice."

I wheel myself out of Maria's hearing, then when I've listened enough times to feel confident, I repeat the words, "*Jo 'e dispiaci utio. Sarà in ritardo.*"

I repeat again in English, "Joe is sorry, he will be late."

Maria's mouth curls into an amused smile. Probably at my dreadful accent. She deals another hand of cards.

"That worked a treat. I don't know if she understood you, but she didn't lose her temper." Matron touches the parcel. "What did you buy?"

"Fancy shmancy art supplies. Maria's been using loose sheets of recycled paper and pages from my notebook. I thought a proper sketchpad and art pencils would cheer her up. She can draw and I can watch. It will take both our minds off the miserable weather."

Once Matron has gone I recline in my wheelchair and watch Maria open her new sketch book. She fans her coloured pencils across the table like a rainbow. I tell her how much she reminds me of my friend, Anna. "We remained friends until her death eight years ago. And although I'm sad she's gone; I feel lucky for the years we had."

Maria glances at the television. There's a parade of horses running in today's Cup, and she starts sketching a horse in full flight. I admire her drawing skill and talk to her about Anna. "We only meet a handful of special people in our lives, and we shouldn't waste a minute." I dab at my tears. "Friends are everything. I shut Anna out when I needed her most."

I think of how judgemental I was. My lovely Anna was only trying to help.

Maria puts down her pencil and pats my hand. She looks up as if she understands me. "Thank you," she says, pointing to the paper and pencils.

"I'm so pleased you love your present. Helping you makes this old woman happy."

Before the big race starts, I ask to eat lunch in my room. There'd be too many visitors crammed into the television area and it's impossible to avoid sad looks from visiting family members. *That poor old lady is all alone.*

Three hours later, Izzy pokes her head into my room. "The hordes have gone and Joe's here. He's waiting at your favourite sunny table, watching the birds."

"Oh my. Already?" I check the bedside clock.

"Did you back a winner on the Melbourne Cup and throw your job in?" I ask Joe, manoeuvring my wheel-chair towards the table.

"Unfortunately, no, but the boss told me I could leave early."

"Wait until you see the horses your mother drew," I say, looking around for Maria.

"Mum's in her room. I'd like to spend a minute alone with you before I fetch her."

"I'm a bit old for you Joe," I joke.

Joe winks at me. "How's the iPad going?"

"Good. Better than good. I'm getting the hang of it. I've looked up things I'd long forgotten. Today, I was looking up the Royal family of Greece. Quite interesting. Like me, the Greek royals had Russian heritage. I'm so old I remember when King George II abdicated... But I won't bore you."

"Russian heritage? You should look up your family tree, Miss Katerina. You're probably related to the Romanovs." Joe makes a thumbs up, like an artist checking their subject. "A lost princess."

"I might do that one day. I can probably do it on the iPad gadget."

"Good, then you can give me pointers on digging

into Mum's history." Joe laughs. "It's amazing the way you pick up new technology."

"Double thanks," I say. "One for the compliment and one for not adding 'for your age'."

Joe pulls his phone from his jacket pocket and smiles a vacant smile. I can almost see the cogs turning in his brain.

I press my lips together and wait.

"I need another favour," he says after a moment. "I was hoping we could try the translator app again, but in a different way."

"What do you want me to do?" I roll up my sleeves to show enthusiasm.

"When you notice Mum in a calm mood, maybe *you* could listen to the robot voice and try talking to Mum in Italian."

"I'm one step ahead of you," I say, "I've already tried it. She's fine."

"Then... you can say no... if you don't mind." He hands me a list. "I've written down questions." His voice trembles. "They're about her youth."

"There must be more to this plan, Joe. You know as well as I do, I'll have no idea what she's saying if she responds."

"As it happens, there is more to my plan." He shows me the microphone icon on his phone. "You have the same feature on your iPad. When Mum responds to the questions, you could press record." He steeples his hands as if praying for me to agree.

"I can try," I say. "But what will we do with the recording?"

"Once you've done a few sessions, I'll send them to a translation service and have them typed up in English."

"What if your mother rambles on about nothing, and it doesn't make sense?" I ask.

"It's worth a try if you're willing," he says.

I pat Joe's hand. "Run through it again and I'll have a go as soon as you leave. While the instructions are fresh."

After Joe's gone, Maria points outside where the late afternoon sun is streaming through a break in the clouds.

"Yes," I say. "Let's catch the last rays. Bring your art things."

I wonder about the possibility of Maria having family secrets she doesn't want to share, but I trust Joe to love his mother no matter what she reveals.

'The Figs Village' is like a woman with a perfectly made-up face and a patch of matted hair. The resident gardener does a fine job of keeping the entry grounds fit for display, but the disused courtyard out back is far from picture-perfect. Out here, tree roots from the giant Moreton Bay fig lift the paving, and scrappy flowers share the company of weeds. It's more a *Do Not Give a Fig Garden*, but I like the air of neglect. It is as messy as love and youth.

When Maria settles with her sketchbook, I get the iPad ready and review the steps Joe's written on the back of his question sheet. Calm Mum first. Ask a question about her youth in Italian. Press record.

Calming Maria down with one of my own tales works as well for me as it does for her. While she draws, I move behind the tree, and practise an introductory phrase in Italian. Taking a deep breath, I say, *"Ho intenzione di raccontarti una storia.* I'm going to tell you a story."

Maria leans forward, eyes wide and says, "A story."

"Oh, Maria, you spoke English." I flick a page in her sketchbook and point to the horse. "The Melbourne Cup. I went there once." I rest my head against the back of my chair. "I'm glad you like my stories, because I have another I need to tell."

When I've finished telling her all about my trip to Melbourne, so many years ago. I translate the first question, press the microphone icon and ask Maria, "What do you remember about your youth?"

Chapter Twenty-Seven

KATERINA

Sydney and Melbourne, 1944

When Father put Aunt Mary's letter back in the envelope, we all commented around the dinner table. Mary, Father's Melbourne cousin, had lost her usual wit and sparkle.

We finished eating, and Mother and Father moved to the drawing room to listen to music, but I didn't return to my room. Instead, I thought about Mary's letter. This could be the perfect opportunity to get out of the house and away from Father's watchful eye. I had a fortnight's study leave leading up to my final exams and Melbourne would make a welcome change from home.

"Poor Aunt Mary," I said. "Perhaps I should visit and cheer her up?"

The looks passing between my parents weren't discouraging, so I offered more reasons for them to agree. "I could help her around the house and keep her company."

They exchanged glances, but I wasn't sure they were convinced. "I'd get uninterrupted time for schoolwork without the distraction of my friends."

"A cheer-up from her favourite niece might be just the ticket for Mary," Father said.

I was pleasantly surprised and didn't care that the tight smiles passing between them suggested they were sick of my moping and would be glad to see the back of me.

Father made the arrangements, and two weeks after the dinner conversation, he carried my bag onto the train, checking I was settled into the private carriage he'd booked to ensure I was safe from strangers. As he said goodbye, he handed me an envelope.

"Don't talk to anyone and give Mary my love. She'll meet you at the station. Tuck this money into your clothing, it's for Mary. I know she manages just fine but tell her it's a treat."

Once the train departed, my pulse quickened, but as I looked from the window to the carriage door, then back to the window, disappointment took over. For twenty minutes, the train rushed past the greyness of buildings and into the greenery of the countryside, and I realised this would not be the romantic Melbourne rendezvous I'd planned.

Nick had delivered a note to Philip, and although he'd responded saying he would meet me on the train, he hadn't turned up. Had he changed his mind and decided not to come?

I missed Anna. Perhaps, I should have invited her to

Melbourne instead of Philip. I had only just resumed corresponding, and Anna had picked up where we left off. She'd written of her belief that young women are more inclined to let feelings spiral out of control and romanticise. She lectured about men's stunted emotional capacity, and quoted words by Ambrose Bierce, whose short stories she was devouring. *Love is a temporary insanity*.

I had laughed when I read her letter, thinking how Anna would change her mind when it happened to her, but at that moment, abandoned in a train carriage, I wondered if she was right.

Half an hour later, my carriage door opened.

"I wanted to be sure no one saw," Philip said, his face a mixture of expectation and concern. "The conductor has checked the tickets and won't be back. Are you sure about this?" His words spoke of caution, but his eyes spoke of desire.

With the door locked, I opened my mouth to complain about the wasted time, but he kissed me full on the lips. I had dreamt about kissing him over and over again, and although there wasn't a sprig of mint in sight, I could smell mint as if we were back in the laneway.

We kissed so hard my lips were plump and tingly, then when I touched his mouth, I could feel the pulse in my fingertips. We kissed again, and I half-heartedly pushed his hands away from my breasts for propriety's sake. I was a little disappointed when he kept them to himself.

It was an hour before we surfaced from our marathon kissing session. It would have suited me to have locked-lips the entire trip, but we needed to rehearse our plan.

We went over the hand drawn map showing Mary's house and the route from the city. Then I told Philip about poor Aunt Mary. "She lost her fiancé in 1917, less than a month before the Great War ended. He had purchased a large Melbourne house before he died and left it to Mary. Like I said in my note. She runs a boarding house now."

"That is so sad." Philip's face showed a sensitivity I'd never seen in a man. Well, certainly not Father. My heart warmed at how compassionate he was towards someone he'd not yet met.

"She wasn't ever carried over the threshold. She walked in all alone."

"She never married?" he asked. His eyes teemed with concern.

"No, and she was only seventeen when he died. But it's too late for her now."

"Why?"

He looked so miserable that I tried to sound chirpy. To point out how long ago it all was. "Don't worry, she's old now. Our mothers' ages. Forty, at least."

I changed the topic and we revised the plan of what Philip would say and do when we arrived. He was to avoid being seen at the station and wait three hours before knocking on Mary's front door. Then he would ask if a room was available for let.

I prised open the flap of the envelope and handed Philip two of the pound notes stacked inside. "This will cover the cost of your board."

"No." The irritation in Philip's voice made it clear he was uncomfortable with this aspect of the plan.

"Stop fretting, Auntie has no idea how much was in

the envelope and she'd never discuss money with Father."

Philip held the cash reluctantly. "I want to explore Melbourne with you, but I don't want use Mary's money. It's stealing."

I thought for a moment. "We're not actually keeping it. You will hand the money straight back to her when you pay for the room."

Philip's shoulders relaxed a little.

"And if you like, you can offer to chop wood or do gardening. For free. This is a win-win for all." I smiled at my ingenuity and lifted Philip's hand to my head, twisting strands of my golden hair around his wrists as if I was binding him to me. I became light-headed with excitement when he smiled.

———

No wonder Mary's letters sounded glum. I'd only been an hour in the living room when those overbearingly dark walls dampened my spirits. I filled Aunt Mary in on the goings-on at home, while keeping one eye on the mantlepiece clock and the other on a gap in the heavy velvet curtains.

After following my plan to walk around the Melbourne Royal Botanical Gardens, Philip arrived. I glanced as he read the "rooms available" sign posted on the front window. We hadn't made a back-up plan for what he would do if the boarding house was full. He closed his eyes briefly, exhaling in relief.

Philip delivered the words exactly as rehearsed, "Can I please rent a room for a few days? I'm looking for work to help my mother."

I was right, Mary immediately softened at the thought of a young man assisting his family. She smiled warmly and invited Philip inside. He didn't make eye contact with me, but edged in slowly, looking at the ground, his shoulders stooping under the weight of his insincerity. When we'd discussed the details, I'd sensed his reluctance to include Mama Bridgett in the lie.

"What sort of work are you seeking?" Mary led him to the stairs.

"Anything. I'm eighteen in two weeks, but I'll put up my age if it helps."

Mary studied him. His clothes were old, but clean and perfectly mended. Although his face retained a boyish quality, Philip's physique was that of a man.

"It's obvious your mother looks after you. You seem honest and strong. There's plenty of work with so many men away at war."

Mary showed him a sparsely furnished room, while I watched from the stair landing. Through the open door I saw Philip's smile of approval as he admired framed pictures on the wall. "What beautiful paintings," he said. "I'm sorry, I've forgotten my manners. Thank you. I would be happy to take the room."

"I'm pleased you appreciate my handiwork."

"Yours? You're very talented."

"Do you paint or draw?" Aunt Mary asked Philip.

I muttered 'No' under my breath, and Mary fixed her eyes on mine, raising one eyebrow. I waited for her to question me, but she turned straight back to Philip. It struck me that it might not be just my presence that cheered her.

Philip handed over the money which she slipped into a pocket at the back of a large, black book. In the front she recorded his name, the date, and the amount paid.

"Two weeks. This includes room and board. We're about to eat dinner if you're hungry. Put your things away and meet us in the dining room."

Mary introduced me to Philip, and I took to the whole charade with glee. It was fun pretending my sweetheart was a stranger. Philip said little, which worked well under the circumstances. He came across as a bashful young man, slightly smitten with both Mary and 'her niece'.

"How is your father?" Mary asked me. "Still looking after Russian subjects of the colony?"

Mary addressed Philip, "Did you know more Russians enrolled in the Australian Imperial forces in the First World War than any other non-Anglo nationality?"

"No, Mrs Alexander."

"Miss, not Mrs." Mary looked sad and glanced at a portrait of a handsome man in uniform. She shook herself upright. "Katerina's father wasn't head of the consulate during the Great War, but he's always been a powerful man."

Mary didn't mention the love who gave his life in the war, but her eyes flicked towards the photo.

Dinner was simple, and we ate quietly. I extended my leg under the table and wriggled my toes to tickle the bare skin in the gap between Philip's socks and the cuff of his trousers. We avoided making eye contact to avoid suspicion, but he moved his foot away when Mary tilted her head to one side and looked from Philip to me and back again.

The colour rose in his cheeks and the moment he finished his last mouthful, he began clearing the table.

"I'll wash these dishes," he said.

"Put those on the kitchen sink, then come straight back, there are things I need to get straight."

She led us both into the formal drawing room where Philip sat, feet together, shoulders square as if posing for a photograph. I dangled both legs side-saddle over the arm of a floral-tapestry chair. Away from my parents, I did not have a care in the world.

"This coming Tuesday is the first Tuesday in November, Melbourne Cup Day. There'll be no looking for work then. The whole of Melbourne stops for the race." Mary clasped her hands. "I haven't been in years, but I think you should come with me, Kat. Young man, you need the work, and I have a dead tree in my yard that needs chopping down."

"Thank you for the offer, Aunt Mary, but I have study to do, so it's probably best if I stay home and miss the horse race."

"Exactly what I expected you to say, but you will come." She tapped her fingernails on the tablecloth and looked at me oddly.

"I'm thinking about Mother and Father, too. I do not think they'd approve of me attending."

Mary looked from me to Philip then back again. "Probably not, but in the big scheme of things they would be infinitely more cantankerous on finding out their daughter is travelling the country with a dashing young man, and the pair are masquerading as strangers."

"I do not know what you mean."

"Don't insult me. Even if I were blind, which I am not, I would feel the tension between you."

Philip put his hands over his face, and I wailed, "Aunt Mary, please. I beg you. Don't tell Mother and Father."

"The dishes are waiting." Mary pointed to the kitchen. "Keep the door open. In the meantime, I will decide what's to be done."

Philip boiled water, turning to me with his finger to his lips. "We shouldn't have lied. I'll go back to Sydney."

"I'm going to tell her the whole story," I said. "The movie, the dance, Uncle Viktor's death. Everything."

We returned to the dining room where Mary sat stony-faced. But despite her manner, when all my words and feelings poured out, Mary picked up the photograph of her fiancé and covered her face with her hands.

Philip and I exchanged looks, then he wiped at a tear running down his cheek and I started to cry.

Eventually, Mary turned to face us. "For me to tell your mother and father would be hypocritical. Before he left for the War, Olaf wanted us to spend time alone. Even though I wanted him with all my being, I refused. I was proud of that strength. But I'm not proud now of doing the 'right thing'. I missed my one opportunity for love."

I was swamped by Mary's sadness. "Philip is going back," I said.

"No. I will either keep both of you in my sight or keep you apart for your entire stay. But for now, show me this dance of yours."

We selected a record with a suitable song and cleared the furniture. Philip and I danced for a while, but although Mary clapped, her smile was tinged with sorrow.

"Dance with Mary." I led Philip over and pulled a reluctant Mary from the chair.

They danced slowly and awkwardly around the room until the song ended. Mary brushed down her skirt and patted her hips. "You will both accompany me to The Cup."

I threw my arms around Mary, dancing her around the room. "Thank you. Thank you so much."

"Now, for the details." She looked at Philip. "I reckon you're close enough in height and build to my late fiancé. His wedding suit may as well get its first outing."

"I don't think I should wear it." Philip looked as if this was sacrilege.

"It will keep his memory alive," Mary said. "Along with thousands of others, my Olaf marched off to war and didn't return..."

Her words trailed off and there were a few seconds where I thought the three of us would fall into a pit of despair. I forced myself to jump up and spin in an arabesque. "What about me? What will I wear?"

"I've no doubt you've brought a pretty dress," Mary said, "but we'll find a suitably stylish hat to match."

As Mary led us upstairs, I placed an imaginary hat on my head and twirled again. Philip smiled at the stair treads, but I felt the warmth of his admiration.

"A horse race," I squealed.

This was going to be exciting.

Mary removed Olaf's suit from a storage bag and brushed it reverently.

"Philip is leaner than Olaf, especially in the shoulders," Mary spoke to no one in particular and ignored Philip's fidgeting as she made slight adjustments and placed shoulder pads inside the jacket. By the time she finished, the suit was more than passable. Philip was every woman's dream.

With Mary's permission, I pulled every hatbox from her cupboard and tried them on, striking ridiculous poses for my aunt and my admiring beau.

"Every hat suits you. You could wear a knotted handkerchief and look chic." Mary smiled and left the room, and Philip helped me pack away the boxes. It was our first moment alone, but he looked at me differently. We'd been hand-holding-lip-kissing-sweethearts but there was a change. "I want you," he said, taking my hand and when I looked into his deep yearning eyes, I sank into them.

Mary reappeared, coughed and gave a stern warning look. I feared she could read minds. Philip dropped my hand immediately.

I was impressed by the military personnel at Flemington racetrack. There was a sea of khaki and navy blue. Even the civilians had toned down their colours in honour of those at war.

"The female officers," I remarked, "so smart, strong and beautiful in their uniforms."

"I agree." Mary nodded. "They outshine women dressed by top couturiers."

Philip shook his head in disagreement. "The two women on either side of me are best on field."

Aunt Mary blushed.

A race photographer interrupted, "A photograph?"

Mary politely waved him away. "Please, Aunt Mary," I begged. "We look such a treat."

"I need to check something first," she said. She spoke to the photographer at length then he set up his camera overlooking the track.

"He's from a private studio, so you won't end up on the society pages of the Melbourne Argus."

I'd never thought about that. Father read *The Argus* every week. I thanked my lucky stars for Mary's foresight.

After the photography session, Mary handed us each a one-pound note. "I had an unexpected windfall in the form of a young lodger. I believe he's also offered to do gardening. Free of charge." She gave Philip both a smile and a wink. "Choose a horse and we'll place our bets."

Scanning the printed program and ignoring the statistics, I waited for a horse's name to leap out. "Sirius," I declared.

Philip and Mary tried to talk me out of my foolhardy method.

"But he's named after the brightest star in the sky, and I've looked at the board. He has good odds."

"Good odds mean he has less chance of winning," Philip explained. "And there are whispers the horse is lame."

I summoned my best persuasive tactics until they agreed to bet on Sirius with me.

"It's not my first pick," Mary conceded. "But come on. Life is short, let's go for it."

An hour before the race, Sirius was declared the hot favourite and as the odds plummeted, Philip and Mary's hopefulness skyrocketed. If Sirius won, we'd make money; if not, all blame for the reckless choice lay with me.

With the race underway, the attention of the crowd was interrupted by the commotion I made behind them. Sirius was winning. I squealed and jumped with absolute joy as he crossed the line in first place. We would all be taking home a tidy sum.

When I wandered to the track to see Sirius up close, Philip stayed with Mary. When I returned, I sensed I was interrupting a private conversation. I took Philip's hand for a romantic stroll around the racecourse, but Mary manoeuvred herself between us as chaperone. They talked easily to each other and I watched furtively for signs of something untoward. Although I saw nothing obvious, my gut disagreed with my eyes.

"Philip," Mary said as we were setting off for bed. "Tomorrow I need to shop in the city, and you will carry my packages."

I was about to offer my help when Mary shut me out.

"Kat, you don't mind staying home, do you? I'm half expecting more boarders to arrive, and it would be wonderfully helpful if you could show them to the empty rooms upstairs."

I stared at Philip, hoping he would be reluctant to go without me, but he looked pleased.

No one sought lodging in the four hours they were gone, and Mary's packages appeared light enough for her to manage alone.

I forced my mouth into a smile. "So glad you had a successful trip."

That afternoon, I tried to take Philip aside, but Mary wanted a new vegetable patch, and apparently the task was urgent. Philip turned the soil and planted seeds and I waited until Mary went inside to ask about the day.

"There's nothing to tell," he said. "I carried things for your aunt."

There was a burning sensation in my chest as he avoided eye contact.

Chapter Twenty-Eight

CLAUDIA

Melbourne, 2018

Our taxi pulls up in front of an old stone house, and I double check Viktoria's email to make sure we're at the correct address. Melbourne weather in Autumn is colder than a Perth winter, and I pull the scarf and jacket tight as I climb out, fighting to stop the wind biting any exposed skin.

"Whoever designed a jacket without pockets should be drawn and quartered," I say, blowing pathetically warm air onto my hands, then shaking them to keep the blood flowing.

"Come here." Dermot clasps my frozen fingers. His touch is like the heat of sun after months of cloud cover.

It's difficult for me to pull my hands away, but I do it with a nervous smile. "Thanks, you've saved me from frostbite."

"As long as they're defrosted enough to knock," he says.

His lips are almost blue, and I wonder about warming them up.

I nod, taking an icy breath that freeze-burns my throat, and ready myself—but stop my fist millimetres from the door.

"Come on, Claudia, it's now or never," Bonnie whispers. "We're going to meet our new sister."

I sigh deeply.

"Don't worry. We'll always be each other's favourite." There's uncertainty in Bonnie's laugh, and I pull her into an *I-love-you-hug*, and we huddle tearfully outside the door.

"It'll all be grand. It's perfectly normal to feel emotional." Dermot wraps reassuring arms around us.

"You'll take notes, won't you?" Bonnie asks. "There's a fair chance meeting Viktoria will be overwhelming—Claudia and I won't remember the details."

Dermot pats his chest over the notepad and pen, and his eyes gleam with as much excitement as Bonnie's. He's ready to crack open this mystery.

When the door opens, there's no doubt we have the right woman. She's made in the same factory as me and Bonnie. Viktoria has Dad's amber eyes, the same ringlet curls as Bonnie, except in silver, and she smiles with a mouth almost exactly like mine. The effect of recognising parts of Dad, Bonnie and me rearranged to create a familiar stranger is both confusing and hypnotic.

I'm astounded at how young she looks. I would have picked her as years younger than seventy-two. I pat the light wrinkles around my eyes, hoping her youthfulness came from Dad's genes.

"Thank you for inviting us," I manage to say, before we become a tangle of hugs and tears.

Dermot takes control, moving us inside before we collapse in a crying mess.

"I'm delighted you organised the visit so soon." Viktoria chokes back tears, grabbing at a box of tissues. "Here." She takes one for herself and passes the box around.

"You look like..." Bonnie starts. The crying start all over again.

Dermot offers to make tea and Viktoria points him to the kitchen, sniffling between sobs. "It's set out on the tray. The scones as well."

The dining room looks like a museum piece, and when the mantle clock chimes, I imagine Dad listening to the same sound seventy years ago. My pulse feels doubly strong, like Dad's heart is beating alongside mine. It's a pity Mary Alexander is dead. I wish I could sit face to face with someone who knew Dad back then.

"Do you really think your father, Philip McLeod, is mine?" Viktoria asks. "I know DNA tests are accurate, but he wrote to Mum using a different name."

I extract the photos of the unidentified baby from our folder. "Is this you?"

Viktoria's holds them to her chest with shaking hands. "Oh, my heart," she says. "That is me. Mum has one of me on my own wearing the same outfit."

"It's clear Dad loved you very much," I say. "He hid those photographs of you in his box of treasures."

Viktoria sobs and I'm unsure what to do, but Bonnie holds her. "You're stuck with us now, and Dermot's never wrong, are you, Dermot?"

He looks up from pouring the tea. "I wouldn't go that far, and even though there are many discrepancies and missing pieces in your family tree—I do believe you are sisters." He hands a cup to Viktoria, then opens his notepad. "Maybe we can solve this together. Your mother was born in 1903, so she would have been forty-two when you were born, but your father was only nineteen."

Bonnie twirls her hand in the air throwing an invisible lasso. "Woohoo, your mother was a cougar. Perhaps, I'll start checking out my son, Will's, mates."

I flick a horrified glare at Bonnie, worried about Viktoria's reaction. I'm relieved when she laughs.

"Would the age difference have been so socially unacceptable in 1945 that they couldn't stay together?" Viktoria asks.

"They weren't worried about older men and younger women back then." I shrug. "But maybe it was different in reverse."

"Dad wasn't going to change his fucking name for something *socially unacceptable*." Bonnie sounds exasperated. We all stare.

"You're right, Bonnie," Dermot says with a voice of authority. "There's more to this, but now that we have Viktoria's help, we'll find out what happened."

"There's not much more to tell," she says. "I know my parents weren't married. I know he sent Mum money and visited when I was very young. There's little else—except the letters I found after Mum died." Viktoria's lips tremble.

I expect Dermot or Bonnie to yell for Viktoria to go get the letters, but everyone's quiet.

I compare her situation to mine. Her own mother is gone, she grew up without a father, and never had children. My life doesn't seem quite so empty after all.

During morning tea, Bonnie shakes up the mood by taking a series of selfies. We compare hands, noses, ears and feet, chuckling at the similarities. Then we talk about our families and our childhood.

By the second cup of tea, I feel I've known my half-sister forever.

"Okay, down to business." Viktoria produces a box with a sliding lid. "Mum's papers," she says taking a letter from the top. "Lived to one-hundred-and-one and got a letter from the Queen." She rests the letter against her cheek for just a second, then continues rummaging.

"All Mum's precious documents," she says of a substantial wad of papers. "I read nothing until two years after she'd gone, and it prompted me to search my family history. I didn't get far at first. It's easier now since records have been digitised."

We move to the dining room and she hands over a large, buff-coloured envelope. "I've made multiple copies of the letters and everything else that seemed the least bit helpful. It will take time to make sense of what's in here."

"Thank you so much," I say, passing the envelope to Dermot. "We'll look this afternoon."

But Dermot can't wait. He empties the meticulously labelled envelopes onto the table. "This is gold!" he yells, looking like he's discovered Tutankhamen's tomb after months of digging with a spoon. "Viktoria, your mother kept everything. Replies from the war office. Letters from Francis Philip Patrick, which is either your father's original name or another alias."

"Can we start with the personal letters?" I ask.

Bonnie dives in before I finish talking. "Dad's handwriting for sure, and now we have his first name. Francis."

"Was that your real name, Dad? Francis Philips?" I lift one of the letters to my ear hoping it whispers a name. It doesn't say a blinking thing.

Dermot holds up photocopies of envelopes complete with post marks. "Names, dates and places. A trail of *who* your father was and *where* he lived for nearly twenty years."

We share out the letters and read through on our own.

"Do any mention depositing money?" I ask. "The two letters I've read mention sending 'a little something'."

Bonnie nods her agreement. "Yes. I reckon there were cheques in these envelopes."

"More likely postal orders," Dermot says.

I shrug, and Bonnie looks on blankly. "Stop speaking Irish," she says.

Viktoria explains, "Rather than a traceable personal cheque attached to a bank account, he would have gone to a post office and bought a money order. They could be cashed at any bank or post office."

Dermot searches through the pile of envelopes. "You and your mother would have been wonderful family historians," he says to Viktoria. "Everything was catalogued. This is a genealogist's dream."

A thinner envelope contains copies of Commonwealth Savings Bank passbook pages. There are handwritten entries showing twice-yearly deposits of between sixty and one-hundred pounds.

Dermot looks over my shoulder at the amounts. "In 1945, the average Australian wage was about three hundred pounds a year. He didn't spend much on himself."

"No wonder Dad didn't have money when he met Mum." Bonnie has tears in her eyes. "And Mum thought he was a squanderer."

My eyes fill too. "That's why he waited so long to marry. He made sure his daughter was supported before starting a new family."

"None of this explains why he changed his name?" Dermot writes 'Philip Sean Francis Patrick Alexander McLeod' in the middle of a blank piece of paper. Then next to Dad's alias, Francis Philips, he puts a question mark. Dermot was right when he said most people in hiding keep some of their real names.

"There are four of us now," he says, pulling a laptop out of his bag. "We can get straight to work."

Without answering, Viktoria fetches her own laptop.

Within minutes, Dermot has assigned jobs and we work in pairs. I'm more than happy to help Dermot search for Francis Philips on old electoral rolls. After finding only one match where name, year and place correlate with a post-mark on an envelope, I lean back in defeat. "It's all going around in my head and I can't see where it fits."

"So many name changes," Viktoria says, sounding as confused as I feel. "I need to map it out." Underneath Dermot's entry, she writes 'Francis Philips' 1946-1956. *Philip McLeod* 1957 – death. She sighs heavily as she writes the word death.

Bonnie and Viktoria are listing the dates on letters and matching them to the bank transactions. Viktoria's eyes are shining. I wonder whether it's the thrill of a mystery, or a sense of pride at knowing how much trouble her father took to provide for her.

"What was Philip's name before 1946?" Dermot is clearly talking to himself. "If he was on the run, which is the conclusion I'm jumping to, we can discount both McLeod and Philips as birth surnames." He flips through the notepad to check possibilities. "Patrick Francis. Sean Patrick ..." His voice trails off as reads what sounds like an endless list of combinations, that could, but might not be, Dad's real name.

I watch the ticking clock and realise every tick takes us further away from whatever happened. *What were you hiding, Dad?*

After a break for dinner, Dermot prepares a new list of questions. "When did he start the premium bonds account?"

"1962. And he was using McLeod officially by 1957 when he signed the airline agreement," Bonnie says.

Dermot throws his hands in the air. "We've swapped one alias for another. No one knew this man."

I race to Dad's defence. "I might not know his real name, but I did know him. He was our father and a good one at that."

"You're right. I'm sorry." Dermot rubs his forehead.

"We're all tired." Viktoria stares sadly at the ground.

I put my hand on hers. "I'm sorry you didn't get to know Dad, but we can tell you *all* about him."

"Except, we don't know *all* about him, Claudia," Bonnie says.

Viktoria groans as she stands and slowly straightens. "We'll have a cup of hot chocolate and cake for energy, then we'll talk about money. Get it out of the way."

Bonnie gestures towards me. "We've discussed it between us and agreed to share Dad's money."

"Oh no." She puts her hand to her mouth. "You've misunderstood, I don't want to make a claim on your money. My—our—father paid a decent amount every year. He continued paying, even after sending a large sum to me and Mum when I was seventeen. We never went without." She knocks her hand on the table as if hammering home her decision. "I want to cover all search and accommodation costs. And if it's agreeable I'd like to help you continue the search."

"Thank you." Bonnie looks very pleased. It's either the thought of chocolate cake or keeping the money.

"You were seventeen in 1962, right?" I ask. "The same year Dad deposited the Premium Bonds."

"I can hear your brain turning, Claudia." Dermot says. "Your dad came into some money around then."

"Just as important," Bonnie says. "This cake is frickin' delicious."

"Mmmmm," Dermot mumbles around a mouthful of cake, reading from his open notepad. "Did your mother tell you how she met your father?"

"Through her second cousin Kat. Francis, or Philip, was, I believe, the son of Kat's family's servant."

"That's something new," Dermot says, jotting it down. "I'm not sure where it fits the puzzle."

I rub my chin. "Dad was proud working class and being a servant's son was the sort of thing he'd brag about. But he never mentioned it."

No wonder I'm confused. Every piece of evidence creates another question.

Dermot looks back at previous notes. "Did he live in Melbourne then? We'd decided Philip was from Sydney."

"Sydney, I think. Hang on." Viktoria opens the antique sideboard. "Mum was quite the emotional hoarder and I seem to have inherited it. Somewhere in here is a photo of Mum, Francis...err Philip and Kat."

She sorts through birthday cards, newspaper clippings and photos. "Here it is." She turns a photo over. "1944 Melbourne Cup."

A tear rolls down my cheek at seeing Dad's face. He was younger than my sons are now. They look so much like him.

Bonnie holds the photo under a table lamp for a better look. "Unmistakably Dad. More hair but the same eyebrow angle, and the same distance from bottom lip to chin." She laughs. "Did that impress you?" she asks Viktoria. "I've gained a lot of expertise from watching detective shows."

"I'm suitably awestruck." Viktoria flashes the warmest of smiles.

I focus on the gorgeous women on either side of Dad. Mary is older, but a fine-looking woman, and I can easily see a young man falling in love. Then there's Kat; young, beautiful and flirty—leaning close to him. Although the black and white photo isn't crisp, their fingers appear to be touching.

"Interesting," I say, taking a photo with my phone. "What happened to Kat?"

"I don't know. She wrote letters until I moved out of

home. I came home to live with my mother before she died, but they weren't writing then."

"Do you have those letters?" Dermot's pen is poised to record anything useful.

"No, and until you just asked, I hadn't realised how strange that is. Mum kept everything personal, but never saved Kat's letters."

Chapter Twenty-Nine

CLAUDIA

Fremantle, 2018

On the return trip from Melbourne, my stomach churns and it's not from the flight. I inspect the Melbourne Cup photo with Dad, Mary, and Kat. Dad hid the woman he loved and a daughter. For what reason? The excitement of meeting Viktoria is dampened with dread —someone has to tell Mum about the new developments.

Before we left Perth, Bonnie told Mum we were following up a lead with a relative living in Melbourne. Same Russian heritage. Apparently, Mum insisted there was a mistake. Her cousin's son's wife had researched their family tree and was definite there were no Russians.

"On Dads' side," Bonnie had tried to explain without revealing our half-sister.

"Even more ridiculous," Mum had argued. "Your

father's family was purebred Scottish and Irish. He told me so, many times."

Bonnie and I joked about the purebred notion. Great Britain's had more invaders than hot dinners. But right now, standing around the luggage carousel, it doesn't seem funny.

"Let's all tell Mum together," I broach the subject with Bonnie and Dermot. My voice echoes. There's a whiny, pleading tone.

Neither of them replies.

"As an unbiased professional," I suggest to Dermot, "you could present the factual information." I turn to Bonnie. "And you can make an off-colour joke to cushion the blow."

Bonnie pokes out her tongue, and Dermot points to his suitcase on the conveyor belt, ducking off without a reply.

"Do we have to tell Mum?" Bonnie bites her lip.

"Are you scared of her?" I ask. I'm surprised my sister is afraid of anything or anyone.

"No, Claudia. I'm not. I don't want to hurt her."

My shoulders droop with guilt at thinking about my discomfort rather than the effect on Mum.

Dermot returns, struggling as he wheels my luggage with Bonnie's bag piled on top, and dragging what might be the last suitcase in the country without wheels. "I thought I'd wait for all the bags, leave you both alone for a while. After all, it is a family matter."

That's it. Dermot is bowing out.

Bonnie opens her mouth ready with an excuse of her own, when her phone rings. 'Mum,' she mouths before she answers the call.

I stare as she listens. "Now? All of us? Hang on, I'll ask."

Bonnie presses the phone against her jeans, covering it with her jacket, but still whispers. "Mum's checked the arrivals; she knows we've landed and wants us all to stop on the way home. She's buying fish and chips."

It's too late to make an excuse.

There's a courtesy bus from the airport to the long-term parking lot, but we decide to walk. Minds tick over in time with luggage being dragged and wheeled along the paths. Intermittent groans punctuate our footsteps.

"Let's not tell her," I say as we reach the carpark.

Dermot shakes his head as if he wants to be left out of the conversation.

"Well, at least, not tonight," I add.

Bonnie's sigh of relief travels all the way to Mum's house.

"Perfect timing," Mum says. "I've just got back from the chippie."

The house has the curious odour of fish, oil, vinegar and salt. I can even smell the paper. Despite my recent queasiness, I'm ravenously hungry.

Mum looks Dermot up and down, lifting the beaded chain holding her extra-magnifying glasses to have a second sticky-beak.

Although Mum's opinion on Dermot doesn't matter, I'm curious about her actions. Was the twice-over because she liked what she saw, or because he's paired black pants with a brown shirt? Mum considers mixing black and brown a cardinal sin.

"Mum, you've heard all about Dermot. The brains behind our search." I'm speaking too fast and overusing hand gestures. I'm like a bad actor who doesn't know her lines, and I haven't yet come to the tricky part of this performance.

Bonnie rips the outer wrapping off the fish and chips, tearing the paper into four equal pieces, then handing them out as '*plates*'.

"Dig in. Grab what you want," Mum says.

Bonnie and I yawn several times through dinner. I'm not sure if Bonnie's putting it on, but I'm desperately hinting at being exhausted. I want to make a quick escape.

"I think it's a funny thing, Claudia," Mum says out of the blue.

"What is?"

"You and Dermot**.**"

I glare at her, hoping to project frickin' laser beams and stop whatever's about to come out of her mouth.

"A few weeks ago, you thought an age difference between a man and a woman was a 'bit iffy.' Yet here you are with an older man**.**"

The laser beam trick obviously doesn't work, and although pricking Mum with my fork would paint me in a bad light—I still consider it.

"Mum. Dermot is our genealogist—you know that. And the actors in the movie we watched had a twenty-five-year age difference."

"How old are you?" Mum spits the question at Dermot, looking to Bonnie for back-up.

"Fifty-four next week," he says coolly, as if he's asking someone to *pass the salt*.

Dermot isn't blushing—he's smiling, and Bonnie is grinning from ear to ear. Am I the only one finding this conversation uncomfortable?

Bonnie ticks the air with her index finger. "That's a point to you, Mum. But if you want to see Claudia really squirm, you have to mention her vagina. Or *beaver*." Bonnie pokes out her tongue. "That's my current favourite."

"Beaver? That sounds very American." Mum frowns when she says the word *American* but doesn't flinch at all at saying *beaver*. It's as if I'm in an alternate universe.

"Is there an Australian slang-word?" Mum asks like she's enquiring about the weather.

Am I so much of a prude that my uptight mother's more broad-minded than me? There's a lull in the conversation. Good. The subject is closed.

"When I was a lad in Ireland," Dermot says, "we used the word '*Gee*' to describe the lady parts."

He seems pleased with his contribution until Mum stares at him as if she's caught him rifling through her underwear drawer. Obviously, her open-mindedness doesn't extend to men.

"And you're supposed to be a professor!" She *oomphs*.

"I was, why?"

"It seems undignified for a man of your position and age to make comments about women's privates."

"My apologies, Mrs McLeod." He looks away to hide his smile.

I'm mortified. What sort of family do I have? I scowl at Mum, but she ignores me and snaps back to business.

"Right," she says. "Out with it. Tell me what you found out in Melbourne."

Bonnie raises her eyebrows at me, while Dermot's eyes are fixed on the saltshaker balanced on his finger.

Not one of us dare a glance at Mum.

"Claudia," Mum says. "You tell it. Bonnie can't be trusted not to embellish. She's too much like your father."

Dermot's shoulders relax and Bonnie coughs in mock indignation as she tries to hide a victory grin behind her hand. They're both in the clear.

I wriggle in the hot seat to buy time, but time slows in a way I imagine might happen waiting at the gallows.

I'm going to tell her about Viktoria... straight outright... after my next breath.

Instead, I stare.

"Claudia," Mum says sharply, locking me in her polygraph stare. The one that always forced out the truth. "Spit it out."

I skirt around it. "We met Viktoria—the woman the DNA results flagged. A close relative. The test wasn't exact."

To avoid eye contact, I begin wrapping the leftover fish and chips and rack my brains to think of other details which won't reveal the truth.

"And?" Mum prompts. "Surely, you didn't fly all the way to the Eastern States to find out what the test already told you?"

"Well, we checked her family tree against the one your cousin's son's wife made, and she's definitely not from your side."

"We already knew that, and I'm not interested in the DMA side of things. Did she know your father, and did she know where he got the money?" Mum's voice is louder than necessary.

"It's N for Nelly, not M for Mike." Bonnie says bravely.

"Who are Nelly and Mike?" Mum looks angry.

I avoid looking at Bonnie. She's shown remarkable restraint so far, but I'm scared we'll both be caught in a laughing fit any second, and Dermot will see two grown women being sent to their rooms.

"No, Mum. We didn't find out where Dad got the money."

When Mum turns her back to clear the mess I poke out my tongue, letting out a relieved breath.

Mum stops and sighs. "He's hidden it well. Years ago, I asked if he was keeping a secret. He joked about being an undercover spy. He hinted there were things he'd done he could never share. Then he laughed and asked me to fix him a Martini, shaken not stirred." Mum gives a knowing nod. "Your father didn't drink Martinis—it was a James Bond reference."

Bonnie rolls her eyes. "We got it without the crib notes."

Mum opens the cocktail cabinet. "I hit him with the Spanish Inquisition, but he laughed again. To this day, I'm not sure whether he was joking." Mum grabs a bottle of alcohol. "Anyone know how to make a martini?"

She laughs at her own joke then falls into her chair. Her mouth opens more than once, but she presses her lips into a puzzled line.

"With your permission, Mrs McLeod, I think we should keep searching," Dermot says.

"No," Mum says firmly. "I'd rather poke my eye out than have my daughters waste more money. Philip was a clever man. If he wanted something hidden, we'll never find it. Claudia and Bonnie, you've got your money, so thank Dermot for his services. It's time for our family to move on."

I'm exhausted both physically and emotionally and there's no fight left in me. Mum has spoken, and that's it.

Dermot shakes Mum's hand, nodding goodbye to me and Bonnie. "Thank you, ladies, it's been an adventure."

I swallow hard as he walks away.

He stops in the hallway and turns towards me. "If you need help give me a call."

"We won't," Mum says and shuts the door behind him.

Chapter Thirty

KATERINA

Melbourne and Sydney, 1944

By the time Mary accompanied us to the station, I'd had enough of us being a jolly trio. Two weeks with Philip, and we'd barely spent a moment alone. While I yearned for intimacy, Philip had cleaned gutters, fixed doors and chopped firewood. He'd made no attempt to get me alone.

As we carried our luggage into the private carriage, I pouted. "We'll be back in Sydney soon and I've hardly seen you. You'll be back at boarding school in two days."

"We saw each other every day," Philip said. "I had second thoughts about Melbourne, but I've enjoyed this break enormously." He pressed his face against the train window.

I too stared at the ants' nest of passengers scurrying about. Mary in her vibrant red, was a splash of colour against the monochromatic Melbourne crowd. When she flapped her purse in the air, and Philip waved a hearty goodbye, I realised Mary was not as over-the-hill as I'd thought.

The train lurched out of the station, and my stomach lurched too.

The engine gained speed and granted my wish. We were finally alone. Two of us, in a carriage designed for many. No stops until Sydney.

"I don't want you to go back to the school." I twisted the pearl buttons on my collar. "Maybe your mama can make Father change his mind and let you stay in Sydney?"

Philip stared at his shoes, his head nodding involuntarily with the movement of train against track. The hairs on my arms prickled, but I didn't interrupt his silence. I was scared to learn what he was thinking. There were many unanswered questions about the day he and Mary had spent together.

"Your father won't change his mind," Philip said eventually. "I don't know what to do."

"I'll send letters to your school. We'll meet up somewhere. We can dance."

"No. That isn't a good idea."

I thought back over the past few days. Mary had laughed more than I'd seen on previous visits. Philip brought out the best in her and perhaps she brought out the best in him. "Is it Mary you'd rather dance with?"

Philip looked both confused and amused, but he pulled me to my feet. "It's you I want. Come on, dance now."

There wasn't enough space between the seats for swing dancing, but plenty to stand close and move to the rhythm of the clickety-clack.

I buried my nose in the crook of his neck to inhale the woodsy scent of his skin. He took the lead, pulling me towards him. His hands gripped my bottom keeping us connected at the hips. I pressed back.

"We should run away together, Katerina," he whispered.

"What?" I blurted out. "Our final school exams? Our families?"

Philip released his hold. Although our bodies were no longer touching, a frisson of fear vibrated between us.

We sat on opposite sides of the carriage and I watched his reflection against the blurred background of trees and buildings. What was he thinking? I considered the consequences of running away. We'd have trouble supporting ourselves. We'd be poor. Then I thought about Aunt Mary and the twenty years she'd lived alone.

I drew the privacy blind and locked the door, shimmying along the seat to lean backwards over Philip's lap, placing my face under his.

"I don't want us to end. We'll run away, but let's finish school first. We can get a job and save money."

I grabbed his collar and pulled his lips to mine. The warm, wet kiss sealed the pact. Nothing mattered now, except Philip.

In that hot rolling box, smelling of stale cigarettes, I tasted his mouth, and our closely pressed bodies rocked in a different dance. Although it was new to both of us, we did what lovers have always done, and when he moved inside me, my heart beat so fast it pounded in my ears. Unfamiliar sounds rose from my throat until I bit them into silence. We rested in each other's arms until the train drew into Sydney station.

As I kissed him goodbye at the carriage door I said, "Tomorrow night at the stables."

"Yes."

I remembered the horse race. "We have some money. Our winnings," I said optimistically.

Philip baulked. "It's a month until our final exams. I'll go north to find a job and come back with enough cash." He blew me kiss and disappeared.

———

There was almost no chance of missing the alarm. I'd rewound the clock-key because I was scared it would stop ticking. If I could not see Philip before he left, my heart would stop ticking too.

My pillow soundproofed the ringing and I watched every jerky movement of the second-hand. I stared at the clock face and the clock stared back.

I was meeting Philip at two, the time of deep, deep sleep. We were both torn, knowing if we were caught, the repercussions would be unimaginable, or rather too easily imaginable. But we could not stay apart.

At the back of my mind was another nagging worry. One of Anna's sex lessons went through my mind. *Conception occurs fourteen days after the monthlies*, she'd said. *If either of us ever do this thing, we must avoid days twelve to sixteen. Just to be safe.* Today was day eleven. At least, I didn't have to worry about pregnancy.

I turned off the alarm bell, then crept towards the stairs. My thudding heart and panicked breaths thudded and roared through the otherwise silent house. I avoided the creaking treads by leaning over the handrail and sliding down. It was difficult to stop momentum as my silky nightwear slithered against the timber, propelling me dangerously fast towards the ground. My determination to prevent a mishap was stronger than the laws of physics.

Although it took longer, I used the side door so the screen of trees would block the view. I was almost at the old stables when 'what ifs' began. *What if he changed his mind? What if he's lost interest now that we've been intimate?* I'd heard many whispered conversations about men moving on once women had given what they'd begged for. Except, he hadn't begged. I'd wanted it too, and I wondered if that made me doubly bad.

I stared upwards at the stable window, searching for signs. Moonlight reflected off the old brass bell once used for scaring intruders.

"Katerina." Philip's voice was almost lost on the breeze. "Katerina. You're here."

"Of course. I haven't slept."

There was enough light to see the worn rungs of the ladder as I climbed to the loft. Though I was capable of climbing unaided, Philip reached to help. His strong grip sent tremors of desire through my hand, and radiating throughout my body.

I admired the love-nest he'd created. He'd spread hessian bags across the splintered wooden platform, and mounded straw sacks into pillows. I removed my silky-dressing-gown, shook it in the air and let it go. The delicate fabric settled like a soft pink petal over the roughness of our make-shift bed.

Philip's tawny-brown eyes shone with desire in the moonlight. I blinked slowly to imprint a picture. To remember this forever. My nightdress caressed my knees, thighs and breasts as Philip lifted it over my head. He held me at arm's lengths and spun me around, gazing at me from head to toe; his eyes eventually resting on my lips.

"You are beautiful." He kissed me softly, firmly, urgently.

I pulled his shirt slowly upwards, tracing one hand over his warm chest and kissing the contours of his torso; inhaling the scent of his skin. He ripped the shirt over his head and quickly removed the rest of his clothing, carrying me to our bed.

The combined sensation of silk, hessian, and warm-hard Philip, consigned the train encounter to the shadows. My rapid breathing made the world spin, and fireworks exploded inside my body.

Afterwards, with arms and legs entangled, Philip stroked my back and my arms. It made little sense for sex to be this enticing. Why weren't people doing it all the time? How long until we could do it again?

"Katerina," Philip whispered. He was on one knee, holding a small box in his hand. "Will you marry me?"

This was so unexpected, I needed to hear more.

"Do you love me?"

"Do you want to know how much I love you, Katerina? To the corner shop and back a dozen times."

"Then the answer is yes."

"Where did you get this?" I kissed him as we lay together on the hessian bed, and held my hand to catch glints of starlight in the diamond.

"The day with your aunt, I spent my Melbourne Cup winnings. Mary said although we are young, we should grasp love with both hands because nobody knows what life will throw next."

I sighed with relief and love, closing my eyes to steal a minute longer. I wanted to savour this moment.

Loud ringing catapulted me from the sweetest dreams, and I shook Philip awake. We'd fallen asleep and one of us had kicked the warning bell.

Lights turned on in the main house and shadows loomed in the dark.

"Get dressed," I whispered. "Run now or we'll be caught together."

He spun around, trying to find his bearings. "I can't leave you alone."

"I'll be fine." I dragged on my nightwear, kissing him quickly as he hurried down the ladder. The moment he disappeared behind the trees, I yelled as loud as I could, "Thief."

Nick and Father approached; their faces and batons illuminated by oil lamps. I clanged the bell again.

"What are you doing, Katerina?" Father's voice boomed over the ringing, but I shook it again to rid myself of nervous energy.

"I got up to use the outside toilet and thought I saw a man climbing over our wall. I came to keep watch."

"Why didn't you wake me?"

Even in the dark, I could see the whites of Father's eyes.

"I wasn't sure. But I am now. It was a man wearing dark clothing."

"Where? Which way did he go?" Nick asked.

I pointed to the vegetable garden; the opposite direction to the way Philip had fled.

"We'll split up," Father said to Nick. My stomach dropped. *Run, Philip. Hide.*

Seconds later Nick yelled out, "Over here."

I followed his voice to a potting shed behind the vegetable garden. Father shadowed me.

Nick held two split pumpkins. "He dropped these as he raced for the wall. He'll be down the street by now."

"Did you get a clear look?" Father asked.

"Mid to late forties. Blonde or silver hair. Stocky build." Nick described a person the exact opposite of Philip. His arms were behind his back as he spoke, and I imagined his fingers crossed.

Father grunted and took the pumpkins. "You two. Back to the house. And Katerina, give me your word you won't take risks like this again."

"Yes, Father." My fingers were also crossed. And the ring hidden.

Chapter Thirty-One

KATERINA

Sydney, 1944

With so many rich meals around Christmas, it took several mornings of squeamishness before I considered causes other than food. I counted back to the day of the Melbourne Cup—the day of my last period. Seven weeks.

Mother and I had never spoken about the 'birds and the bees', and it was too late by then to ask questions. Although Anna and I chatted about most things, I could not trust her with this. She would intend to keep my secret but the temptation to tell her mother would overwhelm her. Although she hadn't exactly broken her promise about the dance, she'd shared confidential information. Anna and I did not hold the same sanctity of secrecy.

I made excuses to stay in my room to conceal my distress, burying my head in my pillow until it was wet with tears. Although I started several letters to Philip, I shredded them. This wasn't a topic for pen and paper. Besides, the 'situation' was unconfirmed.

I'd taped our love notes to the underside of my bottom drawer and memorised his every word. Whenever I was sure I couldn't be caught. I took them out to get the sense of closeness I got from holding them. There was no way Philip or I could meet, but I needed to talk to someone.

My parents made no mention of the incident in the stable, but they became increasingly watchful. Last week, I helped my father move his office upstairs under the pretence of him desiring a better view, but really to watch my comings and goings. I played with a brass paperweight on his desk, before packing it away, and discovered I was born on a Wednesday. The world was conspiring against me. *Wednesday's child is full of woe.*

I needed to see Mama Bridgett. Not to tell her my worries, but because she was the only person other than Philip that I felt really cared for me. For several days, I walked the grounds hoping to catch her alone. Each time I saw her, she smiled and waved. But I thought about Father. What if he caught me? I waved back but returned desolate to my room.

When I could no longer manage the anxiety, I followed her to the worker's cottage. Before she disappeared inside, I whispered, "Mama."

She turned, smiling towards my voice, but her smile evaporated. "What's wrong, Kat? Come in."

Mama slowly scanned the grounds, then put her arm around my shoulder, ushering me inside. She handed me her handkerchief, gesturing for me to sit. "I'll make tea."

While Mama busied herself with the kettle, I traced

my finger around the lace edged handkerchief, willing myself not to cry, or blurt out the disgraceful details.

"Tea might not solve everything, but it never hurts."

At Mama's comforting voice, there was no containing my emotions. I collapsed onto my trembling arms and hid my shame.

She waited for the longest time before resting her hand on mine. "Tell me what's up. There's almost nothing that can't be sorted."

"I cannot," I cried.

"Keeping it inside won't make it go away." Mama gripped my hand as if she'd hold me no matter how far I fell.

After my confession, Mama looked concerned, but there was no judgement. When she assured me everything would be okay, I cried for the entire afternoon.

She decided to ask for personal leave. Someone in Melbourne could help. She asked the address of Mary's boarding house in case she needed somewhere to stay.

"What will happen?" I asked.

"There is no point in explaining my plan until it's in place. I'll tell you the details when I get back."

As I hurried home, I hoped Mama Bridgett would make everything better like she'd done when I'd scraped my knees as a child.

Mama had been gone two weeks and I hadn't heard a thing. Worry strangled me so tightly that sitting at the family dinner table was torture.

"Why aren't you eating the fish?" Mother glared at

me. "I have gone to the trouble to prepare a meal and you push it round your plate like ca-ca."

"Sorry, Mother, I'm not hungry."

Mother pursed her lips in displeasure. "At the very least, eat your vegetables. You've been looking rather pale."

Father eyed Mother's cooking with distaste. "When does Bridgett return?"

"She wasn't definite. I wish to have a word with you about that woman when the children are gone."

"About?" he asked.

"Bridgett refused to provide an explanation for her sudden departure, and I do wonder whether we need her services at all." Mother leaned closer to Father and whispered. Although I couldn't hear her, Father's reply was louder, and I stopped chewing to listen. I was desperate to catch every word.

"Nick and Katerina are old enough to hear," Father said. "Besides, we will have to explain these decisions later. If we terminate Bridgett's employment, where will she and the boy live?"

"Boy?" Mother aimed an imaginary spit at the floor. "Men younger than him have died fighting for their country. Viktor is gone, those people are not our concern."

Father shrugged, and my mouth went dry.

"Anyway, school finished weeks ago," Mother said. "He's gone in search of a job. While he's there, he can find somewhere for his mother."

My parents' refusal to use Philip's name made my head fuzzy with anger. Mother's voice came from far away. I was going to be sick. "May I please be excused?"

"No." Father banged the table with his fist, and we

all jumped. "This is family mealtime and we will sit together."

Mother's voice trembled, but she changed the subject. "King George II of Greece has abdicated."

Nick interrupted, "Please. Something other than politics?"

"There's another letter from your Aunt Mary." As Father opened the envelope, my insides swirled with nausea and wretchedness. What if Mama had spoken to Mary, and Mary was revealing my secret?

'*Dear cousin*,' Father read.

'*I hope this letter finds my extended family in good health. Unfortunately, I find myself in a less than ideal situation. Two months ago, I fell in love with a young man. He left for the war shortly after our love affair. I now find myself—*'

Father stopped reading and gulped his apéritif. "This letter is unsuitable for family sharing."

I gaped at Nick.

"Father," Nick said. "We're no longer children and the gaps you leave in Aunt Mary's letter will be filled by our imagination. In my case, what I imagine is probably worse than the actual words."

Father finished his drink, regarding Mother oddly. Her eyebrows were raised.

In uncomfortable silence, Nick and I stole looks at each other, waiting for Father to decide.

Father refilled his drink, picked up the letter and read on:

'*I know this is a shock, but I refuse to consider it bad news. I lost my fiancé at seventeen and have been alone since. To find love is a blessing. To be with child is a miracle. I have written to my love, and he has promised marriage once the war ends. However, I find myself rather unwell and with a pressing prob-*'

*lem; how to look after the boarding house while staying out of
the public eye until the baby is born.*

*Is it possible for either Nick or Katerina to spend a few
months in Melbourne? I will teach housekeeping and book-
keeping skills and ensure their physical and moral safety.*

Please consider my request.

Mary.'

Mother beckoned Father to join her in the kitchen and
Nick waited until the door closed before pressing his
ear to the wall.

"Mother is talking," he relayed their words in a whisper. "Could solve our problem... Not Nick... enrolled at
university ... Katerina has finished school... too fond of
Bridgett and her son... get rid of them while she's gone."

There was much to take in. I swallowed a mouthful
of water, but it stuck in my throat, so I dampened my
napkin and held it to my forehead to calm the sickness.
It cooled me but didn't stop the questions. *Did Mama
visit Mary in Melbourne? Is Mary pregnant too? Why does
Mama have to leave?*

A week later, Mother took me aside. "Sit here, Katerina.
It's time for a mother-daughter talk." She moved sideways to make room at the window seat. "Your father
was furious about the dance competition, and not just
because of Viktor's death. There are valid reasons for
his anger. Dancing can lead to improper interactions."

I twisted my cardigan to avoid her gaze.

"Your father and I have decided you will act as Aunt

Mary's assistant. You haven't made plans for your future and this will be a time of valuable lessons. You will learn from Mary's experience and also her mistakes. We cannot judge her too harshly, as she is of an age to make up her own mind." Mother lifted my chin to face her. "Father and I want to make it crystal clear that by sending you, we in no way condone her actions. Do you understand?"

I looked down. "Yes, Mother. But what will happen to her baby if she doesn't marry?"

"She should do what countless foolish women have done before her and give the child to a decent family in a position to take proper care. But I cannot tell a grown woman what is right. If you were to find yourself in her predicament, your father's wrath would descend on both of us."

I nodded quickly to hide my fear. No matter what awaited me in Melbourne, it would be safer than staying here.

"That's enough." Mother ended the conversation with a cough and a dismissive wave. "You will leave the day after tomorrow. Father will put you on the train."

I needed to get a message to Philip but asking Nick to post a letter would be dangerous. Several times I crept past the stables to Mama Bridgett's cottage, but her house was still locked.

Even as Father watched me board the train, I wasn't sure if Mary's letter was an excuse to get me safely to Melbourne, or if her dilemma was real. Although the engagement ring had helped cast off doubts about Philip and Mary, visions of them smiling at each other in Melbourne resurfaced with frightening strength.

Chapter Thirty-Two

CLAUDIA

Fremantle, 2018

My shoulders ache from cleaning, but I force myself to tackle one last job. Most of Dad's money has gone towards my new house, and while I've kept an emergency account to fall back on, I need a steady income— and sooner rather than later. When I log on to Job-Finder, I find two positions I'm not only qualified to do but are so interesting I'd almost work for free. One as a forensic accountant, the other doing finances on a cruise ship. A cruise ship? Without ties, I may as well sail out of the harbour.

I polish my resume, send off the job applications, then treat myself to the slice of cake with chocolate ganache that's been calling my name from the fridge. With each mouthful, I think of all I have to celebrate. I'm getting a new house, I will find a fabulous job, my sons and I regularly email each other now, and Bonnie and I are closer than ever.

The cake sticks in my throat as my mind flips; I'm hiding a secret sister from my mother... and I'm no longer spending time with Dermot.

I bin the cake and pick up my phone. There must be some way of talking Mum around. Uncovering Dad's past has given me a sense of purpose and friendship. If I choose my words carefully, she'll understand.

I'm about to dial when I notice five missed calls from Aaron. My hands tingle with anxiety as I press the screen. When three calls go to voicemail, I search for a positive explanation, to stop maternal dread kicking in. If Aaron is phoning, he must be alive.

After waiting for what feels like an hour, but is probably a minute, I press redial. Still no answer.

Who can I call? I twist the buttons on my shirt, giving an outlet to my trembling fingers. Would Oliver know what's going on?

Wendy answers Oliver's mobile on the first ring.

"Claudia," she says in lieu of hello.

"Have you heard from Aaron?" I ask, trying to sound casual.

"It's okay, Aaron's fine. It's Oliver we're worried about."

"Why? Is he hurt?"

"Not physically. He's been increasingly miserable since the house sold. The boys have tried calling him for days, but he won't answer his phone."

My breath whistles with relief. Aaron is fine. Oliver isn't my problem. I'm about to say exactly that but instead I hear myself say, "I'll come over."

During the drive, I ask myself why I'm going. Oliver left. Then I realise that by checking on him, I'm showing my sons I still care about our family.

When Wendy opens the door, she pulls me into a hug, but I don't hug back.

"Where is he?" I ask sharply.

"I'm so glad you're here, Claudia, he won't leave the room. He listens to the same song over and over and he's refusing to eat."

I call through the closed door, "Oliver?" There's a cold pit in my stomach when there's no response. I knock loudly, trying the handle. It's locked.

"Get me a knife," I say to Wendy.

She looks alarmed.

"To turn the lock screw."

I push against the unlocked door with more force than necessary. It opens freely, to Oliver sitting on the floor wearing headphones. My fearful energy turns angry. He has no right to worry our kids like this. I decide against kicking him and I'm halfway through practising my *'grow the fuck up and think about others'* speech when he looks up with pain I've only seen once before. When Aaron was three, he had pneumonia, and Oliver carried our son's limp body into the emergency department, wearing the exact expression. A mixture of fear, sadness and helplessness.

He removes the headphones and slumps against the bed.

"What's going on, Oliver?" My harshness softens.

"I made a mistake," he says.

"What?"

"I know it's too late, but I want you back."

Watching Oliver cry drains my annoyance. While part of me believes the one who *'moves on'* doesn't deserve sympathy—I can't stop my compassion.

"But I don't understand. Did your new relationship

end?"

He kneads his forehead as if he's rubbing away the anguish.

"Maybe you and this woman didn't know each other well enough," I say, "but you'll find someone else."

I find myself wanting Oliver to be happy.

"There wasn't another woman." He doesn't look up.

"But you told me ... I thought ..."

"I left because I knew you didn't love me."

"Oliver. I loved you."

"But I wanted you to love me like I loved you and you never did." He hides his face in his crossed arms.

"No. It wasn't like that. We weren't overly romantic, but we were compatible enough."

"Exactly," he says. "That's how you've always been."

"Oliver. Stop. I realise now that if Wendy hadn't pushed us, we wouldn't have got together. But things worked out okay. Until you left."

He lifts his tear-stained face. "You didn't actually believe Wendy's story, did you? It wasn't her idea. I engineered the double-date. I organised a mate of mine to take Wendy to the dance, so you'd agree to come with me. She played along. For months afterwards, I tried to work up the courage to tell you, but I couldn't. I loved you from the beginning. Fireworks and all."

A thrum of muscles constricts my throat and I take slow breaths to stop the tears.

"Remember this?" He replays the music he'd been playing through the earphones.

The tune is one of Oliver's forever favourites, but this time, I listen to the words. Lyrics about needing nothing else but my love.

I'd believed a lie. He hadn't left me for another

woman. I hadn't left, but I'd never loved him whole-heartedly.

I think about me judging Mum for not appreciating Dad and his flowers.

What is it they say about glass houses and stones? I *am* as cold as her.

"Oh, Oliver. Instead of leaving, we could have worked on our marriage. I would have tried, but I didn't know it was broken."

"I hadn't planned to go." He bites his lip. "I wanted you to feel passionately. After I left, I waited for you to beg me to come home, to tell me you loved me. They were the words I needed. But you never said them."

I sink to the floor next to him. What can I say?

I close my eyes to conjure a happier moment—a moment where Oliver and I were carefree and in love.

The harder I try for that memory, the more elusive it becomes. I find watered down versions, but my mind interrupts. It flashes up Dermot's smiling face.

I scramble to my feet.

"I do love you, Oliver, and you've been a wonderful father, but it's too late. I had no idea our marriage was missing something until you pointed it out. Now, I can't see anything but that."

Oliver reaches out his hand, and I squeeze it quickly, but I keep moving.

I hold myself together long enough to get in the car, and drive away. Halfway home I pull over to the side of the road and climb into the backseat to cry for what I've lost, and for what I've never had.

I think about Dermot and his wife. That's the kind of love I want, and I'd rather live alone than with something diluted.

Chapter Thirty-Three

CLAUDIA

Fremantle, 2018

Except for the bare essentials, my house is empty, and, despite my initial reservations, I'm looking forward to removal day. There's not much furniture to shift, because when I first viewed my new two-bedroom apartment in the converted Soap Factory, I fell in love with the collection of mid-century-modern furniture as much as the house. The real estate agent told me and Bonnie the owners were moving overseas, so Bonnie asked how much extra to buy the furniture. The vendors agreed to sell the lot at a better-than-reasonable price.

I've had time to accept my life will never be the same, so instead of shedding sorry tears as I do a last clean of the conservatory windows, I smile and recall memories of breakfasts with my boys. This was a happy home for many years, and I hope the new owners enjoy it as much as I did.

When I check my emails for responses to the job applications, I'm delighted to be selected for two interviews, and there's an email from Viktoria. When I see Dermot's name cc'd, I realise he and Viktoria are continuing the search.

Mum was definite about ending the quest. After she told Dermot we didn't need his services, Mum not only cried, she begged me and Bonnie to stop, too. In Mum's opinion, it's better to remember Dad as the man we knew, because digging up skeletons could ruin our memories.

After reading Viktoria's email a second time, I consider phoning Dermot, but a pinprick headache begins to *tap tap tap* in my temple like a Morse code reminder of my promise. I wrap my arms across my body, hugging the empty place inside. Searching for Dad gave my life purpose, and I've considered phoning Dermot to catch up as friends, but it wouldn't work. I'd end up asking if he and Viktoria have found anything about Dad's past life. Mum's probably right—not all secrets should be uncovered.

My phone vibrates. When I see Dermot's name I wonder if he's psychic.

"Hey," he says. "Finished packing?"

I close my eyes and picture his disarming grin. I wish there was a way to work this out.

"Yep, I'm ready for the big move." I can't help but smile as I talk to him. I ignore the tapping guilt.

"Viktoria emailed," he says. "She has more information, but I'm not sure whether you want to know. Your mother and all that."

I don't tell him I've just finished reading the email

because I'd deprive myself of a chance to listen to his lilting Irish voice. Surely, there's no harm in that?

"I was majorly disappointed when our efforts to find a Kat, Katherine or Kathleen didn't pan out, so I'm trying not to get my hopes up with this new lead." The excitement in his voice tells me his anticipation is sky-high and my hope soars alongside his.

"Viktoria found a picture of the woman who lived at her house when she was a child," Dermot continues his explanation. "Viktoria knew her as 'Mama' and she hadn't thought about it earlier, but the name on the back of the photo was...wait for it... Bridgett."

"That can't be a coincidence, surely?" I ask.

This could be the lead we need. I'm already keeping the biggest secret from Mum. Dad having another daughter. Finding Dad's mother could be worth the inner conflict.

"Can I do anything?" I will him to say that he'll come straight over.

"Not at the minute. I'll go back to the passenger list information, as I felt sure we were on the right track. Maybe Bridgett was already married even though I noted her as a single passenger. Other than that, it's under control."

I clear my throat and hope not to sound desperate. "I know I wasn't a great researcher, and we've finished working together, but it kept me busy."

"Well, there might be something for you to do. I'll think about it."

"I'm going crazy with boredom," I add.

"Aaah. I better find a task straight away, or as my old Gran used to say: *The devil makes use of idle hands.*"

I'm shocked when I get a visual of what devilish

hands might do, and I'm thankful Dermot can't actually read my mind.

"I know what. We could reach out to social media," he says. "I haven't delved into it much myself, but I believe there are help groups where you post information about lost relatives. Perhaps you could put something together?"

Considering Mum thinks social media is a TV streaming service with shows like *Friends*, there's no way she'll stumble across anything online.

"Will do," I say. "I'll keep you informed."

"Me, too."

Once I hang up, I post a message on a family connection forum, with as much information about Dad, Kat, and Bridgett as I can, but my enthusiasm is limited. I enjoyed the research more when I was sitting next to Dermot. I have no plans to discuss my feelings with Bonnie though, because she'd definitely bring intimate body parts into the conversation.

Then of course, there's the Mum problem. If I tell Bonnie about Dermot, I'll have to admit I haven't given up the search. Keeping things from Mum is one thing, but I don't want to lie to Bonnie, too. Especially not now when I find myself with a sister who is also my new best friend.

Today's the big move, and although I suggested hiring a removalist, Bonnie wouldn't hear of it. She's planned removal day with military precision.

"There's you and me and I've organised three volunteers," she said evasively. I'm guessing she's roped in my brother-in-law Matt and my nephew Will. The third person's probably Mum, I just hope it isn't Oliver. It's a pity my own sons don't live in the state. Whoever we have, I suspect they are *volun-tolds* rather than *volunteers*, but I'm confident we'll move the rest of my stuff in no time.

"Watch out. Incoming," Bonnie's son, Will, calls, as he struggles to carry a packing box up my new stairs. He makes ridiculous forklift noises which make me laugh. Matt is stationed over at my old house, loading things, while Bonnie drives back and forth swapping empty cars for full. I stay at the new apartment to unpack. Bonnie's system is working. There's no mention of Mum or Oliver, but I don't ask about the extra helper. We're doing fine with four.

I stand at the top of the stairs to unpack the first of my packing cartons, and I'm rewarded with the view. The place is perfect—the furnishings sit beautifully under the exposed industrial style beams, standing out against the rough stone pillars and plastered walls. The double-height warehouse-windows are striking on their own, but the way they frame my new view of the Swan River is stunning.

I pause to think how much Dad would have loved it.

Dad, thank you for the money. It can't replace you, but it's a lot less painful living somewhere special.

Starting phase two of my adult life is not as terrifying as expected. Even as a kid, I didn't like change. I've always been that way, so it surprises me how light and carefree I feel; there are butterflies in my stomach instead of elephants.

"A penny for your thoughts." I recognise the voice immediately and spin around to watch Dermot waltz past me, effortlessly juggling a pile of boxes through the door. I'm surprised at his agility

"I'm admiring the view," I say, not sure if I'm talking about the river or Dermot.

"Bonnie asked me to help, and I was too scared to say no." Dermot laughs his musical laugh and my heart sings along. "We'd better set up our research station away from this window though, or we'll be distracted by the view." He deposits the boxes against a blank wall and flashes a smile so broad I feel heat warming my cheeks.

"I hope you don't mind," Bonnie interrupts. "I'm planning an intervention with Mum. Dad might be her husband, but we should be able to look into his past and we need help from 'Muscles' here."

"Thank you." I clap my hands.

"Look at all the boats on the river." Bonnie points. "You'd better close the blinds when you're naked. Those yachties have binoculars."

Will comes over to check what we're looking at, and I'm relieved Bonnie doesn't add a vagina joke to the ongoing gag. Instead, she waves to the boats. "Ahoy, there."

Will makes the realistic sound of a tugboat horn and says, "You'd better keep your gear on up here, Aunt Claudia, those blokes sailing on the river can see straight inside. There'll be a traffic jam."

Dermot starts to say something, then stops.

"What?" Bonnie asks.

"Do you think there's a boat hire place somewhere on the river?" Dermot's eyes twinkle as he laughs.

Will laughs loudest at Dermot's joke. He is so much

like his mother. Although the jokes are at my expense, I chuckle, too.

Deciding what to eat turns out to be the most challenging part of removal day, and after the mammoth task of choosing, Bonnie takes Matt and Will to collect a takeaway meal. As I close the apartment door behind her, she leaves me with a wink and a nod towards Dermot.

When I turn towards him, he looks serious.

"Should we phone your mother? I sense how anxious you are about continuing the research, and in the latest email, Viktoria has asked to visit Perth so we can join forces and solve the rest of the mystery."

"Thank you for offering," I say. "I'll talk to Mum when I'm with both her and Bonnie. Just not yet."

This is something that requires careful handling. I don't want to hurt Mum, but Viktoria has spent her whole life deprived of sisters. I can't say no to her, either.

"Don't worry," Dermot says. "We'll correspond with Viktoria by email instead. It's less of a problem."

"No." My mind is made up. "I'll text Viktoria now."

'*Viktoria: The sooner you come to Perth the better. You can stay with me.*'

Bonnie returns with the meals. She stares as I chew my fingernails instead of eating.

"Everything okay?" She beckons for me to follow her to the kitchen.

"Fine." I don't look at her.

"Come on. Spill."

"While you were out, I impulsively invited Viktoria to visit. Here. In Perth. She's coming in five days and now I have to tell Mum."

Once everyone's left, I throw myself onto the bed, wondering what to say to Mum. For the first time in my life, we share common ground—that patch of Earth inhabited by the lost and lonely. Dad is gone and nothing can relieve that grief, but I want to avoid the unnecessary pain of Mum discovering her husband hid a woman and his child.

After a night considering every explanation and scenario, I decide it's better not to tell Mum about the imminent visit. I need more time. We'll just have to keep Mum away. She's an expert at recognising family likenesses and the game would be over if Mum met Viktoria.

Chapter Thirty-Four

KATERINA

'The Figs' Sydney , 2018

Although I cannot change what I did in bygone days, by telling Maria I'm able to enjoy the perfect memories before it all turned sour. My nightmares have eased, but rather than exiting a dark tunnel, I sense the brightness is the headlight of the train hurtling towards me.

When I'm hit, I need to know Maria isn't alone.

She looks up as I place my hand over hers, smiling and showing me her sketchbook like a delighted child.

Our emotional connection has become almost mother to daughter, and today's surprise is part of my exit plan.

"Joe's coming," I say, waving him over. I haven't yet told her about the surprise.

"Hi, Joe." I pat the empty seat, then look between mother and son. "Today is Pet Therapy Day."

"A new thing?" he asks with a grin. "Your idea, I bet."

"New? Yes, but it was Izzy who noticed the number of dog pictures your mum has drawn in her sketchpad, and decided it would do her the world of good to cuddle a puppy."

Joe crosses his arms in a self-hug. "Mum absolutely loves dogs, and they love her. I've got her old pooch living with me and he's never stopped sulking, or forgiven me for taking his best mate to hospital."

"Pity we can't bring him in, but rules are rules, and as kind as Matron is, she doesn't bend them."

"So, what exactly is Pet Therapy?" he asks.

"Izzy Googled it and found how successful pets are for treating aspects of dementia."

Izzy needed more prompting than that, but she agreed it would be worth convincing Matron, especially if contact with dogs helps as much as the research suggested.

It's impossible to imagine the fear trapped in Maria's mind, and when I'm gone, I believe Izzy will keep looking for ways to make Maria feel less trapped.

"I'll tell her now," I say, opening the English to Italian translator on my iPad.

"Not much longer, Maria. Dogs will be here soon. *Cani saranno qui presto*."

She smiles her way through afternoon tea, and draws three puppy pictures, which I interpret as a sign of understanding. When she holds her sketchpad to her heart, my own skips a beat.

For everyone's sake, I hope she gets to hold one. I've seen her put up a mighty battle for a pair of lost glasses. Imagine how much she'd fight over a dog?

To kill time, Maria and Joe walk around the winding brick paths while I keep watch.

When the double entry gates open and the puppy van drives slowly in. Matron shoos away a dozen residents.

Wheeling towards them, I make barking noises. "Maria! Joe! Come back. They're here."

As she runs to be first in the line, she knocks into George and two other residents. I wheel myself to the scene with Joe running beside me, but Matron gets there first.

"She's just excited," I explain. "Please. I cannot bear to think of Maria missing out."

Matron's expression is firm. "I agreed to this on the proviso we all follow strict rules. Unless we maintain order, the pet visits can't become a regular occurrence."

The wailing sound as Matron escorts Maria inside with empty arms is like a knife opening an old wound in my heart.

A crowd of residents obscure my view of the puppy van, and I do not know which dogs have been handed out. I push myself as close to the front as I can, but the puppies have already gone.

Dejected, Joe and I head inside.

"I hope Mum isn't putting on such a fuss. She'll be banned forever."

I cross my fingers. "Me, too."

Her door is closed, the Leaning Tower of Pisa picture askew. Tartan slippers rest in a messy heap outside her room and squeals of glee reverberate within.

Joe raises his eyebrows. "Who owns those?"

"George."

"I'm worried what we'll find inside." He bites his knuckles.

"Come on. Knock on the door."

He knocks, then opens it to Maria and George sitting beside each other on the bed. Maria is holding a puppy and brushing her cheek against the fur.

Joe pats my shoulder. "I don't want to disturb the puppy love." Tears well in his eyes. "Do you mind sitting with me?"

"It will be my pleasure."

Joe wheels me along the corridors and through the communal rooms. There are puppies galore.

"The place has never been so busy," Joe says. "Don't think we'll find a vacant seat."

"The back garden is usually empty. There's a picnic table under the fig tree. I love it out there."

"Your wish is my command," he says, scooting me along at an almost thrilling speed.

"Mum with the puppy was like a mother with a human baby." Joe's voice trembles. "Motherhood is something special."

I dismiss his words with a hand flick, but my heart flutters. Every cloud has a silver lining, but silver linings have clouds.

So far, I've only told Maria about the joyful, heady days with Philip, but I'm moving close to my life-changing event, and the thought frightens me. Opening these floodgates could bring the terror back. If that happens, I'll have to leave *The Figs*.

Whichever way I leave this place, there'll be sirens.

Will it be the wailing weeeh-oooh-weeeh of an ambulance or the long-awaited alarm-bell of police?

Chapter Thirty-Five

KATERINA

Melbourne, 1945 January

As the dying sunlight flickered, morphing day into night, the train stopped at Melbourne's Flinders' Street station. I wrung my hands in torment—my mood caught in a similar battle between light and dark, relief and terror.

Questions jostled for attention. For better or worse, they'd soon be answered.

What if Mama Bridgett wasn't behind this plan to get me out of Sydney? On more than one occasion, Aunt Mary had remarked on how handsome Philip was, and he certainly enjoyed her company. Where would I go if Mary's letter was an honest plea for help, and Philip was the young man she'd fallen in love with?

Mother and Father would never turn me out on the streets because displaying my condition in public would reflect badly on their standing. Instead, they'd inter me in a home for unwed mothers until the problem was resolved. At eighteen, I was a minor and would have no say. I recalled rumours about young mothers never seeing or holding their baby before it was whisked away.

When the conductor blew his whistle, announcing disembarkation, I struggled through the doors with my suitcases and searched for a familiar face. I couldn't discern anyone among the harried crowds, and steadied myself against a bench.

Mary spotted me first. She tottered towards me in the highest of heels, wearing a dress designed to show-case a slender figure. Her smiling eyes did not match her letters of distress.

With a face as refreshing as lemonade on a hot day, Mama Bridgett appeared at her side. The tension coiled in my shoulders floated away.

During the ride to Mary's house, I sat between them in the back of a taxicab. The two had the air of teenage girls planning a schoolyard prank.

Mary whispered behind her hands, "When Bridgett showed up at my door, I thought she was looking for a room. I was taken aback when she explained."

"Mary blamed herself," Mama added. "Believed she should have sent you and Philip packing once she realised you were a couple. But as I told her; nothing and no one can stop young love."

Pressing her palm against her flat abdomen, Mary giggled. "We're absolutely ready if your parents pop in unexpectedly. Bridgett is amazing, she's fashioned a fake tummy out of a feather pillow, so if your parents come knocking, I can put it on. And I bought a corset to hold you in. It will disguise plenty if worn with a flouncy dress."

Mama nodded in agreement "We are well prepared."

The cabbie deposited my cases on the doormat and Mama explained how they'd replaced the solid front door with a half-windowed affair concealed by curtains. "No one can see in from the street, but we can see who's outside before we answer."

There wasn't a skerrick of ill judgement between them. Their finding such glee in the situation was disconcerting, but I had confidence these ladies would take care of me.

I flooded with temporary relief, but how could they help once the baby was born?

Mary arranged for us to travel to Frankston on the first Friday of every month for regular doctor check-ups. At the first visit, my pregnancy was confirmed, and there were follow-ups to make sure all was progressing as it should. And it was; the baby and I were in glowing health.

Although we were unknown to the Frankston locals, my aunt suggested I use the name Mary Alexander. As unlikely as it seemed, she worried about Father's official contacts, and him being alerted to medical records under my name.

Compared to the dreadful prospect of an unwed mothers' home, everything in Melbourne was done with my best interests at heart and no sign of shame. Mama and Mary were a powerhouse, but they made decisions for me without consultation. I hadn't been asked about keeping the baby, and to be honest, I wasn't sure.

I forced myself to worry about smaller concerns. How to adjust my clothes to accommodate my growing middle, which foods quelled the morning sickness, and what to write to Mother and Father to discourage any visits. Problems much easier to handle than the swirling mess I pushed to the back of my mind, like the terrifying reality of what a baby meant for me and Philip.

Although I never repeated my parents' conversation about wanting Mama out of the cottage, she knew the time had come. When she told me she could no longer delay collecting her belongings, I helped her pack for Sydney.

She looked up as she closed the suitcase. "When I return to Melbourne, we'll need to find a place to live. Somewhere near here—for both of us."

I couldn't contribute much to my keep. "The only money I have is my Melbourne Cup winnings."

Mary appeared in the doorway, her usually small voice growing large. "You will both stay here. And not out of charity. Having you around has taken away the loneliness I've felt for years."

I listened as discussions whirled around me. Mama Bridgett agreed to stay, provided Mary accepted her meagre savings to cover the rent, and Mama made a sign for the front window, offering laundry and mending services.

Selfishly, I didn't warn Mama Bridgett about my parents' simmering rage. I needed her to go to Sydney, find Philip, and make everything all right.

Wrapping my arms around myself, I pretended I was sitting in the big tree with Nick. Both of us avoiding the not-quite-right anger lurking in the background like a black dog. Better to deny all problems and never speak of the yelling and the banging within the walls of the family home. Except now, they screamed in my head.

"Writing another letter home?" Mary asked.

"Yes. This one has a lengthy description of peeling and chopping carrots which should bore Mother and Father to death. They'll never want to visit."

Bridgett had been gone a week, and I'd heard nothing from either her or my parents.

I continued writing, taking joy in making life sound dull. The exercise made me laugh aloud.

"What?" Mary asked.

I skimmed the letter for the most mundane description and shook my head. "I won't read it; it goes on and on and on." This letter writing has become the highlight of my week—a sadistic pursuit.

It should bring groans and yawns around the family table back in Sydney, but there was a niggling worry about my parents turning up at the door.

My letter writing was cut short by a knock and Mary peeked through the curtained window to see if we needed to take action.

She sighed with obvious relief. "Bridgett is back."

Mama Bridgett recounted the events of the past week.

Her trip did not exactly go as planned. My parents were away at the beach house and had organised for Fred, our family gardener, to pack up Mama and Philip's personal possessions, locking the cottage permanently.

"Did you see Philip?" I nodded my head hopefully as if it would make Mama say yes.

"No. But I've left a message with Fred. Philip was set on saving money, so, it could be weeks before he returns. Don't worry, I was discreet when I gave Fred the forwarding address. I trust him, and he's promised to keep a lookout. If Philip sends mail, Fred will forward it here."

I shivered with concern. What if Fred told my parents of Mama living at Mary's house? They'd come immediately. What if Philip didn't return and we never found him?

On the outside I wore a smile, but inside I was a mess.

For the first four months of my pregnancy, there were no visits from home and the bouts of nausea passed. Except for the constant speculation about where Philip was, and why he hadn't written, how could I not be thankful for my confinement? Mary's and Mama's company was more than pleasant, and I owed it to them not to raise my concerns.

When Mama Bridgett explained her plan to sew a patchwork blanket for the baby, I embraced the idea. Mary happily took on the role of sourcing the cloth. She searched through the top of her wardrobe and donated a bundle of second-hand clothes she'd saved for sentimental reasons. "The idea of Olaf's shirt becoming part of a baby blanket brings me happiness," Mary said. "I've only selected fabric that gives me joy. I know it's fanciful, but I can imagine beautiful memories captured inside the quilt and your tiny baby enveloped in smiles."

Mary laughed and Mama Bridgett joined in. "If we're

going with that train of thought, best you choose fabric from someone calm. A baby needs to sleep."

We ended up with quite a pile. Mama had brought the remainder of Philip's clothing with her to Melbourne, and I asked for the shirt he'd worn on the train back to Sydney. It was in good condition, but when Mama saw how much I wanted it, she gave in. I remembered the cravat Viktor had given me to tie my hair and I asked Mama to include that too.

"The colour doesn't really fit," she'd said. "Why do you want it?"

"Because visits from Uncle Viktor were the best days of my childhood, and I want my baby to feel that way, too."

Mama's eyes filled with tears, but I smiled. "Come on let's streamline the quilt-making process."

Mary gathered clothes, Bridgett hemmed the backing fabric, and my part of the production-line was cutting regular squares from the assorted recycled clothing: Philip's shirt, an old dress of Aunt Mary's, Viktor's cravat, one of Mama Bridgett's aprons, the wedding shirt of Olaf's, and a skirt I could no longer button up.

Mary helped me spread the patches over the table and we arranged them into a repeating pattern. Instead of saying 'Blue, white, striped, purple, floral,' I called the pieces by name. 'Olaf, Viktor, Bridgett, Mary, Katerina and Philip.' A patchwork of personalities woven into one.

Although I began singing the names and tapping along in fun, my song slowed and took on a serious tone as if singing each name called them into being.

After the fourth time of singing Olaf's name, Mary

removed a white square of his wedding shirt from its jigsawed place, and held it to her face as she fled the room.

When I stood, Mama Bridgett placed her hand on arm. "Let her go."

Mama took another white-Olaf square and threaded a needle with the finest of cotton, sewing delicate stitches in a rolled hem edge. When she'd finished, she embroidered an O and an M in white, on white, to make a beautiful, sentimental handkerchief.

I fanned my face to dry my tears.

Once composed, Mary returned, but when Mama Bridgett handed her the embroidered cloth, tears streamed again, this time down all our faces.

Mary sobbed, "It's a handkerchief for a bride."

We froze at a knock on the glass and two envelopes fell through the slot landing on the floor. One was a letter from my parents, the other larger envelope was from Fred and addressed to Mama. She slit the envelope immediately and emptied the package onto the side table. A postcard from Philip.

As she silently mouthed the words, I stared at the picture. An advertisement for Victoria Bitter Beer, with uniformed soldiers drinking and laughing. I put my hands over my eyes to make the image go away; I didn't want Philip overseas fighting a war, I wanted him to be fruit picking in Queensland, or some other safe and local job. I wanted him to walk in the door and tell me how much he still loved me.

"What does it say?" Mary asked after what seemed an age.

Mama's hand trembled. "He's enlisted in the Armed Forces and shipped overseas. I'm not sure where, because the location's blacked out. Probably for security reasons."

I stared at a square of Viktor purple in the growing quilt. I knew from the night of his death how much Bridgett mourned for my uncle. He was gone forever, as was Mary's Olaf.

We were three women bound by circumstance.

I threw the quilt onto a chair, to hide the pieces of Philip's shirt. I did not want this bond. This was not to be our connection. Women who had lost their men to war.

After reading the postcard again, we worked silently on the patchwork quilt and I thought hard about the situation.

"Mama?" I started but could not continue.

She removed the dressmaking pins from her mouth. "What is it, Katerina? Are you worried about Philip's safety, or telling him about the baby?"

"Both. I cannot tell Philip about the pregnancy, at least not by letter. He's fighting a war, and I'd rather not add to his worry. Is this the right thing to do?"

Mama continued pinning the squares, but her hand shook, and I knew she was considering my decision. It was ages before she spoke, "I agree. Let him know you love him, then he will return to a beautiful surprise."

I wasn't so sure he'd find the news joyful. After all, he'd run off to the war without telling me.

Chapter Thirty-Six

KATERINA

Melbourne, 1945

I wrote several letters to Philip; talking about the weather, my fun with Mama Bridgett and Aunt Mary, but I never mentioned my pregnancy. When Mary realised I'd been obsessively checking for a reply, she took down the calendar, drawing crosses through square after square. She marked off days for the military to sort letters to each destination, and the voyage over land and sea. Mary's experience in the Great War made me realise it was unlikely he'd received my letter, let alone posted one back.

For the next month, I put aside some of my anxiety about Philip, the war, and the seemingly endless wait. Mary found what she called a *sad bargain* in one of the many post-depression pawn shops. She bought a thin gold wedding band for me to wear with the engagement ring Philip had given on our last night together.

Mama Bridgett would have none of the notion of it

being a 'sad bargain'. We played an after-dinner game where we each fabricated 'happy' reasons for the wedding ring's sale. My favourite was an unexpected inheritance where an eager and suddenly well-off groom had given away the ring bought through scrapings of desperation and love, in favour of a lavish ring encrusted with sapphires to match the eyes of his bride-to-be. Mama warned of the importance of not allowing our thoughts to travel unnecessarily down a pit of misery.

Mary, Mama and I began knitting baby clothes. White and pale-lemon balls of wool rolled across the floor and although we chatted and laughed, anxiety hung in the air. Just as I never talked about my parents' fighting, I never spoke about my fears. And there were many.

I began obsessing over things Philip and I hadn't discussed. I had no idea what he wanted from life. I'd imagined a life of adventure and love, travelling the World. These were the riches I wanted, but they were no longer my future.

I pictured Philip working away from home, earning money for weeks at a time. Me waiting in a dreary room. Yes, there would be love, but would I cope alone with four bleak walls and a screaming child?

While we knitted, Mama told me joyful stories of Philip as a baby. Something my own mother had never done. Because Philip's Scottish father had died, Bridgett cheerfully brought Philip up alone. My complaints would sound selfish to Mama, and I'd never complain to Mary who wished she had a child of her own.

"I'll take the shopping list and get ingredients for

dinner," I said as merrily as I could muster. I couldn't wait to get outside.

The greengrocer on Barkers Road smiled at the wedding band. "God bless," she said.

I wasn't sure what God was supposed to be blessing, but I nodded my thanks.

She pointed to my growing bump. "Is your husband away fighting?"

"Yes," I said.

"I hope he returns safely."

Mary was right. The wedding ring on my left hand protected me from unkindness in those who shared my own mother's view—unmarried pregnant women should be hidden until the 'inconvenience' went away.

The shopkeeper's eyes watered. "I pray day and night for my own two sons."

Her emotion caused my legs to wobble, and she was quick to pull up a wooden crate. I put my head as close to my knees as my belly allowed. If she'd known I was a fallen woman, she may not have served me, let alone brought me a seat.

"Should I fetch a doctor?" she asked.

"No need. I just don't know what I'll do if my love doesn't come home."

"There's been so much bother about young people rushing into marriage because of the war, but I wish my sons had left me with a lovely bride to share the awful wait. And a baby..." She paused to smile through tears. "That would be part of my son in the making."

She found another crate, sat beside me and held my hands. We both sat and cried, and although three customers came in, not one complained.

After more fussing about me being a beautiful bride,

I thanked her, and hurried back to Mary's, confused about the kind-heartedness a stranger had shown because she thought I was married. A simple ceremony and a metal ring changed me from a hussy to a decent woman. It was all an illusion.

I dropped my half-empty bag on the kitchen table, apologising for not buying everything on the list. Then the tears took over.

"My darling Kat," Mama said. "Don't cry, I have something to cheer you. I can't wait to see the smile on your face."

She handed me three letters tied with string.

Philip had written.

My dearest Kat,

Getting your letter changed everything. I had to wrestle with my army mates to stop them from thieving and reading them aloud. They reckoned there must have been magic in your words. The men said I grew taller and wore a grin not fit for a battleground. This morning they joked I was calling your name and moaning in my sleep.

At least I hope they were joking, because I did dream about you. Today, when the other blokes were having a smoke, I held your letter and inhaled memories of you instead of tobacco.

Before I signed up, I tried to speak to you, but your father told me you'd gone away. He said Mama had taken leave and wasn't coming back.

Although in hindsight this didn't make sense, I made a hot-headed decision to ask his permission to marry you. He flew into a rage and told me you'd left home to get away from me. Then he threatened to either call the police or shoot me.

I accepted his word as the truth and signed myself up for active duty.

I'd already been kitted up and shipped out before reason kicked in, and I realised your father saying it didn't make it true.

Please keep writing.

I love you to the corner shop, around the block, and back a dozen times.

Philip.

As I read the letter, I cried and smiled at once.

Philip hadn't forgotten me. I reread the words *I love you*, over and over until they were etched on my heart.

The second envelope contained a letter outlining his dreams—dancing with me, marriage and our future babies. He wanted them to all look like me. The third letter described the food he ate, the voyage, the leeches, and the comradery. None of his letters spoke of killing, or war.

"Happy tears?" Mama asked after I'd finished.

"Oh, yes. He loves me." I held his letter as he had mine, trying to breathe him into life from the pages. "Philip is wonderful. But I'm shocked my own father was so cruel."

Mama bit her lip, busying herself stitching the quilt.

I knew what Mama Bridgett was holding back, but it was something I'd hidden my whole life, and I couldn't face it now, not with my own troubles.

"I think it best Philip stay away from your father. He isn't a man to mess with."

"Father wouldn't shoot Philip, would he?" I trembled at the thought.

Mama steadied my hand. I thought about the many times Mama had brought my own mother cold-herb-compresses to help with her migraines, and how during these spells Mother often had a split lip or bruises.

Father made unkind remarks about Mother's clumsiness. He told her off for tripping on stairs and misjudging doorways, but deep down I knew they weren't accidents.

No matter how hard we tried to hide it, Mama Bridgett knew our family secret.

I clutched a cushion, rocking as I thought about the shouting, the thumping, and the dark mood that weighed heavily in our house. Mother's migraines were an excuse.

There'd been a lot of soul-searching of late and now it was time to own up to the truth. My father beat my mother.

I spoke in a strangled voice, "Isn't there anything we can do to stop Father hurting Mother?"

"They're married," Mama said. "Your mother is your father's property. Although it's immoral, it isn't illegal."

Chapter Thirty-Seven

CLAUDIA

Fremantle, 2018

"So, this is where my sister lives?" Viktoria wanders around my apartment still carrying her suitcase. Despite the flight, she looks chic and refreshed. She puts the case on the floor to use her phone. "I'm taking pictures to imagine you in this background when we talk on the phone."

She makes a familiar bunny-twitch with her nose and laughs. Dad's eyes twinkle back at me. For a moment, I'm looking at him, and I gasp at the resemblance.

"You crying?" she asks.

I wipe my eyes with my sleeve. "You remind me of Dad, and Bonnie too."

Viktoria pats my arm. "I hope it's a good thing."

"A very good thing. I'm glad we found you."

I am glad, but there's a sense of impending doom behind the pleasure. I'm second guessing my decision not to tell Mum.

Viktoria and I spend the morning chatting about life, and her eyes light up as I talk, even when I rabbit on about my sons.

"Sorry for boring you," I say. "You're too polite, and I should stop rambling. No one wants to hear about other people's family."

She squeezes my hand. "They're my nephews, Claudia. They're my family, too."

I breathe in the river-scented air, and it hits me how my life is not all about loss. I've gained someone special.

I remove the wall-hanging, a gift from the real-estate agent. It's useful for disguising the research board in the corner. Mum's pretty nosy, but if she drops in unexpectedly, I'm hoping it does the trick. Viktoria studies the clue cards and looks for patterns. "Did the dance competition come up with any names?"

After searching for copies of Dermot's files, I find the Trocadero lists. "Until we know Dad's real name, we're at a dead end."

Viktoria flicks through the pages and pages of competitors. The Trocadero night club held monthly competitions over five years, and every entrant is listed. "Claudia," she says after several minutes. "There's a Philip listed here whose partner was Katerina. Neither competitor gave their last name."

"Does that mean something?"

She tugs at her hair. "The name of the partner. How could I have forgotten? We've been searching for a Kat, Kathy, Catherine or Kathleen, but Katerina is the full name of the young woman, Kat. The one in the Melbourne Cup photograph."

"Their hands were touching in that picture," I say.

"You still got a copy of it?" she asks.

I scroll through my phone and hand it over.

"It can't be her in the dance competition," Viktoria says. "When I was a child, Mum said how sad it was for someone so young to be confined to a wheelchair."

"What happened to her?"

"I don't know."

I expect Dermot to arrive at four o'clock, but he's fifteen minutes early. The way he greets us both with such ease is enviable.

"I saw a rainbow on the way over." Dermot winks. "It ended right over this place, Claudia. Now I'm excited at the prospect of finding a pot of gold."

For some reason, I blush. I'm sure the gold he's talking about is solving the mystery, but when he looks at me, I feel shiny and valuable.

Viktoria spreads out the photocopies of her extensive family tree, and points. "We have Kat's full name," she says. "It was there all along, but my mother named so many people as cousins and uncles when they weren't, I'd lost track."

There's little in the way of small talk. It's all business and I listen in as Viktoria and Dermot crosscheck Dermot's spreadsheet against Viktoria's. They're on a mission, and I don't want to interrupt with questions. They move on from Katerina to the rest of the family, but Dad's name doesn't come up.

"Viktor and Viktoria, is it a Russian custom to name family members by the male and female version of the same name?" Dermot asks.

"I don't think so," Viktoria replies. "But my mother spoke fondly of her cousin Viktor. He died in the war."

"Do you know which country he fought for?"

"I never asked. He was an officer on passenger liners, then worked on a hospital ship during the war. It was sunk by a U-boat."

Dermot furiously scribbles notes.

I'm out of my depth as Viktoria and Dermot annotate and crossmatch documents, so I assign myself bringer of drinks and snacks and watch from the kitchen. I'm on the outside looking in, wishing I had more to offer. I run my finger around the rim of a wine glass, trying to make it sing, while Dermot nods and smiles at Viktoria's meticulous notes. The thought of my messy index card and post-it-note collection makes me shudder.

Six months ago, I could never have imagined sitting here like this. A completely new house, a new sister, and Dermot—genealogist extraordinaire. It's all good, except for a twinge of emotion I don't recognise. Surely, it can't be jealousy? Whatever it is, when Dermot smiles at Viktoria my cheeks burn.

As if Dermot senses my thoughts, he looks up. "Sorry for not explaining the process, Claudia. It's complicated and if I stop, I'll lose track."

Viktoria wipes her brow in mock exhaustion and pulls another Dad face, then Dermot smiles in a way that immediately pulls me back into their circle.

"At least we've found Katerina's identity," I say, restating the win.

"Except tracing her after 1948 is taking forever," Viktoria says.

Dermot throws his hands into the air. "As my gran

used to say: *Slow is every foot on an unknown path.* We've lost track of her on electoral rolls, so she's probably changed her name. It's unlikely she's still alive."

"And even if she is, we have no clue as to whether she'd even remember your Dad's real name." Viktoria looks as defeated as Dermot.

I stand tall. I have a worthwhile suggestion, "What about census records? You said Bridgett was a servant for Kat's family. Wouldn't Dad and his mother be listed with other names living in the same household?"

Dermot and Viktoria stare wide-eyed.

"You're right," Dermot says excitedly, then frowns as he slumps in the chair. "Unfortunately, the census records between 1921 and 1976 aren't available online."

"We can visit the primary source in the state library," Viktoria says. "You'll both come?"

"I can't," I say. "I have job interviews over the next two weeks, but please go. I'm dying to find out Dad's true identity."

As they make plans, I curl up on the chair in front of the river-view window. I could have asked them to wait a week and worked around the interviews, but with my new regular movie viewings with Mum, I'd have to make an excuse. While I *can* avoid telling her about continuing the search behind her back, I *can't* lie directly to her face.

Viktoria and Dermot are still punching information into laptops at nine o'clock, when I call an end to it.

He leaves reluctantly and I settle on the sofa next to Viktoria. The river is dark, and the boats have been tucked into bed, but a noise makes me jump to my feet.

Shit. The apartment intercom. I stare at the door then at Viktoria, my arms flapping of their own accord as if they're performing magic. If only there was a vanishing act to make Viktoria disappear.

It buzzes three times before I answer. "Hello?"

"Bonnie here. Mum's with me. It's probably much too late for a visit."

My voice rasps through my constricted throat, "It is after nine."

Mum doesn't need an intercom; the echo of her reply bounces up the stairwell in the shared hall. "There was a traffic accident on the highway. Your place was near the detour. I told Bonnie you'd still be awake."

I flick the unlock release for the outside door and press the palm of my hand against my forehead. "Prepare yourself," I say to Viktoria.

In the seconds it takes Mum to walk the two flights of stairs, I play out the most likely scenario. She'll spot the likeness to Dad and clench her teeth in an iron grimace, tightening her jowls into a menacing mask of outrage. She'll point and yell abuse until everything is ruined. I should have been honest. I turn the handle and wait for misery to fill the room.

Mum is smiling when she enters, and my heart tumbles at the knowledge my failed vanishing trick will be the cruellest of acts. Dissolving my mother's smile.

She raises an inquisitive eyebrow towards Viktoria, then back at me. "You should have said you had a visitor."

My heart settles and I let out a long breath. Mum hasn't picked the resemblance. She doesn't know.

Mum slips her handbag over her shoulder ready to leave, and Bonnie says, "Yes. Come on, Mum. Come on. We'll go." Her voice is too hurried and jittery and Mum stops in her tracks, taking slow steps towards Viktoria.

"Your eyes are amber. Amber-gold. Exactly like my late husband's."

Viktoria closes her eyes slowly, pressing her lips in silence.

"Are you related?" Mum asks.

"She's Dad's daughter," Bonnie blurts. "Our half-sister."

Mum's shoulders slump as if all life is draining out. Anger would have been easier to witness than this collapse. She seems older and sadder. "I knew my Philip had someone else, but of all the things to keep hidden—he abandoned a child."

I reach for Mum's hand. "I can explain."

"Stop." She brushes me away, brandishing her car keys like a weapon. "Don't come over. Don't phone."

From the doorway she whispers into steepled fingers, "First my husband betrayed me, now my daughters."

Chapter Thirty-Eight

KATERINA

Melbourne, 1945

The rain was relentless throughout May, and we stayed indoors. For weeks Philip and I exchanged love letters, but I kept my pregnancy secret.

My belly grew rounder, the quilt was complete, and each morning when *The Melbourne Argus* was pushed through our letter box, Mary read the latest news of war. There were increasing signs of Nazi forces in Italy becoming disorganised, but the battle continued. None of us knew where Philip was stationed, and it was unlikely to be Italy, but wherever his unit fought, we hoped the common enemy was close to defeat.

We spent hours discussing Germany's recruitment of women to fight alongside men. The conversation moved to Soviet female soldiers; in particular, the famous sniper, Lyudmila Pavlichenko. While Mama and Mary argued whether Lyudmila's name had hard or soft syllables, and whether she sounded less like a shooter and more like a goddess, I continued knitting the tiny booties. With every stitch and twirl of wool, I hoped that war, with all its evil, would improve the status of women. If I carried a baby girl, then maybe, just maybe, there'd come a day when women wouldn't be blamed and shamed for shared sins, such as mine.

That afternoon, feeling particularly positive about good news on the war front, we stopped knitting to listen to the wireless, steaming mugs of milky cocoa at the ready to clink in celebration. Mary convinced us there would be an announcement. Perhaps the end of the war. No such proclamation came.

I was returning our empty mugs to the kitchen when I was startled by a loud knock. A telegram boy stood outside, his uniform visible through the door's lace curtains. The weight of worry collapsed my legs and I sank into the kitchen chair, calling out to Mama.

He rang the doorbell twice before we summoned the bravery to answer.

Although the telegram was addressed to Mama Bridgett as next of kin, Mary opened the envelope.

"Philip's been injured."

Mama read the telegram, covering her mouth. Although silent, her face flashed sentiment like neon signs outside hotels on Flinders Street. I couldn't identify the specific emotions.

"Any details?" Mary asked.

Although the last thing I wanted was bad news, I leaned in to listen.

The telegram shook in Mama's hand as she inspected both front and back. "The army are shipping Philip home on the twenty-fifth."

The neon message was clearer. It zigzagged between RELIEVED and TERRIFIED.

Philip would return from war alive. But in what condition?

I took deep, then shallow breaths, as if consciously changing the rhythm of my breathing could alter reality. I wanted to believe the injury was minor, but I'd heard many tales of young men patched together and returned to battle. If Philip was being sent home, he was too broken to fight.

Mama stood, appearing twenty years older. With hunched shoulders, she searched through the sideboard. It was hard to imagine anything at the back of a cupboard offering comfort, but she found a candle, and carefully wiped off the dust. Then as if performing a ritual, she set it on a saucer centred in front of Philip's photograph.

It took three attempts to light it and each time the flame failed to catch she gave an almost inaudible sob. When the flame finally burst into life, I let out a breath I didn't know I was holding.

"Let's pray," Mama said.

Then, although I'd never prayed before, I got down on my knees and searched desperately for God.

Chapter Thirty-Nine

CLAUDIA

Fremantle, 2018

After discovering Bonnie and I hid the knowledge of Dad's illegitimate child, Mum refused to talk to us. So, I was shocked when she called this morning, out of the blue, ending the agonising silence and inviting us to her place.

She's been stewing for three weeks, and as Dad often said: *'revenge is a dish best served cold'*.

Bonnie and I are quiet on the drive over. There've been many times where I've wished Bonnie would shut up, but this is not one of them.

"You okay?" I ask.

"Shit-scared."

If my fearless sister is frightened, what hope is there for me?

A stony-faced Mum opens the door, but under the serious mask she looks pleased. She has something up her sleeve.

"Well?" She pushes us both inside. "Do you feel like you've entered the wrong house?"

It takes me a moment to realise she's talking about her new living room décor. I'm stunned. New sofa, new everything.

"I love it, Mum. You've styled it perfectly." For once, I'm not complimenting Mum's decor to get on her good side. It's actually gorgeous.

"F-fabulous," Bonnie says. She never uses the word fabulous. I suspect she just stopped herself swearing.

"My new life," Mum says with a wicked laugh. "I stripped your dad's favourite room. Found a new set-up in a glossy catalogue and asked the store to deliver the lot, including accessories. They took my old furniture away, and I hope they bloody burned it."

"You didn't keep anything? Where's your sentimentality woman?" Bonnie asks.

I hold a swanky new cushion like a shield, marvelling at Bonnie's bravery, particularly after being shit scared on the way here.

"No. If your father got to have two lives, I'm having my second, even if it is in my own home."

I work up enough courage to broach the inevitable. "We didn't want to hurt you Mum. That's why we didn't tell you about Viktoria."

"It's more hurtful being kept in the dark," she says. "Anyway, Dermot turned up while the furniture people were delivering this lot, and I was too slow to lock him out. We ended up having a long chat and it made me think."

"What did he say?" Bonnie asks.

I stick out my bottom lip. Dermot could have warned me.

"He told me Viktoria's age. She was born long before your father met me. You have to admit she looks young."

Relieved tears wash my cheeks. "I'm glad you invited us."

"Stop it," she says. "Even if the Irish fella hadn't come over, I was always going to forgive my daughters."

I blink to stop the waterworks. "Is there anything I can do to make it better?"

"Bring out the box of movies you found in the shed. It's our wedding anniversary and I reckon Dad will be looking down to see if I play our favourite film. When he does, he'll see I've cleared out everything he ever touched." Mum laughs. "Who says you can't get even with the dead?"

While Mum's rummaging through the box, Bonnie tells her about the search, "Dad met you after he'd stopped making child maintenance payments." Bonnie adds, "That's why he was broke."

"I knew he had a secret, but I'm glad he wasn't a cad."

It's weird seeing Mum both teary and stubborn at the same time.

"That's all we've got," I say. "Except Dad changed his name more than once."

Mum bristles. "If all his earnings went to Viktoria, where did he get money for the bonds?"

"We haven't found the source yet," I say. "And we won't now, because we've stopped looking."

"So, the whole thing was a waste of time. I told Dermot as much." She holds up the chosen movie and shouts at the ceiling, "I'm watching this because I liked it, not because you liked it, too." As she removes the large film cassette from the case, a piece of paper falls to the floor.

"Oh Lord. It's from your Dad. A letter from heaven." Mum covers her face.

Bonnie grabs the note and starts reading it:

> *My darling wife,*
> *You might be able to fool others with your brusque exterior, but I know you're sentimental underneath. By the time you read this I'll be gone, and if my intuition serves me correctly, which it usually does, today is our wedding anniversary and you've chosen to watch Breakfast at Tiffany's.*
> *Do me a favour, put on your little black dress and do that chignon thing with your hair. I lied when I said you were as beautiful as Audrey Hepburn. You are better. It's that fighting spirit of yours, Hillary. Incredibly sexy.*

Bonnie sticks her fingers down her throat in a mock gag. "Should I stop reading?"

Mum waves her hand. "Keep going."

> *Before the movie begins, go outside to the Geraldton Wax bush and pick yourself a bouquet. I sprinkled extra love on those plants so I could send some tonight and forever.*
> *Now to the serious bit. If my assessment of events is correct, and it usually is, those feisty*

*daughters of ours will have dug up disturbing
facts. Let me explain. There was a woman I
loved—long, long ago and the events surrounding
the end of that relationship caused me what I
believed at the time to be irreparable heart-
break. I was wrong, Hillary. You mended my
heart perfectly.*

Happy anniversary love.

Philip.

"What?" Mum shrieks and shakes her fist at the ceiling. "You could have written about the money, not
bloody Geraldton Wax." She points at me. "Claudia, get
on the phone to that Dermot of yours. We need him to
finish the search."

After I phone Dermot, we go back to the movie. He
arrives at Mum's door before we've finished.

"I'll get one thing straight," Mum says before he's
had time to say hello. "Sit quietly until the movie is
over. You've missed the good bits, so you've got time
think about my new rule. After the Viktoria debacle,
there's no room for secrets. Every bit of information
must be shared."

Dermot shrugs.

"You were prettier than Audrey Hepburn," Bonnie
says as the credits roll.

Mum tries not to smile.

Dermot scratches his chin, no doubt wondering why
he was summoned.

"It's about this," I whisper, handing over Dad's note.
"It was in the movie case."

"So, when are we going to start?" Mum says.

"Did you find anything in the census records?" I ask.

"I didn't go to Melbourne. Viktoria and I thought we'd caused enough upset."

"You'd better get cracking then." Mum stands as if expecting Dermot to hop on the imaginary plane waiting outside her door.

"There's no need. I went back over the records and it was there all along. Perhaps I should start calling you Mrs O'Patrick."

"O'Patrick?" Mum, Bonnie and I chorus.

"I revisited trails marked as dead ends—like the passenger ship manifest. When I looked through the documents, I noticed a name from Viktoria's family tree. Viktor Alexander was listed as 'first mate' on the passenger ship Philip's mother travelled on from Southampton to Australia."

"What does that mean for Philip?" Mum asks.

"Well, it connects Bridgett to her workplace. She might have been introduced to the Alexander family through Viktor. Since there's no record of Bridgett marrying, I thought it likely that Philip's last name was his mother's maiden name. O'Patrick."

"So, we are really O'Patricks, not McLeods?" Bonnie stamps her foot and wails.

"What's wrong?" I ask.

"Bonnie Ursula McLeod. BUM. I was proud of those initials. They defined me. But all along I've been a BUO. I don't even know what a BUO is."

"I think your personality is set by now." Dermot grins.

"What next?" I ask.

"I'm searching baptism records of a Sean, Francis, or Philip O'Patrick," Dermot says.

"I still don't understand all these connections. Viktoria's mother was introduced to Dad by her cousin, but we're somehow all related?" I shrug.

Bonnie jumps up. "I tell you, there's still a fucking lot of names and missing facts to sort out."

"You're not too old for me to burn your mouth with hot English mustard." Mum gives her *the* stare, but it isn't convincing.

"Give it up, Mum," Bonnie says. "You did your best, but it's time to admit you failed. Despite your proper-ness, you brought up a foul-mouthed floozie."

"Floozie," I repeat, laughing for a moment, but it dawns on me that Bonnie is right about Dad's background. There's a fucking long way to go.

Chapter Forty

KATERINA

Melbourne, 1945 July

For days of end-to-end freezing weather, I'd wriggled into my clothing under the warmth of the coverlet. On a milder day when I got out of bed to dress, my reflection in the dressing table mirror surprised me. I resembled a balloon ready to burst.

I sought out Mama and Mary to show off my blossoming belly, expecting them to be boiling the kettle and warming their hands near the wood stove, but the kitchen was empty.

The whispering from the living room was too soft to make out all the words, but I shook as I put extra wood in the stove. They were discussing Philip. The seriousness of their tone made me shiver.

"Is that you, Katerina?" Mary called from the living room.

They both appeared at the kitchen door, their expressions stopping me in my tracks.

"No bad news, please." I was tempted to cover my ears like I'd done on nights when Mother and Father fought. "You mustn't deliver bad news, or I won't sit with you."

"Oh, it is nothing like that," Mama said. "We didn't mean to worry you."

Mary took my arm and led me into the living room, where Mama patted the seat of an armchair and plumped an embroidered cushion for behind my back. The chair was comfortable, but my hand trembled as I took the cup of tea Mary poured.

With the saucer resting on my swollen belly, I sipped and tried to calm down.

Perhaps the baby sensed my agitation, because it kicked up a storm, bouncing the saucer to the floor. Mama ignored the fallen crockery and placed her hand on my belly.

Her expression was pure joy as the baby kicked her hand. "My grandchild."

"This baby's a wild one," Mary said.

"Philip never stopped moving when he was little." Mama's smile broadened. "More energy than a bag full of beans, that lad."

"Not long now," Mary said to my writhing bump. "We're ready to meet you, but best you wait until your father comes home."

At the mention of Philip, Mama became solemn. "Kat, we are all looking forward to his homecoming but we need to prepare ourselves. Although the follow-up letter indicated a knee injury, Philip might have invisible scars."

Mary and Mama told of men returning from the Great War only to stare at walls. Men who carried the weight of death and were no longer the carefree youths their sweethearts had kissed goodbye.

Mama stopped when she registered my dismay. "Whatever happens, we'll get through it together."

I wrapped my arms around myself, trying to contain my feelings and watched Mary stack logs in the fireplace. The smack of wood against wood competed with Mama's furiously clacking knitting needles.

Being rejected because of the pregnancy had seemed the most terrible outcome, but I now realised how much harder it would be to have Philip return broken.

Loosening my collar did little to overcome my anxiety, so I excused myself to the kitchen to splash my face with icy tap-water. My legs weakened at the thought of Philip having a constant battlefield trapped inside his head, but I held back tears for Mama's sake and returned dry-eyed to the living room.

Seeing my expression, Mary rubbed her hands as if she was wiping off the gloom. "I've an idea. Let's put our nervous energy to use. Philip might not manage the stairs with his injury, so let's convert the dining room into a downstairs bedroom."

She was right, our energy soared as we traded the weight of worry for physical work. Although I wasn't allowed to lift heavy furniture, I did my best to make the room a wonderful welcome-home. It was a splendid plan.

Mary and Mama improved my spirits yet again, by suggesting I move into the downstairs bedroom with Philip.

"Aren't you worried we're not yet married," I asked.

"Too late to worry about that." Mama looked at Mary and laughed. "That ship has sailed."

The following day, an army ambulance pulled up outside, and I bolted into the kitchen where I leaned against the open windowsill and commanded my heart to slow down. A new worry had appeared from nowhere. What if allowing my pregnancy to announce itself was the wrong decision? I should have warned Philip. What if he rejected me because I'd withheld the truth?

Despite the cold draft my hands became clammy.

I listened as the medics helped Philip inside, but I resisted the urge to run out and greet him. The military nurses took forever to settle him into the bed, and I trembled as I waited for the signal from Mama or Mary that everything was okay.

Seconds after the door closed behind the medical team, I heard Philip's voice for the first time in months, and although there was a hint of impatience, he sounded robust and full of life.

"Where is Katerina?" he yelled, impatient and eager.

I edged tentatively towards the door and waited.

"She is outside, carrying a wonderful surprise." I could hear Mama smile.

I looked towards the heavens, then stepped inside, my heart racing with a mixture of love and fear.

Philip's eyes trailed from my head to my toes, up to my middle, and back to my face. His look of astonishment was heart-warming. "Katerina, you look even more beautiful than I remembered."

When he opened his arms towards me, I ran. We struggled to accommodate his injured leg and my growing bump, but found a way to embrace each other in a way that said, 'I will never again let you go'.

Once settled as close as decency allowed, he stroked my belly. "Why didn't you tell me?"

"You had enough to worry about without this." I stretched my dress tightly to show how prominent it was.

"It's unexpected, yet marvellous. We'd best find a priest to marry us. By the look of you, we need to act soon."

Up until then, my pregnancy had been about 'me' and what 'I' would do, but now my thoughts were beautifully of 'we'.

The situation was not ideal, but we were in this together.

Philip's injury might have prevented him from walking, but neither pain, nor immobility barred us from making love. That grand dining room, with four-poster bed, was a haven from the problems of the world.

Mama Bridgett and Mary kindly made themselves scarce, leaving the house often, despite the cold.

There was only warmth to be found inside. Compared to the hurried, urgent lovemaking in the loft, we had all the time in the world, and we took it. His kisses were slow, slow, and oh so sweet. When Philip asked me to stand before him naked, I was surprisingly unselfconscious. He ran his fingers over every part of my body and pronounced me a goddess. He worshipped every swelling curve and I worshipped him.

Our minds and bodies belonged to each other.

Without worry of pregnancy, or being caught, we were in heaven. Within weeks we would become parents, so we stole every moment to bask in love, and lust, and the indescribable magic of us.

We had the perfect honeymoon before the wedding, but Philip wanted us to marry as soon as possible.

Philip and Mama went to visit the priest. Mama half-jokingly suggested putting Philip in a push-along cart, but he managed to walk the four blocks to the church with the aid of wooden crutches and Mama's arm.

When they returned, he looked defeated and I knew it wasn't from the physical ordeal. Mama helped him onto the bed, leaving us together and shutting the door behind her.

"The church won't make an allowance," he said. "We must be twenty-one or have parental permission."

"Yet, you're old enough to fight and die for your country?" I was angry.

"Come here, Kat." He wrapped his arms around my waist and leaned his ear to my belly. "It's only a couple of weeks until I can throw away these bloody crutches, I'll talk to your father then. I'm sure he'll grant permission to marry."

The following day, an envelope in Father's handwriting arrived. Bile rose in the back of my throat. My pregnancy was too advanced to hide it with frills or flounces and hiding an injured Philip would be impossible.

"Open it," Mary said. "We'll think of something. We always do."

Dear Katerina

Your mother and I were planning a surprise visit to Melbourne, but unfortunately, we cannot make the trip. Your mother is plagued by migraines so does not wish to travel. I considered travelling alone, but after reading of the influenza outbreak in Melbourne, I worry about a repeat of the Spanish flu and cannot chance it.

Please pass on my apologies to cousin Mary. We will visit once the winter chills have passed.

Father

We hadn't spoken about such a visit at this late stage, but it had been on my mind. After reading the letter, I tore it into confetti sized pieces and threw it into the fire. The three of us women danced, and Philip clapped us along.

As I danced, I sang a silent song to our baby, "Wait, wait, wait my little one. I hope your daddy convinces your grandfather. Then we can marry before you are born."

Chapter Forty-One

KATERINA

Melbourne, 1945 August

Philip and I entwined ourselves like vines. I could not tell where my body ended and his began.

Lightning hit frighteningly close and the deafening thunder sounded like boulders cascading down the roof, I grabbed his arm and he held me even tighter.

"Are you frightened?" he asked.

"Not with you next to me." I buried my head against his body, nuzzled between the muscles of his chest, and listened to his heartbeat.

Philip pulled the coverlet over our head creating a lover's cave, and we forgot the storm. His voice, deep and mellow, hummed as he whispered sweet words to me and the baby.

"You are both so perfect," he said, resting his head against my abdomen. "I could caress your beautiful skin for ever." He kissed my belly and we drifted off to sleep.

I don't know how long I'd slept when Philip woke me. "Something's happening, Kat, your belly is hard."

I felt it too, from the inside out, but I'd been having mild contractions on and off for hours. "Don't worry," I said. "The doctor said this could happen for days before the baby comes."

I had trouble going back to sleep, so contented myself with rearranging the pillows and watching my beautiful Philip asleep at my side.

The storm stopped, but the contractions continued, and as the aching became stronger, I closed my eyes to distract myself with an unrealistic daydream. We would take the baby to see my parents and they'd fall in love with the little one. Father would be reasonable, and Mother would ignore the gossip. In this rose-coloured version, they would congratulate Philip and me and encourage us to marry. All would be well.

I drifted off on such happy thoughts and began to dream of Philip; handsome and laughing, chasing our child in my family's garden. I tried to follow them as they disappeared behind the trees, but I fell into a puddle and called for Philip to help me.

The puddle was oh so wet, and as I climbed my way out of the dream into wakefulness, I became aware of warm liquid gushing between my legs. I grabbed a towel from the night stand to stop birth fluid seeping onto the bed and counted the seconds as my abdomen cramped with pain.

Only two minutes apart.

I shook Philip awake. "The baby's coming."

He shot out of bed, grabbed his crutches and yelled for help as he hobbled towards the stairs. "Mama! Mary! The baby!"

Immediately Mama replied, "Is Kat all right?"

"I think so."

Mary's voice followed, "I'll get dressed."

"No need for panic," I heard Mama say. "Women do this all the time. I'll stay with Kat and encourage her to keep doing whatever she's doing. Mary, can you fetch the doctor?"

"Shouldn't we take her to the hospital?" Philip asked with a note of panic.

"A hospital? Not unless it's necessary. The staff interfere when nature needs to take its course."

Mama stuck her head through my door. "I'll be there soon, my love. I'm going to assign jobs for Philip, so he doesn't pass out from worry. We don't need two patients."

Mary sat on the edge of the bed wearing her hat, coat, and gloves. "It's almost morning, I'll call the midwife and fetch the doctor."

The contractions came in waves and Mama gave me a glass of sherry. "Take small sips. It'll relax you and dull the pain."

As the ache in my lower back increased, Mama encouraged me to squeeze her hand and reminded me to breathe. Philip's crutches tapped as he paced outside the door, and I took a short breath with each strike of wood against tile. The birth was close, but neither Mary nor the doctor had returned.

"I'm stepping into the kitchen for a few minutes," Mama said to Philip. "It won't take long to get what I need. Talk to Kat."

"Is there anything I can do?" Philip asked me, wringing his hands.

"Pull this baby out of me," I gasped. "I'm afraid I might burst."

"Tell me about your perfect day," he said softly. "I hope I'm in it."

Despite the pain, I nodded yes. I pictured Philip, me, and a beautiful child under a cloudless sky.

"Is the baby in your daydream?" he asked.

"Of course."

When there was a break in the contractions, I told Philip how I'd seen us dressed in our Sunday best beside a lake. "We are all there, you, me, the baby, Mama, and Mary," I said. "And we were crying."

"Tears of joy," Mama said. Until she spoke, I was unaware she'd returned. "Beautiful thoughts," she added. "You'll need to concentrate now, Kat, because you're about to meet your child."

My lower body was being crushed in a vice. Torn apart by horses. I dug my fingernails into my knees and heard screaming that must have been my own.

Mama lifted the blankets to check on my progress. "It's too late for the doctor," she said. "Philip squeeze Kat's hand, it's time for her to push."

"I can't... I cannot," I cried over and over. But I did.

"One more push and we'll be deciding on a name," Mama said as she moved my hand to between my legs. I could feel my baby's head. It was already through. "See. It's here. Come on, Kat, you're doing well."

I pushed so hard I feared I would split in two. Then, I heard new voices. Mary was back with the doctor and a midwife. But there was no stopping now.

I squeezed with all my might and my life changed again. This time, it became all about her.

Chapter Forty-Two

CLAUDIA

Fremantle, 2018

I surprised myself by not asking Bonnie's advice on what to wear to my job interviews. I managed to feel confident and put my best foot forward while banning the negative voice inside my head suggesting I'd only been short-listed because their interview quota had to include a forty-something female. I must have done okay because yesterday I received a commencement advice for my new job in investigative accounting.

To celebrate, I've invited Mum, Bonnie, Matt and Dermot around for afternoon tea. I'm disappointed my boys can't join us, but I have enough time to phone Aaron and Josh with the news before my guests arrive.

I phone Aaron first, expecting to leave a message.

He picks up. "Mumsie? I was just thinking about you."

"Were you?"

The Dancer at the End of His Bed

"Yep. Playing our old game of guessing what clouds look like."

I laugh. "I have news. I'm starting a new job with the Western Australian Police."

"Wow. Following in Josh's footsteps. When do you start?"

"Not as a police officer." I chuckle. "A member of the civilian support team. Forensic accounting."

"Congratulations 007." Aaron laughs and I picture him poking out his tongue. "They're lucky to get you."

In an effort to stop Aaron feeling uncomfortable, I include Oliver in the conversation. "How's your dad?" I bite my fingernail, hoping his reply doesn't ruin my celebratory mood.

"He messaged this morning. Full of new holiday plans."

My shoulders feel lighter. "I'm honestly glad he's happy."

"He's on Instagram now, Mumsie. You should check out his photos. I reckon you'd get a good laugh. Yesterday, he was standing in a teashop staring wistfully at vintage teapots."

"But he only drinks coffee."

"He's trying new things." Aaron coughs.

There's a warmth inside my chest. Pride. Oliver's picked himself up and put his life together. We're both going to be okay.

"One thing I should warn you, Mumsie, before you look at his pictures." Aaron's voice is uncharacteristically gentle, as if he's soothing a child. "Dad's met someone."

I know from recent experience how difficult it is to reveal sensitive information about one parent to the other, so I project happiness into my voice. "Who? Do tell?"

"A woman he works with. She shares Dad's obsession with Greek mythology. He noticed her reading *The Iliad* in the lunchroom. Apparently, she's three years older, and divorced. They're planning a holiday to Greece."

After I get off the phone, I curl up in my river view seat. Oliver has found new love. I let it sit a little, waiting for a sting that doesn't come.

I call Josh to tell him the job news.

"It's all going well for both you and Dad, then." He sounds relieved. "Dad has a holiday planned, you have a new job, and a thing with Dermot."

"Yes," I say. "Dermot and I are on Pop's trail now."

"Not the research. I meant the romance." Josh clears his throat. "Unless Grandma wasn't supposed to tell me."

"What romance? What did Grandma say?" I ask.

"She says you're both in love, but like the characters in her favourite movies, you haven't yet got to the part where you're ready to admit it."

"Your grandmother is a crackpot with too much time on her hands. There's nothing going on." I feel an unfamiliar lump in my throat as I deny it. Perhaps, it's the kernel of truth in Mum's gossip.

I'm relieved when Josh has to dash off.

The intercom buzzes as I'm arranging plates of sweet and savoury snacks.

Mum, Bonnie, Matt and Dermot arrive together, and the first thing Bonnie does is pass her phone to Matt. "I want selfies against the exposed brick. I've dressed to match the décor." She flicks her new earrings. "Steampunk. I bought them to match the industrial vibe."

Dermot laughs, Mum snorts, and Matt raises his eyebrows as he smiles. The man is a saint. Bonnie has an entire bedroom wall housing her earring collection and he finds it endearing.

"Take plenty," she says. "I'll choose the most flattering for Instagram."

"You could follow Oliver," I suggest.

"Oliver on Insta? You're joking."

I shake my head and am about to laugh when Mum gives me a pitiful smile and almost kisses my forehead. She never quite makes skin contact.

"Don't blame yourself about Oliver. You weren't to know he was unhappy. Men and their secrets. How much easier would life be if men said what that they meant?"

"He's found someone now, Mum. He's okay."

To avoid more Oliver talk, I take drink orders, "Coffee, tea or champagne?"

Mum doesn't take the hint. "Are you sure you don't want to give Oliver another chance? I've given one to your father."

"No way," Bonnie answers for me. "Where's the fucking voodoo doll, Claudia? I'm going to give Oliver another stab."

Matt slinks off into the kitchen muttering something about drinks to sidestep the scene.

Dermot, on the other hand, leans in to watch the show. "A voodoo doll?"

"Please. Everyone. I don't want to talk about Oliver. We're here to celebrate my new job."

"Oh, my fucking lordy. I'm not letting it go." Bonnie

holds Mum's shoulders. "Oliver does the wrong thing and you take his side."

"A marriage isn't something to dismiss because of a misunderstanding. Unless of course, Claudia wants to throw everything away, now she's found herself a new friend."

To my absolute horror, Mum points to Dermot. My cheeks burn and I look at the ground hoping for a sink-hole to appear. When I look up, he's smiling. He doesn't seem at all worried by her suggestion.

"New friend?" Dermot says. "I'll take it."

To shut out my embarrassment, I cover my face and pretend I'm here with a normal family.

I open them to Dermot smiling warmly, holding a crumpled paper bag towards me. "A celebration gift. I hope you don't mind the lazy, yet environmentally friendly, version of wrapping paper."

"No gifts," I say. But I reach inside to see what he's brought. "A drawing?"

I know immediately it's a piece by his late wife. It has the distinct style of portraits at Dermot's house. This sketch shows a mother and two small boys collecting shells along a beach.

My voice trembles. "She has hair and a face like mine."

"Maybe it *is* you. She drew pictures wherever she went." Dermot closes his eyes for a heartbeat or two, and I imagine how much he misses his wife.

"You know," he says. "I've always found the woman in this sketch attractive."

Mum's mouth makes a silent 'Oooh' as she lifts her eyebrows. It's an unmistakable challenge. *I told you, Claudia. Now what are you going to do about it?*

I hold my hand against the warmth in my chest. A special picture, just for me.

Then, I remember Dad's painting.

"Hang on a minute," I say, almost hyperventilating in my race to the top shelf of the cupboard where I stored it.

I hold it up to show Bonnie. "Look at the faces."

"You wouldn't recognise anyone from those," Mum says. "I told you, your father was no artist."

"The child is Viktoria," Bonnie's voice is high with excitement. "But the woman isn't Mary."

"Yes," I say. "Katerina is Viktoria's real mother."

"Then who's the dancer?" Bonnie throws her arms around like a grounded teenager.

"What dancer?" Mum asks.

I dash back to the bedroom for the dance medal, then find the Melbourne Cup photo and zoom in. "Look!"

"What are we looking at now?" Mum asks.

"Around her neck. It's tucked under her neckline, but I swear Katerina is the dancing woman. She's wearing a medal like this one."

Dermot leans in and stares at her young radiant face. "What happened to her? She looks the picture of health, but Viktoria said she couldn't walk."

A dropping sensation inside my chest tells me both mysteries are related.

Chapter Forty-Three

KATERINA

'The Figs' Sydney, 2018

Each time I press record, I become more curious about the stories Maria tells. She speaks at length and with animation, especially after I've calmed her with accounts of my youth. Izzy once called us the odd couple, and I think she's right. Yesterday, Maria recounted what appeared to be three separate events, all in Italian. Although she throws in the occasional English phrase, there's never enough to give me a clue about the content. I wonder what adventures Maria enjoyed back in the old country?

If we could have a proper conversation, I'd ask if she too has parts of her life she wishes she could change.

I kept track of my baby girl for a time, but didn't want to intrude in her life. Now, this magical internet wizardry has failed. There's no trace of Viktoria online.

Not that I'd reach out to her, but a picture or name would comfort me. I've revisited my decision so many times, wondering what other path I could have taken. I'd blocked those thoughts for so long I'd almost doubted her existence. But after talking to Maria about my pregnancy, I cannot block it any longer.

I decide to ask Joe for help.

After our usual chitchat about his family history research project, we set out the afternoon tea and admire Maria's latest drawings. The state of her sketches is a window to her mind.

"Your mother's drawings match her mood," I say. "On days where we walk outside and she listens to my stories, she's calm. Her drawings then, measure up to accomplished artists, and sometimes she speaks a little English."

Joe's reaction is unexpected. His eyes fill with tears, and happiness overflows down his cheeks.

"Thank you so much, Miss Katerina. I wish there was something I could do for you."

"There is. I need a favour, Joe."

"Anything."

I pull my iPad from the side pocket of my wheel-chair. "Can you show me how to look up details of my family?"

"I'd love to." Joe saves three ancestral research sites to get me started, and shows me the bookmark symbol to find them myself. "These are free, but there are many more places to look. I'm warning you," he says, "the family history caper is addictive."

"Oh my, it could be just the ticket to occupy me when I'm bored."

"Who knows what we'll both uncover." He feigns horror.

"I do like a mystery," I say. "I could be descended from Russian royalty." I wink so he knows I'm joking.

"I expect a full report—every discovery." Joe wraps his arm around my shoulder and gives me a fond squeeze.

As soon as Joe's gone, I take my parents' birth and death certificates out of my personal folder and delve straight into the research.

Despite spending a large part of the past week researching the Alexander family tree, I've been denied access to many records. It's clear I can't progress without a credit card. Something I do not have.

I watch Maria sitting beside me, drawing up a storm. When Joe turns up, she snaps her sketchpad shut.

"She's produced lots of drawings but she's not showing me," I say.

"Secretive, eh?" Joe winks. "Dare I even look?"

"It doesn't matter what Maria's drawing. I'm spending a lot of time on this family history research and I don't feel as guilty when she's busy. I'm as content as a mother whose child has made friends at school."

Joe laughs. "You shouldn't feel guilty. It's not your job to occupy Mum, and you're not old enough to be her mother," he says.

"I am. Your mother's only seventy-three and I'm ninety-two."

I press the heel of my hand against my eyes to stop the tears. Maria is around the age of my daughter. I look at the ageing Maria. I've lost so much time.

Joe looks thoughtfully at his mother, then turns to

me and nods. "I feel foolish. The age difference between a twenty-year-old and a forty-year-old is so clear, but..."

"That's okay. Most people lump old people into the same generation."

I change the subject to save Joe from embarrassment. "Pass me one of the biscuits, Maria."

Maria taps Joe's hand and holds the almond biscotti close to his face. "*Delizioso.* Delicious."

"She is improving." Joe smiles.

"Yes, and although she's hiding her drawings, she's telling lots of stories and I'm recording them all. I hope they make sense."

"Have you seen any of Mum's latest sketches?" he asks.

"Faceless people, it's as if she catches each memory as the people turn away. I wonder if that's what dementia is like? The memories are there, but they escape before you see the details."

"Imagine this, Miss Katerina: Mum is telling you her life story and illustrating it at the same time. Wouldn't that be a treasure?" His eyes light up.

I visualise my own story illustrated: from my youth, on to when my mother and father were involved in their never-ending personal battle, and on to my own trauma. I shudder to imagine that life in pictures.

Chapter Forty-Four

CLAUDIA

Fremantle, 2018

My phone vibrates while I'm signing the contract for
my new job. I ignore it until I leave the recruitment
office, then retrieve it from my handbag. Dermot.

> Found something.

> What?

> Can't say. This is face-to-face serious.

> Really? Your place or mine?

> Mine. Bring swimmers.

> It's already late afternoon. Won't it be
> cold?

> Heated pool.

> Can you give me a clue?

No. Come in through the side gate, I'll be out the back.

I'll be a while. Have to buy some new work clothes.

The last part isn't quite true. I bought the work clothes before I signed the forms. I'm buying for time now. I'd rather swim in the evening. Preferably in the dark. Swimming requires me to be half-undressed in front of Dermot. Why would that bother me? Maybe subconsciously I do want more.

After collecting my swimwear, I drive back to Dermot's. My mind is fixated on his cryptic messages and I wonder what he's found. While I'm stopped at the traffic lights I reread his text, but still don't have a clue. I don't like written messages. Words on their own are ripe for misinterpretation. '*Your place or mine*' sounds like a Mae West line.

I'm still blushing when I pull up outside his house.

Through the side gate and behind a waist-high limestone wall topped with a hedge that forms an effective screen, there's a narrow rectangular lap pool, I hadn't noticed when we'd eaten our picnic lunch.

After completing a lap, Dermot looks up. His expression tells me he's found something unpleasant. "Come in. I find it calming."

"News that bad?" I ask, trying to raise my eyebrows light-heartedly. The butterflies flying around my stomach grow razorblade wings.

"Let's say we're heading into difficult territory." He rests on the edge of the pool.

"I'm not swimming, but I'm happy to wait."

I sit on a wooden bench, planning to savour my job

news for a few minutes, but I'm drawn to Dermot. He's wearing a pair of navy-blue swim shorts which make his skin look more tanned than usual. He lifts his body up on his arms to sit on the edge before lowering himself back into the water like a gymnast on parallel bars. I've never imagined Dermot without his clothes, but if I had, the image in my head would have been less... interesting. My cheeks burn with self-consciousness.

He disappears, fishlike, beneath the surface and I imagine myself dipping my foot against a jet of water. When I close my eyes, I can actually feel it swirling lasciviously around my heel and licking the spaces between my toes.

When Dermot springs out of the water, he appears to be moving in slow motion and although I know I'm staring, I can't stop. It's just a man getting out of water. Maybe I've developed a fetish? Bonnie would be proud.

Try as I might, I can't be calm with Dermot half-naked.

"Before I show you what I've found, there's something I want to tell you." Dermot drapes a towel around his shoulders.

"This doesn't sound good." What on Earth has Dad been up to? My mind creates a flip book of possible crimes against man and nature. "I love my dad," I say, "and there are many things I could forgive, but some would change the way I feel about him forever."

Dermot's eyes are gentle. "Actually, what I planned to say is how much I admire you. You're a grand woman, Claudia. Strong and no nonsense."

"I'm a woodcutter," I blurt out.

He crinkles his forehead. "An Aussie saying I've missed out on?"

"No. An event. When I was twelve, Bonnie and I were both in a school play. She was chosen to play a princess; I was the woodcutter. Tall and strong-looking, my teacher said."

"You're clever but you're not too cluey." He laughs. "I wasn't talking about the way you look, which, by the way, is pretty good, I was referring to your personality."

I avoid his gaze and look at the pool as I consider taking a dive of shame.

"Come on," Dermot says, "if we don't get inside, I'll freeze to death."

Inside the dining room, Dermot pauses. "Thank you for sharing your woodcutter story." He smiles. "We all carry wounds from the past and telling someone is a big step to healing them."

I give Dermot a gentle hug and brace myself for the news. "Okay. What have you found?"

"Nothing definite, but we need to discuss it."

"Show me," I say.

While Dermot fires up his computer, I look outside, and though it's too dark to see the garden, I realise I have the perfect view of Dermot's reflection.

While he's waiting for it to load, he draws lazy circles on his arm, and I trace the same pattern on my own. I can feel *his* fingers on *my* skin. I don't need a heated pool; I need an icy cold bucket of water.

"Are you okay?" he asks.

"Yes. Yes. Best get straight down to it." My laugh is a mixture of embarrassment and fear.

"I've discovered records from immediately prior to your father's name change." Dermot explains.

Although the browser tab is minimised, I can see the heading: *Australian Criminal Archives.*

"Dad was on the run from the law?" I reach for the computer mouse to open the records.

He puts his hand over mine to stop me from viewing whatever's on the screen. "At least a man by the same name. It's a serious allegation, we can look together and see whether we're going to share it. We might need further investigation, and before we tell anyone I need to triple check."

The way he bites his bottom lip sends a shiver of dread. What could be so bad to make Dermot this anxious?

I'm desperate to see what he's found, but he's stalling for a reason, and I did make a promise to Mum not to keep anything from her.

"Don't show me, it's better I don't know. Once you're certain we have the right person, we'll meet with Mum and Bonnie. I won't keep anything from them."

Chapter Forty-Five

KATERINA

'The Figs' Sydney, 2018

Izzy strolls into the repurposed kitchen where Joe's set up a worktable for me and Maria. "Look what I've got." She's waving a credit card. "You can use The Figs admin card for your research, but you have to sign your life away, so they can bill you at the end of the month."

"Oh my. Thank you. Where do I sign?"

Registering for family history websites means I can now access more extensive document collections. Who knew trying to track down lost relatives would cost the Earth, the moon and most of the stars—but only payable on credit? Izzy is an angel.

She watches over my shoulder as I complete the registration process. "I've never imagined anyone scrolling back so far to find their birth year," Izzy says.

"I know," I say with a wink. "It could take days for me to get past the A.D. dates and into the B.C. years."

Izzy laughs and kisses my cheek. "I'll leave you to it."

Once she's gone, I transfer the family details I've drawn up on paper to the new site. No sooner have I input cousin Mary's name than a green leaf flashes in the top righthand corner of my screen. Amazing. It automatically matches users with common ancestry.

I click on the leaf: *Three Ancestry Hints*.

One option's a link to another user's family tree, but I fumble as I touch the screen and the leaf disappears.

"Arseholes!" I slap the desk. "Whose tree did I lose?"

I'm startled by someone clearing his throat.

"Your sweet image is shot to pieces." Joe laughs. "You're no longer the lady-like Russian princess I knew." He does an overly dramatic brow wipe and pretends to walk away.

"Sit down," I say. "Your mum's not with you?" I look at the clock. "Oh, I've been so busy, I lost track of the time. You've come to say goodbye."

"Not yet. Mum abandoned me to wander around with George. She's showing him her sketches."

"Nothing's a secret from George." I chuckle and flash Joe a conspiratorial smile.

He pulls up a chair. "What happened to make you swear? Maybe I can help? Although if it's another dead end, you may as well yell out *Arseholes* because I'm running into plenty of those in my own research."

"Someone's researching the same family member as me, but I've lost the hint."

"Here, let me." Joe touches the screen, but I stop him.

"I'm afraid."

"Is this person connected to your nightmares?"

"Yes, and they might not want me to find them." I swallow hard. "Do not ask why."

His eyes are kind yet sad. "My gut feeling is it would be good for you to face whatever you're worried about."

I sigh. "I can't, I just cannot contact her after all these years, but I'd like to know she's okay."

"Do you want me to try?" he asks.

"Not today."

"Come on," he says with a shrug. "I need to see Mum before I leave, and you're better with the Italian translator. If you don't mind helping me."

Joe pushes my wheelchair through the Welcome Room and into the courtyard. Maria is chattering in Italian while George admires a picture in her sketchbook.

"Is Mum flirting?" Joe asks.

"Do you want me to chaperone?" I laugh.

He gives me a wink. "Well, she's showing him her etchings. An old pick-up line but a goodie."

"As long as she's happy, I don't care what she's showing him."

Joe eyes widen, then his shoulders relax. Perhaps there's a point in parental relationships where roles are reversed, and children worry more about their parents than parents about their kids.

"Miss Katerina, could you ask Mum to spit in the vial for a DNA test?"

I watch as he unwraps the foil packaging. "Why are you doing a DNA test?"

"I'm hoping it will help me trace my ancestors; maybe I'll find someone who knew Mum when she was young. A cousin, perhaps."

I shudder. "How will the test do that? I've only seen DNA testing on detective shows."

"It will match Mum with blood relatives who've taken the test."

Joe looks intensely and I brace myself for what's he's about to say.

"I know you've told me it's too late to contact this mystery person, but what if you put your DNA in the public domain and they came looking for you?"

I'm not sure if it's from fear or excitement, but my old heart flutters "It would be their choice?"

"Exactly."

The guilt of giving up my daughter has weighed on me for a lifetime, but if the decision to contact is hers, and there's even the smallest chance she wants to, it's a chance worth taking.

"When can you bring me the test?"

Chapter Forty-Six

KATERINA

Melbourne – Sydney, 1945

Advertisements in women's magazines extolled the extra nutrients of specially-designed baby formula, so I agreed to combine breastfeeding with a bottle. Mary and Mama were thrilled, and everyone took turns feeding our daughter. We took splendid delight in everything. Her perfect little hands gripping our fingers, her baby smell, her soft, pink skin. Our baby girl couldn't have been more loved.

When I told Philip I wanted to name her Viktoria in honour of Uncle Viktor, he wasn't sure. Although he had fond memories of Viktor's visits, he preferred the name Bridgett in honour of his mother. Mama and Mary threw in their tuppence worth agreeing with me, and Viktoria became the unanimous choice.

Philip's leg improved so quickly that on the day the war ended, we walked the main streets of Melbourne in celebration. The four of us forming a guard of honour, protecting Viktoria from the jubilant crowds.

We buried our heads in the sand to hide from our dilemma, but three months later, our period of blissful denial was interrupted by a letter from Mother and Father. They planned to visit to Melbourne in a fortnight.

Philip and I disagreed about our next move. I suggested fabricating another excuse, but he didn't want to wait. He insisted we travel to Sydney; introduce Viktoria and ask their permission to marry.

"My father won't take this well. Can we please put it off?"

"I won't feel as if I've done the right thing until our relationship's official. We need the ceremony," he said.

Philip wore me down with reasoning. My father was an intelligent man who would eventually agree. Philip's optimism was convincing and contagious.

I pictured the wedding.

Mary offered me her unworn gown, and Mama proposed restyling it. With talk of flowers and happy days, my head lost the fight against my heart. I agreed to the trip.

We planned the meeting in advance, deciding to arrive unannounced. Mama and Viktoria would accompany us on the train, but Philip and I would go inside to talk to Mother and Father alone. Once we'd discussed the wedding, Mama would bring Viktoria inside to show them their beautiful granddaughter, and they'd fall in love with her. How could they not?

I swayed with fear on the front porch of my family home, and Philip steadied me "Are you sure?" he asked. "We could just run away."

I studied his face. Until now he'd been certain, but his hand had gripped tighter on the walk up the long driveway. Perhaps the heavy atmosphere from the house seeped into the air.

"I'll never be ready," I said. "But if you need a wedding to sleep easily at night, then we must do it. Besides, we're already here."

Mama Bridgett was rocking our baby girl, and Philip whispered, "We'll call you."

She nodded and walked towards the stables.

I removed my shoes out of habit and continued shaking as I stepped inside. The silence unsettled me. When the soles of my feet touched the marble flooring, a deathly cold travelled up my legs. By the time I stood on the stair tread ice was stabbing my insides.

"Anyone here?" My voice was loud enough to reach every room.

Nothing.

"Let's go," I said. As I turned a waft of Father's tobacco drifted down the stairs. Mother was out. He never smoked his pipe inside when she was home.

I called again and Father replied.

"Upstairs. My office." His deep, dark voice bounced ominously off the walls, reverberating inside my chest.

"This is a mistake," I whispered. "We should wait until Mother and Nick are here. Let's tell them all together."

Philip rubbed his forehead. "He knows you're here. We've weighed this up and we can't run forever. It's beyond time to tell him about the baby."

My muscles were reluctant, but I forced my feet deliberately up the stairs. I wasn't expecting pleasantry beyond Father's heavy office door, but I knocked.

"Come in, Katerina."

Father didn't look up from his desk, instead he continued opening envelopes and sorting a pile of mail.

"Father," I said. "Philip and I would like a word."

At Philip's name, Father looked up and spat out his words, "What are you doing here? I thought I'd made myself clear."

Philip pulled out the chair opposite Father and waited for me to sit, then took another and seated himself.

"Get out of my house." Father slammed his fist against the desk.

"No. I can't leave until you hear what we need to say." Philip spoke calmly.

"Go." Father stabbed the letter opener into the dark timber, then stood to face the large curtained window. His strangled breath wheezed like a warning siren.

Father had shown anger many times, but never like this. His face was contorted and unrecognisable. Veins throbbed in his forehead.

I tapped Philip's shoulder, and stood to leave, but he pressed me back into the chair and shook his head. *No.*

"I love Katerina and wish to marry her. While I would prefer to have your permission, I will marry her without it."

My heart beat with both love and fear.

Father's response to Philip was laughter so ugly I held my hands over my ears. He pulled back the heavy curtains and drummed the letter opener violently against the glass. I held my breath, waiting for the window to break.

Father paced across to the other window and peered across the garden. "Leave now, while you can."

Chapter Forty-Seven

CLAUDIA

Fremantle, 2018

In the twelve hours since Dermot shared the news of Dad's involvement in a crime, an awful thought has haunted me.

Murder. Murder. Murder.

I hope to God it's something else.

I pace Mum's hallway waiting for Dermot to arrive. After he confirmed the Philip O'Patrick in the criminal records was Dad, I arranged for him to meet me, Mum and Bonnie at one o'clock. One minute to go.

All I've told the others is Dermot wants to talk to all of us together. I wish there was an easy way to tell Mum that Dad is on a wanted list for a serious crime, but there isn't. I'm relieved to have Dermot break the news.

Mum and Bonnie push me to open the door. He nods a solemn hello. One thing's for sure, whatever Dermot has found, we need to hear it as a family.

Mum makes us all a drink and looks ready to party.

When she winks at me, I meet her playfulness with sadness. It isn't the time for flippancy.

"There's no point putting it off," I say. "Dermot has something to tell us."

Mum leans towards Dermot, saying, "You've a face like a bulldog chewing a wasp. I hope you're not announcing your engagement." She smirks cheekily at Bonnie. It's a pity to ruin her good mood.

"I've discovered the reason Philip hid his past," he says.

"What?" Bonnie puts down her drink and stares.

"This." Dermot hands out copies of the documents.

Sweat beads on my top lip after reading the first paragraph, and I look wide-eyed at Dermot for help.

He pulls ice cubes out of his glass and holds them to the back of my neck. "I'm here with you," he whispers.

I feel less alone, but words can't alleviate the dread of what is to come.

"Could you please read the main points?" I ask.

Bonnie puts down her copy and looks up like a lost child. Mum looks terrified. There'll be no more jokes today.

"I've made notes." Dermot reads from his summary:

"*October 10, 1945. Domestic residence Kogarah, Sydney New South Wales.*

Warrant issued for the arrest of Philip O'Patrick after a physical altercation between him and the owner, Ivan Alexander, a 48-year-old male.

Resulted in the older man's death.

Katerina Alexander, Caucasian female, 19, found unconscious at the scene. Unable to recall anything beyond an argument and her own substantial injuries.

A confession allegedly written by Mr O'Patrick was discovered at the scene.

Police determined Mr O'Patrick decamped before authorities arrived. Despite an extensive police hunt he was never found."

Trembling, Mum throws the criminal records onto the table. "Not my Philip. He wouldn't hurt a fly, let alone murder someone."

Dermot's response is calm, but direct. "I'm afraid it's the same man. Dates, places, and names check out. But it never went to trial—"

Mum interrupts, "Stop."

"He left a confession note before going into hiding." Dermot's shoulders sag under the weight of delivering bad news. "Police handwriting analysis confirmed it as Philip's writing."

Mum shakes her head. "No. We have to find a witness. I know my husband was hiding something, but he was not a murderer."

Chapter Forty-Eight

KATERINA

Sydney, 1945 – St Vincent's hospital

In the first weeks after the accident, more than one policeman attempted to interview me, but between Mother and the hospital staff, they kept the police away. It surprised me how frequently Mother sat at my side. On the days I could open my eyes, she talked about taking me home as soon as I recovered, and she questioned me over and over, but I could not or would not, speak.

Mother told me the police were eager to hear my version of events but warned me to be careful of what I revealed. They'd found Philip's confession and were blaming him for my injuries.

Mother knew it wasn't Philip. "I can recognise evil," she explained. "That young man isn't capable. I should know."

When I became dry-mouthed from fever and too

weak to lift my head, Mother assumed my silence meant I couldn't hear what she said.

"You will get well," she promised. "Your father is gone, and we will open our heavy doors to let in the light."

"When I met your father, he was powerful and protective. Exactly what every young woman wanted in a man. But he was jealous of everything and everyone. Although he held an important job and provided well for our family, he didn't receive the attention he believed he deserved."

"When I first became a target for his control, I made excuses. Excuses for him and excuses to myself. Living without the man I'd married was unimaginable. I loved him and I was sure he would change."

"When you wake up, you can tell me what happened, then we'll make up a story to protect our standing in the community. I know your father was at least partly to blame, but there's no point in smearing his reputation. He's already paid the price."

My breasts tingled with milk, reminding me unnecessarily of the baby who was constantly in my thoughts. I tried locking onto Viktoria's perfect face, hoping I'd soon be well enough to hold her.

My pain became overwhelming and I wanted to scream, but I was too ill to make a noise, or signal my consciousness. For days, I lay in the hospital bed while nurses cooled my fever and administered concoctions to ease the pain.

Even if I'd been able to talk, I wouldn't have told Mother or the police what happened. But nor could I block it from replaying inside my head. Despite the pain, my memories were terrifyingly clear. No blurring of the violence, no version where everything turned out all right.

As if I'd been transported back in time, I imagined Father looking through his office window. "Why is Bridgett out there?" he'd shouted at Philip. "And whose baby is *she* holding?"

"Father," I'd begged. "The baby is our daughter. Mine and Philip's."

When Father turned, the veins on his neck pulsed and the room filled with foreboding. I crossed my arms protectively against the rage building between us.

Father stepped towards me and slapped my face, knocking me from the chair. "I should never have let that Bridgett whore anywhere near you."

Philip seesawed as he sprang to my aid. His eyes darting between Father and me as he decided what to do. I threw my arms around his neck, whispering urgently, "Let's go."

Philip helped me into the chair, braced himself defensively and faced my father head on. I tugged at Philip's sleeve, but he stood his ground.

"Mr Alexander, unless you take back what you've said, you will lose your daughter and granddaughter forever."

From the moment Philip made this threat, events became so awful that I refused to recall what happened next.

I covered my face with a hospital pillow, attempting to smother the memory out of existence.

As the infection spread beyond my wounds, Mother's rambling took on a remorseful tone.

"Please get well, Katerina. I'm sorry for my own unkindness. I suppressed my emotions for so long, I became as bad as your father. It was wrong, but try to understand that by being angry I reclaimed a little control."

My health spiralled downwards, and my Mother, who'd never shown maternal instincts, helped the nursing staff by wiping cold cloths over my brow.

As I drifted in and out of consciousness, she talked at length, "I know your father did this, but we have the best of both worlds now. We keep our good name, and we are both safe."

Believing I was beyond comprehending, she spoke of Philip, "I'm glad that young man has gone. I knew you had eyes for him. There was talk of Philip's Scottish father, but I doubt such a man existed. Your Uncle Viktor brought Bridgett to our house, and there was an unmistakeable tenderness between them."

I tried to hold on to what Mother was saying about Bridgett, to make sense of it, but pain engulfed me, and I allowed myself to drown in excruciating darkness. Unless this all turned out to be a bad, bad dream, I preferred never to surface again. There'd be no more fighting to catch the light.

I almost got my wish, but eventually I came out of my stupor to face the scrutiny of a gaunt man in a white coat. He took my hand in his and rather than shaking it he pulled me towards him. The action matched his words. "We've brought you back to the world of the living."

Turning to a nurse with a starched white veil, he said, "Good work, Sister. It's taken weeks, but our patient has come through."

"Your daughter is lucky," the doctor said to Mother. "Without antibiotics, she would have died."

"So, Katerina is cured?" Mother asked.

"Well, the spreading infection has subsided, but it's not over. As soon as she is well enough to survive the surgery, we must remove all tissue at risk of gangrene."

After theatre, I opened my eyes to a smiling recovery nurse. "They've removed the infected parts. So many sutures they lost count." She smiled as if she was delivering good news.

The surgeon took the seat next to Mother at my bedside. Not once while they talked, did they look at me, it was as if they were discussing someone else. By the time the doctor had finished, I didn't want to lift my head again.

"Thank you for saving my daughter," Mother's voice shook with gratitude, but I wanted no part in acknowledging those who'd stopped me from dying.

I waved my trembling hand to sweep Mother away.

Although I'd closed my eyes to block their voices, I'd heard the truth.

The back injury meant I'd never walk again, and the removal of parts from my abdomen, including my womb, ensured I'd bear no other children.

I shivered despite the pile of hospital blankets. My

heart longed to hold my baby, kiss her tiny cheeks, and run my nose over her fine downy hair. I yearned for Philip to comfort me and tell me it would be all right.

The guilt was overwhelming. Philip, Viktoria and I should have lived our lives without caring about the opinions of closed-minded people. Now, I was without the only baby I'd ever have.

I turned my face towards the window. No doctor would receive thanks from me.

That's when my nightmares took hold.

Once the hospital staff decided the medical team had done their job, I was discharged into Mother's care. From my upstairs bedroom window, I gazed at the family grounds, remembering the long walk up the driveway to ask Father's permission. I blocked out the rest.

My physical convalescence would take months, but as far I was concerned, I hadn't been saved. I'd been sentenced to a joyless life.

Philip was wanted by the law, and even if I wanted to run off with him, how could I? A young woman with a wheelchair would be easy to track down, and if they caught us, he'd be imprisoned, or hung. My Mother would never support an illegitimate child, and I could never care for a baby alone.

Philip had often told me how much he loved my perfect skin and the curve of my bottom. Multiple scars and gouges ruined all that. I could not bear to look at myself. There was no way Philip would gaze at my naked body in the way he had before. The woman he'd once loved was mutilated beyond recognition.

Although it wasn't what my heart wanted, there were valid reasons to reject Philip and my baby, but the most compelling reasons of all— guilt, and unwavering self-loathing.

Faced with this, I decided it best for everyone if I wasted away.

Mother tried to feed me, but the kindness and patience she'd shown in the hospital wore thin.

One morning when I pushed away the food, she made an offhand comment, "I should have asked Philip of Bridgett's whereabouts. I could have paid her to look after you. You always ate what she cooked."

"When would you have asked Philip?" I glared.

"When you were in the hospital. He avoided the police at the gates by climbing the wall. He let himself into the house, carrying a bouquet of wattle flowers, but I sent him away, telling him you wanted nothing more to do with him. I had to. I threw back the note he tried to give me and threatened to call the police. Not that I would have, but he wasn't to know. I found other bunches of flowers over the weeks, but I tossed them onto the rubbish."

I stared at her in disbelief.

"It's best for both of you to stay apart," she said.

Once, I would have seen Mother's action as cruelty, but I was relieved.

She had saved me an unbearably painful task.

"Thank you," I said. "You were right. I do not want to see Philip again."

I wanted to die.

Chapter Forty-Nine

CLAUDIA

Fremantle, 2018

I accept Dermot's second invitation for a swim, but regret starts as soon as I hang up. My favourite swimwear's lost its elasticity and the second pair feel like someone skimped on fabric. I can't display this much flesh. Not at my age. No matter how much I stretch, either the bottom creeps upward or the top creeps downward. Although it's starting to get dark, I hide my body under a sun protection shirt, hoping I don't look ridiculous.

Within seconds of me knocking, Dermot opens the door, and his smile triggers a flush of warmth in the parts my swimwear is struggling to cover.

"Come in." He grabs my beach carry bag and leads me through the house.

"My feet are killing me," I babble as I walk up the stone steps. "I wore heels for work orientation day. Not only are my feet swollen, the other new employees were wearing flats. So much for making a good impression."

Dermot turns to me from the top step. "Don't worry about anyone else. You look great whatever you wear." He holds open the pool-gate, standing back as I walk through. "When do you start the job permanently?"

"Three weeks." I let out a long breath. Thinking about full time work means ending my day-time meetings with Dermot. My stomach clenches. If the meetings stop, I won't discover everything about Dad, and I wanted to discover more about Dermot.

"By the look on your face, you need this swim to take the weight off those feet."

"Is my face that bad?" I rearrange my features, trying for pleasant, but Dermot watches so intently I poke out my tongue instead.

"Much better," he says with a laugh.

Dermot points to a shack beside the pool. "You can change in there."

"I'm good. I've got bathers underneath." I fight the urge to pinch myself. I'm wearing a blinking sun shirt at night. I hide behind my towel to remove my outer clothes, stacking them self-consciously on a wooden bench.

When I turn around, Dermot is staring at me.

I rip off the shirt and crouch at the edge of the pool, dipping my hand, pretending to be engrossed in the water.

The warm water contrasts with the chilly night air. "It's like warm champagne," I say, cupping the bubbles.

"Heated. Dozens of powerful jets." He smiles over his shoulder as he heads towards the shack. "I'll be back in a minute."

I jump in and rest my arms over the edge. When Dermot returns, he whistles at me before diving in. He is so easy-going... and athletic. I swallow hard as he swims towards me, feeling suddenly awkward about my own body. Not that I hate it, I'm just hyper-aware of it when Dermot's around.

He swims two laps under water, then holds me around the waist. Before I know what's happening, I'm being towed towards the pool edge and he's positioning my back against the massage jets.

"There. Let the water do its work."

I move until the swim jets pulse against my lower back and shoulders but I'm careful not to look at him.

"See," he says. "You'll be relaxed in no time."

I nod in agreement, but it's doing the opposite. I'm anything but relaxed. I splash my face, and a voice in my head sings, 'It's getting hot in here, so take off all your clothes...' I wet my face again and pat my cheeks.

It's time to get out.

Dermot drapes the beach towel around my shoulders. "Before we review our research, there's something I've realised."

I stand up straight. Good or bad, I'm facing this head on.

"My life has been better since we started working together," he says, "and not just because it's given me something to do."

I smile to myself and although I've never tried it before, my walk inside is more of a sashay.

"Come on," he says. "We're no closer to finding anyone who knows the truth about your father."

I move the computer mouse to post a message on

another forum and my arm touches his. We move our arms and they touch again.

We both laugh.

"The full moon must be making happy magic." I point into the night sky.

Dermot makes lingering eye contact. "I've certainly fallen under its spell."

I click through the genealogy forums giving me a moment to work up courage. Was he hinting at something between us? Should I make the first move? I open and close every forum tab summoning the bravery to throw down the mouse, wrap my arms around Dermot and declare my interest.

"Stop!" Dermot yells. "Go back."

I freeze.

"New DNA results. The match site has flagged a new relative."

There it is on the previous screen. Katerina Alexander Tremaine.

"Viktoria's cousin?" I ask. "The daughter of the man Dad killed?"

Dermot opens the paper copy of our family tree. "This doesn't make sense. Katerina should be related to Viktoria, but not as close as the DNA test match. This proves Mary isn't Viktoria's mother."

Chapter Fifty

KATERINA

Sydney, 1946

When my weight dropped to a dangerous level, I was re-admitted to hospital. This time to a wing for returned soldiers. The facility was run by the War Repatriation Office, which I found bewildering. The unit was designated for those who'd seen terrors of war and couldn't resume normal lives.

Why was I, a civilian, placed there when my closest contact with a war zone was reading news reports of the Japanese submarine attack on Sydney Harbour?

I learned that the Sydney general hospital staff were only required to treat the physical, and they considered my condition to be one of the mind. Beyond that, they told me nothing.

For the sake of propriety, and after an additional payment by Mother, I was provided with a private room. The bleakness of that sterile, metal-bedded environment seemed the perfect backdrop for my plan to fade away.

Mother visited at first. For a week, she arrived every day to push me out in the grounds for fresh air, but she refused to set foot in the main wing. Apparently, she was sensitive to the smell of tortured soldiers.

"I'm delighted you're avoiding contact with any of them." She held her nose and gestured towards the men. "The arrangement doesn't please me at all. I argued with Matron that surely a women's hospital would be a better alternative, but she'd said, 'Doctors have their reasons,' and shooed me away."

Mother tapped her head, indicating the *'reasons'* were of the mind. She thought I was going crazy.

"When Dr Tremaine, the psychiatrist in charge, returns, he'll fix this nonsense and you can come home."

I sighed. "No one can mend my ruined life."

She studied me from head to toe, her eyes resting on my lower limbs. "It's true you won't regain use of your legs, but at least you have them. Although, I fear, if you lose another ounce of weight they'll snap off."

I looked at my thin calves and ankles protruding below the hospital gown. My white legs looked like a pair of Capstan cigarettes. The beige hospital socks looked like filters. Filtered cigarettes. I laugh-cried so heartily, even Mother's harsh scowl didn't make me stop.

She glared at me as if I'd gone mad.

"Anna has called several times," she said. "I don't know why you won't let her visit."

I shook my head; it was difficult explaining my need to deprive myself of pleasure.

After two visits in the second week, and one in the

third, Mother sent regular excuses with bunches of flowers, but she didn't call again. A situation that suited us both.

At the end of my third week, Dr Tremaine returned. When a nurse explained he was one of the specialists disputing beliefs about the affliction known as shell-shock, I imagined him to be grey-haired, worn-out and smug. He was none of these things. He could have been handsome if he'd stood straighter or carried himself with more confidence. His unusual air of vulnerability made it difficult for me to channel anger in his direction.

At our second meeting, he surprised me by explaining his research. He was animated and knowledgeable, but he didn't address my condition. I'd imagined a psychiatrist probing with well-practised questions then a trite explanation that my mental symptoms were the result of forgotten childhood trauma. This was something I'd read with interest in a scholarly article Anna once 'borrowed' about the famous Dr Freud. I told Dr Tremaine as much.

I would have once laughed at the thought of Anna scanning the pamphlet for references to sexuality, but there wasn't any laughter left. The doctor didn't make eye contact as he spoke, "It is unusual for a y-y-young woman to have an interest in s-such things."

Dr Tremaine's stutter had been less evident when he talked about his work. He really was different to the other doctors I saw, who winked at nurses and bragged about their own importance. He tapped two fingers along his desk as if they were legs making an escape.

"I need f-fresh air and so d-d-do you," he said. "I'm

imp-pressed with your interest in my research so if it doesn't bore you too much, I'd like to tell you more."

"Not at all," I said. Talking about anything other than my condition was refreshing.

He pushed me outside and parked me beside a tree similar to the whispering tree Anna and I once shared at school.

"Do you mind if I talk about my recent conference?" His self-assurance returned, and his eyes shone with zest. I had no idea how his work connected to my condition, but enthusiasm was easier to digest than pity or scorn. "Go ahead." I leaned closer to the tree, picking at pieces of bark while I listened.

"It was believed that mental trauma in returned soldiers was the result of concussion caused by exploding shells. But evidence does not prove that to be the case."

After he'd talked at length I asked, "Aren't you going to enquire why I've stopped eating?"

"It's clear to me already. I requested you as a patient after reading your medical history. Your s-s-suffering is the same as these men. It helps my investigation to have patients experiencing parallel symptoms without having seen battle."

So, I was a guinea pig. I must have shown annoyance because he lowered his eyes and spoke slowly.

"You've undergone a t-t-terrible shock and great loss. It's a natural human response for the m-mind to react in this manner. I've read your notes. Every action you've taken, including your refusal to eat, seems reasonable under the circumstances."

"I don't want to live," I said.

"Well, although it's my job to save you, I don't

intend to force-feed you. If you would agree to eat j-just a little, together we can find a better way to deal with your loss."

I wished for him to go away, but my withering look had no effect other than to strengthen his resolve.

"As you may have noticed, we are short of help. Many of these men are incapable of completing forms to receive r-r-repatriation, and there are many who could do with a gentle ear."

"Do not ask for my help," I said. "I can't assist." Without waiting for a response, I turned and wheeled myself back to my room.

Some days later, Dr Tremaine offered to push me on the winding brick pathway around the sanatorium gardens. Out of boredom, I chose to accompany him, but I insisted on wheeling myself.

"I don't m-mind making the trip easier for you," he said.

"But I do."

While parked under the usual tree he asked me to describe how I felt.

"I can't."

"Don't name any human emotions or tell me what's w-worrying you. Tell me instead about s-something s-mall that's upset you.

It was clear from his unusual request he was experimenting with avant-garde ways of treating patients. While I admired his dedication to his research, I told him I preferred to be left alone.

Dr Tremaine was insistent; he wouldn't leave until I talked. I thought of such an incident and was reluctant at first, but the words spilled out of their own accord.

"When I was a child," I said, "my uncle bought me a

porcelain egg. I thought it a treasure, all the way from Russia. After I came home from the hospital, Mother pushed my wheelchair, knocking the display cabinet. My egg crashed to floor."

"Can it be fixed?' I'd asked Mother.

"She said, 'No. It's broken. It's going in the bin.'

"I cried over that egg more than I can explain. I screamed at her as she carried it through the kitchen. It was only my hysterics that stopped Mother throwing it away."

Dr Tremaine tilted his head to one side, regarding me with interest. I sensed he understood.

"I kept the pieces," I said. "They're in my suitcase."

He wheeled me to my room, then I watched as he unwrapped the handkerchief containing shards of shiny porcelain.

"I'm exactly like that egg," I said. "Ruined forever."

"C-come with me." He pushed me to his quarters, parking me in front of a table covered with an old hospital sheet. We were crammed into a narrow space beside the bed, and I couldn't imagine what lay underneath.

Dr Tremaine unveiled a collection of broken bowls and platters in states of disrepair. Then he threw off another cloth, revealing his finished pieces. He'd repaired the crockery with seams of gold. "Everything c-can be put back t-together," he said.

I inspected the unusual fragmented bowl. "Couldn't you have mended them invisibly?"

"I could, but the-the g-golden joints are integral to the art. It is called *k-kintsugi*, an interred and injured Japanese soldier taught me how."

The more I looked, the more attractive the grouping of objects became. "They're exquisite,"

"Yes." Dr Tremaine's face lit up. "The g-gilded mend is essential. Both objects and people become more beautiful when they're put back together."

I understood his intentions, but while the golden seams were imaginative, mending a broken woman was impossible.

Despite Dr Tremaine's impressive patient results, he never boasted, and I grew to admire his dedication to saving minds and lives. Not long after the *Kintsugi* day, I decided helping others might take my mind off my own misery, so I offered to assist Dr Tremaine with administrative work. I would never be happy, but with less time to think about Philip or my baby girl, the desire to end my life moved to the background, and I began eating.

One afternoon, Dr Tremaine called me to his office.

"It's time to discontinue your therapy sessions," he said.

My throat tightened. The thought of going home to live with Mother was unbearable.

"I wrote to the w-w-war office for a grant, and I've received additional f-funding for a paid position." He regarded me with what looked like a cross between desperation and hopefulness.

"I'm b-begging you to apply. Your effect on soldiers has been positive. I need you to c-continue."

There was nowhere else for me to go. At least there I'd be useful. "Yes," I said.

Dr Tremaine and I worked side by side, discussing

his methods and recording case notes. He listened with interest to my own observations and opinions. Research occupied his entire heart, and that suited me fine. To him, my mind was the part of most value, and I came to realise this was a worthwhile way to live a shattered life.

It was fortunate my quarters were away from the others, because I screamed through my nightmares of the murder, and sobbed with guilt at abandoning those I loved most.

Over the next months, Dr Tremaine asked me to call him Ernest, and I helped more and more with his research. His mind never ceased working. He developed innovative ways to rehabilitate the men who cried out day and night reliving the screams of dying mates who'd died beside them in battle. I was glad to help these men, we had so much in common.

Chapter Fifty-One

KATERINA

'The Figs' Sydney, 2018

There's something troubling about Joe's manner, as he stands in my doorway clutching a spiral-bound folder.

"Oh my, is Maria all right?" I study his face for clues.

He passes the folder from hand to hand like a hot potato and I look behind him, expecting to see Maria dallying about, but Joe is alone.

"Mum's fine," he speaks too quickly, avoiding eye contact. "She's been great since the puppy visits became a weekly affair. I looked in on the way here and she was teaching George the Italian command for 'sit'. The puppy wasn't listening, but George can now sit in response to a hand signal."

His nervous laughter is hiding something.

"You left Maria in her room?"

"Yes, I was hoping to catch you alone." He guards the document as if it holds the political secrets of the free world.

"The translations?" I point.

"Yes, but there's a twist. I don't know how to tell you."

My stomach sinks on behalf of both Joe and Maria. So, she had secrets too? And it seems they are secrets Joe would prefer not to know. Poor Maria. I automatically put my hand over my mouth, horrified at the thought of explaining my past actions.

"We all keep things to ourselves," I say, hoping to put whatever Maria has revealed into perspective. "There are probably moments of your own life you haven't shared with anyone."

"There are." Joe looks no less uncomfortable.

I point to the document. "It cannot be as bad as all that."

"It was difficult to understand at first. There were snippets of recounts about being fed the wrong food at The Figs, and of George stealing her shoes, but then Mum got into a rhythm. She told a life story that made me cry." Joe's eyes water. "I should have stopped reading, but I read every chapter."

Joe fidgets with the folder and looks away.

My insides are heavy. "I'm sorry too, for not asking Maria's consent. We should have got permission."

He changes weight from foot to foot. It's clear there's more. I wait for him to tell me what's on his mind.

"The accounts in these transcripts are as beautiful as they are sad, but most of them aren't stories of Mum's youth."

"I'm relieved about not betraying Maria's trust, but I'm confused. Okay, Joe. You have my attention."

"They're your stories, Miss Katerina. You must have

told Mum what happened to you. I'm not sure how Mum's brain works, but she translated your experiences into Italian, you recorded them, and now they're here." He taps the folder.

My cheeks burn at what he knows, and I press them with my cold hands to cool down.

"This is the only copy," he says. "I can destroy the original if that's what you'd prefer?"

"So, you know what happened?" I force myself to face him, afraid of a judgemental look.

"Some of it, but—" He holds the binder towards me, just out of reach.

"But what?"

"Write the rest of your story. The whole thing. It's a tale I'd want to know about my mother."

I rest my head in my hands. What have I done? "I was sure my secret was safe with Maria."

"It seems Mum's memory is better than we realised." Joe presses his mouth into a sad smile.

"I made a promise not to tell, and I thought she'd forget."

"There's something else," he says. "People are looking for you, Miss Katerina."

I snatch the binder from Joe's hands and clasp it to my chest. "Who?"

"I searched for your name in a forum for lost family members. Philip's daughter, Claudia posted a request. She's searching for you."

I open my mouth in disbelief. "You know about Philip?"

Joe points to my life story.

"He sent me a letter before he died. That's when my nightmares came back."

Joe hugs me. "His daughters want answers, and you need peace. If you're to tell the whole story, it might be easier in written form."

"Me, tell Philip's daughters?" I swallow hard.

Joe shuffles his feet. "Not just them. Your own daughter. Viktoria is searching for too."

"I've wanted to explain to Viktoria, but she'd never understand." My insides writhe in a mass of dread, but amongst the darkness there's a tiny, sad speck of hope. "Do they know where to find me?"

"Not yet," Joe says, "but they've gone to a lot of trouble. They won't give up now."

"I must make a statement to the police, Joe. It's time to make everything right."

"If that's what you want, you can, but you'll need to tell the whole story for that."

My chin trembles. "Okay."

"Read through the account so far, to make sure it's all true," Joe says. There might be sections where Mum has forgotten or mixed up the story."

"I'll ask Izzy to help," I say. "She offered to write my memoirs once. I want to be clear about the facts."

Joe presses his lips to my forehead, and I feel his breath on my skin as he talks, "Don't judge yourself, let everyone make up their own mind."

I nod.

The only real way to put things right now is to clear Philip's name.

I need to open up about this whole sorry business as soon as possible.

Chapter Fifty-Two

CLAUDIA

Fremantle, 2018

We know Katerina is alive, or was a week ago, because she posted her DNA results. Viktoria received the news of Mary not being her biological mother without a fuss. Perhaps, deep down, she already knew.

There's a lot to learn from Viktoria about acceptance. I hope it rubs off on me.

If Katerina chooses not to respond to our messages, we've reached another dead end. I'm not sure what worries me most: having an unsolved mystery taking up permanent residency inside my head, or me and Dermot never moving beyond friendship. There've been moments where I felt we were moving towards more, but now it's all about tracking Katerina. I should be celebrating our success, but all I think about is Dermot. Having such intense feelings channelled nowhere is exhausting. What if, after all this, Dermot shakes my hand and walks away?

My view over the river has been as hazy as my mind, but by my third cup of tea there are patches of blue sky. The light brightens my mood and I decide it's not over yet. I just have to do something about it.

As the clouds fluff and separate, I think about my boys when they were small. We played a game called 'Look for Animals'. No matter what the shape, Aaron would always see the clouds as socks. A folded sock, a sock on a foot, a sock on the floor. I snap a picture, add a message and press send. *What does this look like?*

Aaron's reply is immediate, "A sock on a washing line."

I send a smile emoji in response. My real smile will last for hours.

We might not be geographically close, but since I've begun emailing my sons regularly, our relationships are better than ever.

It's easier to write feelings down. There's no reason I can't do the same with Dermot. I start typing an email when two things happen. The sun's rays shine like a message from God and an email notification pops up on my screen.

> *Sender: Katerina Tremaine.*
> *Subject line: DNA family forum. Can we meet?*

I'm so nervous my fingers refuse to cooperate. It takes forever to send a text message to Viktoria.

> Katerina has made contact. I'm forwarding her email, but she wants me to phone. Would you rather make the call?

My hand shakes as I ready myself for Viktoria's reply. I'm tempted to call Dermot with the news, but I wait. Her response takes ten long minutes.

> Sorry to take so long. I'm too emotional. Can you please call her?

I text Dermot for backup.

> Can you meet me? I need help.

> You okay?

> Nothing life-threatening. Katerina has emailed.

> Where?

I get a flash of our last heart-racing watery meeting and decide it might be less distracting to meet on dry ground.

> Frank's Bar and Kitchen? It's halfway. I'll leave in ten minutes.

I choose a private booth against the wall. The place is warm, but I shiver with anxiety. We're finally going to contact Katerina. My mood is complicated by subliminal images of Dermot climbing out of his pool naked.

I buy a large glass of wine to relax the tic in my left eye.

A few mouthfuls and my nerves settle, but Dermot arrives wearing a long-sleeved body-hugging navy-blue jumper that may as well be see-through. My eye flutters at double speed.

"I hope it's good news?" he asks.

I gulp my drink.

"What's up?"

I feel unfamiliar, impulsive sensations whenever you're around, would be my honest answer—but I swallow those incriminating words. "Katerina emailed this morning about my post in the DNA forum."

"She's alive? In Australia?" Dermot asks.

I open the email on my phone, and he reads her address, "The Figs Residential Care Village, Sydney."

"She's wants us to phone." My teeth are chattering despite the open fire near our booth.

"Do you want another drink? Or should we call now, from the car."

"Now?" I ask.

"She's probably waiting," he says.

"Well, my nervous system won't handle putting it off. I'm close to collapse." I laugh as if I'm joking and swig the last of my wine before putting on my jacket.

"Wait for me." He follows as I race to my car.

After a minute of adjusting and readjusting my seat, Dermot takes my hand.

"Come on," he says softly. "We will be okay."

We? I try to read his expression. Is this a comforting hand hold or the romantic kind? I close my eyes to think. I couldn't bear to make another Troy mistake and jump in too soon.

"I'm ready," he says.

I open my eyes to Dermot writing today's date in his blinking notebook.

Oh, it was a comforting 'we'.

I match my breaths to the phone ringing. Short and sharp. I stop altogether when it answers.

"Hello. Katerina Tremaine speaking."

Her voice is firm and enthusiastic. If I hadn't known her age, I would have imagined a younger woman.

"Hello, Mrs Tremaine. Claudia here. Philip McLeod's daughter."

There's a momentary silence. "I'm with Dermot. The genealogist leading our search."

"Pleased to meet you, Claudia and Dermot. Anyone else there?" Her voice trembles.

"No. Just me and Dermot."

"Excellent." Her voice is low, and she clears her throat. "I'd prefer the meeting with Viktoria to be proper. Face-to-face." There's a pause before she says, "That's if my daughter wants to meet me?"

"Absolutely," I say.

I'm sure I hear Katerina smiling.

"Let's email each other with a date and time," she suggests. "I'm sorry but travelling at my age is difficult."

"We'll fly to you," I say quickly. "I hope you don't mind, but my sister will come too, and I'm worried my mother will also insist."

"Good." She sighs. "I'm sure your whole family have questions about Philip, and Viktoria will have some of her own, but I'd rather not answer them on the phone."

Dermot leans towards the dashboard. "You've made our day, Katerina. I'm looking forward to solving the mystery."

"Looking forward to meeting you," I add.

"You too. I'm almost ninety-two, so the sooner the better." Her laughter is more jittery than joyful.

After I say goodbye, I slump in my seat. "Even good news is exhausting."

"I'll follow you home," Dermot says, "to make sure you get there safely."

I phone Viktoria from the car, but once I've said the words '*we're going to meet Katerina*' the rest of the call is filled with '*I can't believe it*'s' and joyful tears. She's too busy crying to talk and I'm distracted by my infrequent glances at my rear-view mirror watching Dermot drive the car behind me.

I hang up on Viktoria and shake myself to stop looking at him. He's singing along to the radio and I flick through the stations on mine trying to match the song. Dear God, what has happened to me?

We're almost at my place when he stops outside an old house around the corner. I wonder what he's up to, but he disappears into the garden and I continue home. Five minutes later, he arrives at my door, with an armful of lemons.

"I offered to pay the lady for them, but she told me to take as many as I wanted."

I raise a curious eyebrow.

"I'm making you a hot lemon drink to warm you up and calm you down," he says.

When he grabs a chopping board and cuts the lemons, I admire the easy way he makes himself at home. He *does* look at home. When he wears a playful grin and mischief dances in his eyes, I realise I'm not as exhausted as I thought.

"You seem fine now," he says. "You wore such a serious expression earlier, I thought you needed cheering up." He picks up three lemons and juggles with surprising expertise.

I clap my hands. "A man of many talents. Refreshment and entertainment."

"Maybe," he says, handing me a drink.

I rack my brains for something witty and frisky, something encouraging, but chicken out.

"Well, it's all over," he says. "I hope you and Bonnie fill me in on the details when you get back."

My stomach does a miserable backflip and I stare at my empty hands. I won't see Dermot again unless I speak up.

"Dermot..." I start talking before any thoughts have properly formed.

"Yes?"

"Can you teach me how to juggle?" What on the earth am I doing?

"Stand up." He points to a spot on the floor.

I stand close to Dermot, letting my fingers linger against his as I pass him the lemons.

He puts his arms around my shoulders and his hands over mine. I'm like a jellyfish. My hands and arms do nothing, but I laugh as he helps me juggle. I'm a puppet. I wouldn't mind being a ventriloquist's dummy and letting Dermot say the words.

I say nothing and the silence becomes uncomfortable.

"Okay. I'm off," he says. "Enjoy yourself and let me know what happens in Sydney."

The lemons fall from my hands. "You're coming. You have to come. This is our project, and I don't want to finish it without you."

His cheeks change colour to tickled pink.

"Thanks," he says. "I'd love to."

Chapter Fifty-Three

KATERINA

Sydney and Melbourne 1948

On my twenty-second birthday, Mother sent a driver to the rehabilitation hospital to collect me, and, after my party luncheon was over, Nick wheeled me out of Mother's hearing. He told me Philip had made contact. Nick couldn't provide any information other than me being at a hospital because Mother, understanding that their friendship might trump family loyalty, refused to give Nick the exact location.

Nick and Philip tried to find me, but it's not surprising they failed. Even the brightest sleuth wouldn't think to look in a facility for shellshocked soldiers.

Eventually, Philip stopped asking.

Considering the time elapsed since I'd last seen Philip, I was surprised he still thought of me. Part of me hoped he'd found someone new, yet the very idea of that threatened to break me further.

Once back at the hospital, I approached Ernest who was having a day off and working on his latest creation.

"I want you to have these." I handed him my engagement ring and the unused wedding band. "Melt them down and add them to your *Kintsugi*."

Ernest ran the rings through his fingertips. "No. One day you might w-want to give these up, but not today. Your gentle heart holds a p-p-place for whoever gave them to you. Keep them until you're s-sure."

"I can't, I cannot..."

"For your own sake, you must c-confront whatever or whoever you're hiding from." He returned the rings and closed my fist around them. "I'd like to be the p-person you trust to share your t-t-troubles. If I'm not the one, find someone who is."

Ernest was right; it was time to face the mess I'd left behind. I needed to work out a permanent arrangement for our little girl before she grew much older.

That night, I wrote a letter to Mama Bridgett and Mary, requesting to be contacted when Philip planned his next visit. They'd written regularly for two years. Always informing me of Viktoria's health and mile-stones, while agreeing neither to mention me to Philip, nor provide him with my address. It was a huge favour and I was grateful. My daughter was well-loved and well looked after. Although the situation saddened me, it could have been so much worse.

Mary, in particular, insisted the favour was all in her direction. She'd thought motherhood an impossible dream and considered the opportunity to care for Viktoria a gift. She never questioned our arrangement, and I dared not broach the subject. I suspected we were both too frightened.

I took out photographs of Viktoria that Mama Bridgett had sent from her first and second birthdays. I'd hidden the pictures from myself. There was too much of Philip in her darling face, and the pain of losing both was a yearning as physical and ever present as the soldiers who still felt their amputated limbs.

After I posted the letter, awaiting a response tormented me. None of the options available were acceptable, but a decision had to be made.

My apprehension increased as I waited, so I worked overtime to ease the anxious tingling in my head and my fingers.

Ernest was right. I could not handle it alone, so I wrote to Anna, apologising for shutting her out of my life, and organising a place and time where she could find me.

Every morning at four-forty-five, Ernest picked me up from my quarters and drove me to Wylie's baths in Coogee. The ocean was empty and dark so early in the day, which made me less self-conscious when he carried me to the water. I'd permanently lost use of my legs because of spinal injury, but he assigned exercises and encouraged me to work hard. Swimming, he said, would build strength in my core and my arms and shoulders.

We trained for half an hour in what felt like frigid water.

"You're w-working so hard and doing so well," Ernest said, enveloping me in a doubled-up blanket and carrying me back to the car.

There was a new feeling. Pride. This was my

favourite part of the day: the sun rising pink over the ocean, and I closed my eyes absorbing his warmth. He wasn't Philip, but at least with Ernest, I was safe. He wasn't searching for a youthful, spirited affair. This was the only version of Katerina he'd ever known.

As he lifted me into the wheelchair, I noticed Anna, sitting on a bench overlooking the ocean. She'd received my letter.

She patted the space beside her just as she used to in the schoolyard and called, "Sit here and tell me what happened." She stopped, covering her open mouth.

Although I imagine Nick had told her about the wheelchair, she wept.

Once back at the hospital, Ernest made us tea, and left us alone.

"I know you're hiding something, Katerina," Anna said. "It's impossible to believe Philip attacked you. He adored you. And it doesn't make sense that he'd murder your father unless in self-defence."

"I prefer not to talk about that night or any other." I pressed my palm against my forehead to make the thoughts go away, but Anna had more to say.

"On the night of the Trocadero when your father came looking, my mother and I were shocked by his anger."

I'd never been successful at silencing her in the past, so I resigned myself to listening.

"When my mother told your father you were with Philip, he raised his hand to strike Bridgett. I've never seen a woman more scared. My mother told him if he made the threat again, she would kill him."

"Please, Anna. I made a promise."

"Then don't shut me out. Best friends do more than

share secrets, they support friends with secrets they cannot tell."

We sobbed in each other's arms when I told her about Viktoria. She asked what I planned to do. I didn't know.

I couldn't bring myself to tell her what happened with Father.

A week after Anna's visit, I found a telegram clipped to the hospital message board.

Katerina. Philip arriving 26th July. Melbourne Botanic Gardens. Eleven O'clock. Pavilion near the lake. Mary and Bridgett.

I trembled as I read it. The twenty-sixth of July? Viktoria's third birthday. Only three weeks' away.

Although I phoned Anna immediately, it took me ten days to tell Ernest. I was terrified of losing his friendship, but I sat him down and confessed my immoral past. His eyes showed no judgement on hearing I was a single woman who'd become pregnant. He gripped my hand when I told him I'd left my baby with an aunt. I shared everything except the details of my father's death. I intended to keep my promise to Philip.

After I finished, Ernest put his hands to his lips as if in prayer, and, for the first time since I'd met him, he looked frightened.

When he eventually spoke, it was to insist on driving me to Melbourne.

We finished work early the afternoon before Viktoria's birthday, and I couldn't hide my disappointment when Ernest secured my wheelchair in his car. He knew what worried me without words.

"You might not w-walk into the meeting, but you... you have every r-r-right to stand tall."

When Ernest squeezed my hand, a shot of faith travelled the length of my arm.

"Thank you," I said, smiling tentatively

Instead of returning the smile, Earnest wore the look of a man expecting to travel home alone.

We were quiet on the long drive from Sydney to Melbourne. Silence wasn't unusual for us, but this lull was thick with unspoken feelings. When we were almost in Melbourne, Ernest checked us into separate hotel rooms, telling me to rest and ready myself for the big day. It was a long sleepless night, and although I knew he'd be awake working on his research in the next room, I didn't knock on his door. My affection for Ernest complicated an already impossible decision.

The following morning as we entered the outskirts of Melbourne city, Ernest stopped the car. "Katerina, b-before you go in, I need to p-put my cards on the table. I'm sure you know how much I care, and the thought of c-continuing my research without you seems u-u-unbearable, but you've proved capable of l-looking after more than yourself. Despite your physical and mental trauma, you've c-cared for and soothed wounded men, and you've completed research more thoroughly than many academics. N-n-nothing is beyond you."

Ernest's shoulders hunched over the wheel and I swallowed to ease the lump in my throat. When he restarted the car, I stared out of my window to avoid looking at him.

He parked across the road from the Melbourne Botanic gardens and forced a sad smile. "You are b-b-beautiful inside and out Katerina. You are a living *K-kintsugi*. Once you were broken, but you have m-mended stronger than ever. You have my love and blessing to make whatever decision is right for you."

I pinched my nose to stop it running. I refused to cry.

When Ernest walked me to the ominous wrought-iron entrance gates, I felt as if I had a piece of iron inside me, and giant magnets were drawing me in opposite directions.

"I will w-w-wait until dark. If you don't return, I'll know you've left through the other entrance."

I bound my shawl about my shoulders and wheeled myself down the cobbled path towards the lake. When I rounded a bend, I saw Philip. He looked much the same. Handsome even from a distance. He leaned against a pole of the pavilion watching to see who arrived, but although he stared in my direction, he looked beyond me. Philip continued to pace up and down the wooden steps. A woman in a wheelchair was invisible. The Katerina he expected no longer existed.

Mary recognised me and ran towards me holding a handkerchief. Her eyes so puffy and red-rimmed, I knew she'd been crying for days.

Philip followed, then stopped.

At the moment our eyes met, I registered his look. It was awash with sadness and guilt. I tried to turn around, but he blocked my path by falling to the ground at my feet. I shrank into my chair, pushing his hand away, imploring him not to cry. I would rather be despised than a source of distress or an object of pity.

Mama Bridgett bounced towards me, carrying the most beautiful girl I'd ever seen. With every step Mama took, Viktoria's wild curls sprang in the breeze, her hair ribbons threatening to fly away. Those eyes were so much like Philip's that my heart leapt from my chest trying to bridge the gap between us.

Viktoria giggled; she was the only member of our party who hadn't been crying.

She laughed when she touched the wheelchair. "Why a big person like you in a pwam?"

"Because I cannot walk," I said, patting my lap. "Would you like a ride?"

Her eyes widened, and she clambered over my knees circling her chubby little arms around my neck.

"You come too, Mummy," she said to Mary.

Mummy. Hearing this word in her little voice almost broke me.

"No, I'll stay here." Mary smiled, but her voice shook.

"Get better, Mummy," Viktoria said, turning herself forward on my knee.

I pushed down a sob before it could escape. My daughter was kind. A small girl with a bountiful heart.

"I'll push," Philip said.

He wheeled us past the flowers, and under the trees where the dappled light fell across Viktoria's cherubic face. He chatted happily, racing around to make her squeal, and poking out his tongue to make her laugh. He performed a magic trick making his handkerchief vanish, but not once did he look at me. His magic was powerful. I had completely disappeared.

When we returned, Mama was comforting Mary, but she quickly wiped her tears and composed herself. "Lunch is served," she said as cheerfully as she could manage.

There were plates of tiny sandwiches, fruit tarts and sweets and birthday cake. Balloon faces smiled down from the pavilion roof, reminding us this was a celebration even if the festive feeling was absent.

Philip stood by my side and we watched *our* child puff up pink cheeks to blow out three candles on her cake. His smile was strained.

I looked on as Mary lifted Viktoria onto her shoulders and sang made-up songs about items of food. The love between them was both heart-warming and heartbreaking.

While they were playing, Mama took my hand and wheeled me away.

"Mary and I have discussed your visit. We've been torn about this for the past three years. We've always known Viktoria is your baby, yet we've pretended because no matter how much we tried to prepare ourselves; we couldn't imagine how life would be without her."

Tears ran rivers down both our cheeks.

"I have an enormous favour," Mama said. "We know you love Viktoria, but can you please allow Mary to stay a part of her life? She's been a devoted mother and I'm afraid her heart will break." Mama sagged against a tree and wrapped her arms around the trunk as if needing support to stay upright.

"Of course, Mama Bridgett," I said. "You are both her family, and I want the best."

I couldn't tell her anymore. A choice this important needed to be discussed with Philip.

I looked at the lake and surrounding gardens. Although I saw it through the mistiness of tears, the clouds had cleared away and blessed us with a splendid blue sky. Picture-perfect, the wrong day for sorrow.

I called to Philip, "Could you please hire one of the rowboats? This is the most beautiful day I've ever seen, and I'd like to take Viktoria onto the lake."

As Philip carried me into the boat, his hands grazed my hips; no longer smooth and round. Although the look was fleeting, I saw the pity—our love could never be the same.

Mary carried Viktoria, kissing and hugging her as if she'd never see her again. She passed the child to Philip, who sat her beside me on the low wooden seat.

Philip rowed us around the lake, and I touched my little girl's cheeks, played with her hair, kissing every exquisite little finger. I thought carefully. How could I consider taking a child from the only mother she'd ever known? If I left now, perhaps she would never know the awful thing of which her biological mother was capable.

Philip stared at the oars and the ripples in the water, looking up resolutely when I spoke.

"Can you please take Viktoria back? We need to speak privately."

Mary and Mama waited at the shore, wearing pasted on smiles. I called out, "Mary, your daughter needs you."

Mary's eyes locked on mine, and tears spilled as she grasped the meaning.

I embraced Viktoria then kissed her. "Happy birthday, sweetheart. Be good for your Mummy, and remember how much Aunty Kat loves you."

We were in the middle of the lake again before Philip spoke, "I can't visit Viktoria again. The police know where Mama lives and have been asking after me."

"How did they find Bridgett?"

"They aren't sure, but it was after your mother visited Mary in Melbourne. She took an immediate dislike to the child."

I knew immediately my mother was behind it. I swallowed hard at her limitless cruelty.

Across the lake, our little girl skipped in delighted circles. My mother would have 'the child' taken away. I felt a tsunami of frightening protectiveness. I was capable of killing my own mother to save my child.

My voice broke, "Mary and Mama are the only family Viktoria knows. They're the perfect role models and I won't drag her around the country waiting to be caught. We cannot see each other again."

When I broke into uncontrollable sobs, Philip clutched my hand.

"I love you," he said. "We can start a new life together."

"It wouldn't work, unless we told the authorities the truth and you could stop running."

"No. You must promise me now. Never. Ever. Tell."

"Then it is settled. We do what's best for our daughter."

"But Katerina..." Philip started to cry.

"Please, don't. And please do not ask again. I might not have the strength to say no."

I didn't look at Philip until we were back at the shore.

Philip cried silently as he carried me to my wheel-chair, burying his head in my hair as he whispered, "I am so sorry for insisting on talking to your Father. I should have listened."

"It's not your fault."

"Please. I could look after you, Kat. We could leave Viktoria until she's older. I would look after you."

"I know you would, and I will love you forever, but the past stands between us."

"But—"

"We can't, Philip."

I nodded to Mary as she approached, hugging Viktoria again. "If Mummy doesn't mind, I'll visit you again another day."

Mama raced to kiss my forehead. "Thank you. I love you, my girl."

"I love you too, Mama. Goodbye."

With heavy arms, I wheeled myself up the path.

Philip followed, calling from behind, "I love you, Katerina."

As I lifted one hand to halt him, I faltered, my wheelchair rolling backwards. How much easier would it have been to let it roll into his hands? In so many ways, it would have been too cruel for everyone.

I didn't look back as I made my way to the gate.

When I rounded the corner, I found a private place to let out a lifetime of tears.

Just as I composed myself, Ernest appeared, ready to take me home. I removed my rings and dropped them into his hand. As he closed his fingers around them, a look of understanding passed between us.

"I know you are perfectly c-capable of fending for y-yourself, Katerina," he said, looking at the ground, "but I w-want to look after you, and I d-darn well need you to take c-care of me."

Chapter Fifty-Four

KATERINA

'The Figs' Sydney, 2018

Joe and Izzy join me in the sunny corner.

"I didn't expect you today."

"I couldn't stay away," Joe says. "I'm as excited about meeting your family as you."

"I cannot think of anything else. Even my blasted false teeth are rattling." I force a smile to hide the depth of my terror.

When Izzy pretends to shake what could be maracas to break my frozen grin, I smile for real.

"You've recorded the last part of your story then?" she asks.

"Every last secret." I hold my hand over my heart.

A tremor runs through me as Izzy passes Joe the memory stick. There's no going back.

Even with Izzy's encouragement, writing the last chapter of my memoir was tough. For better or for worse, my choices have affected all those will read my story.

Joe checks the to-do list on his phone. "Take recording to the typist. Six copies printed and bound?"

I nod but say nothing.

Izzy puts her hand to my forehead. "You okay? You're pale."

"It's just nerves." I pull away. "Do not fuss."

"Oh, Katerina, I can't wait for everyone to read your autobiography." She studies my face, holding my wrist this time to check my pulse.

I yank my hand away. "Stop it. I really am fine."

"Rest," she says. "I'll pop back tomorrow before I start work, and we'll pick out something especially beautiful for you to wear when you meet your daughter."

"Off you go, before Matron gives you the boot for loitering with me." I flick my fingers towards Joe. "You too. Time to dash."

Once I'm on my own, my head spins out of control. It's only three more days until I meet Viktoria. I hope she understands my decision to give her up.

While I struggle to maintain an appearance of calm. Izzy announces the count down to the meeting, minute by minute, and Joe jumps up every time someone approaches the door.

They arrived early to set up chairs in the courtyard, but their high-fiving and Izzy's shrieks are ruffling the little inner calm I have left. Their exuberance is over-whelming, yet I am grateful to them for making everything happen. Joe's hasn't once shown disappointment at ending up with my story when he was trying to get his mother's, and Izzy's helped with everything. She's even been here on her days off.

Maria's the only one who seems her usual self, so I sit next to her and leave the other two to make a fuss. I watch Maria sketch our faces. If the drawings are accurate, we look a nervous mess.

At unfamiliar voices, Izzy flaps her hands, then smooths my hair.

The stern-faced nurse ushers a group to the door. "S'pposed to be three visitor max," she squawks. "Don't know why they make rules if they don't enforce 'em."

I check each person as they walk in, one man and three women. My heart beats double-time. Viktoria has changed her mind.

The older woman steps forward and points. "Claudia, Bonnie, Dermot, and I'm Hillary."

Philip's wife and his beautiful daughters.

I grasp their hands. "I'm so pleased to meet you. Thank you so much for coming."

Behind my smile, I'm blinking back tears of disappointment. There's a sting of jealousy there, too. Philip had more children and got to watch them grow. Yet, the daughter we shared won't meet me.

Dermot holds my hand longer than necessary. His eyes are warm. "Lovely to meet you, Katerina. We spoke on the phone."

I look over his shoulder hoping for a latecomer, then sigh. Who can blame Viktoria after what I did? I drop my head in resignation.

Joe introduces himself, Izzy and Maria, then performs an almost royal bow as he announces my name. All unnecessary, they know who I am, and I'm no-one special.

The youngest woman, Bonnie, laughs. "Do you mind repeating all that bowing stuff when Viktoria gets here? The cranky nurse in there made her sit down to sip iced water. Said she wasn't cleaning up any visitor mess." Bonnie mimes throwing up. "Viktoria looked green about the gills."

There's a lump in my throat. Somewhere on the other side of that door is my daughter.

Claudia reminds me of Mama Bridgett. "Viktoria's overwhelmed," she says in the kindest of voices. "We all are. We've been dying to meet you."

"Yes." Bonnie winks. "The infamous dancer my dad left behind."

I try not to laugh when everyone else stares at her.

Izzy squeezes my shoulder and points towards the door as Viktoria walks in. I blink back tears, unable to speak.

"I'm Viktoria." Her voice quivers.

I reach my hand towards her and whisper, "I recognise you from the photographs Mary and Mama Bridgett used to send."

But it's more than that, my heart knows her. I close my eyes to an image of my beautiful child, laughing in a rowboat on an almost perfect day.

Viktoria steadies herself before leaning in for a hug. "You're beautiful. My birthmother."

I'm not sure of protocol, but I hold her tighter than I've held anyone. By the time I let go, her shirt is wet with my tears.

"Everyone." My voice is jittery with love and fear, but I try to lighten the mood. "Please make yourselves comfortable. I might not have many years left, but I have all afternoon."

Dermot and Claudia perch on the edge of an over-sized plant pot, while Bonnie plonks herself into the nearest chair. The rest shuffle around in a music-less version of musical chairs, but Viktoria stays so close I feel her warmth.

They all lock eyes on me as if I am the Queen. I blame Joe and his royal bow.

I'm not sure what to say, so I smile tentatively at Hillary. "I'm sorry for your loss." She presses her lips together, but, to my surprise, when I offer both hands, she takes them.

"I read in Philip's death notice that he brought you flowers."

"Yes." Hillary looks surprised.

"I hope he gave you everything you hoped for."

"He wasn't perfect, but he looked after us."

I study Philip's daughters for further resemblances. They have a beautiful familiarity and I see Philip in Viktoria, too. I could sit for hours looking at her face.

Hillary's forehead creases and she opens her mouth but takes a few seconds to speak, "Do you know anything about a lump sum Philip deposited around 1962? We've no idea where the money came from."

Claudia cringes at her mother's question, and Viktoria straightens the blanket over my legs like a shield.

"Hillary has the right to know everything," I say. "There'll be no secrets after today. My mother died that year, and when my brother and I sorted through the paperwork, we discovered Uncle Viktor's will. He'd named my father as executor, but Father had ignored his wishes. He'd left money for Bridgett which remained in a holding account for years." I sigh. "Mama Bridgett sobbed when she found out. She was distressed when she realised how different our lives could have been."

"See?" Hillary sighs, staring at the wall. When she looks back, her eyes are watering. "I knew there'd be an explanation. He got the cash from his own mother?"

"Yes. Mama Bridgett wanted nothing to do with the inheritance. She'd spent years believing Viktor hadn't loved her. Much of it went to Mary for Viktoria and the rest to Philip."

"How would money have helped?" Viktoria asks. "It seems as if society is to blame."

"If your father and I had the means, we would have run away and the whole sorry mess wouldn't have happened." I inhale slowly to steady my voice. "I wouldn't have lived a life without you."

"But why didn't you or my father stay in contact?" Viktoria's hand is shaking.

I have no idea what to say to make this seem right. There's no simple explanation for an impossible decision. "I hoped you'd have a better life. I wanted Philip to have a normal life and meet someone else. And you both did."

Scanning the sea of faces, I see this has generated more questions. Questions no one is brave enough to ask. I firm up my shoulders. "My story tells everything." Then I spin the wheelchair towards the door, determined not to break down until I'm alone.

Chapter Fifty-Five

CLAUDIA

Sydney, 2018

Viktoria looks helpless when her mother leaves the room. "Should I follow?"

"Give her a moment to compose herself. She'll come back." Izzy pats Viktoria's arm reassuringly.

"Surely, someone should go with her?" Mum's expression suggests Izzy is refusing to administer life-saving medication.

"Katerina's okay," Izzy says. "Crying's therapeutic. Tears aren't always a problem, sometimes, they're the remedy."

"If you're sure." Mum doesn't sound convinced. She fishes a purse-pack of Kleenex from her handbag, pressing a tissue to her eyes and passing one to Viktoria.

When Katerina returns looking fragile but composed, Viktoria wraps protective arms around her.

Mum's chin trembles. "I'm sorry I upset you, Katerina. First, I force my daughters to bring me, then I ask silly questions. It's no excuse, but there are so many things I want to know. It's as if my whole marriage has been a lie." Mum dabs her eyes again. "Many nights I woke up to find Philip sitting awake. I'm certain he'd just dreamt about you, but he wouldn't tell me what he was thinking."

I was annoyed at Mum for jumping in, but now I feel sorry for her. This whole crying thing is contagious. I wipe my eyes and Dermot leans his shoulder against mine, squeezing my hand. "It'll all be grand."

Katerina says to Mum, "I'm sure Philip wasn't pining. I was his sweetheart for only a year, and it was over long before he met you."

Mum nods. "Thank you." Then she turns to me and Bonnie, indicating the door with a head tilt. "Best we give mother and daughter some time alone."

I look back through the window at Viktoria and Katerina embracing. They've lost so much time. A wave of gratitude reminds me of the years I had with my sons.

Dermot takes a deep breath. "We all need a snack break."

"There's a vending machine near reception." Mum strides off at full speed, busying herself by buying one of everything. She hands out drinks and packets without asking our preference, and we wander aimlessly around The Figs lawn eating chocolates, chips and butterscotch lollies.

By the time Viktoria joins us in the herb garden, her eyes are red-rimmed. "Would you mind if we leave and come back tomorrow?" She hugs a pile of documents.

"My mother would like us to read the entire account before we ask any more questions."

"Come on." I take out my phone. "I'll call a taxi."

Except for the sound of Mum sucking the butterscotch, we wait quietly outside *The Figs*.

When the taxi arrives, the driver is overly helpful to Mum.

"They taking you out for the day?" he asks.

The insinuation that Mum's a resident doesn't escape her. "No," she says with an *oomph*. "We were all here visiting an elderly friend."

The atmosphere as we drive back to the hotel is mixed. Mum's fuming about being mistaken for a resident, while Viktoria is withdrawn. Bonnie and Dermot play a game of who's first to spot the Sydney Harbour Bridge, and I'm just thankful for family and friends.

We walk into the hotel lobby, while Dermot pays the driver.

"Did you see the look that taxi fellow gave me?" Mum says. "He thought I was a patient. How old does he think I am?"

"I saw the look all right," Bonnie says. "But I thought he was giving you the 'Glad Eye'. You're an attractive woman, old Hillary, and you must be giving out signals. You know the ones. I'm available. Poor bloke's only human."

"It's rude to call your mother by her first name and stop with the old." Mum's second *oomph* doesn't hide her smile.

Inside the shared apartment, we're drawn to the folders Viktoria's dropped on the coffee table. It's like a scene from a movie where we've been given the key to a hidden passage, but we're all worried about what's inside. Dad's secrets are in these pages.

"We can either takes turns reading or pair up," Mum says.

Viktoria picks up a copy, stands slowly, and drifts towards her room.

"Sure you're okay?" I ask.

She nods, closing the door behind her.

"I'll share with you, Bonnie," Mum says.

"Yeah, alright. We can sit on the sofa together, but you better get rid of those butterscotch lollies. The slurping's driving me fucking nuts."

Mum taps the back of Bonnie's head and smiles.

"That leaves us," I say to Dermot, pointing to the tiny hotel table.

We make ourselves as comfortable as possible, but it doesn't take long before the sound of reading out of sync becomes unworkable.

"It's quieter in my room," Dermot says.

I take a breath. "Okay."

As I follow him, Mum's and Bonnie's eyes burn holes in my back.

I overdo the comparison of Dermot's smaller hotel room with the one I share with Mum and Bonnie. There is no table. I press the mattress. "To check how soft," I say, nervously.

"A pillow menu." He laughs, reading a card on the bed. "Feather, down, bamboo, memory foam, high rise."

I close my eyes to listen to his voice. When I open them, he's building a pillow-wall down the centre of the bed. "A barricade."

I try not to show my disappointment.

I read the first chapter of Katerina's story, intending

we take turns, but once Dermot begins, his lilting Irish voice transports me into Katerina's world. He pauses when I can't hold back tears, handing me a box of tissues and patting my shoulder before continuing. Although I already knew about Viktoria, when Katerina surrenders her child, I collapse into sobs. Dermot reaches across the pillow to squeeze my hand, waiting until I calm down to get up and fetch a hand towel from the bathroom. "Heavy duty mop-up. I think we're going to need it."

"Katerina hasn't said what happened when Dad went into hiding."

"It's here." Dermot throws the pillows on the floor. "The night your dad and Katerina faced up to her father."

Wrapping his arm around me, he balances the booklet against my shoulder, and I move into him, my ear against his chest, ready to feel the hum of his voice:

'Letter opener in his hand, Father roared like a wounded bear and lunged at Philip, narrowly missing his head.

I screamed and leapt at Father, but he knocked me aside, twisting to pierce Philip's shoulder with the blade.

Time stopped. I saw the knife about to strike Philip again and instinctively threw myself over him, intercepting the weapon. The point punctured my side, sinking deep into my flesh.

Father lifted me with one arm and threw me screaming and sobbing onto his desk and turned his attention to Philip.

Sharp pains shot down my leg, immobilising me. I turned my head as Mama Bridgett appeared, screeching at Father. Her cries distracted him enough for Philip to roll out of reach.

The pain seared like fire, and I struggled fruitlessly to sit up as Father bellowed and advanced on Philip.

Desperately, Philip kicked, driving Father onto the desk beside me. When I saw his face next to mine, I knew one of us would die.

'First I'll kill the bastard father then your bastard child,' he roared with rage.

When Father moved, his brass paper-weight pressed cold against my hand. I didn't hesitate to seize it and strike his shoulder. He slumped momentarily, then turned, nostrils flaring, his hands convulsively tightening around my throat. Philip wrenched Father's arms, shouting for him to stop, but Father was deaf to reason.

Using every ounce of adrenaline-fuelled strength, I struck. Three thuds in the frenzied fray; the brass against Father's skull, the heavy crash as he collapsed, and the sound of Mama slumping against the doorway.

Blood thundered in my ears but didn't drown out Mama's scream, "He isn't breathing."

The injured Philip carried me from the desk to the dark leather chaise. I bit my lip until it bled, but could not stop crying. He pressed Viktoria's baby quilt to staunch my wound.

"I'll leave a note," he said. "I'll confess to the killing and tell the authorities it was an act of self-defence."

"No. They'll send you to jail."

"Katerina. Listen. I'll hide. After I've earned enough money, I'll come back for you both."

Mama placed baby Viktoria in my arms and my heart broke as I realised the implications of what I'd done.

I squeezed Mama's hand. "Okay, but we cannot let anyone know about Viktoria. My mother will put her up for adoption. Please, take our baby and promise to look after her."

Tears streamed down Mama's cheeks as she reached for the most precious thing I'd known. I pulled my daughter back, gasping with pain, and refused to let her go. "No, I've changed my mind. We'll tell the truth. Or, we'll run away together."

"You need a hospital." Mama Bridgett steadied herself against the wall. "I want to protect my son in the way you want to protect Viktoria, but Philip is right. No matter what story you tell the police... Whether he stays or goes... they'll blame him, and his entire life will be spent in jail, or worse. Then they'll send Viktoria away, and we'll never find her."

Philip's tears fell on my face as he took our baby from my arms and handed her to Mama. "You don't have to lie, Katerina. It will all be in my note. Tell the authorities you passed out and remember nothing." His lips quivered against my ear. ""Promise me. Don't tell anyone what really happened."

Through blurred eyes I watched Philip grimacing with pain as he stooped at Father's desk; the sound of the nib scratching the paper.

He urged Mama to call a doctor and their voices grew distant."

"It's okay, Claudia," Dermot whispers.

"I'm sorry for crying like a baby." My voice catches with the remnant of a sob.

"Don't be. You heard what the nurse said. Crying can be positive." Dermot brushes hair from my face. "The search has been worth it. You know for sure your father was an honourable man, and he ended up happy.

Now, you've helped reunite a lovely old lady with her daughter. Stories do not end better than this."

I relax my body against his. "At least, Katerina wasn't alone entirely. Even though it was only a platonic relationship with Ernest, she had a husband and had her work."

"That's a huge assumption," he says.

"You don't think she married Earnest? She took his name."

Dermot shakes his head. "I mean the platonic part."

"But Katerina said Ernest's heart was in research."

Dermot laughs gently. "It's funny how we fill the gaps of every story with our own version."

"What do you think happened?"

"That a heart can love in more ways than one." Dermot reaches into his pocket for his notebook. "I imagine they explored their relationship in a joint investigation."

"What do you mean?" I peer at the notepad.

"I could explain, but it's better I show you." He turns the pad sideways and scribbles. "What if the doctor made a list of *treatments* and checked Katerina's response?"

"In what way?"

"As lovers."

His skin tingles against mine and my brain almost ceases functioning. "Show me."

"Which feels better?" He runs his tongue across my cheek, then sprinkles kisses across my neck. He laughs but his eyes aren't making fun.

"What else?" I ask breathlessly.

Dermot brushes his warm lips against mine then picks up the pen, pretending to record my reaction.

I press my mouth hard against his. "Maybe this?"

His words are hot on my neck. "How do you want our story to end?"

"Do you think there's a romance?" My voice drips with longing.

"There is if we write one."

I've never understood the attraction for theme-parks, yet here I am with a smile on my face, queuing up for another ride.

When Dermot and I join the others, Bonnie puckers her lips in a kiss. "Slow readers, eh? You two took all night."

"We had a long emotional discussion, then fell asleep," Dermot says, wearing what's either an enigmatic smile or a sign of giddy exhaustion.

"You can tell me all about it in the taxi." Bonnie winks.

I avoid glancing in Bonnie's direction during breakfast in case she interprets eye-contact as permission to make more embarrassing comments. I try to keep my eyes down, but they're magnetically drawn to Dermot. Those lips, his hands, the tips of his fingers. For fuck's sake, I'm even drooling over his elbows.

Although I'm pretending to butter my already buttered toast, Dermot catches me gazing at him and grins. I'm a late bloomer, a ridiculously old version of the love-struck teenager. If I don't look away, my heart might run out of beats.

I am hungry. For love. And for sex.

Dad, you old bastard. I blamed you for breaking my old life apart. But I'm like a piece of Kintsugi *pottery. Love has mended me very nicely indeed, thanks.*

I knock on Viktoria's door, checking she's still happy for us to tag along this afternoon. "Would you prefer today's meeting to be just you and Katerina?"

"No. After reading this," she holds up the memoir, "I need emotional back-up. Besides, Katerina... Mum is expecting all of us." Viktoria bites her bottom lip, looking like Bonnie when she's worried.

I hug her. "I just wanted to be sure."

She inhales slowly. "Claudia, can I ask a big favour."

"Anything."

"You're meeting your son, tonight. Does Joshua have the whole day off?"

"Yes. Why?"

"My mother still carries incredible guilt and wants to clear Philip's name. I'd rather not put her through a police investigation, but I thought... if Josh flashed his police badge and promised to look into the case, it might be enough."

"Katerina is ninety-two. What if it backfires?" How awful would it be if the shock's too much?

"Izzy said Mum still has nightmares." Viktoria bites her lip again. "We've got to do something to help?"

Despite my worry about this going badly, I phone Josh, introduce Viktoria and leave them to hatch a plan.

When she puts the phone down, Viktoria gathers everyone together. "Joshua will visit today on 'official' duties. I'm not asking anyone to lie—just don't say hello."

Izzy leads us to The Figs back garden, where she and Joe have set up a circle of garden chairs near the enormous tree. A table set for a party, festooned with fairy lights and two flower arrangements. One of Geraldton Wax and the other Golden Wattle.

"Mum's flowers," I say. "How did Katerina know?"

"The obituary," Joe says. "Both flowers represent Philip."

I'm surprised when Mum starts to cry. She wipes her eyes, leaning over the bouquet of Geraldton Wax to whisper. All I hear are the words *Philip* and *love*.

I swallow the lump in my throat. *Mum did love Dad.*

Izzy rests her hand on Mum's shoulder. "Katerina's idea." Izzy sniffles. "Your special flowers alongside hers."

"I'll fetch our guest of honour." Joe is forcefully upbeat to counteract the sadness. "Do you want to come with me, Viktoria?"

"Will Katerina be okay on this rough ground with the wheelchair and all?" Mum sounds genuinely concerned.

"She's better in that wheelchair than I am parking my car." Izzy laughs. "This garden's one of her favourite places."

Dermot stands so close to me we're almost conjoined. He laces his fingers through mine. "You holding up okay?"

"I am now."

His touch thrills me, and I don't care what anyone thinks.

When our guest of honour arrives, he whispers, "We've done it."

Katerina's dress is midnight blue, and the sun threads silver through her white hair. Viktoria's eyes twinkle as she pushes her mother over the weed-covered path. With Joe and Izzy walking either side, there's a wedding-like atmosphere. Except Katerina, who looks more like she's attending a funeral.

She scans the circle of chairs, eyes filled with remorse. "So, you know my dreadful secret. Philip was innocent, and I allowed people to believe him guilty for over seventy years."

Chapter Fifty-Six

KATERINA

'The Figs' Sydney, 2018

Hillary waves the memoir. "I've read it, and you aren't dreadful. You're a brave woman, Katerina, and I agree with Philip. He had good reason asking you to stay quiet. That man would die for those he loved."

Tears stream down Izzy's cheeks as she passes around tissues.

Viktoria stands protectively close. "Hillary's right, Mum. You did what you had to. I had a good life because of your sacrifice. Thank you."

I choke with an indescribable mixture of sadness and joy.

Hillary raises her hand. "One more thing. I'm sure Philip will be waiting for you in heaven, and after everything you've been through, I understand why. Thanks for loaning him to me for so many years."

I'm taken aback. "Oh no, Hillary. Philip will be looking for you. I'll stop by to say hello and apologise about not handing myself in earlier, but I have my Ernest. He understood me better than anyone. I never told him what I'd done, but I'm sure he knew."

Maria's the only one with dry eyes, and she looks from person to person like a curious cat.

"It's okay." I blow her a thank you kiss. Without her, Joe and Izzy, the truth would have died with me.

"Excuse me," Joe interrupts, shrugging uncertainly. "Miss Katerina, there's a police officer to see you."

"Yes, sir." I squint, shading my face. "Sorry, Officer, the sun is in my eyes."

"Katerina Tremaine?" the young policeman asks. "I'm here regarding information provided by Miss Viktoria Alexander."

"Yes. Viktoria's my daughter." My voice shakes. I'm face to face with the police after all these years, but the strongest emotion isn't fear, but pride and love at speaking the words 'my daughter'.

"You've alleged that Philip Sean Francis O'Patrick was wrongfully charged with the murder of Ivan Alexander. It's my understanding you wish to make a confession?"

I lift my chin. "Yes, I killed my father. I should have come forward much earlier."

When the officer moves beside my wheelchair, his body blocks the sun and I search for a name badge as I wait for him to produce handcuffs and haul me away. He isn't wearing a badge and the insignia on his uniform says Australian Federal Police. I'd originally put his gentle manner down to respect for my age, but now I've seen his face without the glare, I know why. I could never miss the likeness.

"Based on what I've been told," he says, kneeling

beside me. "It appears the real offender was your father. You and Philip were victims."

He's putting on a strong performance, and I hope this young man is actually in a position to put right the wrongful charge.

"Oh my, can you change the criminal records? Clear Philip's name?"

He juts out his jaw. "It will take time, but I promise to take the project on personally."

The young man's words warm my heart in a way I could never have imagined.

"Thank you. Other than finding my daughter, this has been my greatest wish."

Once he leaves, I look to the heavens, smiling at Philip through a lifetime of tears.

Chapter Fifty-Seven

CLAUDIA

Sydney, 2018

I wasn't confident about confronting Katerina with a police officer, but it seems to have worked. There was a moment where I held my breath, hoping the shock wasn't too much. She's been through enough.

Katerina is serene and relaxed, which is more than I can say about myself. I've never been so highly charged, and when Dermot traces his fingers across the nape of my neck, I tilt my head towards him for more. It's an effort to stop myself from moaning. Once, when Bonnie and I were kids, she made me touch a battery with my tongue. Now every touch of Dermot's skin on mine reminds me of that zap, except this sensation is exquisite. I settle back happily, my face to the sun. We've solved Dad's mystery.

As I watch Viktoria's effortless interactions with Katerina, I become aware of a gnawing unease. Envy. Viktoria's put the past aside to develop this bond, and it's time for me to do the same. I pat the empty chair next to mine and smile at Mum through tears. "Sit here. With me."

Mum moves closer, taking my hand, then she nods approvingly at Dermot. "We're all going to be okay."

Maria interrupts the moment by forcefully unlinking her arm from Joe's and trying to wheel Katerina away. He attempts to restrain her, but she escapes. Her shouts are unintelligible, but the way she points to the door suggests she's worried the police will take her friend, Katerina, away. She clenches and unclenches her fists, yelling words I don't understand, as Joe and Izzy try to calm her down.

Dermot whispers in my ear, "Maria has an extensive vocabulary of Italian swear words." He raises his eyebrows at me, then calls to her. "*Ciao.* Hello. Do you need my help?"

"How many languages do you speak?" I ask, impressed.

He murmurs in my ear, "I can tell you *I love you* in more ways than one."

I turn to kiss him, but Maria starts up again.

She fights off Joe and Izzy, this time setting her dark eyes on Viktoria, who's wheeling Katerina under the tree. This is the last straw. Maria lunges at Viktoria.

"No, Mum," Joe yells. "Viktoria's not hurting Katerina, she's protecting her."

"It's not her fault, it's the dementia," Katerina explains, defending Maria. "She never does well in unfamiliar situations."

"Come, Maria," Izzy says using the gentlest of tones, but Maria's crying worsens.

"Sorry, everyone." Joe grits his teeth. "I don't know what to do."

Dermot's soft, lilting voice cuts through the chaos. He whispers in Italian.

Maria glares at first, making a symbol of horns with her index and little finger. But Dermot responds with a smile and more soothing, sweet-sounding Italian words which only she understands.

Her eyes widen and she appears mesmerised, watching Dermot beckon as he walks to the door. Maria follows, her shoulders relaxing with every step. She's under his spell. Which I understand completely. I'd follow that man anywhere.

Dermot bids an Italian farewell to the group, then they disappear inside.

Bonnie giggles and nudges me. "I know what language you want to hear from Dermot...the language of lurrrrve."

Mum hisses at Bonnie, "Give it up." She pats my hand. "Your sister's a shocker."

Katerina clinks glasses to bring everyone to attention. "This day has been extraordinary. I cannot thank you all enough. First, for finding me, then meeting me, and for making me feel loved. But it would be remiss of me not to mention my favourite part of the day: the Oscar winning performance from the lovely young police officer."

Viktoria's mouth drops open.

"Don't worry." Katerina prods her daughter playfully. "It was a special gift, so thoughtful."

"How did you know it was a performance?" Viktoria asks.

"His Australian Federal Police uniform. I wondered

why an officer trained in anti-terrorism, human trafficking and cyber-crime would be assigned a cold case like mine."

"To which of you girls does the young policeman belong?"

Smiling, I wave, my face warm with love and pride.

Katerina smiles. "And the best part? Looking into that young man's face. He looks so much like Philip it almost stopped my heart." She clutches her chest, then seeing Izzy's reaction, says, "I'm fine. He's not the only one up for an Oscar."

Viktoria hugs her mother and laughs. We all join in.

"Everyone here is incredible." Katerina smiles. "Over the past years, I've convinced myself I deserve to be alone. But it's never too late to find friendship and love." She taps a fork on the table. "Last chance. Any further questions before we break for afternoon tea?"

"I do," Bonnie says. "Do you know who Dad's father was? The DNA results are frickin weird."

"Yes," Katerina replies. "Mama Bridgett told me she'd arranged to meet her fiancé on the ship in Southampton. They were to be married by the captain and planned a honeymoon voyage, but she couldn't find him. She waited for him in her cabin. As the ship was leaving the dock, Viktor, the ship's first mate, delivered a telegram. Bridgett's fiancé had changed his mind.

"Bridgett was hysterical and threatened to jump overboard. Viktor stopped her, she begged to be taken ashore. It was Viktor who convinced Bridgett she could do better than such a heartless rogue. He suggested Australia as the perfect place for a new start. He promised to find her a position in his cousin's house.

"By the time Mama Bridgett landed in Australia, she

was pregnant with Viktor's child. Viktor pleaded with my father, his cousin, to provide a safe place for Bridgett until he could break off his engagement to a woman back in Russia. Mama Bridgett told me she and Viktor were deeply in love, but Viktor's family were set against the relationship.

"On his return to Russia, Viktor's family pressured him to honour his original promise. Mama Bridgett was brokenhearted when Viktor married his Russian bride. Although he didn't continue a romantic relationship with Bridgett, he visited whenever he could. It was a tragedy that three people, Bridgett, Viktor and his wife, lost a lifetime of happiness."

Katerina looks at me and Bonnie. "Your beautiful paternal grandmother, Mama Bridgett, was beside herself. She lived with the shame and stuck with the story of a father who'd died to protect Philip from the truth. He never knew."

"This explains the messy DNA," Bonnie says. "You and Dad were second cousins."

"I didn't know Philip and I were related. Not until it was all over."

"Thank God you and Dad are just second cousins. For a moment, I suspected you might be brother and sister," Bonnie says. "It was creeping me out."

I glare at Bonnie, warning for her to stop. "There've been enough revelations for one day."

Joe looks wistfully towards the door. "Sorry about my mum."

"Don't apologise," Katerina says. "I could not be more pleased with how perfectly this has gone."

"Should I fetch the cake?" Izzy asks.

"Yes, please, and can you bring Maria and Dermot

back?" Katerina waves her hand over the food laden table. "Thanks to the wonderful Joe, we have platters of food and bottles of sparkling apple juice."

"Let's celebrate." Joe fills the glasses.

"Sorry, everyone for taking so long," Dermot says, his arm around a smiling Maria.

She looks around then asks something in Italian. Dermot points to me.

Maria hugs me, chattering excitedly.

"Maria told me a little about her two past loves, so I told her about you," Dermot says. "She wanted to meet you."

"Maria had two great loves?" Katerina asks.

"Yes. She showed me pictures in her sketchpad and started telling some interesting tales about her younger years." Dermot pulls out his notepad. "I hope you don't mind, Joe, but I started writing them down."

"I don't think I could get any happier," Katerina says, hugging Maria.

I raise my glass to Dermot and the group. "Everyone deserves more than one chance at love."

THE END

Acknowledgments

I am filled with gratitude to those who helped shape this novel. Although there are too many to name, I thank you all for bringing this story to life.

Writing is sorcery. My pen seizes thoughts and turns them into words. But the real trickery happens when special people untangle messy sentences, spot sneaky plot holes, and cast spells to keep me on task. A squillion thanks to my magical critique partners; Sue and Linda. Without you, there would be no stories.

A special mention to my beta readers, a fabulous tribe of family and friends, who waded through an unpolished draft and helped me see where the story needed revisions.

To my cheerleaders Robin and Colleen, thanks for your unwavering encouragement and support.

Finally, my husband. He listened as I read the entire story aloud and pointed out sentences he considered too airy fairy. He also brought me coffee!

The readers should thank these people, too.

About the Author

Born in England, Mila Douglas grew up in Western Australia, but has lived most of her life in tropical Cairns, Queensland. There, the rainforest covered mountains gave her a steamy embrace and declared Cairns her forever home.

Teacher, curriculum writer, and professional development presenter turned author; Mila loves people. The characters in her books are as real and quirky as her friends. She stops short at pressing her ear against a wall to eavesdrop, but on occasions she's craned her neck to filch witty dialogue from strangers.

When Mila isn't writing, she enjoys spending time with her energetic family, getting lost in her overgrown garden, buying too many home décor knick-knacks, and lounging about in her head.

Who knows? You might find snippets of your conversations in the pages of her books.

Visit the author's website: www.miladouglas.com.au

Contact the author at mila@miladouglas.com.au

Turn the page for excerpts from the next book in the series!

More from Mila Douglas

The Wolf at Her Heels

Sixty years after leaving Italy, the usually tight-lipped Maria speaks of Mafia connections and dangerous escapes. Are these just cruel tricks of early dementia? Or does Maria have a sinister secret?

1966 Scilla, Italy

When a young seamstress has an unsanctioned affair with one of their kin, the 'Ndrangheta threaten her family. She reluctantly agrees to a proxy wedding and is exiled from her beloved Calabrian bergamot groves headed for fields of Australian sugar cane.

During the lengthy ocean voyage, she forms a friendship with another proxy bride. By the time the women disembark, they've concocted a plan to beat the system.

Present Day, Sydney Australia

Forty-something Joe is suspicious. His mother's verbal ramblings hint that her leaving Italy was more than routine immigration. Unfortunately, he's in a race against time and must capture her stories before dementia steals them away.

Maria agrees to share her story... With conditions... She'll tell what she still remembers—if Joe takes another crack at love. After all, Maria wants the same thing every good mother wants—her son to be happy.

What Joe doesn't know is she already has a woman in mind.